THE DARK ENERGY CHRONICLES:

THE FIRST SPARK

THE FIRST BOOK

T.J. Trapp
and
Japhet Owens

The First Spark

TABLE OF CONTENTS

Authors' Notes

The Dark Energy Chronicles

The First Spark – The First Book

A young research scientist, Alec, is suddenly transported into a different world after one of his experiments with dark energy has unexpected results. On this alien planet he encounters a young woman with a regal bearing but wearing a slave collar. Is she a slave? a princess? or both? While trying to reach her homeland, the two find themselves inexorably drawn into an ancient war between the elves and the orb that has been raging across the multiverse for millions of years. In addition to learning how to fight with sword and staff, Alec must learn to use his medallion in new ways to harness dark energy and stave off certain destruction.

Zero-Point: Beyond the Five Moons – The Second Book

The story of Alec and Erin continues. Alec and Erin are forced to flee the elves and return to Alec's home world, Earth, only to discover that it has become engulfed in the war between elf and orb. Alec finds that he was declared dead years ago and has no identity, and Erin struggles to understand this strange world of cell phones, frozen pizza, and automobiles. Working against time, while struggling to find a new source of dark energy, Alec and Erin must pierce the elves' cover and thwart the secret plans to enslave Earth – and find a way home.

The Dragon of Nevia – The Third Book

The elves are winning their dark quest to overrule the Earth and have unleashed sinister creatures from another galaxy to subdue the human population. Alec and Erin are torn between two worlds – Alec's homeland, and Erin's land that he has come to love. Both worlds are in peril. Only a dragon – the ancient weapon-beast of the True Dragon Queen – has the power to defeat this new onslaught. Before they can capture the dragon, Alec and Erin must restore the dark energy balance on Erin's home world, or risk defeat on both worlds.

Visit our web page to read more: TheDarkEnergyChronicles.com

Map

This small map was derived from the larger maps of Theland that the scholars shared with Alec.

Prologue

They tell me it is not always as it seems, but this is the story as it was told to me. The war between elf and orb has been waged for a thousand generations, maybe more – fought across millions of worlds in this multiverse. It has consumed so many.

I tell this story now not to boast, but to inscribe it beyond the frailty of memory. My narrative is first about two people on an insignificant world so far on the periphery of the multiverse that they were not even aware the great war existed. These two people were my mother and father.

As it was explained to me, the elves claim they are the elder race – the first beings – and that they created the orbs to serve. The orbs did not agree that their purpose was merely to serve. Over the millennia some bands of orbs escaped the elves' control and formed their own societies – some great, some small – eventually spreading to many worlds. But when elf and orb meet, wherever they may be, in whatever form and on whatever world, they fight at every contact, each trying to subvert the other. The elves try to again force the rogue orb into domestication, to transform them into a herd of drones programmed to serve their every need. The wild orbs, however, view the war as a fight for freedom from oppression and unjust subservience.

I, myself, am a cross-breed with the blood of both the elf and the wild orb. I am told that my father, Alec, came from a rogue outpost of orbs, called 'humans,' who long ago lost touch with the multiverse and the true place of their planet, 'Earth,' within it. My mother, the Queen, was also a cross-breed with an ancient elven bloodline.

I write this story now because many people are aware of my parents' undertakings, and even my later deeds, but few are aware of my parents' early life. This account of their awakening is as correct as I could make it, based on events they told me as I was growing up. Some of the events were so horrible they would not describe them in detail to a child. In those cases, I have filled in what I think happened, but wherever possible I have faithfully scribed the story they recounted to me.

I hope this narrative provides valuable insight about my parents and allows a better perspective on the events that the three of us later came to be so well known for.

Remember that the greatest of fires first starts with a single spark. This book is about that first, single spark.

Alecder Leon of Theland

PART ONE

1 – First Encounter

Shake.

Shake and roll. All around were multicolor flashes. Red and yellow. Neon green. Light and dark, dark and light.

Alec grittted his teeth and the flashes slowed; then a wave of nausea swept through him. Breathe. In and out. In and out. The nausea subsided, but the world around him seemed to shift – a strange sensation of time and space realigning.

Alec opened his eyes, still shuddering. *What just happened?* He could feel the ground beneath his feet pitch violently. Or was it him? He could no longer stand – he let his body accept the inevitable and collapsed to his knees, landing on all fours.

I was inside, in the Lab. Now ... where am I? His fingers reached tentatively towards his neck, and he could feel the medallion on his chest pulsing slightly with dark energy, confirming there was still a concentrated dark energy field around him.

Feeling was slowly returning to his body. He could feel his extremities – nothing appeared to be broken.

Am I still wearing my medallion, outside the Lab? Alder was hard on researchers who took a medallion outside the Lab, especially new members of the team. *Like me.*

He had just been in the concentrated dark energy field in the Lab's experimental chamber. He was certain he hadn't left the room, but now he was lying in an open field. The ground beneath him was soft and slightly mossy with an almost purple tint. Around him were clumps of shoulder-high grasses intermixed with low dark bushes. Wherever he was, it didn't look like New England.

≈ ≈ ≈ ≈

Mid-autumn was the best time to be in the Northeast, he had decided. It was the perfect season to be at the North Atlantic Institute, set in the foothills of the Northern Appalachians. The maples, first to turn, were beginning to reach their peak colors and the afternoon sun highlighted the brick-and-stone buildings of the campus quadrangle nicely against the backdrop of red and orange. Alec walked rapidly along the main sidewalk headed towards the research complex on the south side of the campus, cell phone to his ear, oblivious to the students around him.

"Hey," Alec said with a start, as he dodged a young man coasting by on a skateboard, earbuds flying. *Watch where you're going,* he thought.

"What?" said the voice on his cell phone.

"Some kid just tried to knock me over," he answered. "Must be an undergrad. Just zipped by me on a skateboard of all things! Good thing I have the reflexes of a cat or he would have bowled me over!"

"So, am I going to see you tonight or what?"

"Look, Sarah, I told you I'm not sure. I'm still the new guy in town here at the Institute. I've got to put in my time at the Lab, and the project needs to show some real progress here before the end of the month, or our funding report won't look too good. We're just about to make a breakthrough. I've got to put in at least a few hours today, and I don't want to skip another workout, so I'm thinking …"

"Well, <u>Doctor</u>," she said, cutting off his explanation, "I don't understand why it's so important for you to be there today. Your experiments can wait. It's Saturday, for cripes' sake!"

"Sarah, I've told you. The project doesn't work on a fixed schedule. You know that. Your research doesn't either! What I've got to do today shouldn't take too long. And then I'll call you. You know I can't take my cell into the Lab, so when I get done and get my cell out of my locker, I'll call."

"The last time you told me that, I waited until past midnight for you. What is it that you need to do?"

"Sarah, I've told you. It's classified. It's a discovery that could …"

"Change the world?"

"Well, yes, maybe, yes. And I need to be there, this afternoon, to finish some calculations, and try out something there in the Lab that I just thought of."

"Well, Doctor <u>Wizard</u>, you just go do that. And when – if – you're done, you can call me, and – if I'm not busy – maybe I'll answer – and maybe I won't." The connection went dead.

She didn't even say goodbye, he thought, staring at the small screen.

≈ ≈ ≈ ≈

Alec winced. A bright, midday sun shone on his face. He rubbed his eyes. *Strange,* he thought. *It was after 3:00 when I got to the Lab.* He sat up in the spongy dirt and leaned against a clump of the stiff wiry grass. Every muscle in his body was sore. He felt like he had just finished a grueling workout, and his stomach was still rebelling against whatever had happened. Alec shook his head, trying to clear the fuzz from his brain. He could feel a slight wave of heat from his medallion, almost as if he was still in the Lab with the dark energy concentrator active.

Gingerly, he stood up and looked around. In every direction as far as he could see were rolling grasslands, with the coarse gray-green grass flowing endlessly in wind-swept waves, punctuated with the dark bushes. Had he been here before? *Looks sort of like the high plains out West,* he thought, where he had hiked last summer before he met Sarah. Except this grass was much taller, and coarser. And the purplish ground was soft, not like the high desert floor, and punctuated with rocks scattered across the surface. *Where am I?* He had no idea.

His first thought was that he needed to get the medallion back to the Lab before Dr. Alder noticed it was missing. With no better alternative, Alec slowly made his way to the top of the nearest rise. *There must be a road somewhere,* he thought. *Find a road and then hitch a ride to civilization and figure out what is going on.* As he walked his legs gradually regained strength, and his body began to feel more normal. *Too bad my cell phone's still in my locker. If I had it, I could GPS my location and call for a ride.* The medallion continued to pulse, oddly soothing, feeling like it was feeding dark energy into his body.

Alec reached the top of the rise. A slight breeze caught his hair as he looked slowly in every direction. All he saw was the swaying sea of grass, covering rise after rise to the horizon, losing definition in shimmering mirages. There was no sign of a road, or a fence, or a building, or even a path. Nothing. He let out a long sigh.

Then, he paused. *What's that?* On a far hill, near the horizon, something moved. One, two, three, four figures appeared, taller than the waving grass. Were they people – on horseback? *They must know the way out of here,* Alec reasoned. He waved and yelled. At first, they continued their slow lope across the shimmering hill. Alec yelled again. Then the riders saw him and changed their direction to head towards him.

As they moved in his direction, they gained pace, coming into focus. The riders were people, but their mounts were – different. Alec was not fond of horses, but at least he knew what they looked like, and how they moved. These animals were the size and dun color of a horse but looked more like a cross between a horse and a lion – even though they had riders, they had cat-like heads, a shaggy mane and a substantial tail. As they moved smoothly through the sea of grass, Alec could make out their long narrow feet, and as they came even closer, he could see that they had fangs, like saber-toothed tigers of old, and prominent claws, almost like a large raptor.

The riders continued to approach him. Three of them were men, stout and coarsely dressed, each with something that looked like a sword strapped to his side. The men rode the lanky beasts with an ease that could only come from years of experience. Last was a woman, younger than the others, with a slender athletic build, barefoot, and oddly dressed in what looked like a hopsack shift. *Like a flour sack with a neck-hole and arm slits.* It barely came down to mid-thigh and was awkwardly bunched up for riding. She was not riding the same kind of animal – her mount looked more like a cross between an ox and a camel, with a long neck but a flat back. *Maybe a giant llama,* he thought. Her animal lumbered through the grass, but she rode with a grace that made the men look clumsy.

She's quite attractive, Alec thought. Her dark hair was tangled but flowed mid-way down her back. She had a snug metal band around her neck. *Odd jewelry – looks too tight.* She raised her eyes and looked directly at him, and, for the first time, he noticed that her hands were tied together and attached to the pommel of her saddle.

Quit looking at the girl. The riders had slowed their pace as they came near.

"Hey!" Alec called. "Am I glad to see you!"

The riders continued to move slowly towards him, step by step.

"I'm lost," Alec said, holding out his hand in greeting. "Can you tell me where I am?"

The riders stopped. Did the one on the left reach for his sword? Suddenly Alec felt very uncomfortable, and his stomach clenched. *Where am I and what have I gotten myself into?*

"Hey," said Alec, weakly, dropping his hand. One of the men responded in a guttural language that Alec had never heard before. From grad students at the Institute and professional meetings, Alec was familiar with the sounds of Spanish, French, German, and a few other languages. This didn't sound like any of those.

The three men goaded their animals forward, leaving the woman behind. She looked at Alec with concern in her eyes. Somehow, he could tell it wasn't concern for herself; it was concern for him. His apprehension heightened. *Just want to go home and soak out these aches in a hot bath.*

The three stopped about twenty feet from him. Alec noted they were dressed pretty much alike, in dark, heavy clothes. They wore thick boots, leather vests, and ill-fitting leather helmets. They were shorter than Alec, bearded, hairy, and peered up at him intently from under thick eyebrows; their weather-beaten skin was the texture of worn leather, with old dirt tracing the creases. From their dusty appearance and odor, Alec guessed that they had not slept indoors, or taken a bath, in a very long time.

The middle one said something in his guttural language.

"I'm sorry, I don't speak your language. I am lost. Can you take me to your officers?" Alec asked.

The middle man motioned to the man on his left and uttered a brief word in a brusque tone; the girl flinched. The man dismounted and with a couple of steps, he cut the distance towards Alec by half and drew a crude sword from his side.

He is about to attack me! Alec thought. The girl cried out in warning as the sword rose and began a long high sweep towards his neck. Only Alec's athletic reflexes saved him. His body instinctively dodged under the sweep and he rolled on the ground to the right. He came up on his feet. The assailant looked surprised that he had missed. He came forward and swung again. This time Alec backed away. A third and a fourth swing. Each one was getting closer, and any blow that connected would be death. *What can I do?* Running wouldn't work. The men with their mounts could quickly catch him.

Maybe, Alec thought, *this is some strange dark energy test. One of Alder's little games.* He had his medallion. Could he use it? Should he? He didn't have many options, he decided. *Focus.* He felt his medallion pulsing. The next swish of the blade came and missed. *Focus!* The blade swished again. Alec stepped back and tripped over a clump of grass. Now sprawled on his back, Alec watched wide-eyed as the man raised the blade and started a downward slice that would cleave him in two pieces. *Focus.* He felt the dark energy flow – except now it seemed fuller and richer than usual.

Time slowed.

The blade continued its descent but now seemed as slow as if it was moving through thick molasses. Alec rolled to his right. The blade buried itself in the ground where Alec had just been. Alec kicked at his attacker. He felt his kick moving through the thick air around him and into the other man's ribs. Something went pop! and the intruder fell to the ground in a heap, writhing in obvious pain. The leader looked surprised at the outcome but motioned to his other man.

What is going on? Alec thought. *This is not good. I got lucky once, but it won't happen three times. These guys want to kill me!* Alec grabbed a small rock and looked at the leader. *Focus.* He sensed the medallion and felt the dark energy. He picked an aim point in the middle of the leader's face, infused the rock with dark energy, and launched it towards the leader. He knew, somehow, that it would be right. The rock screamed as its velocity exceeded the speed of sound and headed true towards the man's head.

The rock slammed home, midway between the man's eyes, just as Alec had envisioned. But Alec had never imagined the outcome. The leader's head split like a ripe watermelon. Brains splattered in every direction. The third man, half dismounted from his beast, was splattered with gore. The leader slumped from his mount onto the ground. Alec looked in horror at what he had done.

The third man's expression quickly changed from anger to disbelief to fear. He shot Alec a look of panic, hopped back onto his mount, forced it around, and galloped off in the direction he had come. Within no time he vanished into the swirling hills of grass.

Alec stood in shock staring down at the faceless man. Alec had never been in a serious fight; had never killed anything other than a few errant insects; had never witnessed a violent death. The only dead person he had ever even seen was his grandmother on her bier.

What have I done? Was this – murder? Should he report his act to some police authority, somewhere? Or – what if these men were the police? *Did I do the right thing? But – they were trying to kill me.* Alec continued to stare at the body and the dark ooze of blood seeping from the remains of the slain man's head. A body that until a few moments ago was a living, sentient being.

Alec had no idea how much time passed. He might have stood looking at the blood forever if a lilting voice did not poke at the edge of his mind. He looked up. The ox-like creature was still present, with the girl tied on it. She had ridden her mount forward and was trying to speak to him in a language he didn't understand, different from the guttural grunts of the others. The urgency in her voice indicated that she wanted something. *Does she want to kill me, too?*

Alec walked towards her. "I don't understand," he said. The creature, certainly not a llama, glared at him and showed its teeth. The girl motioned to his left. He stared at her.

"What?"

She repeated the gesture.

Alec finally got it. *She wants to be let loose.* He walked to her mount and gingerly tried to untie the knot holding her wrists to the saddle. The creature again gave a low snarl, and Alec shifted warily. Her bonds were well-tied, and the knot was in a position he couldn't easily reach. The girl spoke and motioned to her left again. He looked in that direction and saw the sword from the first assailant sticking from the ground. *Use the sword to cut the rope – that is what she is saying,* Alec thought. Alec grabbed the sword and pulled. With difficulty, it came out of the ground. He couldn't help but think it could be his body impaled by the sword if things had turned out differently.

Sword in hand, Alec turned towards the ox-creature. It snarled again but the girl curbed the beast, and it quieted enough to allow Alec to approach. Alec awkwardly sawed at the ropes – the sword seemed to be quite dull, but eventually the ropes came free, and the girl slid down from the saddle.

She stood before him and stared at him. Her face was angular and striking, tanned as if she was used to the outdoor life, but not weather-beaten like the men. Her hair was jet black, tangled and matted with grass, but appeared to have been well-tended until recently. She had brown eyes and dark brows. She had a lithe, athletic body, about five and a half feet tall. *No fat on her body,* he thought. The sack she was wearing didn't do anything to accent her features, but her features didn't need any help, he thought. It also didn't seem like the right thing for riding.

I have Sara waiting for me at home – why am I looking at her? Alec thought, slightly ashamed.

≈ ≈ ≈ ≈

Erin looked at her rescuer. He was tall – well over a head taller than she, and she was as tall as most men. He wore strange close-fitting blue-colored trousers and brightly-colored cloth moccasins tied in front with colorful strings. His tunic was a simple short-sleeved pullover covered with runes of unknown kinds. *Why would anyone wear runes on their clothing?* she thought. He had a pleasant face, she decided. At first, from a distance she had thought he was a boy, but now that she was close she could see that he was one of the few men who took their beard off. His light-brown hair was cut in an odd short style and was clean, with no evidence of lice. He had nice eyes, blue, and an inquisitive look that didn't appear threatening. He was probably a little older than she, but close to her age, she guessed. He was well-built but not as heavily-muscled as a gladiator or a warrior.

When Erin spoke again, the tall man gestured that he didn't understand. Erin motioned towards the sword, and he handed it to her. She walked over to the first assailant, still lying unconscious where he had fallen, and nudged him with her foot. He moaned slightly. Without a second glance, she rolled him on his back, thrust the dull sword into his chest, and twisted. He writhed and with a final shudder, lay dead. She spat on the man's body and cursed the ancient curse of the victor.

Swiftly she removed the boots and trousers from the body and slipped them on. Not a good fit for either and not at all complimentary, she thought, but much more functional in the grass than the slave tunic she was wearing. She glanced at the tall man before she wiped the sword clean on the dead man's shirt and slid it into a loop on the belt of her purloined trousers.

Now she turned to the tall man and tried again to speak to him.

≈ ≈ ≈ ≈

Alec watched, horrified, as the girl casually killed the unconscious man and stole his clothes. He felt slightly sick and turned away from the man's body.

The girl said something to him that he could not understand.

Maybe she doesn't know English, Alec thought.

"Hola," Alec said. *"¿Quién eres tú?"* She looked at him blankly. *Nope, Spanish isn't it.*

"Guten Tag!" Still no response.

She looked at him quizzically, concerned but not afraid of him. Then she stepped closer to him and held out her right index finger. Slowly and deliberately, she touched her finger to the center of his forehead. Alec felt a torrent of thoughts, and then words, pouring into him and a torrent pouring out from him. The girl started to remove her finger but hesitated, and let it rest on his head a little longer. Finally, she pulled her finger away.

Alec collapsed. It was all he could take. The girl seemed to understand and guided him, crawling, underneath one of the low bushes.

≈ ≈ ≈ ≈

The next thing Alec knew, the sun was rising and the girl was curled up next to him.

"You put out enough heat to make the night tolerable," she said. Then he realized he knew what she said.

"I can understand you!"

"Of course, Alec. I think I can understand your language also."

He thought for a second. "You are Erin." She smiled and nodded, pleased.

"Where are we?" Alec asked. *And how do I get home,* he wanted to add.

"We are here."

"Not helpful."

"Halfway between Arose and Betin. We are in the Grasslands. Toward the morning sun is my land – Theland."

Maybe we're in central Africa? or Eastern Europe?

"Who were those men trying to kill me? And why? I didn't do anything to them."

"They are men from a nomad tribe, the Gryg. They are about sixty warriors, not counting their women, children, and slaves. They terrorize everyone who passes through this region. They heard the disturbance you caused yesterday and came to see what it was. They did not want to let anything that could make that noise live."

Noise?

"What noise?" *What is she talking about?*

"They heard the deep roar and then a loud boom. They are very superstitious. They were afraid that it was the sound of a dragon. I know better: I have seen and heard a dragon, and I knew that wasn't a dragon sound. But they came to investigate. You are what they found."

Dragons? Alec shook his head. Maybe he wasn't fully awake.

"And you. Why were you with them?" *She can't be a member of this homicidal maniac nomad group.*

"I am their slave," she said simply. "See this metal piece around my neck? It makes me a slave to anyone who wants to command me. You can command me. You can command me to do whatever you want."

"Me?"

"Anyone. If I resist, a white pain fills my mind! It becomes increasingly intense until all I can think about is making the pain go away. Then, my body will eagerly do what is commanded, even if I do not want to do it. I am answering your question willingly because otherwise, the neckpiece would cause intense pain." She paused.

"Please don't abuse me as they did," she said softly, her lip quivering slightly and tears welling up in her dark brown eyes.

Alec started to reach for her hand, but pulled back, afraid she would misunderstand.

"How did you get to be their ... slave?" Alec asked softly.

Regaining her composure, she continued her story. "A month ago, I was on a caravan with my brother. I used to go with my father, who was one of the leaders of Theland, my homeland. Father would make this trip every Spring to trade goods with the other peoples. Sometimes I think he made the trip as much to learn what was happening in the lands around us as to sell goods.

"And this year, he is gone. Father had always been so strong and healthy, but he got sick last winter and died. I don't know what sickness he had. It was very sudden. This year, Devin, my brother, thought it was very important to make the annual trip even without Father. He was going to travel alone. Mother did not want me to go with him, because it is always dangerous. But I wanted to get away for a while..." She drifted off and turned her head away from Alec's gaze. Then she again met his eyes. "I was distraught ... I was upset over … I was distraught over a lost love at home and wanted to go away for a while." She took a deep breath. "I talked to our Seer, to see if I would be safe. She told me that making this trip would have a profound effect on the future of my people. So, I insisted, and Mother let me come.

"This is the third year I have made this trip; the first without Father. It usually takes about three weeks. We start after the snows melt. Devin and I joined a caravan that was moving across the Grasslands. We thought our passage would be safe. Usually, only lone wagons are bothered by the nomads."

She paused and drew another deep breath. "But a week or so into this trip, Devin became sick. It was very strange. He just got sicker and sicker, and then died a few days later." She shook her head. "I think he was poisoned because the caravan leader did not seem concerned about his sickness spreading. I was only able to give my brother a brief departing ceremony before the caravan moved on. I had to carry on alone and take our wagon the rest of the way. But I knew I could do it, even without him."

"A week later the Gryg came to the caravan and demanded payment for passage across the Grasslands. I have never heard of them doing that to large caravans! And then …" she stopped, and looked down at her wrists, still red from her bondage. "And then the caravan leader gave <u>me</u> as payment to the nomads!" She swallowed hard, and then spoke faster and faster, as though reliving the event. "I resisted but didn't have a weapon. I started to run, but one of the caravan thugs tripped me. The nomads grabbed me by the hair and pulled me down. Then they put a sack over my head, so I wouldn't know where their camp was, and tied me onto a pack animal. Sideways, like a sack of meal! When they got to their camp, they threw me on the ground and untied me. Three of them held me down while the Gryg leader put this slave band around my neck. It was awful!" Tears again welled up, and she paused; then a lone tear escaped and slowly trickled down her cheek.

"If you are a slave, and do not do as you are told, there is intense pain. So painful that you cannot even see. I had to obey! I could not bear it! The leader, the one you killed, made me his and used me whenever he wanted. He said that with the slave neckpiece he could break me in a day, but that he liked to watch the fear in my eyes when he had me. He said that after this trip he would finally break my mind to his will. He hadn't yet broken me, he said, because about half the people die in the process and he wanted to enjoy me first in case I died." She wiped the tear away with the back of her hand, closed her eyes, and shuddered. Then, she tossed her head back, black hair swirling, nostrils flaring.

"He was a pig," she said angrily. "A dead pig now!" She inhaled quickly. "I would rather die than be broken for the rest of my life!"

Her narrative came to an end, and Alec looked at her as what she had told him sunk in. She had been kidnapped and abused, and she was now free of her captors. Gently he reached towards her and took both her hands in his. She stiffened, and then slowly relaxed as she saw he meant her no harm.

She sighed.

"I think the caravan got what it deserved, though," she said.

"How's that?" asked Alec.

"A couple of days after they captured me, I saw some of Devin's things in the nomad camp." Her lip curled. "I think the nomads attacked the caravan, after the caravan leader sold me to them, and took all of their goods." She snorted. "I hope they killed them all, all of those caravan skarns!"

2 – Preparations

Alec sat near a clump of grass with his knees drawn up, his head resting on his fist, while Erin tended to the horse-beasts.

What's going on? What is this place?

Yesterday he was at his Lab at the Institute, and no one was trying to kill him. Now, this morning, he was sleeping outside under a clump of grass with a girl with long black hair. And yesterday a man had tried to kill him, and he had killed a person in a gory hideous way.

Yesterday had started out normally. He got up, went for a run, left his apartment, ran some errands, read a technical article on potential applications for dark energy, and walked to the Lab and had an argument with Sarah.

He had started his last experiment on dark energy last Thursday morning. That should have been four days ago. Then one of the dark energy compressors had broken down, and it was late in the day before he could get back to his work. That meant it would be Saturday before he had all the data he needed for his next set of calculations. He had intended to go out to the park with Sarah on Saturday, but he had to check his data first. He knew that she wouldn't be pleased, but he didn't have much choice.

Alec felt honored, and somewhat pleased with himself, to be part of the Institute's Dark Energy Research Team. Dr. Alder was internationally recognized as the lead researcher in this field and had assembled a top-notch team here at the Institute. Hooking up with Sarah, Dr. Alder's protégé, was an added bonus.

Alec was amazed at how the equipment at the Lab, including the large dark energy collector, allowed for work far beyond anything he had previously been able to do. Dark energy had so much potential. With a dark energy collector and a special medallion, a person could mentally focus waves of energy and perform incredible actions. Some people called it 'magic.' Alec knew better. He had developed a theoretical basis for combining a dark energy collector with a mental focus, powered by the human imagination, and had written his PhD thesis on this topic. His research showed that dark energy, combined with focused human intentions, could have an unlimited potential for bettering the world – although Sarah laughed at what she called his 'unbridled idealism.'

Much of the research conducted at the Lab had implications for national security and was classified as 'Top Secret' or higher. For that reason, most of the technical research papers were classified and not available in the general scientific literature. A person had to have a security clearance to access the facility or the published articles – even the clerical staff positions required a clearance. Now that he had recently received his own security clearance, Alec felt fortunate indeed to be able to finally read the reports and calculations, and see all parts of the Lab facilities.

As the most recent person to join the team, Alec knew he was at the bottom of the pecking order. The research was interesting, and most of the people on the team were okay. He met Sarah a few days after arriving at the Institute and they immediately hit it off. She actually seemed to be pursuing him, Alec thought wistfully. Soon they were dating and then romantically involved. Sarah seemed to be a favorite of Dr. Alder and helped Alec figure out the ropes around the Lab; but due to the classified nature of their research, he still didn't know what she was working on. It was secret, and they didn't talk about it.

After his first few months on the job, Alec noted that Dr. Alder was more of a technician than he was – Alder excelled at making the equipment work to harness dark energy in ways that no one else could – but Alec felt that he was better at understanding <u>why</u> it worked and how to use dark energy. Alec's current set of experiments involved a new way to use dark energy to create tricrystals. Tricrystals were the heart of the medallions the researchers wore, and the medallions were essential to focus dark energy.

Yesterday he should have been at the park with Sarah, but he thought his research experiment was more important. *Was that just a day ago?* He had gone to the Lab to check on his data. He checked in through the security gate, placed his cell phone and wallet in his locker, which was a security requirement, and entered the secure Lab area. He took his medallion from its container near the Lab entrance, hung it around his neck, and opened the door into the central area.

Someone was in the central chamber, using the dark energy generator. *Who could be here?* Alec thought. *And why is the generator on?* No other researchers had logged in through the security gate that afternoon before he did. For safety reasons, all generator work was supposed to be done with at least two people on site. *Do I need to turn the generator off?* He walked into the dark energy generator room. His medallion started to throb. The room was full of dark energy at levels he had never seen before.

"Who is in there?" Alec shouted.

"Go away!" a voice commanded from within the chamber. "Get out of here immediately!"

Instead of following the command, Alec continued into the chamber. *If someone is in trouble, they will need help!* The lone figure in the chamber came into view.

Dr. Alder stood at the control console. Light from the control panel reflected from his glasses in strange patterns of purple and green. No one else was in in the experimental chamber. Power was pulsing and focusing on a tiny sphere in the middle of the room. Alder's attention was on the sphere.

Alec watched in quiet fascination. Whatever was happening was beyond anything he had contemplated. He could sense the energy being focused in ways he hadn't considered. Slowly the energy started to convalesce into the sphere and then into a ring between Alder and the sphere. The power glowed, and Alder started to turn transparent. Then a slight perturbation occurred in the ring. *Oh no!* thought Alec. *It is picking up on the focus from my medallion!* Alder looked up and saw Alec.

"No!" Alder shouted. "Get out!"

Alec felt the perturbation turn into a massive instability, like a giant roar inside his head. Instabilities could be very dangerous – even lethal – and was one reason why a researcher never worked alone. Instabilities released massive amounts of raw power. The only thing Alec could do now was to try to smooth the instabilities. Although he had read about instability reduction he had never actually done it. With some effort, Alec succeeded in reducing the low-order perturbations and then started on the higher-order effects. He could see that the variances were subsiding, but Alder wasn't helping to quell the flow of power. Instead, Alder seemed to be feeding the instabilities in ways that Alec didn't understand. Alec knew he couldn't keep this under control without Alder's help, and started to call out.

Then suddenly everything was flashing colors and vertigo.

$\approx \approx \approx \approx$

So back to the question. What happened and where am I?

Alec looked up. Erin was looking at him with a bemused expression.

"Where are we?" Alec asked.

"I told you. We are half-way between Arose and Betin," Erin said, as if tutoring a child.

"But I don't know those towns! What state are we in? Or what country?" *Could this be Canada?*

"I don't know what that means," said Erin. "I told you. This is the Grassland. I do not live here. My land is Theland and is far toward the morning sun."

"Who is in charge here?" asked Alec.

"No one rules the Grasslands," Erin answered, "but many travel across it."

Alec sighed and looked up. *Still, no idea where I am*, he thought. The morning sun was well over the horizon now. Three moons were racing across the sky.

"No!" said Alec. "The moons – what – what happened?"

"What do you mean?" she said, puzzled.

"The moons! There are three of them!"

Erin looked at him with a strange expression. "That's because the other two haven't come up yet," she said.

Alec shook his head, exasperated. *Think.*

One of the theories behind dark energy was that alternate universes exist, but no one had proven that. But was it true? Was this a test? The last thing that happened before he showed up here (*wherever "here" is*) was walking into the dark energy chamber, and Alder yelling at him to get out. Then there was some explosion. The dark energy must have thrown him somewhere else – this place – this Grassland. *Is this some alternate universe?* Maybe that was what Alder was working on. *Or maybe I'm in a different point in time.* He couldn't be in the past, because Earth had never had five moons. So, if he was on Earth, he must be in the future. But technologically speaking, this did not seem like the future. It seemed like the Middle Ages. And he was clearly in a different place. *A different universe, then?* The thought gave him a headache.

Erin was still standing in front of him, looking at him awkwardly.

Alec pulled his mind back to the present.

"What do we do now?" Alec asked.

"Whatever you want," she answered.

"What do you mean?"

"I am a slave," Erin said, shrugging her shoulders, "either theirs or yours. As long as I wear this neckpiece, I am a slave. And as long as I wear it, their key will be attracted to it and they can find me and make me do whatever they want."

"Then how do we take the neckpiece off?"

Erin looked at him, her eyes growing wider. "You would take the neckpiece off me? But then I will no longer be your slave!" She drew a quick breath through tight lips. "It will only come off with the key, and the nomad leader had the key. You killed him. But he didn't bring it with him yesterday, and the key is not here – it is back at their camp."

Alec stepped closer and put his hand on the metal collar. He passed his hand over the latch and squinted at the small keyhole. As part of the Lab's commercial applications work, before he had received his security clearance, he had helped a small specialty-metals company make unusual components using dark energy. This didn't look very different from the specialty work he had done there.

"What if I can make a key – would that work?" he asked.

"I don't know," replied Erin. Making a key had never occurred to her.

Alec looked at the keyhole. *What could I use? Chemically it would have to have about the same number of protons and neutrons.* He looked around, then scraped a handful of dirt from the spongy ground and placed it on a flat rock. *Focus.* Alec touched his medallion and could feel the dark energy start to flow. *Focus.* The energy started to pulse, and he started to work it into a form. He closed his eyes, and in his mind could feel the metal band around Erin's neck and the keyhole. He could sense the holes in the fitting. Slowly at first, then quickly like an eel, the small pile of dirt writhed and flowed, transforming into a set of rectangular and cylindrical blocks.

"Done," said Alec with a pleased smile.

"What is that?" asked Erin. "It doesn't look at all like a key!"

"This is just like something I used to do at the Institute," said Alec. "It is a model of the blank space inside your lock. Now I just have to make a key to fit the blanks."

Alec moved his model and piled another handful of dirt on his rock.

Focus. The dark energy moved, and the purplish dirt transformed into a dark metal key.

"Shall we try?"

Alec carefully inserted the key into the lock and twisted. It resisted briefly and then grabbed, and the latch popped open. Erin grabbed the neckpiece with both hands and pulled it off her neck. She shook her head, glad to be free of its weight. Then with a muffled yell, she flung the neckpiece as far as she could into the sea of grass.

"You have freed me. I am thankful and owe you a great debt," she said, bowing her head before him.

"No," said Alec. "I wanted to do that for you. I think it was the right thing to do, and you do not owe me anything." He looked at her cautiously. "But I would appreciate you helping me find my way to safety so that I can go home."

"I can try," she answered. Then, "What is this 'Institute' that allows you to do such things?"

"It is a school," he said. "It is where I learned about dark energy, and how to use it."

"A 'Wizard School'!" she exclaimed.

Alec didn't know how to answer. The old saying about advanced science looking like magic was clearly true.

Alec changed to a more pressing subject. "We need to get you to a safe place and then find a way to get me home. Can we take you back to your … home?"

"No. I cannot go back now."

"Why not?"

"I must have my rings before I return. I will not return without them."

"Rings? What rings?"

"My family's rings! The First Mother's rings! They have been passed down in my family for five hundred years." She paused, then went on, ready to confide in him. "They originally came from the First Mother, the elf Lian, who settled our land. I am a direct descendant of the First Mother. The rings give those descended from her the ability to sense truth and to defend our people against the elves. My mother has two rings, and I was entrusted with the other two – the nomads took them from me. Without the rings, I cannot protect my people."

"Where are they?" Alec suspected he knew the answer.

"Somewhere in the Gryg camp," she said.

Alec clenched his fist and punched the air. "Those guys just tried to kill me," he said angrily, "and they made you a slave, and you want to go and just wander back into their camp to look for some mere family trinkets that might not even be there?"

"Yes!" she said defiantly. "They are not mere 'trinkets'! They are essential to the safety of my people. I can find them! I can sense the rings when I am close to them."

"Why did you bring them with you if they are essential to your people's safety?"

Erin looked contrite. "I was not supposed to bring them. They are supposed to be locked in my mother's vault. My mother would be furious if she knew I brought them, but I thought I could practice using them to sense the people we visited."

"Why don't you just get some more rings when you get home?" asked Alec.

"We can't make rings! The rings came from the elves. We have had the rings for many generations. I cannot go home without my rings."

"We should get out of here and go find help. Then maybe after that we can come back and find your rings."

She gestured towards the hillside where the nomads' bodies lay. "The nomads will be coming for us," she said patiently. "They will see what happened to their leader. They will see that he no longer has a head. They will want to seek their due revenge. And since we are only two, they will certainly catch us before we get anywhere to find help."

The concept of more nomads coming after them had not occurred to Alec. *But of course.* The nomad who fled after the fight with Alec would have made his way back to the Gryg camp and told the others what had happened. They would not be happy leaving two dead members unavenged.

Alec considered his options. He was reluctant to enter the nomad camp to recover the rings, but the girl was determined. Since she was his only link to the world beyond this grassland, he didn't see that he had much choice but to stick with her. At least for a while. *She is pretty,* he thought.

"Where is the nomad camp?"

"It is about a half-day toward evening from here."

Which way is that? Alec was struggling with the concepts of direction in a language he had never heard until yesterday. "How do we get there – and more important – what are we going to do when we get there? Do we need some weapons?"

Erin looked at him. "You are a Great Wizard. I have only heard stories of great wizards. You will defeat the pigs!" She smiled.

'Great Wizard'! Ha! I'm lucky to be alive! "Maybe the first step is to find something to eat," Alec said. "Then we can develop a plan." He gestured in the direction of the nomads' bodies. "Did they bring any provisions with them? A snack, maybe?"

"Yes, they brought a day's worth of food. That is one of the reasons I was along, to prepare food for them. Do you want me to prepare it, oh Great Wizard?"

"Please. I have no idea how to do anything here."

The horse-beasts were tied to a stout bush a short distance away with their saddles and panniers stacked nearby. Erin rummaged through the nomads' supplies and pulled out a couple of small bundles and brought them to Alec.

"What are those things?" Alec asked, pointing at the animals.

"The trogus? Those two are trogus. They are just not very large. They are fighting animals. Riding trogus are larger. The third beast is a drung. It is a beast of burden." She rolled her R's; Alec noted, part of the lilting cadence of her language.

"Oh," Alec said. He was obviously expected to know what a 'trogus' was. *And I guess now I do,* he thought.

Erin looked at him. "Can you make a fire for us?"

Alec thought for a minute.

"If I make a fire, they may see our smoke, but I might be able to do something even better." Alec felt for his medallion, pulsing with dark energy. *Focus.*

Alec arranged four rocks together. Then he thought about lava, deep in the earth. The rocks turned red briefly and then solidified with resounding pops as the surface layer flaked off like so many crickets, just as he recalled from watching lava flows in Hawaii.

There. "Those hot rocks should be perfect for cooking.," he announced.

Erin looked at them suspiciously, but she put her hand over the rocks and could feel the heat rising from them. She spat on one and watched her spit bubble and boil. With the water and supplies from the trogus' packs, she soon had a potful of gruel bubbling on the hot rocks.

Looks like oatmeal, Alec thought. He ate with relish. It was gritty, but not bad, and he suddenly noticed that he was very hungry.

$\approx \approx \approx \approx$

Now it was time to plan. Alec needed a weapon that would give him more range than the nomads' swords. But it had to be something simple, that he could make. Thinking back to his college days Alec thought of playing lacrosse. He could link dark energy with a simple sling, like a lacrosse stick, to give him an advantage. With a little searching he found a stick that would do. *Focus.* The stick transformed itself into a straight rod with a pouch on one end. He collected several rocks for a test.

Erin watched with interest.

Focus. Alec put a rock into the sling. He focused on an impact point on a boulder about thirty yards away, infused the rock with dark energy and launched it.

<u>Zing</u>. A fiery contrail traced the path of the small rock through the air, and with a loud bang! The rock slammed into the boulder. Fragments spewed in all directions.

Erin clapped. "Good show, oh Great Wizard!"

Alec knew better. *No great wizard here. Just a simple guy who wants to go home and take a nice long bath. And a shave.* He felt the stubble on his face. *Definitely a shave.*

If the dark energy field stayed high, Alec knew, he could tap into it, but if the field dropped he would be helpless. He had to use enough dark energy to accomplish his task, but not expend more energy than needed. *Try this again.* On the second try, Alec put less energy in the stone. It hit solidly in the middle of his target without all the fanfare.

The first step was under control. Erin walked around gathering a supply of right-sized rocks for projectiles while Alec thought about the next step. In addition to the long-range lacrosse sling, he also would need a short-range weapon. Alec looked at the two swords Erin had harvested from the two dead nomads. Alec knew that against a practiced swordsman, there was no way he could use a sword well enough to keep himself alive. What weapon could he obtain that would be effective against a sword? Some memory of old adventure movies reminded him that a staff was an efficient weapon against a sword. Maybe he could make a staff and use it for close range.

The next issue was finding a long stick among the tall grass. He searched for an hour looking for a long straight rod. There were none. *Good idea but it's not going to work,* he told himself. Then he thought, *why do I need one straight piece?* He had two swords but only needed one staff. *Focus.* The first sword transformed into a thin rod. Alec had imagined aluminum, but he had no idea whether it was aluminum or iron or even titanium. In the short run, it didn't matter. *This will work.* He poked around the low bushes and took several long branches from a nearby shrub. *Focus.* The branches looped around the central rod and fused together. He looked at the final product. It had a nice curling pattern from the branches and felt very good to hold. The only problem was the ends. They would fray.

He could fix that. *Focus.* Energy swirled, and two metal end caps emerged on the staff. They had the proper light gray color of titanium, but Alec could not tell if he was working to that level of detail. *It doesn't matter,* he decided – the end caps were metal and would keep everything together. If they rusted or corroded in a month or a year, he could worry about that later. Making it through the day was his concern now.

As he finished his staff, Erin returned with a dozen perfectly-sized rocks for his sling. She looked at his staff with interest, but it was clear that she was underwhelmed by the simple piece.

"We need to equip you," Alec said, rubbing his hand along his jaw.

"I could use this," Erin said tentatively, picking up the remaining sword and swinging it. "I know how to use a sword." But even Alec could see that this one wasn't right for her. It was almost a yard long and designed for a two-handed grip.

"How can we make it better?" Alec mused.

Erin looked at it.

"Well, to start with," she said, "it is too long, the balance is wrong, and it is dull as an old tooth."

"Anything else?"

"Well," she said, still looking at it, "it's rather plain."

Alec imagined the sword he wanted. *Focus.* The end of the old sword's blade split off from the rest. *Focus.* Now he had the shape he wanted – *Focus* – and he feathered in a harder metal alloy at the blade's edge to keep it sharp.

Erin picked it up, swung it a few times and tried the blade on a piece of her long hair. It cut without hesitation.

The hilt is wrong, Alec thought.

"Show me your hand," he said to Erin. She stuck out her hand, first palm-side up, then turning it over to show him the back.

Focus – and the hilt shifted and shuddered and shrank until it looked about the right size for Erin's hand. *Focus,* again, and the hilt covered itself with a microfiber style leather that would wick away moisture and keep the grip dry.

Now for the next step. Decoration. *But with a purpose.* Alec knew how to do this well. The ability to create diamonds or other gemstones with dark energy was one attribute that had first attracted him to study this field of science; at one time he had hoped to make large baubles to impress a former girlfriend. The girl departed before he could make any jewels, but his interest in the field of using dark energy to make other materials stayed with him. His mind strayed as he thought how the ability to make diamonds with dark energy had led to a law requiring three labels on diamonds: natural, synthetic, and artificial.

He brought his attention back to the sword. *Focus* – and a thumb-sized diamond appeared on the end of the hilt. *Focus* – and he created a small tricrystal and embedded it in the middle of the diamond. The tricrystal could feed dark energy into the sword.

"Perfect," Erin said, trying out the sword's new grip and admiring the diamond. She poked at the tricrystal frowning.

"Is it a flaw in the stone?" she asked, hesitantly.

"No," Alec said quickly. "It's a crystal. It will … help the sword."

She picked at the tricrystal with her fingernail, clearly not impressed.

"We need only a couple more little things," Alec said. He picked up the sword's dirty sheath. *Focus,* and the now-clean sheath shortened to fit the re-designed sword.

"One last thing," Alec said. *Focus.* Slowly the word 'Erin' appeared on the sword's blade. Alec took the sword, put the sword in its sheath, and handed it to her. "Pull the sword out," he said.

She drew the sword and could see 'Erin' written on the blade in stylized text.

"What are the runes?" she asked.

"They spell your name in my language. 'Erin.'"

"My name in Wizard-runes?" asked Erin, obviously pleased.

"Yes. And your name … the runes … will do one more thing. Let me show you."

Erin handed him the sword, and as soon as he held it, her name glowed like flames. Alec put the sword down, and the glow went away.

"How?" she said, wide-eyed, stepping back.

He laughed. "Don't worry! I will teach you how to make it do that." He pointed to the tricrystal. "This is what will make it glow. A 'tricrystal.' I will teach you how to feel the power crystal and control it. The crystal will also make the sword feel much lighter when you use it, and keep it sharp." He smiled, and turned the sword over, looking at each side in turn. Then he handed it back to her and shrugged. "But until I teach you how to do those things, it will work great as a normal sword."

Erin took the sword and strapped it on her side, quite pleased.

≈ ≈ ≈ ≈

By now the bright sun was high in the sky. It was time to break camp. Erin made a quick lunch and re-packed the trogus' panniers and harnessed the drung. Erin put the saddles and harness on the two trogus and led one towards Alec.

Alec eyed the beast warily. "We have a problem," he said.

"What is that?"

"I have never ridden any animal before. Not a horse, not anything! I have no idea what to do."

"What?" Erin said, laughing. "The Great Wizard can't ride a simple beast?"

"Sorry to disappoint," Alec said, somewhat annoyed. "I am neither a rider nor a 'great wizard.' I have no idea what to do!"

"That's all right," said Erin, still smiling. "I can teach you. I need to have some skills to make myself worthy of the Great Wizard."

Erin patted the saddled animal closest to Alec. "These are easy to ride. Some are very difficult, but these two are relatively docile, and small. Just show no fear. Climb on the saddle, and then direct her with the neck reins."

"Sounds easy."

But it wasn't. Alec's first attempt to mount the trogus was unsuccessful. He managed to get his foot in the stirrup, but as the animal shifted, he hopped alongside it, one foot up, one foot down. Erin got on the other trogus with practiced grace.

"Like this," she said.

Alec again put his foot in the stirrup and attempted to pull up onto the saddle. This time he overshot and came off the other side in a clumsy heap. The trogus turned and snarled at him.

"Hey!" Erin shouted sharply at the beast, and it calmed down.

Third time's the charm. With some effort, Alec made it onto the animal and in the saddle. Then they set off through the grass. Erin went first and set the pace. Alec struggled to stay in the saddle and keep up. Occasionally he managed to look forward and could see Erin gracefully and effortlessly riding her beast.

After about two hours, Alec had all he could take.

"We need to stop," he told Erin. She looked at him and nodded in agreement.

"It is just as well since we don't want to reach their camp tired and unprepared."

"How far away are we?"

"A couple of els moonward, I would think," she said. "The Gryg would not yet have moved their camp."

Alec had no clue whether an 'el' was a measure of distance, time, or something else. Or where 'moonward' was.

"Close, huh?" he said to no one in particular. Erin didn't answer. *Must be close.*

Erin spotted a dense clump of brush and headed for it. They dismounted: Erin quickly, Alec slowly, rubbing his hindquarters as he regained his footing. Erin unsaddled both trogus and hobbled them with a practiced skill that Alec could not imagine imitating.

"What do troguses eat? Will they feed on the local grass?" As Alec looked at the animals' sharp teeth, he knew it was a stupid question.

"They will eat any small animal they can find. These two were fed yesterday and won't need to eat again for a couple of days." Erin gave them a couple of pats on their thick necks and the one she had been riding nuzzled her shoulder. "But be careful. You don't want to be close to their face if they are hungry. They will take your arm off while you watch." Alec backed away from the animal, eying it warily. Erin laughed. "The drung, it is easier. It just eats grass."

Alec heated rocks again, and Erin made another meal of the gritty porridge. The sunlight was beginning to fade. Alec could see a moon through the brush – or was it two moons? Had the other moon set? Or were these different moons newly risen?

Erin was making a nest on the edge of the bushes large enough for the two of them and spread the blanket they had used the night before. Alec looked at it askance.

"We are sleeping together?"

"Of course, just like last night," she said. "We only have one blanket."

"Um … Okay, but … I have a steady girlfriend at home," Alec said. "I mean …" His voice trailed off.

Erin looked at him. "Great Wizard, we sleep together for warmth and protection. Besides, the nomads did as they wanted with me. There is nothing you can do that would be worse than what they have already done." She crawled into the bower. Darkness was falling quickly, and there seemed to be few options besides sleeping with her or staying up all night.

What the heck, thought Alec. *I'm so tired that I couldn't do anything if I wanted to.* The two of them curled up together, under the branches. *But she certainly is attractive,* he thought, and fell asleep.

3 – The Nomad Camp

Erin was already up and stirring about their camp when Alec woke. By now they had a routine: Alec collected and heated rocks while Erin made the porridge.

"This is the last of our food," Erin said. "We will need to do something else tomorrow."

"Okay," Alec answered, and added, "We will get to the Gryg camp today." *If it goes well,* Alec thought, *we will take their food. But if it goes badly … we won't need any more food.* "Can we get closer without them seeing us?"

"That will be difficult. They post guards, and there is little cover so our trogus will be easily seen."

"What if we try to sneak up on them, and just walk in?"

"No one has ever done that," Erin said, mulling over the idea. "It might be possible. We can try. But … if it doesn't work, we have no way to escape. They will run us down easily."

"Hmm." Alec thought a moment. "I wonder … let's try something."

Focus. A shimmering field of grass surrounded Alec.

"Can you see me?" he asked Erin.

Erin looked closely at the spot where Alec had just been standing. "If I really look, I can see you, but otherwise you vanish into the grass."

"Let's try it. The worst that can happen is we get killed." He laughed faintly.

"That is the worst for <u>you</u>," she said, clenching her jaw. "The worst for me is far more terrible."

Alec looked at her.

"Are your rings worth the risk?" he asked softly.

"Absolutely," she said.

This is stupid, he thought. The rational side of his brain said he should leave this girl, run, and find some other way home.

"Okay – we go for the rings." The rational side of his brain wasn't in control this morning.

Alec helped Erin hobble the three beasts and collect the items they would need. Erin had made a pack for Alec's weapons – his sling and his staff – and he put them on his back. They bagged the remainder of the supplies and stashed them under a bush near the trogus. Then they started a slow walk towards the nomad's camp. Periodically, Alec would create a dark energy lens and let the light bend around them, creating the illusion of grass waving gently in the wind.

They heard the first sentry before they saw him: a faint shuffling and loud coughing gave the man away. Alec bent the light around them as a shield, and the two stood stock still and watched as the sentry passed by. The man's trogus was nervous and sensed something, but did not growl enough to alert the sentry.

After an hour of cautious walking, they were on a ridge overlooking the Gryg camp. The camp was larger than Alec had supposed. There were at least fifty gaudy tents for the nomads and twice that number of simpler tents for the slaves and servants. In the corner of the camp were wagons and the plundered gains from various caravans.

"Where are your rings?" Alec whispered, squinting at the tents.

"I don't know," said Erin. "I can sense the rings when I get close to them. I suspect they are in the treasure tent." She pointed to a smallish tent near the center of the camp with red and purple stripes. "That middle tent is where they store the more valuable things that they steal." She scanned the camp again. "I will go closer and sense if they are there."

"All right. You sneak down to the tent, and I will try to create a diversion."

"I do not have to sneak," Erin said. "They know me. They will not be surprised to see me in the camp. If I pull my hair down, they will not notice the slave ring is not around my neck. I will walk to the tent. When I get close, you can distract them."

With that, she slipped off her moccasins and pants, leaving only the slave-girl shift. "If I am wearing more, they will notice," she said, not pleased with what she was doing.

"Take your sword," Alec said.

"Why? Slaves don't have swords."

"And you are not a slave," Alec said, impatiently. "Take it. You might need it."

She looked at her sword. "Well, maybe if I leave it in its scabbard so no one will see its blade … it doesn't look like a Gryg sword." She thought for a moment. "I know. I'll carry it like this," she said, holding it awkwardly over her shoulder, "as if I am on an errand for my master. That should work." Then she was off towards camp.

'Distract them.' Hmpf. Alec hoped her confidence in him was deserved.

His plan was simple. When she got close to the central tent, he would start a fire in a wagon on the other side, away from the treasure tent. Hopefully, in the ensuing confusion she could quickly slip in and slip out. If that didn't work, Alec thought of a couple of other diversions he could try.

Erin moved with confidence. She knew the workings of the camp and if she acted as if she was on an errand no one should challenge her. Using the outer tents as a cover, she entered the camp, walked beside some of the slave tents, and moved towards the center tents.

Focus. Alec started a fire in a medium-sized wagon on the far side of the camp. As soon as the nearby nomads noticed the flames, they started to shout for help. As Alec had planned, the fire created an uproar. Nomads and slaves ran to the fire to help extinguish the flames. Others ran in fear away from the fire.

Men and women passed Erin in each direction, responding to the fire or running from it. By the time she made it two-thirds of the way to the treasure tent, no one had challenged her, or, in the confusion caused by the fire, even noticed her. From his vantage point on the ridge, Alec watched her make her way around the tents and across the camp's open spaces with no one giving her a second look.

Uh-oh. He could see Erin coming around a small tent, with a nomad coming around the same tent from the other direction. Apparently, neither could see the other.

≈ ≈ ≈ ≈

Erin looked up as she rounded the tent corner and found herself face-to-face with a swarthy Gryg. *No!* She thought. *Why him?* This nomad had been a companion of her former master, the now-dead nomad leader; they had treated her viciously, sometimes together, sometimes alone. A sly smile appeared on his face as he recognized her, and she braced herself. Avoiding him was impossible.

"Slave!" he said. "I wanted you last night and couldn't find you. I will have you tonight, I am sure, but first – punishment for not appearing at my tent last night to see if I wanted you." He chuckled. "Down on your knees and pull up your garment, slave! I want your back to remember me tonight!"

"I am on an errand for my master," Erin said. "I have a task I must do. I must bring him his sword."

"Pretty cheeky for a slave!" the man growled. "Do it later!" He pulled a whip from his belt. "Down!"

Erin momentarily felt lost. She had been sure that no one would notice her; that she could pull off her charade with no trouble. The excruciating pain that the slave collar could cause was still fresh in her memory. She clumsily lowered the sword from her shoulder. If she just closed her eyes and let him whip her, she could cancel out the pain in her mind; he would be done in a few moments and then leave her alone. Then she could continue to the treasure tent.

No. Erin felt a new anger boiling in her. Alec's words rang in her ears. *'You are not a slave.'* She was no longer wearing the slave neckpiece – she did not have to submit to this Gryg! She hated him for what he had forced her to do.

Instead of dropping the sword, she felt for its hilt and with one swift motion pulled it from its scabbard and slashed towards her tormentor. He was frozen for an instant, shocked by her resistance to his demands, then stepped back and drew his weapon, his years of fighting saving him.

Erin knew she was one of the best sword fighters in her land, and from his lesser level of skill, she knew she could beat the nomad one-on-one. However, if the fight took too long, others would arrive to help him; while she might successfully fight two or three, she would not last against many. *The Wizard has not had enough time to create his diversion,* she thought. She was on her own. Her best hope was to win this fight quickly.

Although most people in the camp were still fighting the wagon fire, Erin knew it was just a matter of time before her fight was noticed. And soon, from the corner of her eye, she saw three more people come around the tent: a nomad and two slaves. The slaves, of course, did not have weapons, and the other man didn't have a sword – a stroke of luck. At their master's command, the two slaves grabbed long poles and started towards her. She had to end this before even more people discovered her.

Suddenly there was a loud pop! in the sky above the camp. Then a loud bang! followed by a high-pitched whooshing sound. Then, a second loud bang! The sky lit up with red streamers, expanding in all directions like the claws of a giant crab. A third bang! – now white streamers covered the sky.

Then, a bolt of lightning zapped from the sky and slammed into the ground with an audible crack!

The Wizard. Erin did not allow herself to look up, but she could see the two slaves recoil in terror and then flee with their master. Her assailant stopped and looked up at the sky, his hair on end, momentarily distracted from their fight. That was all Erin needed. Her sword flicked out like a snake's tongue, cutting deep into his left arm. He looked at her, startled, and then down at his wound as blood gushed from his severed artery. Erin lashed out with a cut across his throat. He dropped in shock in a pool of blood. Soundless words came from his mouth as the blood gurgled, then he slumped to the ground. Erin silently intoned the curse of the victor, then spat upon his form.

Erin exhaled in relief. She had avenged this stain on her honor.

≈ ≈ ≈ ≈

The Gryg camp was in chaos. The wagon still smoldered near the line of tents, thick smoke hugging the ground. The red and white streamers were slowly fading from the sky, with flickering bits drifting in the afternoon breeze. Nomads, slaves, and servants were running in terror, some trying to protect themselves from the rain of sparks with arms flung high.

"Dragons! Dragons in the sky!" they screamed in their guttural tongue.

Thanks, oh Wizard, Erin thought. The nomad guards were running from the dragon, ducking under wagons and behind tents. People continued to scream and run, this way and that, throughout the campground. *Maybe all is not lost.* She had a few moments before the nomad sentries regained their wits.

Erin sheathed her sword and concealed it in the folds of her tunic. She took a deep breath, and then ran around the corner of the tent, arms above her head, screaming like the others, but heading straight for the treasure tent. *No guard. Good.* The tent flap was sealed but Erin slashed a hole in the canvas with her sword. Several trunks were in the tent; after a moment she recognized her brother's trunk. She grabbed it and pulled open the hidden compartment on the bottom. The nomad thieves had not discovered the secret resting place, and the two ancient rings were still there, nestled among some other family jewelry. Erin grabbed the rings leaving the other things; those could be replaced, but the rings were priceless. She closed the secret compartment and started to leave. Then, on impulse, she stopped and opened a second chest. It was full of coins. She grabbed a handful, scooping them into a nearby cloth bag. *The Wizard may be great at magic, but he seems to have little practical sense.* Someone would have to take care of them.

She ducked and stepped through the hole she had cut in the tent. The people in the camp were still running and screaming in terror of the dragons in the sky. She ran through the crowd towards the edge of the camp and disappeared in the swirling smoke. After a couple of minutes, she heard a low voice. She looked around and then saw Alec waiting for her.

"Good job," he said. "Did you get what you needed?" He handed her the pants and moccasins she had been wearing.

"Yes, I found my rings!"

"I saw that you were in trouble, so I decided to try something new. I made what we call 'fireworks' where I live!" Alec spoke rapidly, enthusiastically, while she pulled on the nomad pants. "I've never done that before! Did you see them? To do that I needed an equivalent number of neutrons and protons in the receiving and giving material," he continued. "Since air is less dense than the fireworks, it took a lot of air. That made a micro-burst that had enough friction to charge the air! It worked!" He chuckled. "Did you see the lightning? That was a surprise! Nice, but unanticipated!"

Erin looked at him and shifted her weight to her other foot as she put on the second moccasin. He stopped talking and looked at her.

"Shouldn't we be moving out of here?" she said.

Alec gave her a hard look. *She doesn't understand anything I just said, he thought to himself. Just like my undergrad students. Tuned me out after the first sentence.*

"Yes," he said and turned back toward the ridge.

"Thank you," she said meekly. "Thank you for sending the fire-dragon works. You did save me."

≈ ≈ ≈ ≈

They carefully worked their way back to their starting point. With the confusion in the camp, no guards were in sight. They reached the top of the ridge in good time, then cautiously made their way down the draw toward their campsite from last night. As they neared the place where they had hobbled their trogus, Erin stopped, put her hand on his arm, and her finger to her lips. Alec stopped next to her and cocked his head.

It's too quiet, he thought.

"Our animals are not here," Erin whispered. She felt for the hilt of her sword.

"Look," he whispered and pointed to the bush where they had left their supplies. The bundles they had stashed under the brush had been torn apart and the contents, meager as they were, strewn around the ground. They looked like someone had picked through them.

"They have found us," Erin said solemnly.

Alec looked at the mess with dawning comprehension.

"They took our mounts, and their saddles and tack. And our drung. They probably went to get reinforcements and will come back with their dogs to track us."

With the mention of dogs, Alec's first thoughts of defense went out the window. He might be able to make themselves difficult to see with his dark energy lens, but he had no idea how to mask their smell.

"Why didn't they use dogs close to the camp? They could have tracked us there."

"Too many people there for them to be useful," she said. "Too many smells."

"How long ago do you think they were here?"

"Some time ago. They will probably be back with help soon unless your fire-dragon distracted them."

"Let's get out of here," he said. They quickly collected their supplies and started out. Soon, he could hear a distant howling sound, brought by the wind.

"Dogs," Erin said. "They will pick up our scent when they get near."

The two of them continued up the draw. The howling sound changed to baying and became nearer.

"This isn't going to work. They will find us before we go another mile," Alec muttered. *I need to think.* "We can't outrun them – we have to out-think them." They picked up their pace.

"I'm going to try something," Alec said after a few moments. "Move over there." He pointed to a nearby boulder. Erin obligingly climbed on top of the big rock. *Focus.* Dark energy swirled around as if he was in the center of an active dark energy generator. *Peppers and paprika.* An odor started to materialize. *Jalapeños.* The area around him filled with the smell. Erin wrinkled her nose. *Maybe that will screw up the dogs' sense of smell.*

"Let's go," he said, taking her hand. "Jump as far as you can. Break our scent trail." They leaped off the rock and then took off at a fast pace. Within a short time, Alec heard the baying change back to howling punctuated by whining barks.

"I think you did something to the dogs," Erin said, with a slight smile.

A little more confident, they proceeded on. It was now late afternoon.

"Man am I hungry," Alec said. His stomach was growling.

"So am I, oh Great Wizard, but we dare not stop now for food."

After another half-hour or so Erin gestured to Alec; they walked up a slight rise, concealed by brush, and looked back. A party of trogus-riders was only a few hundred yards behind them, slowly following a solitary figure on foot.

"They are tracking us," Erin said. "You leave a wide enough swath that I could follow you on a trogus at full gallop. But these nomads are not as good as me. They must be on foot to track us, but they will still catch us before nightfall. What should we do?"

"They will catch us anyway," Alec said thoughtfully, "so let's find a place to engage them where we have an advantage – or at least not a disadvantage."

Erin nodded in agreement.

They found a raised area rimmed by a rock ledge and a small open space. The tracker's trogus would not be able to scramble onto the ledge, but the nomads could easily hop onto it. At least they wouldn't be attacked and eaten by the trogus, but they would have to confront the nomads on foot.

Alec was too nervous to sit. *Another opportunity to be dead.* Erin seemed much calmer on the surface, but he could sense the turmoil underneath. He knew she dreaded being captured again more than she feared dying.

They heard the dogs and thrashing of the animals slightly before they saw them. Several trogus appeared below the rock shelf. Alec didn't have time to count but figured there were probably a dozen nomads. The leader looked up and saw them, then motioned his group to stop. He dismounted and walked up to the rock ledge.

"Look what we have found," he exclaimed loudly. "An escaped prize and her lover!" He reached into a pouch at his side and pulled out a slave neckpiece. "We found this where our skinny slave cast it into the grass. We will have to reattach this to our possession and this time teach it properly!" He grinned, baring a mouthful of yellow teeth.

She's a person, not a 'possession'! Alec thought.

The Gryg turned and looked at Alec. "You are tall and strong and might be of value." He looked up at Alec's face, and allowed his gaze to travel slowly to Alec's feet as if he were sizing up a prize specimen of livestock. "Ha! I will make you an offer. Return our possession quietly, and we will discuss not killing you this night." Erin looked at Alec with horror.

"No," Alec said. "You let me keep her as mine, and then we can talk."

The leader laughed. "You think you have any position to negotiate?" He motioned towards his men. "We know she is a dangerous and skilled fighter, but you don't look very dangerous! Your hands are too soft to be those of a fighter! I will take you myself and let the others take her."

Alec noticed that five of the others had dismounted and were leering at Erin. The nomad leader drew his sword and took a step towards Alec. *Time to do something.*

Alec had his staff in one hand and a rock in the other. He tossed the rock into the middle of the group of trogus. They snarled and spat; one reared up on its hind legs.

The leader briefly looked back at the sound and then turned back and strode toward Alec.

Focus. Alec imagined a molten center in the rock he had thrown. Crack! The rock couldn't hold the stress of the molten center. Fragments shattered and flew in all directions. The trogus were splattered with molten rock and flying shards – they bellowed and kicked, knocking their riders off and fleeing in all directions.

The leader looked back at the commotion, then again turned back towards Alec and took a swipe with his sword. Alec raised his staff, barely in time to block the thrust. The strengthened staff transmitted the force to his shoulders, and he winced. Alec had no time to do anything but instinctively defend himself, countering the sword with his staff. He glanced over at Erin.

Five nomads surrounded Erin. She lashed out with her sword and caught one nomad on his arm, leaving a deep gash and a splatter of blood. The others surrounded her, and any time she attempted to attack the closest man, he would back away.

Two of the nomads brought ropes, knotted with loops. They split up and moved to different sides. One nomad tossed a loop towards her feet. It swished toward her leg, and she dodged but the second nomad looped his rope around her other leg. She tried to cut it with her sword but missed. The nomad jerked the rope hard, and Erin fell to her knees. Another pull and she was on her back. She felt the broadside of a sword hit her hand. Her fingers went numb, and she lost control of her sword. She tried to grab it with her other hand, but a foot kicked it out of her reach. Then a loop of rope caught one of her arms.

"No," she screamed "No! No!"

Alec was barely staying out of reach of his assailant's sword when he heard Erin scream. He quickly glanced in her direction and could see that the nomads would soon have Erin under control. *If I don't do something soon, she will be captured, and I will be dead.* Time to try his 'magic.'

Focus, he thought, and dark energy flowed all around. Time slowed for him. He saw the nomad leader's sword move towards him in slow motion. Alec lunged forward, and the nomad slowly tried to alter the sword's trajectory towards him, but it was too late. Momentum took the blade past his shoulder. Grabbing a new hold on his staff, Alec slammed it into the man's knee and he collapsed, seemingly in slow motion. Alec bashed him across the head, hitting him as hard as he could. If the blow weren't fatal, he figured it would at least debilitate his assailant for a long time.

Alec released the dark energy. He had no idea how long he could have maintained the intense focus, but he suspected it wouldn't have been much longer. He looked towards Erin. Several nomads surrounded her, laughing and taunting as she struggled on the ground.

Chaos no longer dominated the scene in front of Alec. Although several men had fallen from their mounts and some trogus still ran wild, by now most were under control. Of immediate concern were three nomads approaching him with drawn swords.

Alec wasn't sure he could beat even one more nomad, and three of them would surely overwhelm him. *If they kill me, then Erin will be a slave.* The thought of Erin being enslaved again angered him more than the potential for his death. *Do something.*

An idea had come to him earlier that afternoon as his stomach growled in hunger and he thought of a nice steak, broiling on the hot rocks. He didn't like the image that came to his mind, but it might be his only chance.

"Stop!" he yelled at the three nomads advancing on him. "Submit, or I will kill you all!" he yelled with false confidence. The man in the middle of the three attackers just looked at him with amusement and motioned for his compatriots to spread out and circle Alec.

Too bad, big guy — you are going to be my guinea-pig, Alec thought.

Focus. Alec's medallion vibrated with new vigor. The lead attacker's bemused look changed to one of concern, then distress; and then he made a strange gurgling sound. Suddenly both of his eyes popped out of their sockets. Blood gushed from his mouth and nose and oozed from fissures appearing first on the skin of his arms, then on his legs. Alec was almost sick when he saw the result of his work. The other two nomads saw the first man drop, saw the blood leaving his body, and stepped back.

"Now leave! Or you are next," Alec roared. *How could I have done this to a human being?*

The two backed off. One of the men surrounding Erin looked over, saw the fallen man — now lying in a pool of his blood, his body convulsing — and nudged the others.

"Let her go," Alec yelled at the men around Erin. By this time her feet and hands had been lashed securely, even though she continued to struggle valiantly. The men looked at him dumbly.

Then one of them drew a knife and put it to Erin's throat. "Cease and submit to us, or she will be dead!" he bellowed.

"I would rather be dead than a slave! Let them kill me," Erin shouted.

Alec felt sick as he resolutely started what he had to do. *Focus!* Dark energy flowed. The man holding the knife at Erin's throat went gray. Blood flowed from his face and oozed from his skin. He collapsed in a heap on top of Erin. The other nomads slowly backed up to the edge of the shelf, looking at the dead bodies, then at Alec, then back at the bodies.

Alec looked at them. "Get out of here!" he yelled. None of the nomads moved.

"Now! Or I will make you like them!" He waved his staff.

With that one of the nomads bolted. The others slowly backed away never taking their eyes from Alec. Once off the ledge they jumped on their trogus and galloped as fast as they could down the draw and over the next ridge. Alec watched until they were out of sight.

Alec felt sick. Killing wasn't his thing. He had read treatises about how all technology could be used for either peace or war, but had never understood the consequences of that. Killing was terrible. And he had just killed two men. He retched, dry heaves wracking his exhausted body, and felt like he was going to faint.

≈ ≈ ≈ ≈

At the edge of his consciousness, Alec heard sounds coming from across the ledge. Finally, it registered.

"Great Wizard are you all right?" Like a mantra, it was repeated over and over.

He glanced around and saw Erin, lying in a heap across the open space on the ledge. She had wriggled out from under her dead assailant and through his pool of blood but was still bound with the ropes that held her. Alec slowly walked over to her sword and picked it up. A few paces back to Erin, and he cut the ropes around her wrists. Then he handed her the sword and sat down on a rock on the corner of the shelf, shaking with deep sobs.

Erin finished freeing herself and came over to him. "Are you all right?"

"No," he said, catching his breath. "I feel like I did something terrible."

"You saved our lives and ran the nomads off," she said.

"I know."

"How did you do that?" she asked.

"I boiled their blood." He swallowed hard. "They boiled from the inside out. Like meat on a fire." He wiped his face on the sleeve of his shirt. "I got the idea when we were cooking the other night. It worked, but I hate it. I hate killing people!"

She touched his arm. "But you saved us," she said, softly.

"Can't you see! I'm not like you! In my world, we don't go running around with swords and knives killing people!" He gasped, a deep sobbing gasp of agony. "I'm not like you! I can't just slash somebody's throat like you can, and then spit on them and go about my business like nothing was wrong. Those were human beings! They had lives! And I killed them!" He closed his eyes and shuddered.

Erin looked at him, then wrapped her arms around him and held him close for a long while as the afternoon sun warmed them both.

4 – Crossing the Grasslands

Finally, Erin spoke. "It will be night soon. We need to find a place for the night and something for you to eat. This has been a hard day, even for you, Great Wizard." She stroked Alec's shoulder.

Erin took Alec's hand and bade him follow her. Erin was adept at finding good campsites in the Grassland, and a short distance upwind she found a secluded nook in a knoll.

"This will make a good campsite," she said.

Alec took it upon himself to hunt for food. He hoped that moving around and foraging would improve his mood. When he was a teen, he had hunted squirrels with his grandfather in Washington State. Surely he could do that again. Erin had pointed out several kinds of small game animals that lived in the Grasslands. Soon Alec spotted a small antelope-like creature that hopped around the tall grasses – "bounders," Erin had called them, and with good reason. Holding his breath, he slowly approached the little fellow, his sling in hand. *Focus.* Dark energy flowed. One flick of his wrist and a well-aimed rock took out the bounder. *It almost isn't fair.* Alec field-dressed the creature and brought it to Erin. She nodded approvingly, filleted the meat with her sword, and cooked it to perfection.

"I'm starving!" Alec said, breathing in the tantalizing smell of the grilled meat. He was pretty sure that he ate more than his share, although Erin ate ravenously as well.

A flicker from the corner of his eye brought Alec out of his contented state. A four-legged creature stood at the top of the knoll; the animal was a little over knee high with long shaggy fur and a humped back. It snarled at them, showing its long yellowing canine teeth. "A hyra," said Erin, calmly pulling out her sword.

Alec pulled out one of his rocks and tossed it at the animal. The rock hit the animal in the shoulder. It let out an angry grunt as it scurried into the grass.

"They hunt in packs, so there are more of them. The smell of blood must have attracted them. They are scavengers and will attack defenseless animals. They will attack us in our sleep if we give them a chance."

"Why won't they go after the dead bodies over the hill?"

"They are afraid of trogus and probably can still smell the dead ones. Until they are sure all the trogus are dead they will seek other prey."

"What do we do? We can't run from them, and it will be dark soon," Alec asked.

Erin started to dig into the hillside with her hands. "We need a cave to provide us protection."

"You're going to hurt your hands," Alec said. "Let me help you." He scratched at the soft dirt; he could dig into it with his bare hands, but it was slow going. "It will be dark soon. I'm going to try something," said Alec. "Scoot."

Erin stepped away from the hole.

Focus. A blast of dust came out of the ground, and a burrow appeared where Erin had started to dig. Twice more Alec created a disturbance before the hole was large enough for them both to fit.

Erin climbed into the cavity – the entryway was barely large enough for one person to fit through, but the inside was large enough for them both. "Nice," she said. "There are some advantages to traveling with a Great Wizard. Can you make us a soft bed to sleep on?"

"I don't think so," said Alec, assuming she was serious.

"Then maybe there aren't that many advantages, after all," she said with a smile, as she collected enough grass to provide some padding against the dirt. Then she slipped their packs into the burrow and began to undress.

"What are you doing?" asked Alec a little surprised.

"I am not going to sleep in these filthy, scratchy rags," Erin replied.

Alec swallowed hard and tried to figure if her should watch her undress or not, considering that she was sitting very close to him and there was really nowhere else for his eyes to look. In the dusk in front of their little burrow, he could see that her back was crisscrossed with oozing red welts.

"What happened to your back?"

Erin tried to look over her shoulder to examine her back. "That is where they beat me. They would beat me until I would squeal. For the first few days I refused to squeal, but I learned that the sooner I started squealing and begging, the sooner they would stop."

"Do they hurt?"

Erin gave him a look. "Of course, but it doesn't do any good to complain." Then she wriggled into their burrow.

Alec slipped off his shoes, and after some consideration slid out of his bloodstained pants and shirt before he also climbed into the burrow. "Now let me see if I can make us a door."

Focus. The entryway was sealed with only a small area at the top for airflow.

He felt Erin's warm body beside him on the grass mat and sensed the pain that she had suffered. Instinctively he put his arms around her. She sobbed softly underneath her breath as she relaxed in his arms. *She trusts me,* he thought, *I can't let her down.*

She curled up close to him but flinched whenever her back touched anything. "Let's try something," Alec said, speaking softly into her ear. He focused, and pulled a small amount of dark energy. Then he pushed the dark energy into her and let it flow through her body.

Erin's body relaxed, and she slid into a deep sleep.

≈ ≈ ≈ ≈

The next morning, he awoke early and could feel Erin's body nestled against him in the half-light of the burrow. He could tell by her breathing that she was awake, but neither moved nor spoke. They lay together for a long while absorbing the feel of each other. Finally, Erin spoke.

"I almost lost hope, but you, my Great Wizard saved me – and gave me back hope." She sighed, thoughtfully. "We have a Seer at home. She is not a great wizard like you, but she does have some spells, and sometimes she sees the future. Can you see the future?"

"I don't think so," said Alec, "but I have never tried. Dark energy and time are linked together so it might be possible," Alec mused. "But I have never done that."

Erin continued. "I wanted to learn about the world before I had to settle down. When I was trying to decide whether to travel on this trip, the Seer came to me and said she had seen a very disturbing vision." Erin pursed her lip. "Her vision told her that if I didn't go, my people would all die. But if I went, I would suffer but shouldn't lose hope for I would return home and find what I had lost. Now you have given me hope."

They were silent for a while. Then, since she had spoken of her home, Alec ventured a question that had been bothering him.

"Do you have a special person at home?" he asked, although it seemed to him a strange question to ask someone lying naked beside you.

"I did," Erin answered, "but he died a year ago."

Maybe this was not a good thing to ask her, Alec thought. But he wanted to know. "Do you ... do you want to tell me about him?"

"Leonder was his name." Erin put her arms under her head and looked at Alec. "Leonder was my first real love. I met him at the Queen's court. He came to Theland from the moonward land when his father, Leon, came to be a member of the Queen's personal guard. My mother thought I was too young to have a serious love." She laughed softly, remembering her past. "Leonder wanted to be a scholar and not a fighter. At first, Mother thought I should have someone more ... warlike."

"Did you ... were you ... How long ago was that?"

"I first met him about four years ago. We spent many days together, talking about our wants and desires. After about a year, we coupled, both for the first time." She smiled wistfully, remembering. "Leonder was my love. My passion."

"That first summer we spent many afternoons in the woods near my home enjoying each other's company, both mentally and physically. We wanted to consort then, but there were two problems. The first was that I was still young and needed my mother's permission."

"The second problem was that we have an old custom from our warrior past that is still part of our law." She scowled. "It is a barbaric law that was originally intended to produce the strongest people. To make the strongest pups. Warrior pups."

"What is that?" Alec asked.

"For women of my position in our society, it is imperative that we have the strongest mate, so that we will produce the strongest pups. So, once I announce a proposed consort arrangement, anyone else who wants to consort with me has three days to post a claim. Then the claimants meet in a public fight to the death, and the winner claims me as their consort."

"What?!" Alec exclaimed. "That sounds like wild animals – lions or gorillas – not civilized people!"

She shrugged. "It is our law," she said simply. "We have ancient customs. They must be followed. "

She paused and clenched her jaw. "A disgusting man, a bully named Brunder, also wants to consort with me. Brunder is one of the best fighters in Theland, and everyone knew Leonder would be no match for him."

"Last year, I went on a two-week trip with my mother and told her of my desire to consort with Leonder even though he was not a great warrior. Mother had thought about great warriors a lot. She told me there are different ways to be a great warrior. She said that some great warriors have strength of arm and some have cleverness of mind.

"Mother worried that if we tried to consort, the one who would suffer would be Leonder. If the two of us were sure we should be together, though, and Leonder accepted the risks, she would allow it. She agreed with my consorting with him.

"Mother is very clever. She came up with a plan to thwart Brunder. She decided that she would announce our plans to consort after Brunder went on his annual hunt with his father. They hunt in the mountains every year, several days from our home. We would send a messenger to inform Brunder of the arrangement. We thought that by the time he heard of the proposed consort and returned to make his challenge, the three days would have passed and Leonder and I would be consorted.

"But it was not to be. When Mother and I returned from our trip, we learned that Brunder supposedly had taken Leonder on a boar-hunting trip while we were gone, and that Leonder had been gored and killed by a wild boar. My Leonder was dead! Mother was right, I made Leonder suffer because I wanted him, even though he was not a great warrior!" She stopped, and Alec gently stroked her arm.

"I'm sorry," he said softly.

"I did not even get to give my final farewell because the departing ceremony was performed while I was gone!" She curled her lip. "Leonder did not like to hunt, so I do not believe that story! He would not have willingly gone with Brunder in any case. I think Brunder found out about Leonder and me and decided to eliminate a rival."

"Did anyone do anything about it?" Alec asked.

"When this happened, his father, Leon, was out of town with us, as part of the Queen's guard. When Leon returned and found out about Leonder's death, he was very angry. He accused Brunder of foul play and challenged him. They fought the challenge at the circle in our city's arena. Leon was one of the best of the Queen's guardsmen, so everyone came to see the fight. Leon and Brunder had a tough fight. But eventually Leon slipped, and Brunder sliced the tendon in the back of Leon's heel so he could not walk. Then he disarmed Leon and spent a long time tormenting him before he finally killed him." She clenched her fists and Alec could feel her body stiffen as she recounted the fight. "Finally, after Brunder tired of playing, he beheaded Leon right in front of me. Then Brunder cut off the male parts from Leon's dead body and tossed them at my feet. It was a clear message to anyone who might be interested in me! I was distraught!"

She drew a deep breath. "Brunder is a crowd favorite, and the spectators thought it was the best fight in a long time."

"Sounds absolutely barbaric," Alec muttered.

"Leonder's death is my fault," Erin said, and then began to sob. "If I had not decided to consort with Leonder, he would still be alive. It was my love that brought about his death!" Alec held her as she sobbed in his arms. Finally, the sobs abated. "I will never find another like Leonder. Brunder will kill anyone I want as my consort unless they are a great warrior."

"But you don't have to … consort … unless you want to, do you?" asked Alec.

She exhaled sharply. "While Father was alive, he protected me, and let me recover from the pain of losing Leonder. Since Father died this past winter, the pressure for me to consort has increased."

"My older brother – Devin – told me that after this trip I would have to consort. He told me that if I didn't find someone suitable then Brun, the head of our Council, would force me to consort with Brunder. Devin knew I detest Brunder but said 'politically it would be a good match' for me. It would tie the two most powerful families in Theland together. Brunder is the greatest fighter in Theland, but he is an egotistical pig who wants to bed every girl in Theland. I do not want him!" She turned her head and spat into the grass mat.

"My brother told me several times to quit complaining and consort with Brunder. Devin said that I didn't have to like Brunder, just occasionally sleep with him and have pups with him. The rest of the time, Brunder would be too preoccupied with his other 'interests' to bother me.

"That is not the kind of consort I want." Her lip quivered, and Alec could see she was fighting back the tears. "I wanted Leonder," she whispered. "I wanted Leonder, and now he is gone. Brunder killed him so that I could not have him."

She turned to Alec and buried her face in his chest, and he slid his arms around her and held her as she sobbed.

≈ ≈ ≈ ≈

The sun had risen high in the sky by the time they emerged from their burrow. Alec looked at Erin's back as she reached for her clothes. "Your back – look at it! The welts are gone."

Erin craned her neck around to try to glimpse her back, and rubbed gently against the bush. "It feels much better."

Then with mock seriousness, she turned towards Alec. "My brother always said that men only think about one thing. He never told me it would be my back!" Then she turned away from him and started pulling on the rough dirty clothing she had discarded the night before. "My brother told me that I am too hard and thin. He said men like curvy, soft, girls. He said that I would have to stop riding and training and develop some curves if I wanted to be attractive.

"I know that I am not curvy in the front. Is that why you only noticed my back?"

Alec flushed red and just stood there for an instant. "I don't know about your brother, but … I think … I think you are beautiful," he stammered.

"Thank you," she said seriously, and began to poke around their small camp, retrieving some scraps of left-over meat from the stash in the burrow. After a while, she asked quietly, "I told you my story. But how did you arrive here, my Wizard? Why are you here?"

Alec had quit correcting her. Maybe he was a wizard. Anyway, he was a wizard to her.

"Well, I was in my Lab when something happened, and then there was an explosion, and then suddenly I was here." She looked puzzled.

"'Lab'?" she said. "'Explosion'?"

"The Laboratory where I work, at the Institute – that's a big school where thousands of people study things. The Lab is a big building where people like me study science – 'magic' – and do experiments, so we can see how to use scientific phenomenon. How to use 'magic.' We do not have wizards at home. I am a scientist, not a wizard." *Why am I calling 'science' 'magic'?*

52

"I have spent years studying something called 'dark energy.' That's the stuff that allows me to focus energy and do what you have seen me do: change things and move things. Like when I made your sword, or the 'fire-dragon-in-the-sky,' or the hot cooking rocks." She nodded.

"For some reason, dark energy is much denser here than it is at home, so it is easier to use. At home, we must build big concentrators – big machines … um … big pieces of equipment – to focus enough energy to do anything. Even little things are hard to do. At home, I don't think I could do the things I've done here."

"Oh – I see," Erin said. Alec knew that she didn't. "And the 'expulsion'?"

"Explosion," he corrected. "I don't understand it. I was in the Lab, and I was talking to Dr. Alder … one of my other … wizards, and then there was a big flash, and then I was here."

"A flash like your fire-dragon?"

"Well, yes, sort of like that." *Not really.*

After they had eaten their meager breakfast, she stuffed their supplies back into the packs.

"And you have a special person?" she asked, casually, combing some leaves from her dark hair with her fingers and pulling it back into a knot. "You said you have a 'girlfriend.'"

"Well, yes – I mean 'no,' not really," Alec answered, slightly flustered. "I have … I mean, 'had' … a girlfriend, Sarah. We've been seeing each other for a while. Several months." *Should I explain Sarah to Erin? How?* "But we aren't that serious." *Are we? Were we?* He swallowed. "Neither of us has decided that we are the right person for the other," Alec said truthfully. "We aren't ready … weren't ready … to commit to each other." *And how would he explain Erin to Sarah? If he ever saw Sarah again.*

"Things haven't been going too well with Sarah recently," Alec continued. "I think we both understand that we are at a stage where we either patch things up or drift apart. But I don't even know if I will ever see her again."

Erin hugged Alec tightly. "Now I understand. You want to be faithful until you decide she is not the right one. That is wonderful. I want my consort to be like you, not like that rutting pig, Brunder."

Alec returned her hug, and then looked over her head at the endless waving sea of grass and stepped away from her. "I don't know if I can ever find Sarah again. I don't know where I am, how I got here, or how to go home. I don't even know if it is possible to go home!" Alec shook his head. "I don't want to think about it, but this could be a different world – a different universe – than mine. There might be no way home!" Erin looked at him blankly.

"Were you a great warrior at home?" she asked, trying to change the subject.

"I am not a warrior at all," replied Alec. "I am a scientist. I know nothing about fighting or warcraft."

"But you saved me twice from the nomads. That is what great warriors do." With that statement, Erin became preoccupied trying to sort out Alec in her mind.

Alec grabbed his medallion from his pile of clothes, hung it around his neck, and shook out his clothes. *No vermin.* As he dressed, he thought about the two women, both attractive to him, but very different from one another. Sarah was more petite than Erin, prettier, in a way, with her snub nose and short styled hair, and trendy clothes, and always nestled closely in his arms when they slept together. Would he ever see Sarah again – or did that matter anymore? Erin had ignited a spark in him that he had never felt before – even if he found Sarah would he still feel the same about her?

He had no idea where he was, or what world he was on. He didn't understand this place where people and beasts attacked with little provocation and fought viciously to the death. The gore of the headless nomad leader flashed through his mind, unbidden. Alec was aware that even more fundamental than sorting out his feelings for Erin and Sarah, he needed to figure out how to survive in this world.

Erin broke into his reverie. "What is our next step?" she asked.

"Take you home," Alec answered, tersely. "How do we get to your home?"

"My home is ten days towards morning," said Erin. "Also, I have a confession."

"What is that?" he asked.

"When I recovered my rings from the Gryg camp, I took enough coins to pay for my father's goods, plus some. We have coins if we need them." Erin pulled out the bundle of coins she had taken and showed them to Alec.

She unwrapped the two rings. "These are very special," she said. "They have been in my family for five hundred years. This ring is mine," she said, and she put it on her finger.

Alec asked, "May I look at it?"

Erin handed him the second ring. "They are alike," she said.

Alec looked at the ring and then focused, collecting a small amount of dark energy, and pushed it towards the ring. Suddenly the ring sparked, and he almost dropped it. Then he tried to pull dark energy through the ring. He slipped the ring on his finger; it fit perfectly. *Interesting,* he thought. The rings were somehow connected to the dark energy that was all around him.

He could suddenly sense Erin looking at him in shock. *I heard your thought,* she thought to him.

Alec looked at her and thought, *I can hear you also.*

Erin stood wide-eyed, still staring at him. "Mother said my grandmother and grandfather could sense each other's thoughts. Mother could never learn how to do it. Grandmother died young, before she had a chance to finish teaching Mother. I never knew her. Mother said Grandmother could do many more things with her ring – my ring – than Mother could ever do with hers. How did you make the ring do it?"

Alec looked at the ring for a long time. "I think the ring is a very sophisticated version of a medallion. Except it uses negative dark energy instead of positive dark energy. Negative dark energy is like antimatter. The universe has a balance of the two kinds of dark energy." Alec sensed the frustration in Erin's mind. "Oh, sorry. The details don't matter. You should be able to use your ring like I use my medallion."

"How do you make your medallion work?"

"I use a mental focus. I focus my mind. Try it."

Erin tried to focus, and nothing happened. Alec could sense her frustration.

Let me guide you, he thought.

Alec focused and pulled energy from the ring through Erin.

"Oh!" she exclaimed. "The world is so much brighter! I can sense you and your feelings. I can feel a flock of bounders over the hill. I can even sense the ground creatures and prairie skarns looking at us."

Alec released his focus. *Try to do it without me,* he thought.

Erin laughed. "Now that I know what to do, it is easy. Almost like it is natural, and I should have always been able to do this. This sense of the world is how my mother described my grandmother's vision."

Alec took the ring off to give it back to Erin. She shook her head and pushed it back to him.

"Please wear it because I think we may need to communicate before we finish this journey. The only other person I ever allowed to wear this ring was Leonder." She looked at Alec shyly. "But I could never sense his thoughts, nor he mine, even though we tried many times. You are much like him in many ways, and he would want you to wear it."

Alec looked at the ring, and then put it back on his finger. Immediately he had a sense of Erin's presence – a comforting feeling.

≈ ≈ ≈ ≈

Erin led Alec back to the battle site to see if there was anything worth taking. The area was starting to smell. Besides the dead nomads, there were three dead trogus. Scavengers had come during the night and ripped flesh from the bones of both trogus and nomads. Erin and Alec retrieved the trogus panniers, rummaged through them, and found a bit of food, a small knapsack for Erin, a blanket, a knife, and a couple of pots that were worth taking. The rest they left behind. Then they started walking through the Grassland towards morning.

Their days fell into a pattern. Alec was not accustomed to multi-day hikes and looked forward to the point in late afternoon when Erin suggested they find a campsite. Erin was skilled at locating a good nook for a camp amid the large clumps of grass. They had not had any more encounters with the hyra or other predators. Erin could sense everything around them, so they had avoided several encounters with wild trogus.

They developed an efficient camp routine. Erin set up camp while Alec went out hunting. Small game was abundant, but Alec found the little antelope-bounders the easiest to catch, as well as tasty. When he found one, he used a rock and a dash of dark energy to take it down and then bring it back. One night, Alec volunteered to cook and tried his hand at it, but the small carcass turned into a mess, charred on the outside and raw on the inside. With a gale of laughter, Erin pushed him aside and took over. The result was edible, barely, and their unspoken agreement after that was for Erin to cook and Alec to hunt. After their meal, as the five moons traversed the sky, they had time to talk, or sit quietly and listen to the noises of the Grasslands.

It was on one of those late afternoons that Alec had cleared his mind sufficiently to let his scientific inquisitiveness come to the fore. *What can I do with the local energy*, Alec thought. *So much stronger here than at home.* So far, he had heated items, pushed them, converted them from one thing to another, and somehow in the heat of battle concentrated enough energy to slow time. *What else can I do?* Alec decided to experiment. One of the first things he had learned in graduate school was how to make crystals. He took a rock and focused. The rock quivered, then with a dull popping noise converted into an emerald the size of his fist. *Showy, but not useful.*

"Nice," Erin said, somewhat impressed.

Then Alec took off his medallion and tried to feel the energy. He could detect the energy swirling around. *Focus.* It was hard. There was only a trickle, not the torrent that he felt with his medallion. Still, he managed to convert a small pebble into a small emerald.

"Nice, but not so much as the first," said Erin.

Every night, Alec and Erin would curl up together for warmth. Alec felt guilty about sleeping with Erin; he worried about his relationship with Sarah and didn't want to violate her trust. However, he found Erin more and more desirable, and she seemed to feel the same about him. Even so, Erin respected his boundaries and they did not cross that uncertain line that separates friends from lovers.

Their trek across the Grasslands was not easy. The days were the same, walking cross-country through a sea of shimmering gray-green grass and rolling hills. Sometimes scudding clouds would race overhead, and a light rain would fall, enough to give them drinking water for a few days. Erin knew which of the dark bushes had edible berries and which of the low understory plants had edible roots or fruit, giving some variety to their diet of wild game.

The long grass had saw-like edges that could make painful cuts. The spongy rolling ground was full of rocks and protrusions. Alec had been wearing a T-shirt, a pair of jeans, and tennis shoes at the Lab when he was transported to this place – not the best clothes for this kind of travel. His shoes were starting to look and feel worn, and his jeans had lots of small tears from the grass. His shirt stunk.

Erin was even worse off. She had started the journey with her slave-tunic and the scavenged clothes of the nomads – the nomad's clothes were made for riding, not walking. Her pants were filthy. Her moccasins were not designed for the rocky soil. Twice they had ripped. Both times Alec had done a crude repair job that didn't hold up. She was proceeding without complaint, but he could see everything was wearing on her.

After the fourth day of walking through what seemed to Alec to be endless prairielands, they came to a rough path. "We will follow this route," said Erin, pointing.

5 – The Inn

After a day walking along the path, they saw a small village tucked between the hills of the Grasslands.

"Do you know where we are?" asked Alec.

"I've never been to this village," she answered. "But every village has an inn. We should stay there. It will be warm, and they will have food." She smiled. "Tomorrow we can equip ourselves for the rest of our journey to Theland." With that thought, her gait picked up.

Okay, thought Alec. When they were wearing the rings, they didn't need to speak aloud to each other since they could feel each other's thoughts.

"Village inns can be dangerous places," Erin said, "especially for women, but we need to be there, or the local merchants won't deal with us." Alec could sense her apprehension.

"Is there any place else to stay?" he asked.

"Probably not, but if we are together, we should be all right. Inns are almost all the same. They will have a big common room to feed the travelers and for the locals to use as a gathering place. They will serve some food, usually stew, and have ale, wine, and probably something special like purple mushrooms, if you like to get high.

"They will have a few sleeping rooms – usually five or six – besides the common room. We want one of the sleeping rooms instead of sleeping in the common room, because any woman in the common room is considered available, and I don't want that. Besides, there will be several inn-ladies working the common room."

"'Inn-ladies?' You mean, like 'servers'?"

"You might call them that, but I think in your language that is not the right word. Women who let men use their bodies, for sex."

"Oh."

"The innkeeper gives them food and a place to sleep as well as a small share of what they earn from the men. Most of the inn-ladies are older – working an inn is one of the few options available for them if they do not have a consort or family to depend on. The local men might bring in their women if they need coins, or they might trade a few days of their wife's or daughter's time in exchange for a night of drinking and gaming. That's why you might see a few younger women. And some men — well, some men just prefer very young girls."

That's disgusting, Alec thought. *Women here don't sound very well treated.*

They aren't, she thought, then spoke aloud. "Places like Gott and the Grasslands treat their cattle and trogus much better than their women. Theland is not like that. In Theland, a woman is her own person. Women can be soldiers, own property, handle coins, go to school — things that are not allowed in these other places. It's a better place for women. Most other places do not even allow women to learn to swing a sword or hold a spear."

But you can't choose you own consort, thought Alec to himself.

≈ ≈ ≈ ≈

The village was small and dirty. Animal waste and trash littered the street side. The late-day light cast long shadows over everything. Only a few people were out, and they looked around cautiously before they scurried from place to place.

"We will have to bargain for the cost of our lodging," Erin said and handed him a few coins. "I can't be seen with coins. Here, only men can negotiate prices or pay coins."

"I would be perfectly happy if you did that," Alec said.

No — that is not the custom, Erin thought to him. A quick tutorial on coins and prices left Alec at least marginally conversant in proper currency and bargaining etiquette. Their plan was simple. Alec would negotiate, and Erin would hold his arm and let him sense her opinion. *Act as if you have only a few coins,* she admonished. *It will reduce the chance for mischief.*

The inn was near the crossroads in the center of the village. They found the door facing a side street — Alec had to duck his head to clear the low frame — and went in. The innkeeper appeared from behind a curtain, looked them over, and quickly decided Alec wasn't worth a second look but that Erin might be.

"A room for two nights," Alec said.

"I have space in the common room for three small coins a night. I can let you both stay free if you let me sell her for both nights. I can use another inn-lady this time of year."

Alec shook his head. "No. We want a sleeping room."

"Two gold coins," said the innkeeper.

Alec felt a tight grip on his arm and sensed Erin's opinion. "We are poor travelers and just need a place to sleep, not a palace with servants," Alec said.

The banter went back and forth for a few moments as they argued over price. When Erin was satisfied with the innkeeper's price, Alec agreed and took a few coins from an almost-empty coin purse, looking sorrowfully at each one.

The innkeeper pointed to their room, up narrow rickety stairs. It was small but appeared serviceable. Erin pulled out the bag of coins from her pack. "I need somewhere to leave this. The innkeeper will rummage through our room while we are eating."

Alec thought for a minute. *Focus.* Dark energy swirled. A cavity appeared in the rough-hewn planks of the floor, and Erin stuffed the coin bag into it. *Focus.* The cavity closed and looked like the rest of the floor.

A wash basin stood on a side table with an ewer of water, so they could clean up a bit. Alec gingerly patted down his week-old beard. He had never before grown out his beard and wondered what it looked like; he had not seen a clean-shaven man since he had arrived in this world and felt that with a beard he would be less conspicuous. Erin undid her knotted hair and combed it out as best she could with her fingers.

"That's better," she said.

Alec nodded. "Your hair looks nice."

They went downstairs to the large common-room for supper. The meal was a stew, heavily spiced (*Probably to conceal the state of the meat,* thought Alec), but an improvement from their fare of the last few days.

There were a surprising number of people in the common room, more than Alec would have expected based on the small number of people he had seen moving about the streets. Most of the men wore the loose dusky drab tan clothes of the Grasslanders; a few wore dark blue or dirty white. At some of the tables a woman or two sat drinking beer, each hidden behind a man, but Alec noticed a few women who did not seem to be with anyone.

Who are those women? he thought to Erin.

They are inn-ladies, she thought back.

There were six or eight of them milling about the room, smiling at the men or dutifully sitting on a wooden bench to the side of the dining tables, one idly chewing on a root. One was taller than the others, with dark hair; the others were older, shorter than Erin, and plump. They were all dressed in a similar manner: a loose knee-length robe, open in the front, leaving little to the imagination; some in bright colors, some dull. Each had a heavy belt around her lower abdomen, fastened with a lock. As Alec watched, a man rose from the table, finished his last swill of beer, wiped his mouth on the back of his hand, and took hold of the taller inn-lady by her arm. The man waved at the innkeeper to gain his attention. The innkeeper ambled over; the man handed him a few coins and the innkeeper unlocked the heavy belt and removed it, allowing the inn-lady's loose robe to fall freely open. Alec was startled to note that the inn-lady was wearing nothing underneath the robe. The inn-lady smiled at the man, wrapped her arm firmly around his stout waist, and led him towards the common sleeping-room.

I don't see any kids running around the inn. What happens if an inn-lady get pregnant? Alec thought.

Usually they don't, Erin answered. *If you chew on the jinja root, it will keep you from pupping. If they become heavy with a pup, it is bad for them. The innkeeper probably will throw them out, and they starve.*

Whew! thought Alec, and left the rest of his stew uneaten.

As Alec and Erin stood up to return to their room, a rugged-looking heavy-set man put his hand on Alec's arm.

"You're passing through our village? Join us for a little game of cards," the man said, obviously a regular at this inn.

"Not tonight," Alec said, "We have been traveling and are very tired."

"Then tomorrow night," said the stranger.

"Maybe," said Alec. He pulled away and went up the stairs with Erin to their room.

≈ ≈ ≈ ≈

The next morning started with bright sun shining through the cracks in the shutters. Alec wasn't convinced the crude inn bed was better than sleeping on the fresh grass. *I am taller than this bed is long,* he thought. Erin was anxious to start the day. The first step was breakfast in the common room. It was a porridge that was oddly seasoned. A very bitter drink went with it that must have been the local equivalent of coffee.

"First things first," said Erin.

"What is that?"

"Clothes!" she said, and smiled.

A short distance away, they found a tailor shop on the main square, with a cobbler next door. The usual order of business was to make clothes to specification for customers to return later to collect, but the seamstress did have a small supply of clothing that was already made. After a couple of minutes of mutual gesturing, with Alec trying to describe what they wanted and negotiate prices, the seamstress gave up on him, and Erin took the lead. Then things went quickly. They found several items that were very serviceable and worked well for Erin. Alec was outfitted with two sets of local clothes. The trousers were heavier and looser than his jeans but reasonably comfortable. The undergarments were heavier and rougher than he was used to; he could tell that he was going to miss the wonders of microfiber boxers, but at least these clothes were not filthy and torn. At the cobbler's shop, Alec found a good pair of boots to be picked up tomorrow. Erin also found a set of boots and then insisted on a second pair also.

The town also had a bathhouse, and Erin and Alec were at last able to bathe in the lukewarm common bath. *Not as nice as my shower at home, but still a relief,* Alec thought to himself.

Erin came out of the bathhouse with her damp hair neatly combed back, wearing her new clothes – women's trousers and a long tunic top with a V-neck and belt. The change from scavenged to fitted was amazing – Erin had converted from beggar to beauty.

Alec gave a low whistle. "You are lovely," he said.

Erin was pleased. "You finally notice my looks after all this time."

"I have always noticed your looks, but I have never seen you look like this." He smiled. "I may have to fend everyone off you," he said in jest.

"That won't be a problem," she said in a more serious tone than his. "Most men don't like my looks. They prefer much more … rounded and softer women than me."

For the first time, Alec could feel Erin's deep vulnerabilities. Using the ring, he allowed his deeper feelings to swell up so that she could see them – the depth of respect, admiration, and appreciation that he had acquired for her, beyond his appreciation of her looks.

Erin almost blushed. She winked at him as she thought, *My Great Wizard, thank you. I will see if I can live up to those feelings.*

The next stop was the livery stable to procure a wagon. Erin wanted to purchase a wagon like the one she had lost to the caravan, and the stable had a used wagon that would serve the purpose. It needed a few modifications that would take the ostler a day to complete – he told them that they could have it mid-day tomorrow. The ostler also sold them two drungs to pull the wagon. Alec noted that they didn't have fangs and were feeding on something that looked like oats – not meat and not people's faces.

The rest of the day was spent obtaining supplies for the wagon and the rest of their journey. Foodstuffs, pots, blankets, feed for the drungs – the list seemed to run forever, but finally Erin looked satisfied. By the end of the day, the two of them had become proficient at working together while negotiating, sensing each other's thoughts. Erin had doled out a portion of the coins she had taken from the Gryg camp to fund the day's shopping spree; Alec noted that by the end of the day he had spent most of the coins that they carried.

Alec was tired as they came back to the inn but saw several ill-kempt men in the common-room who had not been there the night before. Erin led the way up the stairs to their room.

Erin thought, *I don't trust those people. They don't seem right.*

Alec agreed. *Should we stay up here and not eat?*

No, we need to eat but be careful. Something isn't right.

≈ ≈ ≈ ≈

Soon it was time for dinner. Alec again concealed the bag of coins beneath the floorboards of their room, taking only a few to the common room. The room was crowded; they sat in the far corner of the room and ate, quietly watching the assembled people. Some were travelers, like them, and some were regulars. The collection of inn-ladies milled about; Alec could not tell if they were the same women as the night before. There were many locals, some eating the stew, some just drinking beer, some gathered by the big open fireplace swapping tales, some joining in the loud card game going on in the middle of the room. After their meal, Alec and Erin made their way towards the stairs to their room, but before they reached the bottom step a large man stepped in front of them.

"You must play cards with us tonight," he said.

Alec thought, *Is this the same man who invited me to play last night?*

I don't think so, thought Erin back to him. *Be careful.*

"Not tonight. We are tired," Alec said. "Maybe some other night."

"Oh, you must join us tonight," the man insisted. "We would be very insulted if you don't." He gestured broadly towards the other card players.

Watch out, thought Erin. They could both see the man's knife blade flash briefly in the lantern light.

"Join us," the man said in an oily voice, "or you might be looking for a new lady." He laughed as if he had made a joke. Maybe he had. Maybe not.

Alec and Erin knew that they could handle the situation if it digressed into a knife fight, but neither wanted that.

Maybe it would be best to play along for a while, Erin thought.

Okay, but I don't know the game, Alec thought to Erin.

I do, she thought back. *I will show you what to do.*

Alec could tell this was a set-up. *They are after our coins.* He was certain the men had searched their room for coins during the afternoon and found nothing; the men probably assumed the coins were on one of them. *They know we have more coins somewhere, since we will need them to complete our purchases tomorrow.*

You are a stranger here," the man said. "I am Jitsu. Traveling through our little village?"

"Yes," said Alec, not volunteering his name.

Alec sat at the table, Erin sat seemingly-meekly behind him. He looked at the rest of the table. There were four other players. Across from him was Jitsu, who looked like the ring-leader of the group. Behind him sat a curvaceous woman in skimpy clothes, like the inn-ladies, but with no locked belt. Alec gathered that her name was Lily. She didn't seem to be Jitsu's consort, but seemed to be with him. One of the other three players looked like a compatriot of Jitsu. The other two looked like slightly-tipsy rich kids, apparently local young noblemen, just here to play cards and get drunk and maybe purchase a moment with an inn-lady. *They look like the undergrad students at the Institute,* thought Alec, with a pang of nostalgia.

The game was straightforward. It looked like a local version of draw poker with one hold card to bet on. Alec was good at poker and knew how to calculate odds. Maybe he could use that to his advantage. The first few rounds went well. He won a few hands and lost a few, but something wasn't right. The cards weren't playing to the odds. The distributions of numbers and suits among the five players were wrong.

Alec was suspicious of Jitsu but couldn't see him cheating. The night wore on, and with conservative play, Alec was keeping about even against the others. One of the young nobles was losing heavily, and the other youth was playing about even.

Alec thought, *I wonder if I can sense the cards.*

Focus. The hand was dealt, and the hold card was down. All he could sense was a fuzzy world. He thought to Erin, *This guy is cheating, but I don't know how. Somehow, he is changing cards.*

Erin thought back, *I can tell when Jitsu switches cards, and I can sense what he feels about the cards he has.* Erin also mentally told him the feeling of the other players. Since Alec now knew what kind of hand each player held, he could rely on his knowledge of the other cards.

Eventually one of the young noblemen was out. Alec had already collected about half the youth's money over the course of the evening. Alec was holding his own: the combination of playing the odds and closely watching Jitsu was working. Jitsu was too good for Alec to see when he switched cards, but Erin could detect Jitsu's deception every time. Whenever Jitsu played the cards straight, Alec stuck with the odds. The others were playing based on whims and hunches. Playing the odds kept Alec gaining coins but let him lose enough not to look suspicious. Whenever Erin sensed the cards were switched, Erin would mentally tell him about the other players' cards and he would play based on this knowledge.

After an hour or so of play, two gruff but well-dressed individuals sauntered into the room. Erin poked Alec to make sure he saw them. *Those are the local marshals,* she thought. *If you break the law here, they will throw you in their dungeon and decide what you must do to get out. Not a good idea to get on their bad side.*

How do we quit this game? Alec thought to her.

Try being tired and see what happens.

After the next round, Alec yawned, raised his hand, and said, "Jitsu, my friend, this has been very entertaining, but I am ready to quit for the night."

"That is well and good," Jitsu said with a toothy grin, "but you owe us your pot." Alec looked puzzled. "We play until one person wins everything. That is the rule of the game." Jitsu's grin turned menacing. "Isn't that right?" he said to one of the well-dressed marshals.

"That's right," the marshal said, obviously conspiring with Jitsu.

Alec thought about it. He hadn't started with enough to be a loss to them. He didn't want to lose the coins he had won, but they weren't worth the risk of whatever trouble Jitsu intended if he continued playing.

"Ok, you can have my coins," Alec said, pushing them towards Jitsu.

"Just a second," Jitsu said. "Did you think that we would let you in for only those few coins?" He laughed. Then he suddenly leaned forward. "Your ante included her," he hissed, pointing at Erin.

Erin gasped at that.

"You can buy her back in the morning," Jitsu said, "and then finish your errands."

"No way!" said Alec.

Erin poked him. "Don't worry, I can take care of myself," she whispered, then thought to him, *If I must, I will go with them, kill him, and meet you later.*

Alec shook his head. "No! She's not part of it."

The marshal laughed. "She was part of it when you started. Now honor your debt. Either toss her in or play on."

Alec realized that they wanted this to play out to the end. Desperate to come up with a plan, Alec said, "Okay, I'll play on." He sat back down on his chair with a thump. He looked around. It was clear the marshals were with Jitsu and in on his scheme. They had the two exits covered, so running was not going to work. Others in the room had noticed the confrontation and began watching the card players, perhaps anticipating a good fight.

The marshal wasn't satisfied that Erin wasn't going to run, so he grabbed Erin's arm and roughly pulled her to her feet. The second marshal came over and pulled out a pair of leather cuffs, put them around Erin's wrists, and looked at Alec. "A little insurance to make sure your ante doesn't flee. If she did it might cost you your life." Then to the first marshal, "Where do you want me to tie the cuff rope?"

Before Alec could react, Erin spoke up, "Tie me over there with her," she said, pointing to the woman behind Jitsu. I am tired of this loser anyway."

The marshal obliged and pulled Erin over beside where Lily was sitting. He took the opportunity to let his hands roam over Erin' body, and he whispered, "Maybe I will see you later tonight."

Jitsu also looked at Erin. "You aren't my type – too skinny – and I already have her," he said, jerking his thumb towards Lily. "Don't think you are buttering me up by coming over here. I am going to sell you to the innkeeper at the end of the game."

Erin thought to Alec, *I can see Jitsu's cards from this side so that I can help you more.*

Alec played mechanically over the next few hands while he considered the situation. Then he decided it was time to get this game down to the two of them and force a crisis point. Alec suspected a piece of the strategy all along had been to whittle the game down to the two of them – *Jitsu and me.*

Alec started aggressively playing his cards and quickly knocked Jitsu's friend out of the game. Then, both Alec and Jitsu focused on knocking out the other player, the rich young noble, who was running low on coins. With their more-skillful playing and a little card knowledge thanks to Erin, Alec and Jitsu soon had the youth at bay. Now was the time to try the next piece of the plan. Alec waited until Erin told him that Jitsu had changed a card. *Focus.* Jitsu turned the card over, but instead of the changed card, it was the original card. Jitsu looked at it in slight surprise but then went on with the hand. *It worked,* thought Alec.

The young noble bowed out. Now almost everyone in the inn was watching the two of them: Jitsu and the tall stranger. Alec was on one side of the table and Jitsu, Lily, and Erin on the other side. The crowd could tell this was more of a match than usual but had no sense that the game was rigged.

Alec thought to Erin, *Be prepared: we may have trouble.* They played several more hands, staying about even. Then on a hand where Erin told Alec that Jitsu felt he had average cards, the big man stroked his beard convincingly.

"I am all in," Jitsu said. "Do you match, or do you concede?"

Alec knew he had the better cards. "I am all in," he said.

Erin informed Alec what Jitsu's last card was. Alec thought back, *That is the same card as I have!*

Then he must know what card you hold, Erin thought.

Erin could sense the scam. Jitsu was going to turn over the winning card and ask Alec to concede. If Alec did concede, he would lose Erin and be penniless but alive. If Alec did not concede and then turned over the same card as Jitsu, he would be accused of cheating. The marshals would determine his card was the fraud and haul him off to jail. Jitsu would get Erin and all the money and Alec would have an unfortunate fatal accident.

Alec met Jitsu's gaze. "I will match," he said evenly. *Focus.* The cards swirled, and Jitsu confidently turned over his hand. Then his jaw dropped in amazement – the cards he turned over were not the ones he expected.

Seize the moment. Alec laid down his winning cards. A murmur rippled through the assembled crowd.

Focus. A card appeared on Jitsu's sleeve and drifted to the floor. "Did you drop something?" Alec said calmly and pointed to the floor. Jitsu's winning card lay on the floor.

The two young nobles gasped. "Cheater!" they shouted. "This man is dishonorable! He is a cheater!" The two young men rushed towards Jitsu. Jitsu eyed his henchmen, the two marshals, but they were the local law. They could and would help Jitsu against outsiders, like Alec, but there were too many village people here for them to help against a serious cheating accusation by local noblemen. Jitsu saw the game was up, swept the cards off the table, and dashed towards the rear exit. Someone stuck out a foot and tripped him. The two youths were on him, kicking and gouging. Several locals joined in; Jitsu had cheated many. The marshals interceded to break up the fight.

Alec focused, and Erin's leather bindings shredded. The two of them backed to a corner and waited to find an opportunity to slip out of the fray. In the confusion, one of the marshals grabbed Jitsu as if to cuff him and then shoved him out the back door. Within a few moments, without Jitsu or any other reason to vent their anger, the fight broke up; one of the young noblemen wiped his bloody nose on his sleeve.

One of the marshals turned and saw them in the corner. "Cheaters forfeit their ante. Jitsu's ante is yours," he said to Alec. "Everyone else's ante is returned to them." The two nobles counted out their initial ante and left. Jitsu's companion was nowhere to be seen. The marshal passed the remaining coins to Alec, slyly pocketing a handful as he did so. Alec scooped up the coins, then picked up the two changed cards from the heap on the floor. *If anyone looked closely at these, they might be able to tell that they are not quite right,* he thought, and casually tossed the two cards in the fire.

"What about me?" a plaintive voice whined. Slithering out from under the table was Lily. The marshal looked at her, licked his lips, and then stopped.

"You were part of Jitsu's ante, so now you belong to him," the marshal said, pointing at Alec.

Erin snickered.

Alec raised his hands. "I don't want you. You can do whatever you want."

In a little voice, Lily said, "I have nowhere to go and no coins. You must take me." She looked at him pleadingly. Alec started to hand her some coins and send her off, and then remembered that women couldn't hold coins.

"I guess we have no choice for the night, but we need to figure something out tomorrow," said Alec.

The three of them made their way up to the room. Alec looked at the small bed.

"We won't all fit in this bed," he said.

"We will all fit fine," Erin and Lily both said.

Lily turned to Alec. "Which do you want first, her or me?"

Alec blushed and stammered.

Erin interceded, "He has someone else he is trying to be faithful to. Climb into bed and don't bother him."

Both women undressed and burrowed under the thin blankets for warmth. It was hard for Alec to come to grips with a society where people blithely and routinely slept nude with people they had barely met. Alec stalled around checking that the door and the shutters were latched and then decided to face the situation, stripped, and climbed under the blankets.

He suspected that being in a bed with one woman he might feel aroused, especially if the one woman was Erin, but to be in bed with two women would be worrisome, not exciting. The two women nested together, feeding off each other's warmth. Alec slept poorly, feeling like he was constantly elbowed or kneed in all the wrong places by one or the other of the two women. He thought about sleeping on the floor, but Erin was right – in this land people slept together for body heat to ward off the night chill. As he finally drifted off to sleep, he again thought longingly of his home and his large bed.

6 – The Aldermen

The next morning Alec wanted to find out Lily's story before they decided what to do next. After being freed from Jitsu, and a good night's sleep, she was much more pleasant than the night before. She was fairly attractive, Alec decided, in the curvaceous way that the local people seemed to prefer, and about Erin's age, but without the fire in her eye.

"So I guess I won you in a poker game," Alec said. "Who are you, and where did you come from?"

"I'm Lily," she said, "from a village about a four-day ride from here. But I left there about a year ago. I've only been in this village for about a month. I joined Jitsu a couple of weeks ago."

"How did you wind up with him?"

"Like I said, I left my home village about a year ago – I was getting to be too old to stay there. There were no men in the village who interested me. Besides, I wanted to see what it was like outside my village. So, when a nice peddler-man came through, he asked me to go away with him, and I did. We snuck off one night, sort of as a lark, but we got on well, and it gave me a chance for some fun, and adventure! We didn't tell my parents we were leaving, but they didn't mind – at my age, I was a drain on them. They weren't going to get any coins for me from any of the local boys. They were glad to see me leave, and it was a bonus that it was someone who would take care of me.

"We had a good life, my peddler-man and me. He was fun and made me laugh. We traveled around, and I got to see more of the Grasslands. He would trade things between towns and sometimes get extra coins as a storyteller. I set up our camp and took care of things. Cook, clean, manage the animals, and things like that. It was a good life." She smiled a wry smile. Then her smile faded.

"Then about a month ago, we were caught in one of the Aldermen raids."

"Stop!" said Alec. "Who are the Aldermen?"

Lily shrugged. "No one knows who they are, but they are fearsome raiders. They started showing up over the last year or so, maybe less. They are raiding and savaging the Grasslands! They have fearsome weapons that make them impossible to fight – some people say they throw the dragon's teeth! We all fear them!"

"Hmm," said Alec. *Dragons again.* So many tribes and lands to remember. *Word association. You can remember this tribe because they sound like Dr. Alder back at the Lab.* "Please, continue with your story."

"About a month ago, we came to a village, Cantin, and things were fine. I set up camp outside the village. We like to set up on a brook so we have easy access to water. The best location was a few els from town. My peddler-man had gone into town. Then I heard loud noises and saw smoke. I feared for him!" Lily shuddered at the memory.

"I hid beneath our wagon for a long time. But I was too scared to stay at camp by myself! When the noises stopped, I ran as fast as I could into the village, but it took a while to reach it. By the time I got there, it was too late. The Aldermen slavers had come through town, taken what they wanted, captured as many people as they could, and moved on." She shook her head. "There was no sign of my peddler. I do not know if he was captured or killed. At first, I went back to camp and cried. Then I went to town to beg for help." She scowled.

"First an innkeeper took me in and told me he would let me work for food and a place to sleep. Then the next day, he told me I had to agree to a contract if I wanted to stay. He lied to me! He said it was just a village formality and nothing to worry about. I can't read! I didn't know what his parchment said, but I trusted him! I was a fool!" She snorted. "I agreed and put my drop of blood on it like he said. That night after I cleaned up the common-room, he started to beat me. I threatened to leave, and he laughed, and just beat me harder. He told me my contract said that I could only leave if I paid him five gold coins – that's more than I could earn in a year! And more than the worth of the food and board he offered me! He knew I had no coins and could not pay him anything! He said I had agreed in that contract to do whatever he wanted! So I couldn't leave!" Erin patted her arm sympathetically, and after a moment to catch her breath, Lily's hysterics subsided.

"After that, he made me clean and help in the kitchen in the day and serve as an inn-lady at night. If he thought I wasn't enticing enough to the patrons or if any of them complained about my performance, he would beat me!" She pulled back her sleeve and showed Alec the purple and green marks of old bruises on her arm.

"A couple of weeks ago, Jitsu passed through town, liked how I satisfied him, and purchased me from the innkeeper." Lily crossed her arms over her breasts, hugging herself. "Jitsu is mean and cruel, but I had to stay with him because he paid for me. I had no choice! The other night I threatened to run away, and he told me he would catch me and kill me painfully." She looked up at Alec, her eyes pleading with the look he had seen last night.

"Please help me! If you don't take me, I will become the property of the marshal. When the marshal tires of me, he will sell me to one of the inns." She looked like she was about to burst into tears.

Don't be a sucker for a sob story. We've got enough problems as it is, without her!

Alec was about to tell her they couldn't help her when Erin said, "Of course you can stay with us! We are headed to Theland, and we will need someone to help with our camp during our journey." Erin wrapped her arms around Lily and hugged her.

"Thank you," said Lily tearfully, burying her face in Erin's sleeve. "Oh, thank you!"

≈ ≈ ≈ ≈

The three went downstairs. The common room had been cleaned and put back in order after last night's melee. The innkeeper did run a tight ship, Alec noted. Breakfast was more of the porridge for the three of them.

Today was a repeat of yesterday's rounds. First to the seamstress. At Erin's request, the seamstress was able to equip Lily in clothing suitable for their trip. Then it was off to add more food and supplies. Finally, they went to pick up the wagon. Everywhere they went the card game of the night before was the main topic of gossip.

Lily seemed positively cheerful with new clothes and something to do. She helped carry their bundles to the wagon and put things in order. By late afternoon they were ready to leave.

As they made their final inspection of their loaded wagon, and out of earshot of Lily, Erin made a request. "Can you please use your wizardly powers to make a hidden compartment on the bottom of the wagon? We need a safe place to secure our valuable things." As soon as Alec was finished with this task, Erin stored their remaining coins and both rings in the compartment.

They didn't travel far before the sun was starting to set, so they stopped for the night. Lily gladly took care of the drungs and set up camp without any direction.

Alec laid out several rocks. *Focus.* The rocks heated and steamed. Erin had warned Lily, but she still gasped at the heated rocks and almost burned herself when she tried to touch them to see if they were truly hot. Lily quickly figured out how to use the rocks and cooked a better supper than they had been served at the inn. Both Alec and Erin were more pleased with the arrangement than they had imagined.

The wagon was designed as a cover for a sleeping tent with the sleeping bay under the wagon. The three of them crawled under the wagon, undressed, and slept.

The next week passed uneventfully. They continued to follow the rough path. They passed no one else as they crossed the rolling Grasslands, but that wasn't unexpected. When the third moon waned, Erin estimated they had another few days before she would be in familiar territory – then they would leave the Grasslands and enter a forest at the edge of the mountains that were still mere shadows on the horizon.

As they travelled, Alec spent time experimenting with how he could use the local dark energy. He also continued teaching Erin how to sense dark energy. She was progressing slowly but steadily. She could feel small amounts of dark energy, and she could use the energy to light her sword.

Occasionally they would stop. Erin would put on her ring and sense the location of a flock of bounders and Alec would hunt to give them fresh meat. *Things are going well. Maybe too well,* Alec thought.

≈ ≈ ≈ ≈

Erin was driving the wagon when she saw a column dust rising high above the next hill. She kicked herself for not noticing it earlier. "Riders are coming," she said with some concern. "Enough riders to stir up dust. That's not good. Can you hide us or blur us with your magic?"

"At this range, my ability to bend light won't be good enough to obscure something as large as this wagon, and the drungs," Alec answered. "If we can get a little way away – maybe a quarter of an el – I might be able to blur things enough that the riders would miss us in the grass."

Erin started to turn the wagon off the path into the tall grass – another few hundred paces and Alec might be able to obscure them successfully. Too late. The riders had seen them and changed their direction to intercept the wagon. Erin could count ten well-armed riders on trogus. She could see the riders were all dressed in functional dark blue clothes. This was not a gang of rag-tag bandits. It was an organized team. *Soldiers? But whose?* She hoped the riders would give them a cursory look and pass on by.

The riders again altered their course so that they would come across the wagon in the next few minutes; however, they never changed their speed and did not appear to be in any hurry to approach the wagon.

Alec's staff was laying in the front of the wagon, and he wore his medallion in its usual place on his chest. Erin had her sword out and close to her side. Erin had been teaching Lily how to use weapons, so Lily had a long knife by her side. Alec felt that Lily was inept with a weapon – she wasn't going to be much help if it came to a fight, but she needed some way to protect herself. Erin also had been teaching Alec how to use a sword. His athletic abilities made him capable, but she could see that he would need long hours of practice to be even half-way proficient as a warrior. They had also practiced combat moves with his staff, and now he had a better feel with it and a more natural sense of how to effectively use it. Plus, Erin had pointed out, few sword fighters ever face a staff, so they were rarely prepared to fight it effectively.

The lead rider approached and stopped directly in front of them. The others spread out around the wagon. Erin had been hoping that they could keep their heads down, keep plodding along and that the riders would let them pass. *Not going to happen.*

"Where are you three heading?" the lead rider asked.

Erin replied "We are heading home after trading our goods in Arose. We are from Theland."

The leader looked at them with no apparent concern. "We will have to inspect your wagon. Get down."

Since discretion still seemed like the better option, the three of them slowly got off the wagon. Alec hopped off the left side, and the two women stepped down from the right. Alec noticed that Erin had taken her sword with her.

I should take my staff, Alec thought. He reached back into the wagon to grab it but as he turned, although he never saw anything, he felt a whoosh of air near his face. Something connected with the side of his head, everything went dizzy, and he lost consciousness as he felt himself falling groundward.

≈ ≈ ≈ ≈

Erin had stepped warily from her side of the wagon, looking with concern at how the riders had surrounded them. She looked across at Alec just in time to see a soldier in Alec's blind spot pick up his cudgel and bat Alec across the head.

"No!" she yelled, but it was too late. Alec had fallen in a heap.

She drew her sword and looked at the troops. "Let us go," she said. "We haven't done anything to you." Lily cowered behind her – did she have her knife?

They ignored her plea. Three of them dismounted and came towards her. She slashed at one of them with her sword, but he just stepped back. She could see they didn't appear frightened by her. A fourth member pulled something from the side of his saddle. It looked like a big pile of ropes.

They are going to have to fight me and win before they can tie me up, she thought. With a practiced hand, the fourth solider flung the collection of ropes at her. It spread in a wide arc over her head. Erin had never seen a net before, but she instinctively raised her sword to fend it off. The gaps of the net were widely spaced, and her sword pierced the air.

The center of the net settled over her head; her sword was outstretched through a gap.

Maybe I can still fight, she thought, as the edges of the net settled around her knees. The soldier gave a pull, bringing the net tight around her, and left her off-balance. She stumbled onto her knees and hands, losing her sword in the process. She tried to lunge forward to pick it up, but one of the dismounted riders grabbed it. Two of them pulled the net tight around her knees and tied the net to the pommel of the trogus. Her head and shoulders were on the ground, her arms were tightly tangled around her side, and her feet were in the air lashed to the beast. Erin tried to kick and squirm, but the trogus had done this many times before and ignored her. She was stuck.

The riders weren't particularly worried about Erin escaping and turned their attention to Lily. Lily stood holding her knife and staring at them. They gestured for her to drop it. Lily had no idea how to defend herself. She dropped the knife.

"Down on your knees," one of the men barked. Lily dropped to her knees and complied.

The lead rider looked at the haul. "Probably doing just what they said – returning from a trading trip." He gestured to his men. "You three – strip them and take them back to camp! We will add them to the other slaves." He eyed the wagon and drungs. "Take that wagon, too; we need more wagons and drungs to carry supplies. The rest of us will continue to patrol." The remaining soldiers mounted and rode off with their leader.

≈ ≈ ≈ ≈

The three soldiers approached Alec and started removing his clothes. Erin saw one soldier remove Alec's shoes and cast them off into the tall grass. One of the men tore off Alec's pants and underclothes while another tore off his shirt. They rolled him over and saw the medallion on his chest. One soldier cut the strap holding it. He squinted at the medallion briefly as it caught the sun and tossed it towards the wagon so that he could look at it later. His aim was bad, and the medallion hit the wagon's sideboard and caromed into a patch of high grass and disappeared from view. They tied Alec's hands together and roped him to the pommel of one of the trogus. All Erin could do was watch and squirm in her upside-down position.

The three men then turned to the women. First, they approached Lily. By now Lily had figured out she was better off cooperating. By winking and smiling, she made sure they knew that she would do whatever they wanted. They motioned for her to undress and she quickly stripped everything off and dumped her clothes on the ground around her. She gave several suggestive wiggles, but the men weren't interested. They tied her hands and looped her rope over the pommel of the third trogus.

Then they turned to Erin. *I won't make this easy,* she thought. But it was. With practiced efficiency, they pulled the net up enough that her lower body was exposed and all her clothes below her waist were off. They rolled her on her chest and put a harness with a bit through her mouth to control her head. A twist and she was face-down on the ground. Her remaining clothes were torn off and left in a heap. Her hands were tied, and she was roped to the trogus with Lily, still wearing the harness on her head.

One of the soldiers climbed onto the wagon, clicked at the drungs, and started moving in the direction the riders had come. The first rider mounted his trogus.

"Come along, or be dragged," the soldier said.

The trogus started slowly. Alec had regained just enough of his senses to stumble alongside the trogus with the second soldier. The two naked women followed the third trogus, attached by about ten feet of rope.

Erin desperately looked around for a landmark in the grass – a bush, an animal burrow – anything – so that she could locate this place again. She knew that somehow this medallion was very important to Alec and that he would want to be able to find it again when they got free. But there was nothing obvious that she could see. The only hope would be if some of their discarded clothing stayed close to the clump of grass where the medallion had landed; however, the slight breeze was already blowing her tunic down the trail, so she knew it was but a faint hope.

7 – Captured

Alec started to regain consciousness.

My head. His head throbbed and he felt as though he could see sparks behind his closed eyes. He could tell his hands were tied together firmly and he could feel the grass rubbing against his skin. Then he realized he was naked. *Now what?!* He opened his eyes and blinked a few times to clear the clouds of darkness from his vision.

As his mind cleared, he could see their new wagon heading off in the distance, and two naked women tied to a nearby trogus. *Erin and Lily!*

"Your turn," his captor said. "Stand up." Alec looked up and saw a man in a blue uniform standing over him. He got to his feet drunkenly and instinctively felt for his medallion. It was gone. *A raider,* thought Alec.

His captor mounted his trogus. A jerk on a rope commanded Alec's attention, and he realized he was attached to a tether tied to the trogus saddle. The animal started off at a slow pace. The rope pulled tight, and Alec stumbled and almost tripped before he could match the animal's gait and walk behind it. The trogus did not seem to be affected by the saw-like grass blades or the small rocks on the path and wandered along the easiest walking route. The short length of his tether and the constant pace did not allow Alec to avoid the grass – soon his legs were covered by dozens of grass cuts and his bare feet were slashed by the rocks. He had to keep his eyes on the path ahead and could not look around, but he figured that the two women were suffering the same fate.

Alec was ready to collapse when the trogus came over a small rise. He could see a camp below with about fifty soldiers in uniforms like his captor's and a dozen or so others. His commandeered wagon was entering the camp ahead of them and joining other wagons. As they came to the edge of the encampment, they passed a pack of dogs; most were chained but a couple roamed loose. *Sentry dogs,* thought Alec, *to keep us from escaping.*

In the center of the camp's circle of tents and wagons were two groups of naked people, huddled in a central cleared area – about fifty men on one side of the clearing, all tied together, and about the same number of women tied together on the other side about a hundred paces away.

Slavers! thought Alec. *Slavers have captured us!*

≈ ≈ ≈ ≈

Erin and Lily were pulled roughly behind a trogus as it made its way along a faint trail through the tall grass. The pace was set to cover ground, but not totally exhaust the new captives. The rope that tied them to the trogus chaffed Erin's arms, and Lily whimpered and cried incessantly. There was not enough room on the path for both women to walk side-by-side and they tended to bump into each other. Erin was experienced with rough terrain and knew to step adroitly between the rocks, but she could see that Lily was having a very hard time. The soldier riding the trogus turned once to look at the two naked women. Lily shook off her tears and gave him a very suggestive gesture and a wan smile. Erin spat at him.

He laughed and turned back to watch the path. Erin could see their wagon being driven off ahead of them, moving considerably faster than they were; soon it went out of sight over the hill.

What about Alec, she thought. *Is he alive?* She turned and looked back, but no one was behind them – the other soldier and his trogus with Alec must be ahead of them.

They walked for a long while with Lily becoming progressively slower and her limp more pronounced. Finally, they topped a rise and could see a camp with many captive men and women, separated from each other on different sides of the camp. Their captor untied them from the trogus and herded them towards the women's side. Erin took one last look over her shoulder towards the men's side and saw another trogus pulling a naked man along behind it. *Alec,* she thought.

≈ ≈ ≈ ≈

Alec was led to the men's side of the cleared area. For the first time, he could see Erin and Lily, no longer tied behind a trogus, being led towards the women's side of the camp. From Lily's limp, he could tell that they had been affected by the trek much as he had.

Alec could smell the group of men before he could make out their faces. The stench, a ripe smell of old body odor and human waste, hit him like a wall. Alec almost gagged. There was no sanitation and no bathing.

Alec's captor came up to another man in a similar uniform. "Found them out on the plains. Captain says to add them to the catch."

"All right."

A few more soldiers came over to inspect the new capture. Two of them pinned Alec's arms and strapped a leather collar around his neck; the collar had a short rope leash. Then his hands were set free. The slave-keeper popped him twice on the rear with a small whip – Alec jumped both times.

"You behave, and you won't have any trouble. Cause trouble, and you will regret it. Do you understand?" the slave-keeper said.

Alec nodded his head.

The slave-keeper led Alec by his leash to a group of four other men. Each of them had a leather collar, and each had a three-foot length of rope leading from the collar to a common metal ring. Alec realized that all the captured men were joined together in groups of four or five, each man tied to a center ring. No man could move independently – they had to sit or stand or move as a clump. *Hard to go very fast,* Alec thought, *with five people tied to a ring.*

The slave-keeper poked the group with his crop to make them stand up, quickly tied Alec to the center ring, joining him to the four others, and left. Alec looked at his neighbor's collar. It was a plain leather collar with a cotter-pin fastener. Alec could see that the pin couldn't be removed by hand, but a simple lever could probably fasten or unfasten it. *Not much hope of that in a place like this,* he thought. He felt something squish beneath his foot and realized he had stepped on a pile of human excrement.

Alec's ring-mates sat down, forcing Alec to sit also; he moved enough to avoid sitting in the pile of shit. He noticed the central ring that held them was not attached to anything.

"Why haven't you tried to escape?" Alec asked. The men looked at him with no hope left in their eyes.

"Try, and the dogs will get you," the man next to him said.

Another chimed in. "You don't want the dogs to get you! That's a terrible way to die!"

"Misbehave too much and they will let the dogs play with you for sport while they cheer and then they will use whatever's left of you as food for the trogus," a third man said, running his words together, and speaking with the hollow tone of one who had seen it happen.

The fourth man just stared into space and said nothing.

They sat for an hour or so until they heard the clang! of metal against metal as a slave-keeper banged a spoon against a pan as a signal to the captives.

"Food time. Come on," one of the men muttered. They awkwardly scrambled to their feet, impeded by the addition of Alec who did not yet have the rhythm of moving as part of the group.

Alec estimated that there were about twelve sets of ringed groups in the camp for the male captives. The groups formed a loose line and headed towards a low plank stretched between two rocks. In time, Alec's group came to the front of the line. A large wooden bowl sat in the middle of the plank. Nearby a cauldron hung over the remains of an open fire. A serving woman, dressed in a loose-fitting smock, hair covered by a sunbonnet, trudged over from the cauldron and threw a pot of mush in the wooden bowl. Alec's four ring-mates surrounded the bowl, squatting on their haunches and pulling Alec down with them. The captives reached in and scooped up handfuls of the warm dripping mush, lowering their heads and shoving it in their mouths as fast as they could. Alec looked at the stuff in the bowl.

"Eat quickly," one of them said. "We don't have long." Alec scooped a little of the mush on his fingertips, smelled it, and tasted it. *Pasty.* Alec looked at his mates. They had already eaten most the mush and made a mess as they slopped it out of the bowl. It was all over one of them, the quiet man. Alec scraped a mouthful from the bottom of the bowl.

"You'll get used to it," the first man said.

After almost no time there was another signal from one of the slave-keepers.

"Time to move," one of the others said. They all got up, pulling Alec along with them. The next group behind them came up to the bowl, and the serving lady threw another measure of mush into it. Although he could not see them, Alec could hear their slurps and grunts as they slopped up the mush.

Alec's group meandered from the eating area and sat down again, next to another ringed group. Within the men's area, the groups jostled about but seemed to have no defined place to sit, and no organization. Alec noted with studied fascination that the hair of a man in the group next to him was crawling with lice; another had an oozing cut on his back that seemed to be infested with maggots.

As always, as soon as the sun began to set the air temperature began to drop. Alec looked around. Although the soldiers began moving towards their tents, there seemed to be no shelter for the captives.

"We are out here for the night," Alec's first ring-mate said, patting the bare ground. "We have to use each other to stay warm enough to survive the night." The five of them huddled up with another group to generate enough body heat to stay warm. Occasionally the men shifted positions as a person on the outside of the pile moved closer to the center for warmth.

Exhaustion took its toll and Alec dropped off to sleep. He was roused from a fitful doze by a whimper and a yelp; in the half-light of the double moon, Alec could see that two men from a different ring had pinned a teenaged boy from an adjoining ring. Alec could hear the cries of fright, and the whimpers from the boy and the rough grunts of the men as the two of them abused the boy long into the night. There was nothing Alec could do. He couldn't reach the boy, and even if he could, he might just become the next victim of this group. *Even in adversity, we can't pull together,* thought Alec.

≈ ≈ ≈ ≈

Erin and Lily were led to the group of women. Their captor turned them over to another soldier, dressed in a different uniform. He put a leather collar around Erin's neck. Then he led her to a ring that had three women tied to it. The slave-keeper attached Erin to the ring and went back to Lily. As he started to put a collar on Lily, she looked up at him and smiled coyly, playing with a strand of her hair.

He gave Lily a long look, appraising her. "The Captain says we need more help around the camp. Can you work?"

"What do I have to do?"

"Help feed the captives during the day and help keep the men happy at night."

"Oh yes," said Lily.

The guard stroked her bare rump, letting his hand linger, then said, "Go over there," and pointed at a fat lady wearing a smock and a sunbonnet. "She will put you to work."

Lily breathed a sigh of relief and went over to the fat lady. "The man told me to come over here, to help you."

The lady looked at her skeptically. "I hope you are some help! Because I need help – not another sniveling lazy-bones – but if you aren't I will have them feed you to the trogus!" She squinted menacingly at Lily.

"I will be very helpful," said Lily, meekly.

"You will be a serving lady, and you can start right now," the fat lady said, and directed her to a tent where Lily was handed a smock and bonnet; then was ushered outside to a big cauldron to stir simmering mush with a big wooden paddle.

≈ ≈ ≈ ≈

Erin felt like a chained animal. She warily eyed the other three women tied to her ring. They sensed her fierceness and did not try to converse with her but did try to point out the camp routine. The first day, however, Erin refused to eat and growled at the slave-keeper as he tried to push her face into the mush.

"Bitch!" he shouted at her and lashed her with his whip. Then he commenced whipping the other three members of her ring. "If you can't keep her in line you can all suffer," he said to the women.

"Why?" one of the women hissed at Erin. "Why did you do that?"

Another of the women in the ring spat at Erin. "We do not want to suffer because of you!" The third woman glared at her darkly.

Erin learned quickly that peer pressure was a very effective form of control. After that, she ate the mush. *I must keep my strength up,* she rationalized and looked for some way to escape.

≈ ≈ ≈ ≈

Dawn seemed to come early. Alec welcomed the first light since it promised warmth from the night's cold. He had slept very poorly, jostled amongst the other captives. His feet hurt, and his scratched legs ached. He was a little worried that his grass cuts would become infected. To make things worse, there were no sanitation provisions. Everyone was sleeping in their urine, and Alec smelled – *Forgive the pun!* he thought to himself. *I smell like crap.*

Breakfast was the same drill. The groups lined up for their time at the food plank. When it was their turn Alec's group settled around the bowl as the serving lady threw in their measure of mush. The others ate eagerly. Alec was hungry and knew he had to eat, so he scooped some out and ate it. *There is no way to eat this slop from that bowl without spilling it all over yourself,* he noticed. *I'm going to look just as grungy as those other guys in no time.* Very soon the signal was given for the next group to come forward, and his group stood to leave. Alec was slow getting up and felt a whip lash his leg as they moved away.

The slavers were bustling about, breaking camp and packing their tents and supplies into the wagons. With whips and shouts, the slave-keepers herded the groups of men into a long line, connected to each other by a rope passed through each of the rings. The rope was attached to a pair of drungs in front. With a whistle, the beasts started off, plodding slowly, and the captives trailed along behind. The pace was relatively easy but relentless. It was very hard to walk with five people attached to a ring. The path was rough and there was no way to avoid stepping on rocks and brushing against the sawgrass. The people on the edge of the trail barely had enough room to stand straight.

Around midday, they stopped, and each of the rings was given a water-skin. They drank and shared the water although Alec was sure that a couple of members of his ring drank a lot more than the others. The line soon started up again and continued until late in the afternoon when they stopped for the night. Alec had spent the day looking for ways to escape but hadn't found any. In the first place, he couldn't get the leather collar off his neck, and in the second place, he couldn't get away while attached to the others. The rest of the evening was a repeat of the night before. Everyone again slept in their filth and huddled together for warmth. He heard the whimpering of the teenaged boy again.

The next day began much like the previous day: prods by the slave-keepers to rouse the captives; a measure of mush; the rings of men tied to a team of drungs. About mid-morning the line of men was ruffled by a commotion occurring somewhere ahead of Alec. The pace of the roped line slowed slightly as the men, captives and soldiers alike, turned to see what was going on, their combined weight pulling on the drungs.

The teenaged boy who had been abused had somehow figured out a way to unfasten his collar; when the monotonous pace lulled the slave-keepers, the boy took advantage of their inattention to make a break for it. A murmur ran through the chained men as they craned for a better view of the running boy – a few snaps of the slave-keepers' whips quelled any other thoughts of disobedience. The drungs grunted and recovered their steady pace, jerking the lines of men along. The soldier near Alec looked at the fleeing boy and shrugged. *I hope he makes it,* thought Alec as he watched the boy run away from the line. However, days in captivity had hindered the boy's ability to move quickly, and he stumbled as he ran. Then Alec heard the baying of the dogs. About fifty paces from the trail the first dog caught up. It snarled at the boy, who turned and went the other way. Then a second dog appeared. The boy turned back to avoid it, and the first dog grabbed his leg. The boy fell, screaming in pain. The second dog attacked from the other side. Alec could see that at least one more dog joined in. The dogs continued to tear and torment the boy until he could scream no more.

Alec felt sick.

"Too bad," said one of Alec's ring-mates, under his breath.

"Why?" said another. "The kid is better off dead."

"Yes," said the first, "but now that bunch will just have to find someone else to abuse."

With that thought fresh in his mind, Alec spent the rest of the day looking with increased urgency for some way to escape.

$$\approx \ \approx \ \approx \ \approx$$

The third day on the trail started the same as the others; however, Alec was surprised to see that the serving lady filling the food bowl this morning was none other than Lily. Alec started to say something to her but didn't have a chance, and by her frown aimed in his direction, she obviously did not want him to.

They marched half of the morning. The combination of rocks, grass, and nonexistent sanitation were turning Alec's legs into a festering mess and the places where he had felt the sting of the whip had raw welts; the pus attracted small biting flies. As he felt the aftertaste of the morning's mush fill the back of his throat, he wondered when dysentery would set in. Perhaps it was his imagination, but it seemed there were fewer men in the large group than when he had first been captured. With a sick feeling, he realized the trogus looked well fed.

The soldiers stopped near a slight rise and started to make camp. Off in the distance was a small village.

"They will raid that village later today," Alec's more talkative ring-mate mused. "We will have some new companions by tonight."

Indeed, Alec could see more activity going on in camp than on the previous stops. The soldiers were preparing their beasts and getting ready to fight. The supply wagons had been pulled up in a tight circle. The slave-keepers marched the captive men past the wagons to a stopping point on the far knoll. As his ring passed near the soldiers, Alec saw one of the raiders pull something out of a heavily-sealed wagon.

Alec stopped and stared.

It was a rifle.

Alec gasped. Although he knew little of munitions, from a distance, the gun had the look of the hunting rifles he had been around back home. As he watched, two other guards pulled out things that also looked like rifles. Alec stared in shock and tripped as his ring-mates gave him a swift jerk. They grabbed his arms and pulled him along at their pace until he regained his feet.

"Are you a fool? You will get us all whipped! You know if one misbehaves all are punished!"

"That was a rifle!" Alec exclaimed, trying not to raise his voice.

"'Ry-ful?' No – that is their magic death rod!" Even the silent man in their group looked back and shuddered, and they all quickened their step.

"Don't you know of the death rod? It can kill anything, man or beast, from a great distance! No one can stop its magic. Even the sound of it can cause men to go deaf!"

The second man chimed in, "It beat us at my village. So many fell dead from its bite! Its tooth ripped right through our shields! There was nothing we could do to stop it – most of us ran, and I think the others surrendered or were killed. They captured the ones that ran. Like me."

"Can't that village see us?" asked Alec incredulously. "Why doesn't everyone run away?"

"Because they think they are safest behind the village walls," the first man explained. "If you run from the raiders in the open, the dogs will chase you down, one by one. You saw what that means. The dogs will tear you apart. Behind the village walls, people can fight as a group and are usually safe from raiders – except for these Aldermen raiders, because of the death rod – but the people don't know that until it is too late."

The rings of men were taken to their usual place on the left side of the camp. Alec could see a cloud of fine dust rise from the prairie as the raiders rode towards the village. Alec's group sat down.

"All we can do now is sit and wait," one of them said. "They won't feed us or give us water until the village raid is finished. That will take most of the day and probably some of the night."

Alec settled down on the hard grass. *Rifles. But how?*

8 – Escape

On her third morning in the slavers' camp, as Erin squatted down for breakfast she saw that Lily was the serving lady hauling the slop. She hissed softly to Lily in recognition.

Lily leaned over so that her bonnet hid her face from the fat lady and the slave-keepers. "The soldiers are leaving soon to go on another raid," she whispered hurriedly. Erin's ring-mates were noisily slurping their mush, paying no attention to Erin, or Lily. "When I signal to you, make a commotion. It may be the only way that Alec can escape."

After their feeding, Erin and her ring sat at the edge of the women's area, and Erin watched the raiding force ride off from camp.

Then Lily walked by, carrying a dirty bowl as a ruse, and said softly, "Wait a few moments, and then do something. This may be his best chance."

Erin waited until the shadow of the feeding plank moved about a hand's-width, pushed by the morning sun. *It must be time,* she thought.

Suddenly Erin leaped to her feet, half dragging her startled ring-mates and lunged at a near-by girl in the next ring.

"You! You stole my man!" Erin screamed. "You purple-striped trogus!" The girl recoiled in surprise.

"What?!?" she said, flabbergasted by Erin's assault.

Erin grabbed the girl's hair and started to pull her to the ground. The girl reached over her head for Erin's arms, and the four other women tethered to her ring fell on top of her. One of the women on Erin's ring tried to punch Erin, but again, the ring of women fell into one another. Soon it turned into a shouting and wrestling match, with some of the women trying to pull away and some of the women fighting each other. Because of their tethers, all nine of the women were quickly entangled with each other, and it wasn't clear who was fighting and who was cowering.

The slave-keepers, hearing the commotion, ran over to see what was happening. "The bitches are at it," one yelled in delight. The women's slave-keepers were joined by some of the other camp men, amused by the spectacle of nine naked women engaged in a mud-wrestling match, cheering the women on and occasionally poking them with a spear handle or slapping their backsides. The other rings of captive women also began to yell, some enjoying the fight, some wanting it to stop, and some yelling just to release their pent-up voices.

However, after a time it was clear that Erin was getting the upper hand and might kill the long-haired girl. The slave-keepers decided it was time to break this up and started whipping the women to stop the fight. Two large men grabbed Erin's head, pulled it back, and stuck a bit and harness in her mouth to pull her off the other woman. They spread Erin on the ground, beat her with their short whips, and then beat the rest of the women involved in the fight. All of them lay there on the ground, panting, bloodied, and beaten.

I hope that worked, Erin thought, wincing from her lashing. *I hope Alec got away.*

"Why did you do that!" one of her ring-mates asked angrily.

"She stole my lover back home," Erin said, gesturing towards the long-haired girl. "I hate her for that. I saw her and couldn't hold myself back anymore! My emotions got the best of me." Erin hoped she sounded a bit contrite.

Erin's lie seemed to quell the anger of her ring-mates but did not make them happy. From then on, they treated Erin more harshly.

≈ ≈ ≈ ≈

Alec heard a commotion coming from the women's side of camp: women screaming and yelling and men cheering. The few slave-keepers guarding the men went over to see what was happening. A serving woman appeared from behind a wagon and bustled over to where Alec and his mates were sitting. She reached down, and using a small tool, sprung the leather collar from his neck. Alec rubbed his chafed neck, gingerly feeling the raw spots, and looked at her in surprise.

"You! Come with me, and be quick and quiet about it," the smocked figure said loudly. "I need something carried."

Beneath the woman's bonnet, he recognized the face peering intently at him. *Lily!* He quickly scrambled to his feet – painfully, because of the cuts and welts – and followed her.

As he limped off, he heard one of his ring-mates say, "Too bad – the ones they take off alive are used to feed the trogus."

"I didn't like him anyway," grunted another. "Too tall. Too inquisitive."

Lily pushed him along in front of her. Soon they were past the edge of the camp and over the knoll.

"Go," Lily said urgently. "This may be your only chance! The soldiers are off on their raid, and they have taken most of the dogs with them. Only the dogs they left behind the caravan path remain, in case the Aldermen are followed. Now run! Or risk being caught and killed!"

"What about Erin?" he blurted.

"You fool – she is giving you this opportunity to escape. Now go!" She shoved his naked body towards the open grassland. He almost fell headlong but recovered his footing and moved as fast as he could into the cover of the tall grass.

He walked very warily through the clumps of grass for the first few hundred paces, expecting the dogs to find him after each step. Then he broke into a slow trot, running as fast as his sore feet and legs could take him. Eventually, he felt he was outside the dogs' range. *I'm free,* he thought. *I hope.*

He hunkered down next to a clump of brush on the lee side of a small hill and inspected his legs and feet. *Okay, I'm out of the slave camp. But – so what?* And then there was the question that haunted him: *What about Erin?*

One part of his brain said, *'Forget about Erin and just take care of yourself.'* He could make it out of here on his own, and then maybe – maybe – find a way home. And back to Sarah. And his apartment. And a shower. And his clothes. And his life.

But ... The rest of his brain told him that was ungrateful – he had to help Erin. And, going through his thoughts, he realized that he was deeply attached to her, and in a much stronger way than he had ever felt with Sarah. Whatever happened next, he knew he had to find a way to free Erin and get her back to her home.

Then reality struck as he felt the deepest cut on the bottom of his foot. *Ouch.* Here was one naked guy with sore feet and infected legs against fifty or more well-armed soldiers, some of whom had long-range repeating rifles. And he was going to take them on? Maybe when he had his medallion, but not like this.

First problems first, he thought. *How am I going even to survive?* What was there to eat, where was water, and how was he going to keep from freezing at night?

A low growl brought Alec back to more immediate problems. A small hyra had come out of the nearby thicket, only twenty paces from him. Erin had told him they were opportunistic. They would not take much of a risk to bring down game, but if there was a hurt animal, they would willingly kill it. The hyra was approaching carefully but confidently – obviously, it put Alec in the 'hurt animal' category. *Got to change that impression,* Alec thought. He picked up a rock and flung it at the creature. Without his sling, the projectile didn't have the power he was accustomed to, but his natural athletic ability sent the rock straight at the animal. It hit the hyra in the side with a reassuring pufft! The small creature jumped and pulled back to the edge of the clearing, looked at Alec for a few seconds, and then vanished.

Good for now, thought Alec, but knew it would come back under cover of darkness to see if he was vulnerable. *If I sleep, I may be hyra food.* He sighed. *Need to do something,* he thought.

As Alec sat on the hillside, with the smallest moon crossing the sky at an oblique angle, his mind slowly sank into despair. He was tired and hungry and been captured by slavers and beaten. This was barbaric. He was supposed to be a premier research scientist, working in a safe, comfortable Lab with proper restrooms. Instead he was out here in God-knows-where, having to kill people and eat dead animals. Tears welled up in his eyes. *It's hopeless,* he thought. *I'm no Boy Scout! I don't know how to do this!* What could he, a university research genius, do out here to survive? He didn't even know how to make a safe place to sleep. Erin always did that part. Erin knew how to survive. *Erin.* If only Erin were here, she could show him. *Erin.* And with Erin, he could keep warm at night. *Erin.* The thought of Erin gave him a feeling of hope, an anchor against the sea of his fear and darkness.

No, I can't give up. And be eaten by dogs or those fanged trogus. I must figure out how to make it. Alec looked up at the waning moon, crossing through the sunlight, and took a deep breath. Then he realized that it was no chance opportunity that allowed Lily to get him out of the slave camp. *Erin did something – something – to set me free.* He smiled a bit ruefully. *Erin thinks I am a 'Great Wizard' – but she is the one who knows how to succeed!* He gingerly slapped his sore thigh and stood up. *She is counting on me.* With that, his spirits lifted, and he felt as ready to tackle his situation as anyone who is naked and hungry, on a lonely plain with wild beasts waiting to eat him and slavers ready to re-capture him, could possibly be.

≈ ≈ ≈ ≈

Late in the day, the Aldermen soldiers returned from their raid. First, the war party returned. Then a second party arrived with stolen wagons and goods from the village. Slightly later a third party returned with captives from the village. The captives had been stripped naked and pulled along behind the drungs. Erin guessed there were another twenty women added to the group. She could see they were divided among the various rings so that they would not be with people they knew.

One of the captured women had not been able to make the walk. Somewhere she had fallen and been dragged the rest of the way. Erin could see a trail of blood where her mangled body had been pulled across the rocks and saw-grass. The woman was still alive, although breathing raggedly, and had been left, unattended, lying on the ground while the slave-keepers attached the other women to rings. Now the slave-keepers returned for the downed woman. The dragged her to a butcher's block near the animal pens and laid her across it face down. They stuffed a rag in her mouth. One of them took an ax and chopped off her arm. The woman reflexively screamed, but the rag muffled the sound. Then her body shuddered a couple of times and went still. The slave-keeper chopped the arm into two pieces. Then he chopped the hand off. He tossed the hand to a nearby trogus. The beast caught the tidbit in mid-air and messily chomped it down. Erin watched with horror as the man continued to chop the body into pieces.

"Trogus food," said her ring-mate. "Cut up parts like that are how they usually feed them. If the soldiers get bored and they want a spectacle, they will put a live person in the pen with the trogus and let several of them feed at once. The trogus like to eat the hand and feet first, and they like hot blood. The soldiers like to hear the person scream for a long time, while the trogus eat their arms and legs." Erin thought she was tough, but this turned even her stomach. Also, she suspected that her ring-mates would not grieve if she became trogus fodder.

≈ ≈ ≈ ≈

Okay. What first. Alec exhaled heavily. *Maybe some way to defend myself.* He looked around the clumps of tall grass – not even a good long stick here – although there were plenty of rocks around. *If only I had my medallion, I could take care of this.*

A new thought came to him. *There is so much natural dark energy on this world that I can feel a small amount of dark energy even without my medallion. Can I use the local dark energy to make a new medallion to use as a focus? I know how to make tricrystals.*

Alec thought back through his research notes. The theory of dark energy implied that the stronger the focus, the easier it would be to work with dark energy. *Let's see. Dark energy and time are related. Dark energy is related to time.* The amount of dark energy available and the strength of the focus would reduce the time required to use it effectively. Anything could be done; it was just a matter of how long it took. *And, oh yes, there is that one little problem. If I lose my mental concentration, the dark energy will move away from the focus and into an unstable form. It will release itself energetically, but I won't be here to worry if that happens. Boom!*

Alec couldn't think of any other option, so he got to work. Sitting in front of a flat rock, he carefully put a small pile of rock-dust in the center of his rock. *Start with something simple.*

Focus. It was very difficult to feel the free-floating dark energy, but finally, he found it. *Focus.* The dark energy concentrated. Alec felt himself right on the fringes of losing control; he strained to maintain his mental stamina. And then he was done.

He looked at his rock. *Success! Sort of.* Barely visible was a tricrystal on the rock, not much larger than the head of a pin. Alec could feel that it was a focus crystal, but it didn't provide much more focus than he could create without it. *Let's try again,* he thought. He made a second tricrystal and then a third, each of the three about the size of a pin-head.

The next step was to put them close together and see if anything happened. He moved the three small tricrystals close together and was disappointed with the result. *Slightly more power than before, but not enough.* He sighed and idly picked a louse from his hair.

He looked up. While he was making tricrystals, the day had gotten away from him – the sun was starting to dip towards the horizon, and already he could feel the temperature begin to drop. *Let's see.* Alec did a quick mental calculation. *I would need ... oh ... about ... around twenty thousand of these to replicate my medallion.* He thought a bit more. *If I can make, say, six of these a day, how many days will I have to be here on this godforsaken plain before I have twenty thousand tricrystals?* The answer was disheartening.

Damn, he thought and slapped his rock in disgust. The three crystals moved slightly from the force of the slap. Alec felt a sudden jump in power, and then a decline as the pebbles slid away from each other.

What just happened? he thought. *Have I got the shape wrong? Maybe I don't need them all to be close together.* Maybe a spread-out array of crystals would work.

Where should they go? He reviewed the dark energy theory in his mind. Maybe they should be placed along the lines of the attractors. With a supercomputer and a couple of days' time, he could calculate those points exactly. *But that's not going to happen.* He didn't even have a cell phone here, much less a computer. Was there another way to do it? Maybe he could let the field strength tell him the right locations.

He broke a twig from the bush and began to move his tricrystal pinheads gently. First, nothing happened, and then the focal strength increased dramatically. *That's close,* he thought. It was still much weaker than his medallion, but it was almost usable.

What now?

'Make more crystals,' was the obvious answer. Using the three tiny crystals as a focus, he made another twenty small crystals. He looked up at the sun. The last twenty had only required a few minutes to do, unlike the whole afternoon for the first three.

The pattern for twenty-three was different than the pattern for three, so it took most of the next hour before he found the right arrangement. The tricrystals were still laying on the flat rock. The next step was a container for them he thought.

A snarl interrupted his thoughts. With the last light of day, the hyra had returned with two others. Alec was about to be their fine dining experience, he could tell.

Not tonight guys, he thought. Earlier, he couldn't have done much, but now he could. *Focus.* His initial thought was to boil the creature's blood. *How dare someone try to eat me!* he thought with unexpected anger. *Nah, the little guy is just trying to live. He thinks I'm the best thing for dinner.* Maybe something less dramatic.

Focus. Alec's hands were on the sides of the flat rock. Dark energy swirled. A patch of hair on the rump of the first hyra burst into flames; it jumped in fright and went squealing off into the brush. The other two followed it. *That should teach you not to invite me to join you for dinner,* he thought. *Ha!*

Now back to the next task. *Focus.* He created a large flat diamond, about the size of the palm of his hand, to enclose his tricrystals. *Might be the world's largest diamond,* he thought. He tested the focal strength. It was good – as strong, or stronger, than his original medallion. The focal lines felt cleaner also. *Quite a step forward,* he thought. *I need to write this up. This will change a lot of thinking when I get back to the Lab.* Then he stopped himself. The Lab. The Institute. Would he ever get back? And deeper down was the question that he hadn't yet asked himself: if getting back to the Institute and the Lab meant leaving Erin, did he want to go back?

But for now, naked, sore, shivering, and exposed to the elements on a cold night, he was a long way from making any kinds of long-term decisions. *Got to survive the night. How would Erin do this?*

Alec found a suitable place under one of the low bushes, as Erin had shown him, and made a clumsy cave. Without her body heat, he would need something else to keep warm. There was some dried grass that he could use to cover himself, but it would not be enough. *Rocks.* He carried several medium-sized rocks and put them next to his sleeping spot. Then he heated the rocks. They gave off enough warmth that he wouldn't freeze. *But it's still cold.* He missed Erin's softness curled next to him.

As he lay under his grass blanket he was keenly aware that the hyra were right – he <u>was</u> a wounded animal. His legs throbbed where infection had set in and the bruises and welts ached. *What can I do to stop this, so I can sleep?* Could dark energy help? *Focus.* Alec let the dark energy flow through his body. After a few minutes, he started to feel better. The dark energy gave him a feeling of calm, and gradually a sense of euphoria. Even if he didn't know how to perform medical miracles with dark energy, he could at least minimize the aching.

9 – Rescue

Alec awoke to a bright sun shining into his cave. He had slept far longer than he was expecting and felt much better, but he was shivering from the morning cold. He rolled over onto his rocks – they had lost their heat and were cold. *Focus* – the rocks were warm again and he could feel the heat soak into his body.

But the first thing on his mind was not the cold. *How is Erin doing?*

He brushed the grass from his body and looked at his legs. *Much better this morning!* The infection was gone and the cuts no longer oozed pus. The scratches were still present but partially healed, and even his feet had recovered to the point that he felt like he might be able to walk comfortably. *Did bathing myself in dark energy have healing capability?* Was it some other unknown effect of dark energy, or just the result of a good night's sleep? He didn't know and didn't have any way to figure it out right now.

His stomach was growling. Even the slave-camp mush sounded good. He crawled out of the cave and started looking for something to eat. Within a few minutes, he spotted a small bounder. *Focus.* The rock went true to its aim, and the animal was down. He walked over and picked it up. *Now what?* He wasn't going to skin it without a tool. He knew that in the Old West, the natives could skin an animal using a chip of chert or sharp rock – Alec had tried to do that once as a boy and only succeeded in cutting his hands.

Focus. He created a sharp edge on a small rock, and after a few rough tries he had most of the bounder's skin off. He took a bite of the raw flesh and almost gagged. *That's not going to work.* He spit out the remainder. *Focus.* Soon he was grilling the bounder's carcass on a hot rock. It was burned on the outside and undercooked on the inside – *But better than raw.*

≈ ≈ ≈ ≈

Cautiously, Alec retraced his steps from the day before. About midday he came over the crest of the knoll and saw where the slavers' camp had been the day before. All that remained was flattened grass, cold campfires, and a mess of human and animal waste.

If he was going to rescue Erin, he needed to catch up with the slave caravan. *I am going to have to follow their trail,* he thought. *They are not moving too fast.* And then what?

Alec decided that first, he needed some clothes and supplies. The little village that the slave raiders had attacked the day before looked like it would be the best source. He could see the village walls in the distance. *Okay. Get to the village first, get some stuff and then follow the slavers' track.* It should be easy to find the slavers – *Just by following the smell alone,* thought Alec.

Alec's feet were still raw and sore, so it took him a couple of hours to reach the village. The outer gate had been battered down, and the place was eerily quiet. He cautiously entered the village gates. Only a few stray dogs moved on the street, looking at him warily, tails between their legs.

Finally, Alec called out, "Is anyone here?"

There was no answer.

Alec walked up to the first building, located near the village gate, and pushed aside its broken door. It had been a guard-shack but now there was a stack of dead bodies against the wall, starting to smell of death. He could see that they had all died of bullet wounds.

He walked around the corner to the village square. It was strewn with several dead bodies, mostly old people, women, and children, including a few babies. *The ones who wouldn't make good slaves,* thought Alec. Some looked like they had been torn into pieces. The sight of the mauled bodies brought back the scene of the runaway boy from the slave line; Alec was sick to his stomach when he realized the slave-raiders had allowed their dogs to feed on these bodies.

Across the square was a large heap of discarded clothing. Alec walked towards it, passing more bodies on the way – these people looked as though they had died defending their village. Most had been hacked to death with swords or spears, but bullets had killed a few. A couple of the local dogs were scavenging on the bodies. Alec's stomach turned in disgust, and he bent to retch his half-cooked breakfast.

No one seemed to be left in town. No large work animals either, just the dogs. Alec rummaged through the pile of clothes – it seemed to be a mix of men's and women's items, in no particular order. He soon found a pair of mostly-intact trousers that would fit him. No underclothes that he wanted to touch, though. He shook out the trousers and put them on. He dug on through the pile and found a serviceable set of peasant sandals and a shirt. All of the boots were too small for his feet.

Alec was amazed at how much more confident he felt with clothes on than he had felt when naked. The Aldermen raiders understood that emotion and used it to keep people subservient.

He hadn't found anything that resembled a weapon, not even a knife. He looked around the silent streets and crossed the village square to a nearby house; as soon as he entered, he could see the place had been ransacked. He tried the next house. *Same.* Every house had been searched and anything or anyone of value taken. *Not much left.*

The villagers must have taken all their weapons to the outer wall for defense, Alec reasoned. He did find a sturdy rake and converted the handle into a staff for himself.

The raiders had taken most of the food. He found a few left-overs from yesterday's meal on a table in one of the houses and shoved a piece of bread into his mouth to quell his nausea. From a small smokehouse out back he could smell cured meat, and in the straw on the floor of the shack he found a ham of some kind that had been missed by the raiders. The only reason Alec found it was that a dog had dragged it down and started to eat it. *Oh well, better to eat dog food than starve,* he thought, and picked it up and took a bite out of it.

Standing by the shed, Alec thought he heard a sound. He looked around and heard it again. Beside the shed was a small outhouse. He walked over to it and heard a whimper.

"Help me, please," a small voice said.

Alec opened the outhouse door and looked in. At first, he didn't see anyone; then he looked in the toilet hole. Down in the filthy sump was a boy, probably about ten years old, too short to climb out on his own.

"Can you help me? I can't get out," the child said. The sides of the pit were higher than his head, and there was nothing to grab. Alec could see the claw marks along the sides of the privy pit where the boy had tried to climb out.

Alec flipped up the outhouse seat, reached down, and gave the boy a pull. He scrambled out easily enough but was covered in filth. Alec almost gagged at the smell. Once out of the pit, and standing on the outhouse floor, the boy looked at Alec suspiciously.

"Are you one of them?" he asked.

"No," said Alec, and then, seeing the boy's uncertainty and disbelief, added, "I am trying to get rid of them." Alec led the boy out into the sunlight. "What's your name?"

"Ilave," was the answer.

"Well, Ilave, let's get you cleaned up, and then figure out what to do."

The village well was on the other side of the square. They went over to it, and with a little work and the use of some of the discarded clothing for rags, cleaned the worst of the mess off the boy. *He's improved from 'disgusting' all the way up to 'filthy,'* thought Alec.

"Now let's find something for you to eat."

Alec and Ilave went back to the house where Alec had left the ham. The dogs had grabbed it again and pulled it back on the floor after Alec left, but the two of them shooed the dogs out.

After Ilave had eaten, Alec asked, "What happened?"

The boy burst into tears.

Ilave told his story between sobs. "They came to the village. We all ran inside and closed the gates. We have had raiders before, and they never bothered anyone inside the gates." He wiped his nose on his sleeve. "My dad always told us not to stray far from the village wall. The raiders look for stragglers, he said, and take them to be slaves." The tears came again. "These men were different! They looked more like soldiers and they came right up to the gate! They had a terrible weapon that made a great sound – our village guards all fell dead. I don't know what it was." Terror swept over his small face as he recounted the scene. "The raiders pulled our gates down with ropes and their drungs. No one could stop them! Our guards were all dead! There was blood all over! Then the raiders came through our gates.

"We all ran. I was watching when the gates came down, and I saw them fall – they pulled them right off their hinges. I was too close to the gates, and I had nowhere to go. I couldn't make it back to my house." The boy again convulsed in sobs. "I didn't know what to do! So, I ran away from the raiders and towards this outhouse. I hid inside but I was afraid they would pull it over and find me, so I jumped down the hole. I hid down in the latrine!"

"You're safe now," Alec said, trying to sound soothing. *Poor kid!*

"I could hear the fighting, and at first I could see a little between the boards of the outhouse wall before I jumped down the hole. The fighting seemed to end. Then I could hear the raiders yelling to search every house.

And they had dogs! I could see just a little bit and some of the dogs looked terrible."

"Those men and their dogs searched every house. If they found anybody, they dragged them to the square. In the square, they tied their hands behind their back, and put a bag over their head." The boy looked at Alec to see if this tall stranger believed him.

Alec nodded reassuringly. "Go on," he said gently.

"They were there for a long time. They lined everybody up. Then they took the people, one at a time, out of the line. It looked like how we shear our flocks every spring. A couple of men would hold them, just like we hold our animals, and they would cut off their clothes, just like a fleece. Then they were naked. Then they put a collar around their neck and tied them to the person in front of them. I think that they were going to tie them to drungs because there were several there.

"I saw them take my mom, and my dad, but I never saw my big brother. I don't know where he is. Maybe he was out there. Maybe he's dead now. There were so many people." The boy paused.

"And then I saw them do things to people. Horrible things!" He broke down again, his thin body wracked by deep sobs. Alec let him cry for a few minutes.

"Like what?" Alec said softly, although he figured he knew.

"Well, anyone who was old – anyone who couldn't walk, those men beat them with their whips until they bled, and then ..." The boy stopped and shuddered. "And then, they set their dogs on them. Their dogs ... they just ... the dogs would bite the people and chew on them. The dogs were killing them. I saw them throw two babies to the dogs and the dogs ... the dogs just tore them apart!" He covered his eyes – trying to erase the scene.

"And then they came back through the village, with their dogs, looking for anybody they missed the first time, I guess. I was scared. I was so scared!" The sobs welled up again.

"That's when I jumped down into the bottom of the latrine pit. But I thought, maybe that wasn't so bad because I thought that maybe the dogs couldn't smell me there, because, you know, of all the smells that were already there." Ilave sniffed and wiped his nose on the back of his hand.

"I couldn't see anything after that. There was a lot of noise, and I could hear the drungs snorting and the men yelling. And then after awhile, it got quiet. So, I thought they had gone. But I was afraid and decided I should stay hidden for a while longer. I could tell when it got dark. It was so quiet. No voices in the village. Just the village dogs. I decided it was safe to come out, but then I couldn't. It was very slick down in the pit. And it stunk. I tried and tried …" he made clawing motions to show how he tried to climb, "but I couldn't get out. I was afraid I would be there forever!"

He looked hard at Alec. "When you got here, the village dogs started to bark, so I knew that someone had come back to the village. At first, I thought it was one of them, so I kept quiet. But when it looked like you might leave, I had to call for help. I knew I couldn't get out of here by myself.

"So, thank you for pulling me out of the pit."

After telling Alec his story, Ilave was exhausted.

"Where is your house?" Alec asked.

"I'll show you," the boy said. The two of them walked across the village to Ilave's house. There were a few scraps of food for Ilave and then the boy climbed into his little spot and fell asleep, comfortable in the safety of his bed.

Alec stayed awake well after dark, very disturbed by the boy's story. Also, he was undecided about what to do with the boy – take Ilave with him? But where would that be? Or leave him here, to an uncertain fate? Eventually, Alec went to Ilave's parents' bed and crawled into it, glad to feel the warmth of a real bed and real blankets. He felt guilty sleeping in a bed when Erin was out in the cold, but he did it. And he dreamed of fighting with Sarah.

≈ ≈ ≈ ≈

The next morning, Alec was up with the sun, but not before Ilave.

"Ilave," Alec said to the boy, "I am going after the men who raided your village. It is going to be dangerous."

"I can fight them," Ilave said enthusiastically, his ten-year-old bravado showing. "I am tough!"

"I know you can," said Alec, "but I need you to do something else. If I rescue your parents, they will need someone here to take care of their stuff and the rest of the village until they get back. Can you do that? By yourself?"

Ilave brightened up. "I know how to draw the water and keep everything running. I can make porridge, and I know where the food stores are in the shed." He nodded. "I can do that for mum and dad."

Alec wasn't sure what kind of fate he was bestowing on Ilave, or how Ilave would feel surrounded by the sights and smells of death, but Ilave had more chance here than coming with Alec. It was mid-morning by the time he had Ilave settled.

"Goodbye," he said to Ilave and hugged the grimy little boy.

"Safe journey," the boy said and waved until Alec was out of sight.

≈ ≈ ≈ ≈

Alec gamely started out on the track of the slavers. He had the stick made from the wooden rake handle – not nearly as good as his other staff, but functional – a pocketful of rocks, and a simple sling. He had briefly thought about taking the time to make a new staff but decided his new medallion would determine the outcome of any fight, not a staff. He had taken the time to fashion a pouch so that he could wear the medallion around his neck.

Instead of following his previous path, Alec walked diagonally across the Grasslands to intercept the path of the slavers. It would save him a good portion of the day, and he was concerned that time was important. Even then, he almost missed the track of the slave train. Only a step that almost landed in a pile of human excrement alerted him to the path. Looking around he saw that he was on the far side of the caravan's swath. A little further and he would have missed it.

It was harder to follow the path than he expected. That, combined with the fact that he cautiously approached every rise to make sure he wasn't detected, slowed him considerably. Alec saw several of the hyra as he walked, but apparently they thought he was too healthy for them and gave him a wide berth. Evening found him with no sight of the caravan. He briefly thought about walking through the night but decided he would most likely lose the track if he did.

Alec made a quick camp and heated some rocks for sleeping. He had bagged two little game birds during the day as he walked, and now he skinned them and cooked them on a hot rock. Again, he singed the outside and left the inner portion barely cooked, but it was better than his previous attempts and satisfied his hunger.

The next morning, he continued following the slavers' trail. He figured he was moving about twice as fast as the caravan, so he expected to catch them today. He decided that when he found them, he would take some time to observe them and develop a plan to free Erin. He didn't know why Lily was now a serving lady – had she defected to the Aldermen? –or whether he could or should try to free her also.

Alec was slightly lost in thought when he heard a growl at the same time he sensed movement. *One of the sentry dogs!* He twisted around with his shaft and struck at the dog; it rolled away from him and started to lunge at him. He swung his shaft and hit it again. The dog backed off and growled. That gave Alec the moment he needed. *Focus.* Dark energy swirled around the new medallion in satisfying patterns. Alec had no love for these dogs – they had torn people apart in front of him – and he felt no remorse in heating the dog's blood to the boiling point. The animal collapsed in front of him before it could howl and alert more of the pack.

Lucky, thought Alec. He crept to the top of the next rise. He could see the Aldermen's camp in the distance. It looked like they were setting up for the night. In the far distance, he could see another village. If things were true to form, tomorrow would be a raiding day for the group. *A good time to see what I can do,* he thought.

He circled the campsite, moving upwind from the dead dog. If other dogs were released, perhaps they would be attracted to its smell and not to him. The best shelter turned out to be on the far side of the camp, the same side as the next village. He found a rocky spot where with a little help from dark energy he could create a cave. He climbed on top of the rocks to a vantage point where he could survey the camp. The setup looked familiar. The women were camped on one side the men on the other side – there were more people in each group now, due to the raid on Illave's village. The wagons were in the middle. The trogus were positioned in the front and the other livestock situated behind the wagons. The camp appeared animated with the usual activities of feeding the captives and the animals as well as the slavers preparing their gear for their next raid.

As the sun set, Alec crawled down into his cave and sealed the opening. Only a small air hole was left. Twice during the night, he heard growls and footsteps. His smell must have alerted the dogs. He didn't know if the sentries would discover the missing dog, but he hoped there was no scent link from the dog to his hiding place.

Okay, I'm snug in this cave, but how am I going to find Erin? Maybe he could sense her. He let the dark energy expand out over the camp. He could feel lots of bodies. Finally, he felt a familiar focus. That had to be Erin.

I am coming to rescue you tomorrow, he thought to her. *Be ready.* He smiled, thinking of Erin. He slept fitfully and dreamt that she was telling him to come quickly, or it might be too late.

≈ ≈ ≈ ≈

Erin lost track of the days. Each morning after eating they were herded along the path again, walking long hours under the blistering sun. Erin was feeling filthy. Huddling close together at night, sleeping in everyone's urine and crap, and eating the messy mush was horrible. Little biting flies buzzed about, attracted by the smell of blood and filth.

At night she would try to sense Alec; she felt that he was alive. Every day she felt like he was getting closer. Maybe that wasn't a good idea. Maybe it would be better for him to leave the grasslands without her. Then she realized that she didn't even know if he actually <u>had</u> escaped the slavers. She hadn't seen Lily in a while and knew nothing of what was happening in the men's side of the camp.

After a few days, they stopped earlier than usual to make camp. Erin could see a village in the distance.

"A chance for more captives tomorrow," one of her ring-mates muttered.

Late in the afternoon one of the slave-keepers came, grabbed Erin's arm, and untied her from the ring. Her ring-mates nudged each other, aware of what would happen next.

"Come with me," the slave-keeper said. He pulled her over to the trogus pens. "Time to feed the girls," he said cheerfully. The trogus began to stir and come over to them. Erin had a very bad feeling about this. The man sneered at Erin. "Trouble-makers make good trogus food."

A uniformed man stepped out from a nearby tent, apparently alerted by the expectant whines of the trogus.

"What are you doing?" he asked Erin's keeper, sharply.

"Going to feed the trogus, Captain, sir," the slave-keeper said, jumping to attention, but still holding Erin's leash.

"Not tonight, you fool. We need the trogus to be in a fighting mood tomorrow, and I don't want them fed before a raid!"

"Yes, sir. Sorry, sir."

The officer relented slightly. "You can feed them when we get back tomorrow night if they are still hungry."

"All right, sir. Very good, sir."

The slave-keeper sullenly led Erin back and tied her with her ring. Her ring-mates were surprised to see her.

"You missed the evening feeding," one finally said. Erin didn't care – she couldn't have eaten. *At least I wasn't the meal,* she thought. Being consumed alive by carnivorous beasts was not her idea of fun.

That night Erin had a dream. She felt that it was Alec telling her that he was coming to rescue her tomorrow. She needed to be ready. *I love you, please come quickly*, was her thought to him. *Or else it might be too late.*

≈ ≈ ≈ ≈

The sun peeking into the air hole woke Alec the next morning. He took a careful look outside his cave to make sure there were no unpleasant surprises in store for him, then opened the entrance and slid out.

Alec was apprehensive. He was too excited to eat, so he didn't even try. He crept to the top of the rock outcrop and looked towards the camp. All was quiet. They would not be feeding the captives until after the raid.

He could see the raiding party already well on the way to the village. His plan, such that it was, involved waiting until the raid started – then the slavers would be too occupied to return to camp to fight him. Alec saw the raiders approach the village and the village guards frantically closing the village gate.

Crack! Crack! Crack!

Alec could hear the noise of bullets, carried by the wind. The rifles gave the slavers an advantage that would quickly swing this battle. The village gates were designed to stop mounted intruders with light archery or swords but would not protect against gunfire.

Maybe there was something he could do to help swing the battle against the raiders and further the distraction. He looked out towards the village. The slavers had taken a single wagon with them on the raid. That must be the ammunition for the rifles.

Focus. Alec pulled in dark energy. Different materials affected the dark energy background differently. He could feel a clump of material in the distance that might be gunpowder in the wagon. *Focus.* Nothing happened. *Must have been the wrong thing.*

He focused the dark energy and again let his senses wander over the battlefield. He had never tried to sense materials from this far away before, and he could feel himself sweating from the exertion. He felt another material. *That might be it. Focus.* A few seconds later he heard a lone shot on the wind. *Found it.*

Focus. This time Alec simultaneously heated the powder in all the bullets. He heard a massive burst of noise on the wind and then everything went silent. *Hopeful sign,* he thought.

Now for the slavers' camp. Maybe he could do the same thing here.

Focus. The dark energy swirled. He could see the powder wagon and could feel the powder in the protected wagon. Again, he heated the powder. A massive outpouring of sound erupted. The wagon caught fire and started burning. The captives started to yell in fear – if a fire swept through the camp they would likely perish.

At the great sound, the animals in the camp reared and screamed in terror, breaking their halters and running free. One of the trogus escaped from its pen in a panic, and as its keeper tried to corral it, the animal crunched down on the man's arm. Blood spattered everywhere, but instead of devouring the man the beast brayed and continued to run, crazed, through the camp. The few remaining soldiers and slave-keepers started running after the animals to corral them, yelling at the cooks and other camp helpers to try to fight the fire.

Here's my chance. Alec trotted down the hillside and into camp. No one was trying to keep intruders from getting into camp. In fact, no one was trying to keep people from doing much of anything. A person was easier to recapture than a trogus, so the men in the camp were intent on capturing the frightened animals.

Alec slipped down into the men's camp. He had prepared a tool to release the leather collars, and released about a dozen people, including his former ring-mates. The men stood and looked at him.

"You are free!" shouted Alec, raising his arms and shooing them like barnyard chickens. "Grab some weapons and let's take over from these slavers!" The freed men just kept looking at him blankly as he released more of them.

Finally, two of them seemed to come to life.

"Come on, come on, let's get ready and take over!" With that, the rest started to move.

Thank goodness, Alec thought, *someone still has some hope left.* Then, with a start, Alec realized the two men organizing the other captives were the same two that had abused the teenage boy. *What a world,* he thought.

≈ ≈ ≈ ≈

The morning after her dream, Erin could feel that the camp seemed filled with adrenaline as the soldiers prepared to raid the nearby village. Erin was dreading every second. She knew when the raiders returned her slave-keeper intended to feed her to the trogus.

The morning wore slowly on. Erin heard a sharp noise carried on the wind from the distant village – crack! crack! crack! She didn't know what it was, but she knew it was somehow tied to the raiders' overwhelming advantage over the villagers. Then she heard a loud bang! being carried on the wind. *What was that? Did the raiders destroy the village?* How could anyone fight against that?

A few seconds later Erin heard a crack! crack! crack! very close by. Then there was an overwhelmingly loud sound as one of the wagons in the slavers' camp spit pieces everywhere and then burst into flames. Erin clapped her hands over her ears to try to stop the ringing sound inside her head. All the animals in the camp seemed to go crazy from the noise, and trogus and drungs alike pulled free and ran about.

"Dragons! one of her ring-mates yelled. "We've been attacked by dragons!"

"Fire!" yelled another woman. "We will all be burned alive!"

That must be Alec! thought Erin. *He doesn't know how to do anything quietly.*

Then she heard shouts on the other side of the camp and looked to see what was going on over there.

"The men are free!" a woman captive shouted, pointing across to the men's side. The captive men were running towards the few slave-keepers left in camp; the slave-keepers saw the danger, turned towards the captives, and drew their swords, but they were outnumbered. Five men, even armed with swords, were no match against fifty desperate men armed with sticks and rocks. In no time the slave-keepers were taken down.

Erin saw the guards fall and the captive men continue to beat on them. And then Erin saw a single man running towards her.

"Alec!" she shouted, and for the first time since her capture, began to cry.

10 – Freedom

Alec heard Erin's cry and ran to her. In a moment she was in his arms, and he was lifting her off her feet in a bear hug, totally oblivious to her state of filth or that she was tethered to three other women. She let him hold her for a moment or so, while her ring-mates looked on in wonder.

Finally, the reality of their situation and the utter silliness of her appearance struck her. She laughed through her tears.

"Do you hug every naked lady you see?" she asked.

Alec snapped back to the moment and pulled out his tool to unlock her collar. It quickly snapped off, and she was free. Alec freed the next woman on Erin's ring and then handed her the tool.

"Free the others," he said to her. Then to Erin, "We have to get out of here. Fast. Let's find our wagon."

Their wagon was easy to find among the others and had been loaded with loot taken from the village raids. Their clothes were still in the wagon and Erin grabbed enough to feel presentable, although she knew she was as filthy as she had ever been. She also checked the concealed compartment. It had not been disturbed; the rings and coins were still there.

"Let's dump the stuff we don't need, grab a couple of drungs, and leave," said Alec.

"I don't think that will work," said Erin.

"Why not?"

"If we try to run, the mounted soldiers are much faster than we would be in our wagon – they would soon catch up with us."

Alec looked back towards the village. The raiders who had survived Alec's 'magic' were beginning to straggle back to the slave camp.

"Yeah. You're right. They will be back before we can get out of sight," he said. "I guess we are going to have to fight our way out of here." The two of them made their way back into the center of camp where the captives – men and women, now free of their collars and tethers – were milling around in confusion; a few were sitting on the ground, hunched up, face buried, hugging their knees and shaking.

Alec stood on a serving-log and addressed the throng. "The raiders are starting to return from that village. They'll be here before long. We will have to fight them. Who has experience in setting up a fighting force?" Alec shouted.

"I do," one man said, stepping forward.

"Who are you?" Alec asked.

"I am Harl," the man answered. "I was the guard subleader at Octavin."

Alec had no idea where or what Octavin was, but the man seemed confident and did not have the hopeless look in his eyes of some of the captives. Also, Alec noted with relief, the man was not one of those who had abused the boy.

"Good," said Alec. "They won't be expecting that you have been freed from your collars and can fight. Let's surprise them and try to take them down."

"But what about their death rods?" said Harl. "We can't win against those!"

"I destroyed the fuel supply for them," said Alec.

"You what?" said Harl, in total confusion. "The fuel? The death rods have fuel?"

"He is a Great Wizard," said Erin, holding Alec's arm.

"Are you a Wizard?" said Harl in amazement – or was it disbelief?

Alec paused, and instead of objecting to Erin's explanation, gave in and just said, "Yes."

"Good!" Harl said delightedly. "Then maybe we do have a chance! What magic can you do?"

Alec didn't want to tell him that he might not be able to do much.

"I can launch projectiles … uh, send rocks through the air," Alec said, "and I can set their animals' tails on fire."

Harl paused and looked at him. "Is that all?" Harl asked, looking somewhat dejected.

I guess the idea of burning trogus tails isn't too exciting, thought Alec, then added, with a bit of a swagger, "I can do more – but that should be enough."

Someone had located the soldiers' armory and was handing out swords and spears to anyone, man or woman, who could hold one. In the meantime, Harl and Alec briefly discussed their options and agreed on a course of action. Harl arranged the rag-tag group in accordance with their plan.

≈ ≈ ≈ ≈

The slave raiders were clearly annoyed. For the first time, their plan of attack had not worked. Their death rods had blown up and killed three of their members. Without their magic weapons, they were merely an ordinary band of marauders; the village walls were designed to hold off raiders like them, and the slavers had not been able to breach the gates. For this entire trip the slavers had been relying on their magic weapons to give them an advantage over the simple villagers, and, without their magic, they weren't very skillful marauders.

After their death rods blew up, and a few feeble attempts to attack without them, the leader of the raiders called for a return to the slave camp. Without the advantage given by the death rods, the village wall was going to hold. The leader thought that they could return to camp, get more death rods from the armory, and come back and finish decimating the village; there would be grave retribution for its impertinent resistance.

As the raiders returned to their camp, the leader heard a loud 'bang!' ahead of them. He was surprised but felt that it wasn't an issue – his men could deal with whatever it was after they got back to camp. He continued to lead his crestfallen raiding party at a slow walk. There was no reason to hurry – the mounts were tired, and several of the men were injured. They weren't going to attack again until tomorrow, so there was plenty of time.

But as he came closer to camp, the hubbub of activity didn't seem right. Something was wrong.

"Draw weapons," he called to his men. A rival raiding party? He wasn't afraid – he still had at least thirty good soldiers. There wasn't anything out here that could take down that many armed men.

The leader came closer to camp. Then he felt his mount flinch. He looked back. Instead of an orderly array of troops following him, his riders' mounts were bucking and bolting in a frenzied panic. Each trogus had flames coming from its tail – they had caught fire and were burning, and the acrid smell of singed hair filled the air. Trogus were charging in every direction, colliding with each other; some were rolling in the grass and the dust to stop the burning. Blue-clad riders were running from the beasts but were being trampled and mauled right and left. The wagon drungs were also bleating and trying to escape the scene.

Then, as his own mount began to yowl, the leader became aware that his trogus also was on fire. He turned and swatted at the burning tail with the flat side of his sword. He had a very well-trained beast, and it stood the test, enduring the pain until his swatting succeeded in putting the fire out. The leader looked around and saw that he was the only one still mounted.

Then a rag-tag bunch of mostly-naked men and women charged out from a gully that bounded the camp, running towards the raiders; they started beating on the downed men with sticks, kitchen tools, and swords from the armory.

≈ ≈ ≈ ≈

Alec watched from the knoll as the raiders retreated from the village walls and slowly returned to the camp. *Harl has done a great job of organizing these guys,* Alec noted appreciatively. Most of them were still naked, but they had clubs or spears, and a few even had swords. Harl had positioned the captives in concealed spots along the edge of the gully. It was a good staging point. They couldn't be seen until the raiders were almost on top of them.

Harl had pointed out to Alec that without help, the raiding party would make quick work of the freed captives; it would be Alec's job to dismount the riders. Alec was amazed at how much everyone trusted him. *'Great Wizard,'* he thought ruefully.

Erin had found her sword in the soldiers' armory and stood by his side. Alec suspected that she intended to protect him at any cost, but he didn't want it to come to that.

The slow-moving retreating raiders came near the gully. It was time. *Focus.* Dark energy flowed, and Alec felt the power of his new medallion. Although he had lost the first medallion in the scuffle when they were captured, he had grown comfortable with the new one. Maybe it was even better than the old one.

As Alec and Erin watched, dozens of small fires erupted. *Maybe I overdid it,* thought Alec.

With their tails in flames, the trogus ran screaming and braying through the grass. Small fires ignited in the dry undergrowth, and billows of thick grass smoke blew towards the downed soldiers.

Harl gave the signal and the captives charged from the gully. Their chore was simple: kill the raiders. Alec was amazed at how much discipline Harl had instilled in the captives in this little time. Were these the same men that so recently had looked at Alec with hopeless eyes?

"One soldier is still up," Alec pointed out to Erin.

She nodded, "I think it is the leader."

The man had managed to put out the tail fire on his trogus and was now charging towards the mob of former captives.

"That trogus could overwhelm all of our people if it gets to them," Erin said.

"Time to go to work again," he said.

Alec pulled out one of his rocks and put it in his sling. *Focus.* The rock sang as it left the sling. It hit the lone soldier in the back of the head, and he fell with a thud to the ground. His trogus spooked and took off across the Grassland like a frightened rabbit.

Five of the dismounted raiders succeeded in joining forces and formed a defensive position. They were better equipped than the ill-armed captives, but it still wasn't going to be a sure victory since they were badly outnumbered. However, the captives were reluctant to attack the soldiers.

From his position a short distance away, Harl saw their hesitation. He rushed over to handle this last part of the fight. Alec and Erin followed. The three approached the soldiers slowly, with the captive mob following uncertainly behind them.

"Surrender, and we will not kill you until we have determined what is just," Erin shouted to them. They looked at her and laughed.

"Hah! A woman who thinks herself able to give us orders!" one soldier rejoined, and he spat in her direction.

That was the limit for Alec. *Focus.*

In a moment the soldier's hands flew up as he grabbed his throat; blood spilled from his nose and eyes, and he collapsed to the ground with hot blood steaming from breaks in his skin.

"Anyone else want to question her?" Alec said. "Want to wind up the same way as him?"

After a shocked pause, as the scene before them sank in, one of the remaining soldiers asked, "Do you promise that we will live?"

"No," said Alec, "I don't promise anything." One of the soldiers took a step backward. "The only thing I promise is that I will not kill you right now if you surrender," Alec said.

One soldier dropped his weapon, and then the others followed suit. Then, with muttered curses and angry shouts, the mob of captives started to surge forward.

"Stop!" yelled Harl.

The mob hesitated and then stopped.

"We need to find out any information they have," said Harl. "They can't talk if they're dead!"

Harl picked three people to tie up the soldiers and watch them. By mutual agreement, Alec and Erin left Harl in charge of securing the battle scene and scavenging the raider's possessions for anything useful.

$$\approx \ \approx \ \approx \ \approx$$

Erin and Alec walked back towards their wagon in the main part of the slavers' camp. As they approached, a smocked figure came running up to them.

"Lily!" Erin exclaimed with delight.

Lily threw her arms around Erin in a long hug. "I am so happy that you are all right, and that both of you are free!"

Erin hugged her back. "Thanks for what you did. I know it had a price."

Lily looked at her and then her self-assured façade cracked. Tears welled up in her brown eyes. "It did," she said in a quiet voice. "The soldiers took advantage of us serving ladies because they knew they could find others willing if we didn't do whatever they wanted." She sighed. "But I guess it wasn't much worse than being an inn-lady."

"It's over now," said Erin, and hugged Lily again.

Lily turned towards Alec. "I knew you would return and I knew you could free Erin. I had confidence in you and your magic, and you did it."

Their reunion was interrupted by the arrival of Harl and the former captives bringing their spoils from the battlefield.

"Harl, this is Lily," Erin said. "She is a companion of ours and was captured with us. She was forced to work as part of the slavers' staff."

Harl looked at her, and his face brightened. "You know the workings of the camp? I can organize our fighting force, and the others, but since they held me as one of the slaves, I have seen nothing of the workings of the camp."

Lily nodded. "I do."

"Then would you be willing to help me organize the camp? I know nothing of the food supplies or kitchen. We have a lot of people we need to feed … or else they are going to be very grumpy," he said with a cheerful wink.

Lily nodded her head in agreement and looked at Erin.

"Go," said Erin with a smile.

Harl and Lily headed off towards the kitchen tent, and Alec heard him telling her "… and besides food, we need to figure out sleeping, security, a latrine, and …" with Lily nodding and adding her ideas on re-arranging the camp and tending to the former captives.

≈ ≈ ≈ ≈

Erin and Alec returned to their wagon, cleaned up, and unloaded the slavers' loot. Most of their belongings were still in the wagon under the ill-gotten booty. Erin checked through their clothing and took inventory of what was missing from their supplies. She opened the secret compartment where she had stored the rings and put one on her finger. She put the other ring on Alec's finger.

Alec poked around the wagon to see if his medallion was there.

"What are you looking for?" asked Erin.

"My medallion. They tore it from my neck when we were captured."

"It's not here," said Erin. "I saw them lose it out on the Grasslands with all our clothes when they captured us. The only thing they kept was my sword, and I found it in their armory."

"I can't find my staff, either," said Alec, looking under the wagon seat. "They must have discarded it."

"I didn't see it in the armory," said Erin.

No staff. No medallion. Just a rake handle. Alec thought briefly about attempting to return to the place they were captured to see if he could find the medallion. Then he thought about the impossibility of that. It was lost a week back, some place on the Grasslands where there were no identifying landmarks. It was beyond his skills. *Well, the new medallion is working fine — must make do with it.* Now that he knew how to make medallions, perhaps he could make an even better one.

They set up their wagon so that they could use it this night for sleeping, then walked back towards the center of camp. They could smell food and heard the bell that had called the soldiers to their dining tent. Neither of them had eaten that day. *Better to be fed, then to be fed to the trogus,* thought Erin.

At the dining tent, Lily had established an orderly line and was giving everyone directions. Lily saw them and motioned to them.

"We are feeding everyone the soldiers' food tonight. We have enough of their rations for a few days, and it should make everyone happier. We set up a special tent for you and the other camp leaders. Your food is over there with Harl." Lily pointed to a smaller tent nearby.

They joined Harl, who introduced them to three others.

"These three and Lily are my lieutenants," he said. "We need to get this group organized and move out of here. We can't stay here – we have limited food and water, and most of us have no idea how to get home. Lots of us are pretty sick or lame from the conditions we endured as captives and will have a hard time walking." He stuck a spoon in his food and smiled at the first bite. "But that is tomorrow's problem," he said, eating with gusto and scooping up a bit of gravy with a hardtack biscuit. "Today's problem is to get everyone fed, and then impart enough order so that we can keep a veneer of civilization in this camp."

Alec ate in deep silence. The soldiers' fare was not gourmet cuisine, but it was much better than the pasty mush the slave captives had been fed. Or half-raw game meat.

How did I come to oversee a camp-full of half-starved, battered, ailing refugees? Alec thought. *Why do I feel like I need to rescue everybody and why did I feel justified in boiling that soldier's blood?*

≈ ≈ ≈ ≈

It was getting dark by the time they headed back to their wagon, holding hands, and talking softly to each other. So much catching up to do.

As they walked between the soldiers' wagons, they heard a muffled whimper.

"What is that?" Erin said.

"I don't know, but it came from over behind those wagons," Alec said. They went around the corner to find a crowd of about ten men overlooking a scuffle. Alec tried to push his way through to see what was happening.

"Wait your turn," said the man in front of Alec, not looking at him. "We can all get a chance at her."

Alec pushed the man out of his way. In front of the men was one of the younger girls, captured at the most recent raid, lying naked on the ground beside the wagon wheel. One of the men Alec recognized as the abuser of the teenage boy had cornered her and now stood over her, unfastening the pants he had taken from a fallen soldier.

"Stop that," said Alec.

The man turned towards Alec and leered. "Who's going to stop me?" He did not recognize Alec.

"I am," said Alec.

The man re-fastened his pants. He looked at the young woman and snickered.

"Don't go anywhere without me. I'm not done with you. This won't take me long."

The tough man had taken possession of a soldier's sword and now picked it up. His comrade abuser was also there and stepped up, also holding a sword.

"You think you can take us on," said the first man. "You don't even have a weapon! Just run along and leave this to us men!"

Alec sensed Erin pushing her way forward. *This is my fight,* she thought to Alec.

You're right, Alec thought. *It's yours.*

Erin stepped up to the bully and drew her sword. Her name, etched into the side of her sword, came alive and glowed in the evening's half-light. Those around her had the impression of a flaming sword. The crowd stepped back, and more than a few decided to leave. The two aggressors stepped towards her, not particularly impressed with the pyrotechnic show. Since she was a mere woman, they did not make a coordinated attempt to attack her.

The second man swiped clumsily at Erin. She stepped to his right side so that she only had to face one opponent. He swung again. This time she caught his blade and twisted. He ended slightly off-balance; his return slash flicked inches from Erin but left him open to a quick blow. Erin aimed true and sliced the inside of his sword arm. Her razor-sharp sword flicked through muscle, bone, and the main artery deep in his forearm. His blood began pouring out, and his sword fell to the ground. Erin turned to the other opponent, the ring-leader of the abusers.

His sneer faded, and he began to take Erin more seriously. He engaged Erin in a tight fight. Alec knew that Erin was the better fighter, but the captivity of the past several days had left her weakened, sore, and stiff. The man was fighting more conservatively, parrying Erin's thrusts and stepping back from her sword. Although he had the same disadvantage – weak from days in captivity – he was bigger than she and was trying to out-muscle her.

On the ground behind her, crawling from the pool of his blood, the other man managed to grab his dropped sword with his left hand and scrambled to his feet. From her vantage, engaged in swordplay, Erin could not see him.

Alec stepped up behind the injured man and banged him on the head with his staff. There was a satisfying thud when it hit, and the man again slumped to the ground.

The fight was almost over. Erin's opponent was tiring and made a misstep that left him open to her blazing sword. Erin slashed across his neck. The man fell with a gurgle and a crash. Erin's sword still glowed, ember-like, and she looked at the others.

"Isn't it time for you boys to quiet down for the night?" she said. "Or does anyone else want to try to harass this young lady?" The others all answered by mutely slinking off.

Erin turned to the trembling girl and hugged her. "It's all right now," Erin said softly. "You're safe." *For now,* she thought darkly.

Harl, Lily, and one of the other lieutenants arrived, running between the wagons, drawn by the ringing sound of sword on sword.

"We heard you, but couldn't find you fast enough," Harl said. "We saw the end of your fight."

Lily took the young woman from Erin's arms. "Was she..." her voice trailed off.

Erin shook her head. "No. Not this time."

Lily helped the shivering girl to her feet. "I will take care of her for the night," she said.

"We'll take care of these two," Harl said, pointing to the two fallen men.

≈ ≈ ≈ ≈

Erin and Alec were again alone, but the event had shattered their jubilant mood. Erin was starting to shake from the aftermath of the fight and the chill of the night air. Alec put his arm around her shoulders and pulled her close as they walked away from the two bodies on the ground.

"Let's go to our wagon," he said gently. Once there, they spent a long time laying in their sleeping spot, nestled under proper blankets for the first time in over a week, holding each other and telling their stories of their captivity and rescue. Alec stroked the bruises and welts where Erin had been beaten. She winced slightly when he touched a particularly deep cut.

"Let me try something and see if it heals you, or does anything," he said.

"Okay."

With that, Alec pulled dark energy through his medallion. He did not focus it on anything specific but just allowed it to soak into both of their bodies. He could feel the euphoria brought about by the dark energy and could sense that Erin was feeling it also. Maybe it would help her as it had helped him.

"I knew you were a Great Warrior. Mother used to say, 'braggarts talk but great men do.' You have done more than any other warrior of Theland ever did. No one else could have beaten fifty men to rescue me."

"I don't feel like a warrior at all. I didn't want to be without you, so I did what it took to get you back."

"I missed you but I knew you would come back and rescue me," she whispered, nuzzling into his beard. "You are so warm."

A sense that they belonged together filled them both. They were drawn to one another and gave in to their feelings. Soon his arms were around her, and his cheek was against her face, her hair smelling of dirt and leaves and blood. An animal sort of smell, he thought, and he found himself reacting to her presence – her smell, her bare body, her warmth, her dark eyes, her resolute fierceness. He was kissing her before he realized what he was doing but was very aware that she was responding to him in kind. As their bodies came together his only thought was to make love to her, and as they coupled the terror and angst of the recent events dissipated and they felt the deep comfort that physical bonding can bring. Afterwards they lay quietly in each other's arms for a long time before dropping into a deep sleep, safe together.

Mornings always seemed to come too early. *Maybe the nights are shorter here, what with all those moons and all,* Alec thought idly. He lay under their wagon enjoying the warm feel of Erin against his side. He knew their moment of leisure couldn't last – there was too much to do today. Erin rolled over, satisfied, and smiled at him.

"I sleep well in your arms," she said.

Alec looked at her body as she moved towards him. He thought her beautiful, as always, but more importantly, there were no bruises on her.

"We did something," he said, elated.

"Of course, we did," she purred.

"No, no – feel your bruises." He ran his hand down her back.

"My bruises – oh! They've quit hurting!"

"They look like they've healed. Let me see the welts on your legs," he said, running his hand down her thigh.

She looked at him, one brow arched, with a sly smile playing on her lips. "At least you are interested in more things today than just my back. Is this another ploy for the Great Wizard to feel me?" she said, nestling tighter next to him. The she whispered, "You were wonderful and might not need a ploy to feel me."

The two of them would have continued if someone had not interrupted them.

There was a knock on the side of the wagon. "Begging your pardon, sir, and ma'am," one of the new lieutenants said, coughing discreetly, "but Captain Harl wants to have a council in an hour and would like you there, if possible."

"We will be there shortly," they both said in unison, quickly rearranging their blankets.

They dressed and stopped by the dining tent for a quick bite to eat.

"Not much left," the serving lady said. "Most others have already eaten." She served them scraps of the main food on a hard tack biscuit, but they were satisfied with the fare.

"Let's go take a quick look at the wagon that exploded before we go to the council," Alec suggested. They walked over to the ruins of the wagon that had fallen victim to Alec's 'magic.' The soldiers had parked it some distance from the other wagons, probably for extra security in the event of a fire, so none of the other wagons in the camp were damaged when Alec caused the stored ammunition to explode.

"Yes, the dragon made short shrift of this one," Erin said, squeezing Alec's arm.

The body of the wagon was riddled with holes. The force of the simultaneous firing of all the ammunition had pushed the wagon over on its side. Two wheels were broken beneath its weight, and the axles were fractured. The canvas covering had caught fire – the wagon carcass was a charred hulk.

As they circled the wagon, Alec pulled in dark energy to see if he could detect any gunpowder. Most of the powder had burned, but he could feel a little residual. He wanted to feel the signature of the gunpowder so he could recognize it. He suspected he would sense it again.

They both kicked through the charred wood and bits of equipment lying around, but it was Erin who made a find. She picked up a burned piece of metal with a small loop and showed it to Alec.

"That's a trigger from a gun … one of the death rods!" Alec exclaimed. Erin brought it over to him for inspection.

He turned the charred piece of metal over in his hand. It had been blown apart when the shells in the rifle magazine ignited, and it had burned afterward, but there was a little metal button with something inscribed on it.

"Runes," said Erin, poking the piece with her finger.

The inscription said "safety" with a little arrow. Alec felt sick.

"What?" Erin asked.

"It's in English … it is in my language," he said. *How can that be?*

"Well, of course," said Erin. "Of course, wizardly tools would be inscribed with runes of the wizardly language." Erin wasn't surprised at that but was surprised that Alec was surprised.

≈ ≈ ≈ ≈

Erin and Alec entered the council tent only a few minutes after the others. Harl's lieutenant was bringing the prisoners out for questioning, one at a time. The first of the captured soldiers were made to kneel before the council, still bound hand and foot.

Harl began the questioning. "What is your name?"

"Zag."

"You are a soldier?"

The man nodded.

"To whom do you owe your allegiance?"

"We are Aldermen," the prisoner said, a bit impudently for a man in his position, Alec thought.

"He speaks the truth," said Erin to Alec. Then to Harl, "With my ring, I can sense truth, and I can tell when someone lies."

"What are Aldermen?" Alec asked.

"We are the force of Alder, and you will all obey the force!" Zag threw back his head and looked directly at Alec. "Treat me well, and I will put in a good word for you. If not ..."

Alec wondered if the man thought their positions were reversed. *He speaks as though he is in charge, not us,* thought Alec to Erin.

"What was the purpose of your raid?" asked Harl.

"We are to gather as many slaves as we can and destroy the Grasslands villages that we encounter. We are to bring the slaves to the Fortress."

"What is 'the Fortress'?" Alec asked.

Zag shrugged. "It is a Fortress. I have never been there."

"Where is this Fortress?" Harl asked. "As a soldier at Octavin, I knew of many enemy encampments and fortifications, but I never heard of a fortress that needs large numbers of slaves."

"Somewhere." Zag shrugged again, and then, perhaps sensing that Harl was not pleased with that answer, added, "The Captain knew where we were going but didn't tell us foot soldiers. He told us that we were to be gone at least a few more weeks."

"Why did you need so many slaves?" Harl asked. "What were you going to do with them?"

"I have no idea," Zag said.

"All that this man has said is true," Erin said to Harl.

Like Alec and Erin, Harl had been captured by the soldiers to become a slave. But, unlike the other two, he had been taken from his home. The disaster that had befallen his village weighed heavily on his mind. His line of questioning changed.

"Did you go on raids to villages?" asked Harl. The man nodded.

"Did you kill anyone in the villages?" Harl asked.

"I didn't kill anyone," the man growled, looking down at his knees.

"That is a lie!" said Erin. Then, with a little kick towards the man, "Tell the truth."

"Okay, okay! Okay, maybe once I had to kill a person in self-defense."

"Still a lie."

"Did you murder any unarmed person?" Alec asked.

"No." He turned his head away.

"Lie!"

"Did you kill any children?"

"No."

"Did you kill any of the people you captured to be slaves?"

"No."

"Did you steal from the villagers, or from your captives?"

"No."

"Lies! All lies!" said Erin contemptuously.

Harl motioned to his lieutenant to take the man out and to bring in the next prisoner. After questioning all four of the captured soldiers, Harl and his lieutenants conferred.

Harl said, "Three of these men are murders and thieves. Under the traditions and customs of our land, they must not be allowed to go free. The other man seems to be more of an underling and did not participate in the raids; or if he did, not to the same extent as the others. He could go free." Harl looked at Erin and Alec. "Do you agree?"

"Yes," said Erin. "That is a just and fair punishment."

Alec was still a little put off by the idea of casually killing people, even if they had committed a capital crime, but realized that he was not in his world, and this was not his justice system. "Umm," he nodded.

"Bring the four prisoners before the council," Harl said to his lieutenant, who left and brought the four men back inside the tent.

"The council has conferred," said Harl. "You three ..." he pointed to them, one by one, "have committed crimes for which we cannot let you live. You three are condemned to be stoned to death." The three men shuffled their feet and looked at one another. Harl turned to the fourth prisoner. "We have determined that you have not committed the heinous crimes of the others. I am going to let you go, but you must leave this camp immediately."

The man breathed a quick sigh and swallowed hard. "Can I have my weapons and my mount?"

"No," said Harl. "We are giving you your freedom. That should be precious enough. You can have a day's supplies and a knife. If after an hour we ever see you again we will assume you have returned to do us harm and will kill you." He lunged at the quaking man. "Begone!"

The man jumped quickly to the side. The lieutenant took him out of the tent for his promised provisions. Then the man was released to the fate of the Grasslands.

The other three men were led out to the camp's central common area, still bound and under the control of Harl and his lieutenants. Word quickly spread through the camp, and soon a sizeable crowd of men and women assembled to take part in the punishment. The stoning was quite a spectacle, and many of the former captives took out their animosity by continuing to stone the bodies long after they were dead. Alec and Erin did not stay to watch.

≈ ≈ ≈ ≈

"I have another chore to attend to," Alec said to Erin.

Many of the former captives had located family and friends and had established groups related to their home villages. Alec and Erin walked among the small groups, greeting people they knew. Alec asked where the people from the last village raided were and was directed to a cluster of about a dozen people.

"Are you from the village raided last?" he asked the closest couple, and they nodded in assent.

"Do any of you know the boy Ilave?"

An older man looked at him. "I knew the boy," he said.

"Do you know his parents? Are they here?" Alec asked.

"They are his parents," the man said. He pointed to a couple standing nearby. "They have had a struggle with this," he said, "being separated from their sons and all. I hope you are not bringing them bad news."

Alec walked over to the couple. "Are you the parents of Ilave?" he asked.

"Yes," the man said. The couple looked at him with dread in their eyes.

"We have been looking all through this camp, trying to find him," the woman said, clutching her hands together until her knuckles were white. "Do you ... Is he ..." The woman hesitated, not wanting to get her hopes up; wanting to know the fate of her son; not wanting to hear that he had died.

"He is alive, and in your village," Alec said, and tears of relief ran down the woman's face. Alec told them his tale of finding the boy in the village,

124

rescuing him from the latrine, and leaving him at their house for his safety. The parents, overjoyed by this news, grabbed Alec's hands, hugged him and thanked him a thousand times. Their excitement was contagious, and others from the village shared in their joy. Alec was elated by their happiness and hugged many of the villagers as they thronged around him.

Erin watched the whole encounter quietly, then took Alec's arm as they walked away.

"You are a good man, as well as a Great Wizard. You have given their life hope – it has raised your spirits too. My ring allows me to sense many things besides the truth. And one thing that I sense is deep goodness within you." Alec looked at her face and smiled. He was beginning to understand.

11 – Medallions

Harl prepared the camp to move. He saw that the group of former captives, some recently-arrived, and some acquired long enough ago to have broken spirits, needed to have something to do rather than sit idly by. Some still did not have clothing; none had proper sleeping accommodations; and food and water would soon be in short supply. The captives needed to act to recover their lives.

It took longer to get the camp moving than it had under the strict regimen of the Aldermen slavers. Harl and his few assistants did not care to use the whips and ropes to motivate the former captives to get up, get fed, and get started in some semblance of order along a trail that was hard to make out. Most of the trogus and some of the drungs had escaped into the Grasslands, which further complicated the logistics of moving several hundred men, women, and teens. If the group remained on the open Grasslands they were susceptible to retaliation from the Aldermen, or attack by other raiders, thieves or slavers.

The goal of the first day was simple: reach the edge of the first village – the one the soldiers had attacked with their death rods the day before, but failed to raid – and spend the night. They approached the village wall slowly, but as the ragged band came near, armed men appeared at battlement positions along the wall. The village gates remained closed. It appeared unlikely that the surviving villagers were aware that the Aldermen had been overthrown.

Harl, Alec, Erin, and a couple of others walked up to the gate.

"Halloo!" Harl shouted. Then after no answer from within the village walls, he shouted again. "Hail! We come to ask entry."

"Go away," a voice shouted. "We don't want you here."

"We need your help," said Harl.

"No. Go away."

"Please. We need help. The same slavers that harassed you captured us. We overcame them and killed them. Now we seek refuge." Still no answer.

Harl tried again. "It was only because of us that the raiders left you and did not come back. We helped you and thwarted their efforts to enslave you. Now we need your help."

"Go away! We cannot help," the voice said.

"What?!" said Alec to Harl. "This is not what I was expecting! We helped them and saved them from the raiders! Don't they owe us some consideration in return?"

"Yes, maybe, but not surprising," said Harl. "I probably would have given the same answer to a horde of escaped slaves from a slaver band. You have to admit – some of our people are a little … rough." He rubbed his jaw. "These villages have a bare existence with just enough food and supplies to live on, and not much extra. They probably couldn't handle this many more people – and if they open their gates to us, they might think that this band could overrun their town. From their point of view, that could be just as bad or worse than the slavers' raids."

"I guess I see," said Alec, mulling Harl's words. "I guess we'll have to camp outside the village walls."

≈ ≈ ≈ ≈

Harl had won the trust of most of the former captives, many of whom still appeared to be shell-shocked and frightened. Alec noted that the band seemed to be content to let Harl be in charge. Harl directed setting up camp that night near the village walls where they would have some protection. After their camp was established Harl called another council meeting. Alec noted that a couple more people had joined Harl to help run things. *Lord knows he needs the help,* Alec thought. Two more men and two women seemed to be functioning as junior officers and attended the council meeting as well as Harl, Lily, and Harl's other three lieutenants.

"As I see it, we have two choices," Harl said, gesturing towards the village walls. "They are not going to let us in. So, either we can head back towards the last village the soldiers raided before this one, and return some of these people to their homes, or we could try to storm the walls of this village and force them to give us provisions."

The group was evenly split between heading back towards the previous village or storming the walls.

"I am not going to be any part of storming the walls of this village or any other," Alec said, shaking his head. *How did I go from being a research scientist at a respected institute to being part of a discussion on 'storming village walls and killing people?'* Alec thought to himself. *Barbarians.* But he had boiled the blood of more than one man. *What does that make me?*

Harl continued to lead the council discussion and found that none of them had any experience in storming walls, or how to do it, or what would be needed to succeed. They understood, however, the consequences of failure. Slowly a reluctant consensus emerged for the group to backtrack along the slavers' route. They could slowly repatriate members of the group in their home villages if anything remained.

Alec and Erin were at a crossroad. They could stay with Harl's band and continue to help them, or return to their original task of heading towards Erin's home. The slavers' path had taken them in the wrong direction from Theland. They were, at best, an additional week from her home, if nothing else befell them.

"It is still a long journey, My Wizard, but we could save a few days, perhaps, by cutting across the Grasslands instead of following the slavers' trace," Erin pointed out.

"Well," Alec said, thinking through their situation, "it would save time." Then, to Harl, "But I feel that I am part of your group and that I would be ... abandoning you ..."

Harl reassured him in his hearty voice. "We will be fine. We are functioning well, the people are willing to follow me, and everyone wants to try to go home. Go, sleep on it, and we will talk about it in the morning." Lily nodded in agreement.

Back at their wagon, Erin and Alec talked until late in the night, going over different options – stay or go? – and different ways to get to Theland. Alec became acutely aware that despite her brave demeanor and tough talk, Erin was still a homesick young woman who yearned to be home and see her mother again.

They met with Harl and Lily at breakfast. Although she oversaw the serving ladies, Harl ushered Lily to their table, his hand on her shoulder, and made sure that she was seated and served with the others.

"We have decided to go our separate path," said Alec. "Erin needs to return to her home, Theland." Then to Harl, "I am amazed at what you have done in such a short time. You have created a little 'village' here – but one that is on the move, instead of sitting in one place." He clapped Harl on the shoulder and Harl embraced him.

"Thank you, my friend."

"We have a long journey to make, and we will be heading out of the camp this morning, as soon as we can get ready. We need to start on our trip." Then to Lily, he said, "Lily, we owe you a deep debt of gratitude. You are welcome to come with us or stay in the camp." Alec understood in just a few days, Lily had become Harl's indispensable support for camp functions.

Lily looked relieved at being given the option. "Thank you, kind Alec. I was afraid that you would make me go with you," she said. "At first, I was hoping that I would find my former companion, my peddler, among the captives here, or that I would see another familiar face. I knew no one here when I came, but now I know so many." She turned and looked at Harl. "I want to stay and help Harl."

Harl also looked relieved. "Miss Lily, you are indeed a flower in this camp. Of course, I … and the others, I'm sure," he added quickly, gesturing to his lieutenants before continuing, "would be most grateful for you to continue to be among us."

Everyone clasped arms and said farewells, and Erin and Lily hugged. "Stay safe, my friend," Erin said to her. "Until we meet again." *If we ever meet again.*

"We will take the supplies we started with," Alec said, "and leave before mid-day."

"As far I am concerned, take anything you need, or want," Harl said, and the others nodded in agreement. "We would still be slaves if it weren't for you two."

≈ ≈ ≈ ≈

Alec and Erin hitched up their drungs and left quietly. By evening they found a small brook coursing through the Grassland and decided to stop.

"We are filthy and we both smell," said Alec. Erin's nose wrinkled in agreement. "Let's stop here for the night and see if we can't do something about that," said Alec.

Alec created a small depression for the brook to fill. Then he heated a few rocks to warm the water. When pool was full, he said, "You first, or me?"

Erin stuck her foot in the water and found it warm. She didn't give Alec a chance to go first – she was out of her clothes and into the warm water before he even had time to notice her back.

"You can join me, my Dear Wizard," she cooed, patting the surface of the water beside her. Alec was also out of his clothes and into the warm water.

"Let me wash your back," Alec said, ulterior motives front and center. He washed her back, and her front, and her hair. They spent over an hour in the pool washing the filth from each other and stroking their tender spots. The stroking progressed until they lay exhausted in the warm water wrapped in each other's arms.

After they were out and dry, Erin said to him, "If you keep that up, you have a lot of wizarding abilities that would make me want to stick with you." With a laugh, she smacked his bare backside. "I'm talking about warming the water, of course!"

Alec surprised himself by thinking; *I hope we do. I hope we do stick together.* Then remembering that he was wearing her ring, wondered if she knew he had thought that. He wanted to talk to Erin about his feelings and their future but couldn't figure out how to start the conversation.

The next few days were repeats – driving their wagon and their drung across the open Grasslands. If they found one of the small streams that crossed the plains, they would stop early and enjoy their time together in the warm water.

≈ ≈ ≈ ≈

Sitting on a wagon seat behind a plodding drung gave Alec a lot of time to think. Still a research scientist at heart, he spent time considering how he could use dark energy more efficiently and what improvements he could make to his focusing techniques. His new medallion was working fine but he thought he should make one for Erin, and he had a new idea he needed to experiment with for himself. One evening they stopped early at a stream.

Alec decided it was time to create a medallion for Erin. It was laborious work. First, he created twenty-three small tricrystals. He laid them on a flat rock and adjusted their locations until he was happy with the focal strength. Next, he encapsulated the tricrystals in a diamond. He slowly modified the diamond until it was perfectly faceted. Then he created a gold loop and chain for it.

When it was finished, he came over to Erin. "I have something for you," he said shyly and showed her the diamond that he had made.

"It is beautiful!" Erin exclaimed.

"Wear it," he suggested.

She put it around her neck and snuggled into his arms. "Thank you, my Wizard."

There will be time to work on using it later, he thought, as it was becoming clear that her immediate interest was not focused on tricrystals.

The next morning, Alec suggested they take a day off from their travel to let him work on a new staff. It was okay with Erin – she was bored with the repetitive travel. She spent the day scouting the landscape and hunting, ending up with several days' worth of meat and roots.

Alec spent the first part of the day making tricrystals. He knew a three-dimensional pattern would generate a stronger focus than a flat pattern, but it had never been possible to make a large enough single tricrystal that didn't shatter. The distributed tricrystal pattern of his current medallion opened the possibility of making a three-dimensional focus medallion. He wanted to try it for the top of his new staff.

He created one-hundred-fifty-seven small tricrystals. Then he started creating a complex pattern. It was very difficult to create the complex shape by feel. With a supercomputer, he could have calculated the correct pattern easily, he thought ruefully. With just his hands, eyes, and senses, however, it was a long process. He would focus and create a tiny glass thread and attach a tricrystal to the thread. Then he would repeat the process. By the time Erin returned from hunting, he had almost finished what looked like a pin cushion. She watched as he placed the last tricrystal in place. He stepped back and smiled at her. As a last check, he felt the dark energy. It was an extremely strong focus. He then fused it into a single diamond.

"Ooh," Erin said appreciatively, not exactly sure what he was making, or why.

"Tomorrow, when we have more light, I can finish this," he said. "I don't think it will take me very long."

"It's too bad we don't have a lantern so that you could work at night. I didn't think to get one from the slavers' camp. We haven't even a candle."

How stupid I've been! "I think I can make one," he said. He scooped a handful of sand and laid it on a flat rock.

"Something new," he said, waving his arms dramatically in an imitation of a cartoon wizard. "I am going to make a fluorescing globe that uses a small tricrystal to generate light. I used to make these as sensors for the dark energy concentrators back home. "

Focus – and he had a translucent round globe. Then he created a small tricrystal in the bottom and an internal wicking path inside the globe. *Focus* – and he had an internal fluorescing media. Next came a catalyst at the top of the globe. Then he picked it up and focused on the tiny tricrystal in the globe. The globe lit in his hands.

"Nice," Erin smiled.

Alec handed the globe to her and it stayed lit. She turned it over in her hand, in wonder. The only artificial light she had ever seen was from an oil lantern or candle. The steady light of the globe looked like true magic to her, and it did not burn her hand as a candle could.

"I watched, and saw, and felt what you did, but I don't know how you did it or why it works; I could never repeat it," she said in wonder, the bluish light highlighting her cheekbones and dark brows.

"It's easy," he said. "It is a simple chemical reaction. I built a globe and then made a fluorescing material inside. When it reacts …" He stopped his explanation. On reflection, it wasn't simple. He had a PhD from a good university, had spent over ten years studying this stuff, and still had a hard time understanding the basics of the process. Today he had just improvised on a process that had been developed long ago by others and then used to measure dark energy.

"Well, maybe it isn't so simple," he acknowledged, "but they are easy to use. I'll show you." Alec took the globe and felt the focus. He let the energy drain from the crystal. The globe went dark. He handed the globe back to Erin.

"Now just feel the crystal and let a little energy flow into it."

She did and jumped when the crystal glowed for her, almost dropping it. "Ahhh!" She stared at it with wonder.

"How long does the light last?" she asked.

"If you stay within about twenty feet of it … three or four paces from it … and don't release the energy, it will last indefinitely," he answered. "But if you go farther away the energy will start bleeding off, depending on how good our focus crystal is. Then it will go dim. This one should last for a couple of hours."

"Oh," she said, trying hard to understand what he was telling her. "Three or four paces."

"Let's make a couple more while we are at it. You can make them, and I'll help you with each step."

By late in the evening they had three more good globes. Erin could replicate each step in the process with Alec's guidance but had no idea why the step was required. Her ability to focus dark energy was significantly less than Alec's, but with practice she could focus well enough to make the globes. They discarded a pile of rejects that, for various reasons, hadn't worked.

Erin sat back on her heels and admired her handiwork, the small globe in her hand glowing softly in the twilight. "Did you know that you are a good teacher?" she said.

He smiled. "Thanks." He looked intently at the globes, now throbbing with light. "At one time, I thought that's what I wanted to be in life. A teacher. Teach kids about science. But then I moved into research and found it more exciting than teaching. But I always enjoyed teaching when I did it in graduate school."

"You taught other would-be wizards?" Erin exclaimed, impressed. "Were they your apprentices?"

"Well, I was teaching others about science," he said thoughtfully. "I guess you might call that 'the study of wizardry.' After they finish school, they go out and find jobs in the real world. But at home we have a different system that doesn't involve apprentices. I guess. Maybe it used to, in times gone by. But now it is correct that the older, more experienced people, like me, teach the younger scientists. So maybe they are apprentices." *Maybe Alder was the wizard, and I was his apprentice.*

The sun was well towards mid-morning when they finally roused the next morning. After a leisurely and tasty meal of fresh game and roasted roots, Alec returned to work on his staff. He wanted it to be available if they encountered any more problems. Making a new staff was easier this time. He was much more comfortable using dark energy, and the new medallion was stronger than his original one.

With a little work, he finished the new staff. Again, it had a narrow metal core and a fibrous outer surface. He clad the bottom in a metal boot. As a final addition, he fastened the diamond focus medallion that he had fabricated the previous day to the top of the staff. He reshaped the crystal surfaces so that it could glow like the lights they had made last night. He pulled a little power through the focus in the diamond. He could feel how clean and crisp it felt compared to either of his other two medallions. *Three-dimensional focus medallions are more powerful,* he realized. Then he focused and pushed a little dark energy into the diamond. It glowed brightly for a second. It shimmered as he rotated it and the light reflected from the various facets.

Erin had been watching the end of the process. "Now you truly look like a Great Wizard," she said, clapping her hands together. "You are my Great Wizard and my Great Warrior," she said with emphasis. Then she looked a little concerned at what she had just said.

By this time, it was late enough that it wasn't worth the effort to break camp and travel. Erin was very interested in Alec's background and spent the time that afternoon extracting the story of his life. It wasn't that he didn't want to tell her, it was just hard to tell, and it didn't seem interesting to him. It turned out to be far harder to explain things like cell phones and moon landings than he would have imagined. He was determined to not resort to calling it 'magic,' but could see that for every step forward away from 'magic' he would fall two steps backward in another area. He could see that much of his explanations were so far from Erin's framework of knowledge that she struggled to understand.

Erin was most interested in his family story. He told her his mother's story.

"Well, my mother met my father in college ... school ... like 'wizard school' ... and she said that he was tall and handsome and that she fell dearly in love with him. They got married ... they consorted ... and then she became pregnant with me!" Erin nodded. She understood this kind of story much better than stories about dark energy and wizarding. "And then ..." Alec shrugged.

"What happened then?" she asked, leaning forward, sensing that something disturbing had happened.

"And then, before I was born, my father left Mom, and she never saw him again."

Erin put her hand on his knee. "Where did he go?"

"It was like he just disappeared. No one ever saw him again."

"Oh," said Erin softly.

"So, it was just Mom and me. My father left Mom a large sum of money ... coins ... so she had enough money to raise me. I had a good life, but I always wondered about my father. Mom didn't talk much about him. I spent a lot of time with my grandfather – Mom's dad – and we went hunting and such. I grew up in a place called 'Washington State.' On one side of the state there were trees and mountains and on the other side there were open plains and grass lands, sort of like this stuff, but dryer and hotter." He looked around at the endless Grassland.

"Did you father come back?" Erin asked.

"No, he never did. I've never seen my father. I only know his name."

≈ ≈ ≈ ≈

The next day was uneventful as they rode across the plains. Alec spent time thinking about the continual fighting they had experienced. He had never been a pacifist or joined in the college protest movements, but never liked to fight.

"Erin, fighting here will change. The sword and the spear cannot match up with the death rod. In my world, the death rod replaced those long ago, and then the death rod was replaced with even more terrible weapons. If one army's death rods can be countered by wizards, then the other side will use their own wizards to make stronger weapons." He frowned and sighed.

This issue of fighting bothered Alec for the remainder of the day as he stared blankly at the rear end of the drung. Erin could see he was lost in thought and didn't try to engage him in idle chatter.

That night, after eating, he told Erin he had some ideas for defending against other wizards. "We should practice," he said. *Need to think about how this would work.*

"All right," she said. "What do you want me to do?"

"Okay. Use your medallion and fling a rock at me." He took several paces away from her. "Not a big one." He couldn't see what she was doing. "And be sure to miss me, don't hit me!" he yelled.

The rock zipped by him, and Alec felt a touch of dark energy. "Okay, now send a few more!"

The next two rocks zipped by as Alec felt the dark energy flow. On the third rock, he felt the energy flow start, and then he started to smooth the flow out. The rock froze in mid-air, suspended in space, held by the dark energy flow.

"Try to make it move!"

Erin tried again to make the rock move, and nothing happened. Then Alec relaxed and released his dark energy focus. The rock came zipping by his head.

12 – Consort

The next afternoon, one of the wagon's wheels broke, obviously a common event since the wagon came with spare parts for repairs. After trying unsuccessfully to repair it in the conventional way, Alec decided to cheat. With the use of a dab of dark energy, the wagon wheel was repaired, and they were traveling again.

After that, Alec became very conscientious about inspecting the wagon each morning. When he saw any part that looked even slightly suspicious, he used dark energy to rework it or replace it with a better part. Over the next three days, he went over the wagon and made an essentially new wagon. The only thing he wasn't happy with was the sleeve between the wagon and the axle. He kept trying to imagine how he could replace the sleeve with a roller-bearing arrangement, but finally decided it was easier to keep fixing the sleeve and use dark energy to create more of a grease-like substance to lubricate the joint.

Late one afternoon, they could see a mountain peak on the horizon. "That is Mt. Eras," said Erin. "It is the tallest peak in the mountains on this side of my homeland. We will continue to travel across the Grasslands until we get closer to the mountains and then we will go along the edge of the mountains. Eventually the mountains turn into low hills and the Grassland ends and a forest begins. In a couple of days, just before the Grasslands and forest meet, we will find a trail. There will be a good trail from then on, and we might even encounter some of my people. We will have three days of travel after we join the trail."

That evening Alec's curiosity about the rings got the better of him, and he asked, "You have used the rings to help us before. Show me how the ring works. I mean if that's okay."

Erin held out her hand, the ring sitting dully on her finger. They tested it with various truth, half-truths, and outright falsehoods.

"In my world, we can fly through the air."

Erin looked surprised but said, "true."

Erin continued, "I am a toothless old hag that has trapped you with a magic charm."

"I know better," said Alec, "but I don't sense anything."

Alec nodded and said, "In my world, I can use a cell phone to talk to someone anywhere in the world."

Again, Erin looked surprised but said, "true."

"My world only has one moon, and we can travel to it."

"Partially true," said Erin.

"I am a Princess, and my mother is the Queen," she said smiling slyly.

"You are my Princess, but I can't tell anything with my ring," said Alec sweetly. Then, unexpectedly and unbidden, Alec blurted "I love you and want to spend my life with you."

"I have hoped you felt that way," said Erin quietly, "and I love you and want the same." She allowed Alec to sense her feelings to know she was speaking the truth.

"I can sense you are a Princess among warriors. I don't think I am good enough for a Princess," Alec added, dejectedly.

Erin laughed. "I felt the opposite. I did not think a mere Princess was good enough for a Great Wizard."

Alec grabbed Erin and hugged her tightly. "I knew when I escaped the slavers that my life would not be worth living without you."

"What about your other person? I do not want to take you from her."

"Sarah? I have thought about her. Sarah and I never had a bond. I always felt she was more interested in keeping tabs on me than on loving me. I suspect that by now she has moved on and found someone else. You and I are meant to be together."

"You are my very own Great Wizard. Mine and no one else's," said Erin, smiling at him. Then, still looking into his eyes, her smile faded.

Alec could still feel that Erin was concerned. "Is something still bothering you?"

She looked at him, and said simply, "Yes." She paused, choosing her words carefully. "There are things about me that I haven't made clear." Her dark eyes searched his face.

Alec swallowed. Fearing the worst, he said, "I am with you." Then, "Maybe I can help you with … whatever it is."

"I told you my father was one of the leaders of our people. I didn't tell you about my mother. She is the Queen of our people." Erin threw her head back a little.

Alec took this in stride; it seemed less of a problem than he was expecting. *No wonder that she seems so … regal.*

"So, your father is … was … the King?"

"No, silly," said Erin. "We do not have kings in Theland. In our land, the Queen is the true ruler. Her consort – 'husband' I think you say – is a member of the Council, but not the ruler. I am the Queen's daughter and so I am next in line to be the ruler of Theland after my mother."

"So, you <u>are</u> the Princess," Alec said softly. Slowly the significance of this began to sink in. "Should I be bowing to you?" said Alec, only half in jest.

"What? 'Bowing'?" asked Erin, not understanding.

"In my country, we do not have rulers as you do," Alec said. "We do not have kings or queens. But in the olden days, in other countries in my world, there were kings and queens. Very powerful. Some places still have them." Alec bowed deeply, and then went through a brief description of the customs of European royalty. Erin listened with amusement.

"We have nothing like that," she said, laughing. "They have customs like that in some of the surrounding lands, like Gott, but we do not. Those customs seem so silly."

"What does the Queen do?" Growing up in the United States, Alec wasn't sure what any queen did.

"It is simple," Erin explained. "The Queen lives in Freeland City, in the center of Theland. Her role is to make decisions for the good of Theland. The Queen can determine who is speaking the truth, and the people know that she speaks the truth. If some issue comes up, regarding our safety or the welfare of our people, then the Council brings recommendations to the Queen. The Queen considers the recommendations and then brings her decision to our people. They know it is the truth when the Queen speaks."

"How does she determine the truth?" asked Alec.

"There are two ways. The Queen can use the Stone of Truth. It lights with a golden glow when we tell the truth. With it, the people can see the glow and know that we speak the truth.

"The ring – this ring – also allows Mother and I to sense feelings. We can tell when someone is telling the truth. There used to be five sets of rings. Over time three sets have been lost. Now, my mother the Queen has one set, and I have the only other set – the rings we are wearing."

"Then life is wonderful," said Alec, hugging her tightly.

"Not quite," said Erin in a more confident voice. "There is one more issue. Since I am next in line to be Queen, I will be forced to consort when I return from this trip. The Council has already told me that. The future Queen must be pure when she consorts."

"Pure?" He thought of her experience in the nomad camp. And, of course, her relationship with him.

"Yes, we have thought for centuries about what that means. Wars have been fought over it. We agree that the future Queen can have sexual relations with someone before consorting, but after the Queen and her consort are bonded, her consort must be the only living person to have had relations with her. That way, there can be no false claims brought by former lovers."

Alec stood still, processing this. Finally, he asked, "What about the nomads?"

Erin snorted. "Either you or I killed all the ones who used me. They aren't the issue. But if one of them were alive, my consort would be expected to lead a war party to bring back the offender's head."

Her former lover, Leonder, was dead. *That leaves me,* Alec realized. *I am the issue.*

"Yes, my dear Wizard," she said aloud, sensing his thoughts. "That just leaves you."

Alec stood there, holding her hands in his, looking into the dark pools of her eyes, love for her pouring out from his very being. For the first time in a very long while, he knew what he wanted, and where he belonged.

"I want to be with you. I don't know your customs," he said softly. "What should we do?"

"When we reach Theland, my people will see you. I cannot deny I know you because Mother's ring will show the truth. If you were to run, hunters would search for you until they found you and brought you back. Then they would probably make me disembowel you in a particularly gruesome manner to show my distance from the past events and my fealty to my consort. That only leaves two options." She stepped back from him and slowly drew her sword, holding it menacingly before him in a fighting stance.

"You have only two choices, my Dear Wizard," she said sternly. "You must either decide to become my consort, or I will have to behead you," she said. Then she could hold her pretense no longer and began to giggle, sheathing her sword and falling into his arms.

Alec laughed too, amused by her mock fierceness, and stroked her hair. Sensing where Erin wanted this to go, he asked, "As I said, I do not know your customs. Is there some process we need to go through?"

"Usually what happens is that if two people decide they are willing, a match-maker works with both families, and a consort arrangement is reached. Once the agreement is reached the two people formally bond to finalize the relationship. Sometime afterward often there is a big feast or ceremony to make sure both families come together in the union."

"And what happens when one is an outsider, like me?"

"It happens so rarely that I don't know. In fact, I don't remember it ever happening before."

"What about Leonder?" Alec asked. "I can't replace what he meant to you."

Erin looked at him. "I don't want you to replace what Leonder meant to me. I will always remember and have him in my mind, but I want to spend the rest of our lives bonded together. If Leonder were alive, you would be his idol. You are all the things he wanted to be. I think Leonder acted from the beyond and sent you to rescue me, and take care of me."

Alec held her close, moved by her acceptance and acknowledgment that her past love for Leonder was, indeed, in the past. Thoughts and emotions swirled in his head, colliding and cementing with his new reality in this strange world of five moons. His past, also, now seemed to be merely his past, and not something he would ever regain as his future. Her world had become his world, alien as it was.

Finally, he said, "In my world, we have customs, too. When a man and a woman agree to be together – to consort – usually he gives her a gift. A gift to show his love and faithfulness to her."

Erin pulled back and looked at him with surprise. "The man? Gives a gift to the woman?"

"I know what I need to do," he answered her, with a small smile threading his lips. "Give me a few minutes to get ready." With that, he left her and went behind their wagon out of her view. *I have wanted to try this ever since my college girlfriend,* he thought. *I hope it works.*

Erin was sifting through her thoughts, and doubts, about this sudden, unexpected turn of events. *I haven't known him that long,* she thought. *He didn't accept my invitation to be my consort. Maybe he thinks I am too skinny. Maybe he just wanted to untie the drung so that he can flee without me.* She fingered the hilt of her sword, the first gift that he had made for her. What would his next gift be? *Another sword? Some kind of staff? A ball of light?*

After several minutes, which seemed like a short eternity to her, he came back around the wagon. She could see that he held something in his closed hand, something small. *Not a sword.* She again reached for the hilt of her special sword.

Alec stood before her. "You can put your sword away," he said gently. "I do not want you to behead me."

Then he knelt on one knee before her and took her hand. "Erin, this is how we do it back home."

She wasn't sure what to expect next. But, then he said simply, "Erin, will you marry me?"

She could feel that his heart was pounding, and her ring told her that his heart was true.

"If you consent to marry me, I will consent to be your consort, and with these two rings we will seal our bond." With that, he opened his hand and showed her what he had made — two rings with a set of large diamonds on one and a single row of small diamonds on the other.

Erin, feeling the solemnity of the moment, even though she did not understand his customs and said "Yes. I will." Then Alec put the ring with the large diamonds on her finger and the other ring on his finger.

"They look nice alongside my family's rings," Erin said softly, looking at the four rings on their two hands. Alec fed dark energy into tiny focal points in the diamonds on both rings, and they glowed with a light of their own.

"They are beautiful — I have never seen anything like this," said Erin. She wrapped her arms around him and held him close.

Alec grinned. "I have always wanted to make a diamond wedding ring for my wife — consort — ever since I started working with dark energy. At home, I wouldn't be able to make it glow, but here with all the background energy, you and I can make it do that."

Then Alec turned serious. "Will this work?" he asked. "Will this show that I have agreed to be your consort?"

Erin started to say 'yes,' then realized she was still wearing the ring and Alec would sense her feelings and know the truth. "I don't know," she finally said. "Before I was getting ready to leave on his journey, there was an undercurrent of things happening at home. Political things. I thought my father would explain them, but he died before he could tell me very much."

"Okay," he said, trying to sound reassuring. "We'll figure things out as we go. You will have to help me – I don't know your customs, and I was never very good at social etiquette."

The next morning dawned with a bright sun; brighter than any day before, it seemed to Alec. He was next to the woman he wanted to be with. They were close to reaching her home. He still wanted to figure out where he was, but he was no longer concerned about when – or whether – he got back to his world. Curled up with Erin seemed like home. Life certainly seemed good.

13 – Coming Home

"We are only two days from home," said Erin, pointing to a stone cairn. "That marker is the border of Theland."

The countryside had continued to change as they rode along the trail. The high mountains to their left had given way to low hills; then they entered a wide tree-covered valley running between two mountain ranges.

Erin gestured. "This valley runs through the center of Theland. My land stretches between those two sets of mountains."

The land seemed fertile, with fields of well-tended crops. The faint trace they had followed across the Grasslands had widened into a regular road, running through woodlands, alongside the fields, and passing the occasional house or cluster of buildings. Wagons, riders, and people on foot passed by, travelling in both directions.

Alec thought about this land. It wasn't that different than where he had grown up. He could live here if they would have him.

Erin was soaking in the view, the sounds, and scents. It was her land, and she was home. She felt both joy and relief, returning to land she thought she might never see again; yet marred with sadness that she was returning without her brother. Occasionally a rider passed by who recognized Erin. In that way, she knew the news of her return would be carried to her home, and to her mother, in advance of her arrival.

On their second afternoon in Theland, they were within a few hours of Freeland City, Erin's home. They were trying to decide whether to travel on and arrive at her mother's home late in the evening, or spend one more night in their wagon and reach the city tomorrow morning. The decision was taken from them when a rider galloped up to them.

"Greetings to you, Princess Erin, and to your escort."

"And greetings to you, as well," Erin replied.

"I bring sad tidings," the messenger continued. "Your mother, our Queen Therin, has heard with great delight the news of your imminent arrival. However, your mother is very ill. She may not survive the night. She bids you please come quickly."

"Ride back to my mother and tell her that, indeed, we will come as quickly as we are able," Erin replied, her lip quivering. "Where is she?"

"As you wish. The Queen is at her Residence," said the rider, and sped off.

Alec clucked to the drungs to quicken their pace. He wanted to hold Erin tightly to comfort her but sensed that she needed her peace to come to grips with this unwelcome news. They were quiet on the rest of the journey. The drungs were tired this late in the day but sensed the urgency of this part of the trip and pulled hard until the end.

At dusk they entered Freeland City, the largest city Alec had seen in this land. Alec was lost in the spectacle of the place. It was neat and well maintained with many large walled estates. They pulled up to one of the estates and the guard opened the gates and let their wagon in. Erin directed them around to one side. They dismounted from the wagon and entered a large compound that reminded Alec of a palace. "This is the Residence," said Erin. "It is my home. I grew up here."

They went through the door and into a grand receiving room. Alec looked around the room in wonder, but Erin strode purposefully towards a side door. She walked through a sitting room and into a bedroom, Alec following in her tracks.

"Mother," she cried, running the last few steps towards a figure reclining on a couch-like bed, flanked by a few attendants around her.

"My Erin! Daughter, it is wonderful to have you home!" The woman raised up on an elbow and opened her arms to enfold the sobbing Erin. "It is so good to see you. I wasn't sure I would ever lay my eyes upon you again."

"What is wrong, Mother?"

The woman shook her head slowly. "The healers don't know. But I am getting weaker and weaker. Every night it is questionable whether I can make it through the night ... and who is this?" she said, noticing Alec for the first time.

Erin grabbed Alec's arm and led him to her mother's bed. "Mother, this is Alec. Alec is my Consort! He is a Great Wizard and a Great Warrior. If it weren't for him, I would be dead several times over!"

Her mother reached out and took Alec's hand. "Greetings," she said. "I am Therin, Queen of this realm. If Erin has chosen you, then you must be a just man." She looked at him a moment, appraising him, then asked, "Will you take good care of my daughter?"

"To the best of my ability," he said.

"I can see that you speak the truth." Alec noticed that she wore a ring like Erin's.

Then she shook her head sadly and said, "I have done you a great wrong, my daughter. If I die tonight, you might be able to rectify the wrong." She sighed. "If I live through the night, then I have done you wrong." She sank back on her pillows.

"Mother, no!"

"Let me die," she whispered. "It is enough to see you back and hold you once more."

Alec gently nudged Erin's arm. *I might be able to help, and give her some healing, to ease her pain,* thought Alec.

Can you save her? Erin thought back.

I don't know, but I can try. It might work.

"Mother, Alec can help. He can make you feel better," Erin said, pleadingly, her dark eyes searching her mother's face.

The Queen looked at them. "No, let me pass without help. If you try and fail, they will blame you for my death. If you succeed … then I have wronged you, Erin, and it will certainly mean the death of Alec."

"No Mother, you can't die on me! Not so soon after I lost my father and brother." Erin broke down and sobbed.

Alec came up to the Queen. "Take my hand and let's see what I can do," he said quietly.

"You would try, knowing it means your death?" the Queen said.

"I would try because it is the right thing to do. We will face tomorrow, tomorrow." Alec reached for her hand. "You know the old saying, 'tomorrow never comes.'"

Alec took the Queen's hand and pulled dark energy through his medallion. He fed the energy through his being and bathed both the Queen and himself in dark energy. As the energy flowed into her body, the Queen sank back on her pillows, her eyes closed. Her handmaidens moved forward, uncertain as to what this tall stranger was doing.

"It's all right," Erin said to them, and they stepped back to their appointed positions.

Alec held her hand for hours, feeding dark energy into her body. Sometime in the night, Erin took his hand and helped him. Alec knew that something felt right when Erin helped.

146

≈ ≈ ≈ ≈

The next morning dawned dimly in the Queen's chamber. Alec and Erin had found a corner to sleep in between sessions of flushing dark energy through Erin's mother, and one of the attendants had brought pillows and blankets for them. The Queen woke first, and saw Erin and her Wizard curled together in the heap of blankets in the corner. *How good to be young,* she thought.

The Queen stretched and sat up. She hadn't felt this good in years. She got out of bed carefully. She was a little unstable from lying in her bed for several days, but everything else felt good. An attendant quietly appeared and led her away to dress and perform her morning rituals.

A short time later the Queen was back with two servants and a tray of food.

"Wake up! Even lovebirds cannot sleep forever," she said. With the sound of her voice, the two sat up.

"Mother! How are you?"

"Whatever your Wizard did worked. I haven't felt so good in ages. Even my back hurts less than it did. Thank you, Wizard."

"Alec," he said, correcting her. "You are most welcome."

"Where are you from, Wizard?" she said, ignoring his name. "And how did you meet my daughter?" Alec and Erin told her a short version of their events while they ate.

"And you, Mother? How have you fared since I last saw you?"

"Not so well," the Queen answered.

"What is the matter – is there a problem with the Council?" Erin asked. *The Council is often at odds with my Mother, and is led by a bully named Brun,* she thought to Alec.

"Let me tell you of my folly, said the Queen, sighing. "Even before you left, the Council was concerned about my status as a widow, and Brun was pushing me to consort with him. Then after you were gone, a peddler came around, bringing news of your brother Devin's death and the loss of your caravan. Everyone on the Council thought <u>you</u> were dead as well. But I knew you were not dead. If you had died I would have sensed your death just like I sensed your brother Devin's death, long before the peddler brought the news.

"Brun continued to insist that the Queen must have a consort in order to rule. 'The people will not feel safe if the queen does not have a consort,' he said; after all, The *Book of Queens* states that the Queen should have a Consort who is a warrior who can work with the Queen to protect our people.

"I knew he was right, but I was still mourning the death of your father. Since I am past child-bearing age, he insisted we consort and that his daughter be in the line of succession after you. He said that would prevent uncertainty amongst our people."

The Queen paused and looked at Erin. "I resisted his demands until he hinted that he had taken your younger brother Colin as a hostage and would kill him if I did not consort! I knew he could do that kind of vicious action! I was so distraught that I didn't even feel for the truth with my ring. I could not stand to lose my last son, so I agreed."

The Queen looked at her hands and twisted the ring on her finger. She hesitated before plunging on with her story. "Brun bonded with me on the floor of my audience chamber with my retainers all watching. I was so shocked and embarrassed that I didn't protest. Since agreement and bonding are the only requirements to consort, Brun quickly informed the Council and the public that he was my Consort."

The Queen snorted. "Brun has been very uninterested in me since that first bonding. He only wanted the power of being my Consort and of having his daughter, Amelia, as heir. I do not like her. She is shallow and stupid, and not suitable to take my place as Queen, but she is a direct descendent of the Original Five."

"The Original Five?" asked Alec.

"I am sorry, I forgot that you do not know our history. Theland was first settled five hundred years ago by five clutches of elves who wanted a different life away from the rest of the elves. They established this place, and named it Freeland City, to commemorate their new order. Each clutch had a set of rings with them. Erin and I are direct descendants of Lian, the First Elf Mother. Brun's daughter is a direct descendent of another original elf, Gwyn, and a merchant's wife here in the City is also a direct descendent of the Original Five. The other two elf lines have died out.

"Only the descendants on the Original Five can use the elven rings to sense truth. Some like, Erin, are very strong in their abilities. Others, like

Amelia, are much weaker in their abilities. In fact, I don't think Amelia can use the rings at all.

"A few days after Brun and I consorted, Colin returned from his trip in the mountains. Brun lied to me – he had not captured Colin and was not holding him hostage! But by then I was consorted." She gave a deep sigh. "I feel that I have let your father down," the Queen said sadly, "and you and Colin as well." Erin gently touched her mother's arm.

The Queen composed herself and continued, "Now comes the worst of my folly. Forgive me Daughter, because I did it for your own good. After we heard that you were lost, I sensed that you were alive. I thought we needed to send a rescue party to find you. I needed the Council to agree. But Brun refused to consider a rescue party. He said that you were dead, and my feelings were just the refusal of a mother to give up hope."

"I knew better so I came up with a desperate scheme. I told Brun that I would agree to last year's consort request from his son Brunder, and told him I was sure you were alive and in trouble. I told him that Brunder was honor-bound to find and rescue his intended consort." She looked at Erin.

"Brun and Brunder were both furious, but knew I was right. That meant that Brunder had to go on a rescue mission to save you or else lose all standing in the eyes of our City. He had been delaying starting the rescue trip with one lame excuse after another. When the news arrived a few days ago that you were alive and returning, Brun has been insisting that you consort with Brunder immediately upon your return, and the Council agreed."

Erin sat back, in shock.

"I am so sorry, but I thought it was the only way to save your life." The Queen looked at Erin and shrugged her shoulders.

"Mother you picked the biggest pig in the whole land! I would have never agreed to that! I would have preferred to die!" Erin blurted out. She reached for Alec's hand. "I am glad that I have already chosen."

The queen continued, "The situation is not good. If I had died last night, the consort agreement would have died with me, so you might not have been bound by it. Since I am still alive this morning, both your decision and mine cannot stand. Either you two must flee, or the Council will insist that the two choices for consort resolve the issue in open combat."

"Flee Erin's home? Forever? That doesn't sound like a good idea," said Alec.

"Then you may have to take on Brunder," the Queen said.

"What does that mean?" Alec asked.

The answer was interrupted by a commotion in the reception hall outside the Queen's chambers. With an arrogant swagger, a muscular young man strode into the room.

"Why are you here? You were not invited!" said the Queen. "Leave!"

"Queen Therin, my dear step-mother, and soon to be my mother-in-law, calm down. I am here to see my intended," said the man. "I heard that she has returned from her long absence, and I want to see her."

"Brunder," said Erin. "How good to see you. I would like you to meet my Consort, Alec."

Brunder's eyes shifted from arrogant to wary to angry as he looked at Alec, then shifted his gaze back to Erin.

"You are promised to me," he hissed.

"Well, it is too late. I consorted while I was traveling," said Erin.

"No, no! Your mother, the great Queen Therin, promised you to me. You cannot break her promise," said Brunder.

"I did not know the situation," said the Queen. "I did not know that she has already selected her Consort."

Brunder turned to Alec with rage in his eyes. "You are the problem! You! I challenge you to a personal dual to resolve this." He turned and glared at the Queen. "That is the law, is it not my Queen?" He leaned forward and stared directly at the Queen.

"It is," she said, after a moment's pause.

"This afternoon, then – on the City combat field!"

Then Brunder stomped out of the Queen's chambers. They could hear his heavy footsteps cross the Great Hall and the heavy outer door slam.

≈ ≈ ≈ ≈

Brunder stormed out of the royal Residence onto the common grounds, fuming. A buxom young woman was waiting for him. She came up to him and entwined her arm with his.

"Tonight, my sweet? Come to me tonight."

"Not tonight Zari," he said, brushing off her hand. "I have something else to do tonight. Tomorrow I will have time for you."

"What is more important than me?" she pouted.

"Bah! The Queen's daughter has returned! We all thought that she was dead." Brunder spit into the dust of the commons. "Now I have to make her consort with me. But she brought someone with her – some strange man. She says she has selected her consort! This stranger! Hah!" Brunder's eyes darted back and forth as he planned his next moves.

"I must kill him this afternoon in an open duel. Once he is dead, I will have to spend tonight riding that skinny wench to seal our consort arrangement." He looked at his mistress, and a hint of a smile flickered across his mouth. "She will be squealing in delight, just like you, after I ride her a few times!" He patted Zari's rear. "I will see you tomorrow. She will be the appetizer; you, my little cabbage, will be the main course." He nipped her ear. "And the dessert."

"Why not me tonight and her tomorrow?" Zari said, squirming under his arm.

"Because," he said impatiently, "the only one that will defend her after her champion is dead would be her younger brother Colin. He is still out wandering around poking at slugs and managing the Queen's affairs in the valley. I need to seal this union before Colin can round up any opposition. No one will oppose me tonight, no matter how much the fair Princess or aging Queen object. So, I must bond with her tonight to become her consort." He slapped Zari's round rear. "Be ready for me tomorrow."

≈ ≈ ≈ ≈

Erin and Alec left the Queen's chamber and went to Erin's suite of rooms. Erin looked at Alec with fear in her eyes.

"Brunder is the toughest person and the best fighter in the land. He doesn't lose fights. I fear for you." She turned and stared out her open window at the gardens below. "It's too bad you didn't just kill him when he came into my Mother's room."

"That wouldn't have seemed right," Alec said softly. Then, scratching his head, "What kind of fight is this?" *Why does it seem like every time I get to a new place, someone wants to kill me?* he thought. Then, with surprise, *and why does this now seem sort of . . . normal?*

Erin turned to explain. "This will be a traditional duel. You fight at the City arena in the center of town, and you fight to the death. It is traditional that the contestants fight naked, but you can bring as many weapons as you can carry in your hands."

"May I use any weapon any way that I want?"

"Yes." She thought for a moment. "We have never had a wizard fight, so there are no rules against using any wizard power." Then she took hold of his arm and said earnestly, "You should finish him as soon as you both enter the ring. Don't give him a chance to do something sneaky, because he will."

Alec mused about what he was facing. *So here is the Queen, who is now married to Brun. And here is Brunder, who wants to be married to Erin.*

"Brun and Brunder are similar names," said Alec. "Are they related?"

"Yes!" replied Erin. "I guess you don't know our naming customs. They are father and son. The 'der' is added to the father's name to name a son. 'Brun,' – 'Brunder.' When the father passes, the son drops the 'der' part of the name. Your son," and then she realized the implication, "our son, would be named 'Alecder.' Alecder. Alecder." She repeated it twice. "It is a good name. I like it."

A knock at the door broke her explanation. The Queen entered the room and addressed Alec. "You must have a second for the event this afternoon. Since you know no one, do you want me to find you a second?"

"That won't be necessary," said Erin.

"You will find him a second?" asked the Queen.

"No, I will be his second."

Queen Therin looked at her daughter. If she was surprised, she did not show it. "That will not make Brunder happy," she said.

"Too bad," said Erin.

"So be it," said the Queen, and left them to prepare for the duel.

≈ ≈ ≈ ≈

Erin and Alec walked to the arena arm in arm. Alec had played in a few big sporting events in college, and this felt to him like one of those events. His stomach was fluttering. A crowd had already gathered. Venders were roasting sweet-smelling grains and roots and were selling food and ale. *A carnival atmosphere,* thought Alec, *to watch me die.*

Brun stood at the back of the crowd. The return of Erin was unexpected. He had paid the caravan master to take care of her permanently. This would not have been his plan. *But this will work,* he thought. *My son relies on violence when treachery would work better, but he will certainly dispatch the outsider. Then I will have two paths to control Theland. One through Brunder and Erin and one through Amelia.*

As they neared the arena, Erin saw a solitary figure come out of the crowd and walk towards her. Since Erin had grown up here, she knew everyone, and she recognized Zari when she approached. Zari came up to Erin and took her arm.

Zari whispered in Erin's ear, "Don't be too good with him tonight – I want him back. He has explained the political reasons why he must bond with an important person like you, but know that he is mine." Then in a conspiratorial tone, she added, "He is particularly hard and good after he kills someone. Please don't enjoy him too much!"

Erin was surprised and flustered at the comment. She started to remark back, but Zari released her arm and faded back into the crowd. Alec gave Erin a questioning look, but by now they were at the arena's ring.

Alec guessed the ring was about thirty feet in diameter, edged by a well-defined circle of stones. Brunder was already on the other side, boasting to the crowd; a smaller man stood nearby as his second. Brunder would have drawn an admiring glance in any gym back home, Alec thought. He was a dominating physical specimen, several inches shorter than Alec but well-muscled and good-looking. Alec suspected that he also had the training and quickness to complement his strength. This would not be easy. *Better body than mine,* thought Alec, *and knows the local customs. Knows how to be a 'consort.' Maybe Erin would be better off with him than me.* He looked at Erin, and the look on her face dismissed those thoughts.

Alec stripped and handed everything to Erin. The only weapon he carried was his staff. He missed having his medallion around his neck but was comfortable using the medallion in his staff. Since there was no local taboo or inhibitions about nudity, seeing a naked body was not unusual for either sex. Most of the crowd were seeing Alec for the first time, and Erin sensed that more than a few of the single women were thinking it was too bad they wouldn't have a chance to see him in bed with them. Taller than most of the men in Theland, his was a leaner physique than the warrior-gladiators of the realm, but he moved with an athletic grace that was foreign to the more muscular men.

Alec looked at Brunder. Brunder was still standing ten feet away from the ring, holding three weapons: a knife and a sword in his left hand and a small axe in his right hand. Alec turned to Erin.

"I love you," he said.

"Come back to me," she said.

Alec looked at Erin to make one last comment before he entered the ring.

"Watch out!" Erin grabbed him, jerking him aside and saving his life. Brunder had been looking for just this chance. When Alec turned to look at Erin, Brunder had thrown his axe at Alec from outside the ring. Only Erin's pull had saved Alec from being impaled by the axe, but the shaft of the axe caught the side of Alec's head. Alec was momentarily stunned and lost his focus on dark energy.

Brunder was across the ring to Alec in only a few strides. he had switched his sword to his right hand; the sword came up and swung towards Alec. Alec, still dazed, awkwardly caught the sword on his staff. Brunder brought the sword up and took a double handed swing. Alec caught the blade awkwardly again. For a third time, Brunder brought his sword up and slashed it towards Alec. Again, Alec was off-balance, and the staff came out of his hand and rolled across the ring to the other side. Brunder brought his sword up for a killing blow to Alec. The sword swept down toward Alec. Alec rolled, and the sword plowed into the ground.

Erin looked on with concern. This fight had started badly for Alec. She reached towards her sword in case she had to save Alec, knowing that if she helped him, they would have to flee her homeland forever. She would do that for Alec but wanted to wait until the last moment.

If Brunder had followed up rapidly, the fight would have been over, and Alec would have been dead – he could have chased Alec around the arena and harassed him such that Alec could not recover his staff. Brunder, of course, knew nothing of dark energy or the value of the staff to Alec – he saw the staff only as a simple weapon, and a decorative one at that. Brunder was a bully and wanted to show off his victory as well as lord it over Erin. He looked at the crowd and raised his hands in victory. Then he looked at Erin, grabbed his crotch and made an obscene gesture toward her.

Alec continued to roll towards his staff fearing a sword in his back at any time. Reaching it before Brunder looked at him, Alec grabbed his staff and crouched, ready for a sword blow. He saw that Brunder was still on the other side of the arena playing to the crowd.

Brunder turned back towards Alec. "You look like a scared bounder!" he roared. "I will make you squeal and make sure you suffer before I kill you. You will not die quietly after having tried to steal my woman!"

The only retort that Alec could come up with was, "Beware of cornered animals – they can be fierce!"

Brunder looked around, puzzled. "There are no corners, here, you fool – this ring is a circle."

What a waste of a good saying in a literal society, thought Alec.

Then Brunder strode slowly and confidently across the ring towards Alec, ready to land the killing blow on what he thought was a cowering figure. This time Alec used the focus in his staff and felt the dark energy flow. Alec knew he could do as Erin wanted and end this quickly, but felt that would weaken Erin's position in her society. Based on what he saw of Brunder's strutting and stirring up the crowd, Alec felt that he also needed to make a show of this. Brunder swung his sword in a broad arc, but what now looked like slow motion to Alec. Alec stepped aside and used his staff to pop Brunder on the nose.

Brunder looked startled but came with another swing to decapitate Alec.

Alec moved aside and bashed Brunder across the back of the head. A few people in the audience cheered, and more than a few laughed.

Brunder was now angry. He took a two-handed swing toward Alec. If Alec had tried to block the swing, it would have knocked him down. Instead, Alec moved slightly and watched the blade sweep past him in slow motion. The swing carried Brunder past Alec, causing him to lose his footing. Alec took his staff and hit Brunder in the rear. The hit caused Brunder to sprawl outside of the ring. The crowd roared with laughter at this indignity.

"That is cheating," said Alec, "you are out of the ring." Brunder got up, now enraged and embarrassed. He had never had this kind of experience in any fight and had never before heard a crowd laugh at him.

Alec thought, *I could end this now and be safe, but for Erin's status and my future as Consort, I need to put on a little more show that they won't forget.* With that, he felt for little dark energy and lit the crystal on top of his staff. It glowed as brightly as the sun.

Brunder was blinded by the crystal's light but swung again. Alec dodged and slapped Brunder with his staff. Brunder fell to the ground. Again, after almost no pause, Brunder was up and charging towards Alec. Brunder tried a cross-handed roundhouse swing, a dangerous plan against a staff. Alec pushed the sword down and hit Brunder behind the head, driving his chin into the ground.

Brunder was up in no time and tried the same tactic again. Alec popped him behind the head, and again Brunder's face impacted the ground. This time he did not get up. Fearing a ploy, Alec let him lie for a few moments. Then Alec prodded him with his staff. Only a slight sound came from Brunder. Alec rolled Brunder over. He could see Brunder's knife sticking deep in Brunder's side where he had fallen on it. He wasn't dead, but the wound was certainly fatal, and everyone in the stands knew it. There was a murmur from the crowd, and then silence. Alec put out the light on the top of his staff and stood over his opponent. He was unsure what to do. Should he kill Brunder in cold blood? Or try to revive him?

He was saved from the decision. A flaming sword flashed at the edge of the ring as Erin stepped forward and took one sweep through Brunder's neck. The head and body separated and rolled in different directions.

"Pig," she said and spat on his torso. Then she loudly uttered the ancient curse of the victor. "'Begone, my foe, lie in death's shadow, and do not defile this world again!'"

Then she turned to Brunder's midsection and with another cut separated his male parts from his body. She caught the parts on the bottom of her sword blade and flicked them to the feet of a sobbing Zari. *He is yours now,* she thought. *Enjoy.*

Then she turned to the crowd.

"I stand before you as your Princess of Theland! This is my rightful consort, the Great Wizard, Alec!" she shouted. "Does anyone here question my choice?"

For an instant, Brunder's second looked like he would say something but then shrank back; trying to fight flaming objects was beyond him. Brun stood by the side of the arena, looking at his decapitated and mutilated son, and said nothing.

"Then let it be known that no one has challenged my intended. All hail my Consort, Alec." After a brief hesitation, one man in the crowd cheered, then the others joined in, some weakly, some with gusto. There were no hisses, and no one spat.

"Come, my Consort, we have much to do." With that, she took Alec's hand and led him from the arena. He could still hear the applause as they walked away from the field.

PART TWO

14 – Winter in Theland

In the weeks after Brunder's death, life in Freeland City seemed idyllic to Alec. The majority of the population readily accepted him as Erin's Consort. He shared Erin's suite of rooms – apartment, really – in the royal Residence. The Queen had taken to Alec immediately. Alec found that he liked Erin's younger brother, Colin, and they meshed as two brothers should.

The only blot on the situation was Brun. Alec could tell that Brun hated him – and Erin – and not because he had slain Brun's son. Brun was Queen Therin's consort in name only and never spent time with the Queen or the family; he only showed up at formal occasions when required in his role as official Consort or as the head of the Theland Council. At those occasions, there was a clear standoff between Brun and the remainder of the Queen's family.

As the hot humid days of summer faded into the cooler clime of autumn, Erin and Alec had time to relax and enjoy their new life together. After the hardships of their captivity and their arduous journey, Erin was relieved to be once again pampered and treated like the royal princess that she was. Alec decided that having servants, including a personal valet, was a nice perk of being a royal consort. He adapted to the local styles of clothing, let his hair grow a bit longer, and wore a short beard. Erin introduced Alec to her friends, showed him the local sights, and took him on long rides in the surrounding countryside.

The approach of autumn and colder days meant more time was spent indoors, often by a nice fire in the large fireplace in their quarters.

"All we need is a dog curled up at our feet," Alec said one evening as they sat by the fire.

"Dog?" exclaimed Erin. "What for! We have no food refuse in here!"

"Not to eat garbage," Alec said. "You know, like a pet."

"Pet?"

"An animal like a dog or a cat that you keep for companionship," Alec said. Suddenly he realized that he had not seen any pets in Theland, just the village street dogs who seem to scavenge garbage – and the hate-filled sentry dogs. And cats didn't seem to exist here.

"You mean you would keep an animal – a dog – for no other reason than to provide 'companionship'?" said Erin, arching her brows. "That seems like a waste of time, and food. And you would let it enter your residence?"

"Yes, to curl up in front of the fire."

"But what work would it do? What would it do to earn its place?"

"Well, I guess you could have a dog that worked. Like help hunt, or round up cattle, or pull a little cart. But mostly, just to have around, to be a pet."

"A 'pet' – that sounds like nonsense!"

"Well, if you spend enough time with a pet, you become quite fond of it," Alec said.

"Fond of an animal!" Erin snorted.

≈ ≈ ≈ ≈

The Queen began to demand more of Erin in order to prepare her for her future role, and Erin spent time with her mother learning the day-to-day business of the governing the realm. Occasionally, Amelia, Brun's daughter, joined the two women – more as a formality than anything else, Alec decided. Erin told him that Amelia was so inept – or disinterested – that she could not keep the simplest concepts of government straight or remember the names of the current ministers or other government officials.

Alec had no problem keeping busy. Queen Therin introduced Alec to the local scholars, who were very willing to show off their knowledge to the Princess' wizardly Consort. The scholars could recount every ancestor of the Queen all the way back to the Original Five. The older archivists maintained the country's historical records but taught their younger apprentices largely through rote recital instead of scholarly research – many could not read. They had detailed records of every event for the past five-hundred years but seemed to have no records before that.

"Why is that?" asked Alec, surprised.

The archivist huffed. "I do not know why anyone would be the least bit interested in events that happened before the Founding!" he replied. "Our story starts with our Original Five. There is no point in reciting the things that happened before then, if there even was a time before then."

"But, surely, there was a reason that those five people – 'elves' – came here to create Theland," Alec pressed.

"Well," the old man said, looking over his reading glass at Alec, "I suppose that perhaps they did have a reason to start the world here. I have heard – but this is just a story, mind you – that some events before the Founding were inscribed in *The Book of Queens*; but only the Queen can read that book. I have never seen it, and I know of no one else who would have knowledge of these things."

Alec did note a strange coincidence. All the Queen's ancestors had precisely three children, a son, a daughter, and then another son. One evening when he was talking to Erin about their future, he asked about this.

"I have been going over the history of your country with the scholars. I have noticed that the records show that all of your ancestors had three children; no more, no less. Is that what you want to happen with us?"

Erin looked surprised at the question. "Of course we will have three children! There is no other choice."

"What?" Alec said, confused.

"That is one of the marks of a descendant of the founding elves. The direct descendants of the Originals always have three children: a boy, a girl, and a boy. Then we have no more children. When you and I are ready to pup, our first will be a son, and he will be wonderful just like you. Our second will be a daughter, and she will eventually become Queen after me; and our third will be a son, like Colin. We need to have two males, because so many are killed in battle. But I am not yet ready to pup. I want to do more before I settle down and raise our family. And I think you do, too."

"So our future is pre-ordained," Alec said, stroking his beard. As an only child, he had thought it would be nice to have more than one offspring, but had not thought about how many, or their genders, or that he would have no choice.

Alec also spent time with the scholars trying to understand the geography of the area. The steep jagged mountains he had passed on the road to Theland reminded him of the Cascade Range in Washington State along the Pacific coast, but when he questioned the scholars about geology or volcanology or plate tectonics, he was met with blank stares. The scholars had very detailed maps of the land between the mountains and less-detailed maps of the surrounding regions, including the Grasslands, Gott, and the Elf Mountains.

They had no maps beyond that, and no notion that there might be lands beyond, or what they might be. The concept of a round planet was too ridiculous for them to consider.

$$\approx \ \approx \ \approx \ \approx$$

One fall evening, after an afternoon quizzing the archivist, while they dined with the Queen, Alec used the opportunity to ask about the book. "My Queen, the scholars talk about a book called *The Book of Queens*. They talk reverently about the book but claim that only you have access. May I ask: what is the book?"

Queen Therin paused, then answered, choosing her words carefully. "Yes, there is a *Book of Queens*. It was written late in the life of the First Queen of Theland as a guide to her daughter. The First Queen requested that the *Book* be read only by the current queen and passed down to her daughter when it was time. And so it has been passed down, through our line of Queens, to me." The Queen stopped and thought for a while. "Maybe it is time to tell Erin about the *Book*. You may listen if it is permissible to her."

Erin nodded her agreement, and her mother continued. "There is much in the *Book* that might be upsetting, so, please do not repeat to outsiders any of what I am about to tell you. The secrets of the Queen are just that – secrets of the Queen only. I have not even shared the contents with my Consort, although he has pressed me to do so." Erin and Alec pledged their agreement.

"The First Queen of our land was an elf named Lian. Lian was a full elf, not a cross-breed, and in the *Book* she claims that she was the first elf born on this world. She was born about five-hundred-fifty years ago in the elf colony called the New Haven, not long after the elves arrived on this world. In the *Book*, she claimed her mother was not only not born on this world but wasn't even born in this universe. Until I heard your story," and the Queen nodded towards Alec, "I thought the concept of being born on another world was fanciful and invented – perhaps an allegory for a time before knowledge. Now I am not so sure – maybe she actually meant that her mother came from outside this world.

"Lian claimed her mother was a direct descendant of the 'Dragon Queen.' I have not heard of such a being anywhere else, and I do not know who – or what – that might have been. Or what that meant. Lian's elf-clutch – family – and many other elves came to this world because they did not want to be part of a civil war among the elves – she called that conflict 'the War of Dragon Succession.'

"In the *Book*, she writes that initially the elves established a settlement in the Elf Mountains – the New Haven. They also established herds of a race they called 'the orb' in Gott and in the land on the other side of the Elf Mountains. I do not know the name of that far land, or even if it really exists. Lian wrote that the elves captured free orbs and made them slaves. She called that 'culling,' and the culled orb slaves, 'drones.' The elves apparently used the drones to provide for their every need.

"The people of Gott, and the people in the land on the far side of the Elf Mountains, are descendants of the elf drones, not the elves. The Gott would not like this story. If they ever heard this – that they were descended from slaves – they would be very insulted and might cause a war to defend their honor." She looked sternly at Erin, and Alec, and they nodded.

"According to *The Book of Queens*, Lian and her family and her drones, along with four other elf families and their drones, came from the Elf Mountains to escape from the regimented life they lived there. She formed a new elf settlement in our valley. Those families were the Original Five. They settled here in peace."

"The elf war from beyond the sky somehow expanded to this world and the elves in the mountains became engulfed in that war. Lian and her settlement decided to live a quiet life here in our valley and let the war pass them by, so they distanced themselves from the elves in the mountains. That's when our land, Theland, became a separate realm. The elves chose Lian to be their ruler – she was the First Queen."

"But the scholars told me that they felt there was no time before the founding of Theland – that time began with the Founding," Alec interjected.

"Well, yes, they think that, because they have not seen nor read *The Book of Queens*," Queen Therin explained simply. "They think that because our oral history starts with the Founding, they have no reason to believe that anything happened before that time. That is the history they know."

"Are there still elves here in Theland?" Alec could hardly believe that he was asking a serious question about elves.

"Over time, with the passage of the generations, the pure elf lineage has died out here in Theland," the Queen explained. "For reasons that have to do with the elves' strange biology and reproductive life, very few purebred elves were ever born in this valley, and none have been born here for several hundred years. Lian must have consorted with someone who was not a pure elf, because her daughter was part elf and part orb: a cross-breed. The daughter, who became the next Queen, passed along that genetic heritage to all of Lian's descendants. *The Book of Queens* dwells for many pages on the genetics and lineage of elves, orbs, and cross-breeds. When you have time to spare, Erin, you may read it; it is difficult to read because the parchment is fragile and the runes are of the old language and the ink is fading. The important thing for you to remember, however, is that many of the people of our land carry the mixed blood of both elves and orbs. Just as I do. Just as you do."

Erin let this sink in, and then asked her mother, "What about the Stone of Truth? Where did it come from?"

"The Stone is said to be an artifact that Lian's family brought from the mountains over five hundred years ago. It has rested in the center of Freeland City since the beginning of our times. In *The Book of Queens*, Lian mentions that the stone had been in her family for centuries, but does not dwell on its property of revealing truth. I suppose that since back then all of the women elves had rings like ours, and could sense the truth, the Stone of Truth wasn't really very interesting to them. But our annals show that later on, our Queens began to use the Stone to show the people that they were making true decisions. Apparently in times past, some of our citizens doubted one or another of our predecessor Queens. So over time the Queens began to use it more often. I myself use it, though only sparingly, for matters of deeper consequence or where there is contention among my subjects."

"If she didn't need it to tell truth, then why did she bring it here?" asked Alec.

"According to Lian, the Stone's original use was to determine 'when the dragon blood runs true' in a person."

"'Dragon blood?'" questioned Erin.

"Lian does not explain that. I don't know what 'dragon blood' refers to. It might have something to do with the reference to 'the Dragon Queen.' The *Book* simply says that 'only she with a strong vein of the blood of the dragon' can make the Stone change colors, and that 'transparency comes with strength of blood.' I take that to mean that the more transparent the Stone becomes, the stronger the user's blood line. I can make the Stone rather transparent, but it is still milky. I am sure that you will be able to do the same. I suspect, however, that Amelia would never be able to use it very well, because she is of a different lineage than us."

"I have 'dragon's blood!'" exclaimed Erin with playful delight. "I always wanted to soar through the air like the dragon I saw." Alec rolled his eyes.

"Lian writes of dragons with the same awe that you have, Daughter. She viewed them as formerly-grand creatures that the elves subverted and turned into terrible war machines. Her writing hints that the war the Original Five were trying to avoid had something to do with the dragons."

Alec was now beyond being astounded at stories of flying dragons and warring elves and stones that changed color, here in a world of five moons where the most learned scholars thought that their planet was flat. He felt that all of these phenomena must have something to do with the dark energy fields in this world. That, or too many sips of the juice of the purple mushroom.

As Erin flapped her imaginary wings, Alec broke in, changing the subject. "I keep thinking of your rings, and why they work the way that they do. I understand how my medallion works, but your rings must be as complex as my medallion. I don't understand where the rings came from. Certainly, the rings had to come from somewhere else – are they discussed in the *Book*?" asked Alec.

"The Original Five founding elf clutches each brought two rings with them. Over the generations, three sets of the rings have been lost. There is no mention in the *Book* where or how the rings were originally made, but I suspect the elves brought the rings with them when they first settled on our world. Lian's writings indicate the rings were very precious and were very difficult to replace."

"Mother," Erin interjected, "Alec taught me how to use my ring to gain greater powers. You should work with Alec to see if he can teach you also." Queen Therin nodded in agreement.

Then the Queen's attendants entered with the next course of their evening meal. The Queen gave Erin and Alec a look that said that they must not continue their discussion about *The Book of Queens* around the servers, and the dinner conversation transitioned to the Queen's plans for the annual harvest ball and associated fall festival.

≈ ≈ ≈ ≈

Erin introduced Alec to the local Seer – the old woman who had given Erin the prophesy before she had left Theland. The Seer was a disappointment to Alec. She had a rudimentary focus crystal that could barely concentrate dark energy. She used her crystal to develop fuzzy images which she then interpreted as prophecies about the future. Alec could feel a flow of energy around the Seer but wasn't sure what it involved. Alec asked the Seer about other wizards.

"I have heard of other wizards, like you," she said, stabbing her gnarled finger towards Alec, "but I never met one. Most people claiming to be wizards are charlatans – imposters." She frowned at Alec.

One night at dinner, Alec asked Queen Therin about the Seer.

"If I had known what she told Erin – what she said that made my daughter go off with her brother on that caravan – I would have had her flayed alive! Now am I content to let her spend the rest of her days as a doddering old woman." The Queen spat. "When her daughter takes over as Seer, I will have a long talk with her about the proper limits. Especially when she is talking to a Princess!"

"But why does she have a dark energy device – that old crystal – in the first place?"

The Queen shrugged. "That old crystal has been handed down through the Seers, from mother to daughter, since the Founding. I don't know where it came from, but legend has it that many generations ago the Seers had a very important role in our society: to nurture our future generations, protect our people from ill will, and discern omens. Now the Seer's role is mostly ceremonial; sometimes I'm not sure why we keep her on. But – it's our tradition. We have so many traditions!" The Queen laughed.

≈ ≈ ≈ ≈

Throughout the autumn Alec and Erin both practiced every day to improve their fighting skills. They worked together to improve Erin's special sword that Alec had made and increase her mastery of commanding its special powers. Erin redoubled her weapons training, and Alec worked hard to develop a rudimentary proficiency with various weapons. While Alec became marginally proficient, Erin continued to excel and was better than any of the local weapon-masters. Often in their practice sessions, two masters fighting in combination could not beat her.

They spent quite a bit of time honing their ability to read each other's thoughts when they were wearing their rings, and to converse in this manner. Additionally, Alec spent time working with dark energy and learning different ways to use it. He also tutored Erin in what he learned. Erin found she could focus small amounts of dark energy but could not handle significant amounts like Alec. In fact, Erin found that using dark energy in combination with a medallion limited her sensitivity to her ring; she decided that she would concentrate on learning to use her ring and leave most of the dark energy business to Alec.

Alec was the first to notice a new ability that Erin had acquired when she wore her ring. "Erin, when I am focusing dark energy to slow down time and accelerate myself, you can sense where my sword stroke is going even before I start to make it. When I use dark energy, you know where my stroke is going."

Erin thought for a second and said, "You are right. I do know where you are going to make your next strike. I can sense it almost before it happens."

"Then you should learn how to take full advantage of that ability. Anything that gives you an advantage will make you a stronger fighter. If you use the dark energy crystal on your sword in combination with your ring, it will give you an extra advantage."

≈ ≈ ≈ ≈

Even though he had never met the man, Alec wanted to do something special to honor Erin's father, Consort Devin, and decided that the annual fall festival would be a good time to do it. Alec spent days preparing for it. He located a suitable spot in the Residence's main courtyard. Having found a natural spring up-hill from the courtyard, and using dark energy, he built a gravity-fed aqueduct and pipe system. Then he created an elaborate spraying fountain, reminiscent of those he had seen in Italy, complete with a stylized image of Erin's father. He discretely left a spot next to Consort Devin where he could add an image of Queen Therin later.

Erin loved the fountain. She had never seen anything like it in her life. The fountain was unveiled at the harvest celebration, where the Queen and her court saw it for the first time. All were impressed and applauded Alec's work. The Queen was quite perceptive, however. After lavishing praise on the work, she turned to Alec.

"I notice there is a space next to the image of my dear Consort Devin. What is that space for?" she asked.

Alec stammered and didn't quite know how to answer.

"Is that where you will put my image when I am gone?" she asked.

Alec nodded his head in a guilty and contrite manner. "Um, yes ... I mean, it could ... go there."

"What a wonderful tribute!" she said. "Why wait until I am dead? Go ahead and do it, so that I can enjoy it for a while."

Alec was relieved. "Of course, Queen Therin. I will do it tomorrow."

Alec used the fountain project to solve another problem. Part of the lower town, the poorest part of Freeland City, had no water supply. The people living there had to haul water to a central cistern. Alec routed the excess water from the fountain to the cistern to give the lower town a continuous and clean source of water. The poor were honored that someone had done something to make their lives easier.

≈ ≈ ≈ ≈

Alec was consciously trying to turn himself into a contributing member of Theland. He noticed that the dirt road into town tended to rut out after rain. He replaced about two els of the road with a cobblestone pavement that would be unaffected by rain. It worked so well that nobles and other townspeople petitioned the Queen to have him fix the roads in front of their residences; after initially grumbling in Council meetings about Alec's "meddling," Brun then began to complain about Alec's inability to satisfy the demand.

From Alec's point of view, one impediment to enjoying life in Theland was the Governing Council. As Erin's Consort, Alec was an official member of the Council and expected to attend Council meetings. The Council had the power to make consequential decisions that could affect the country's customs and economy but seemed to Alec to rarely use this power. *These are worse than the faculty meetings at the Institute – just a bunch of old men bickering over trivia,* he thought. Brun was the head of the Council and resented Alec's presence, but made few comments in the open forum.

Alec felt that the Council placed impediments in front of him at every turn. Alec wanted to create a "wizard school" and train promising youths to help improve the community. Everyone agreed it was a great idea, but then the problems started, as Brun began to ask theoretical questions and pose arguments. Who would pay for the wizard school? How would the wizards charge for their work? Who would prioritize the wizards work, the Queen or the Council? How would their wizarding abilities be used? And who would monitor them to ensure the youths stayed out of mischief? All of these and other issues bogged down the school project in endless hours of discussion.

Finally, Queen Therin explained the real issue to Alec. "Brun is afraid of having more wizards here. For a long time, Brun has been using the council to try to usurp power from me, the Queen. He knows that Erin is already the greatest of our warrior-riders and will probably lead our warriors if need be; by consorting her with Brunder, he could have limited her role. But now, Brun has to contend with you. You have new abilities that Brun fears. Brun wants to be all-powerful – he is concerned that the changes you suggest would reduce his power."

≈ ≈ ≈ ≈

On many long evenings, as autumn waned into winter, Alec, Erin, the Queen, and Erin's younger brother Colin enjoyed long after-dinner conversations by the big fireplace, sipping goblets of wine. They talked about philosophy on many evenings so that Alec could understand Erin's worldview and Erin could understand his. The biggest difference, Alec thought, was in how they viewed human life. Alec found it difficult to accept the casual way that Erin's society viewed killing people. He understood war – although in his prior life he had abhorred the thought of having to participate in one – and he understood the American justice system and its use of capital punishment for murderous criminals. However, fighting a duel with someone merely to settle a disagreement seemed to him like vigilante justice – or no justice at all – even though he himself had done this in self-defense and to defend Erin.

And I'm becoming more like them, Alec thought. *I have these conversations with Erin about who to kill, and when. That's not who I was!*

Of great concern to Alec was his nightmarish ability to boil the blood of an opponent. Alec had thought long and hard about it and concluded it was not a humane way to fight, although he knew if it came down to saving Erin, he would do anything without regret. He rationalized that it was like nuclear weapons in his world – something that existed but that you never wanted to use.

Erin listened to his concerns and his explanation. She felt the sincerity and the truth of what he was saying but didn't understand the underlying issue.

"Dead is dead," she said flatly. "It doesn't matter how you get there. There is no difference between boiling someone's blood and chopping off his head. It is the same result. You have defeated your enemy." The concept of 'rules' for conducting warfare also was foreign to her. "War is to resolve issues in any way possible, not to fight like a couple of schoolchildren playing some game," she chided. "But I respect your feelings, and I know that this bothers you."

≈ ≈ ≈ ≈

One blustery winter day Erin and Alec went to the Square of Justice to see Queen Therin consult the Stone of Truth. The main portion of the square was a stone-paved plaza with small shops along the edge. In the center was an elevated platform large enough for several people. The Stone of Truth was in the middle of the elevated platform – a perfect sphere half buried in the platform. The part that was exposed was waist high and black. Erin had seen her mother make many pronouncements after laying her hands on the Stone of Truth.

They reached the square long before the Queen and were escorted to a special area reserved for dignitaries. Most of the other members of the Council were already there. Only Brun and Amelia arrived after they did, Brun almost dragging his daughter by her arm. Amelia looked very annoyed. After the pale sun moved a hands-breadth, Alec watched the Queen enter the square, flanked by her attendants. She walked confidently to the raised platform, mounted the steps, and put her hand on the jet-black stone. The stone turned from black to a milky translucent color.

Then the Queen made a pronouncement about the need to extend justice to all the citizens of Theland and to discern the right path, and the stone glowed with a golden hue. *Her statement is truth,* thought Erin. Alec nodded.

A man was brought forward in chains. A justice presented the charges. "This man – a nobleman of our City – has been convicted of brutally murdering his neighbor, a peasant, in a dispute over a woman. The punishment is death by beheading. Do you ask for the queen's intercession?"

The man yelled, "No! I didn't do it! That is not what happened! I am innocent!"

The Stone of Truth turned black.

"That is not the truth," said Queen Therin in a loud but troubled voice.

"Well, I did kill him, but he deserved to die! I am a nobleman! He was not! He wronged me – he was trying to take the girl I wanted. She was too good for him."

The truth stone glowed with a golden hue.

The queen shook her head. "I cannot change your sentence. The Stone has confirmed that you have performed a murderous act; even though your victim was of a lower class than your standing, he did not deserve to die in such a violent manner."

The justice pulled on the man's chains and took him off. Everyone there realized that the man was being led to his execution.

Erin took hold of Alec's arm, watching the man being led from the Square. "Mother likes to say that 'fighting is easy, but governing is hard,' and she is right. She often must make decisions in cases where everyone has a true and valid position. It is not unheard of here for nobles to take advantage of the lower castes; many nobles would agree that killing a peasant does not deserve a death sentence. I hope that I do not become queen for many years."

Alec nodded in agreement.

At the end of the inquisition, Erin went to talk with her mother; from his seat, Alec could see that the Queen looked as if she was exhausted from using the Stone. While Alec waited for Erin he saw that Brun and Amelia were still in their seats and having a heated argument. Not wanting to intrude, Alec continued to face away from them, watching Erin. However, he could clearly hear the high-pitched whine of Amelia over the murmuring of the dissipating crowd.

"Father, I don't know why you insist that I come to these events."

"Someday you may be Queen; you need to know how to govern," Brun growled.

"I won't ever be queen! I don't need to know this stuff. Queen T will live a long time, and then Erin is next. When she has a daughter, her girl-pup will be next in line before me. I don't like wasting my time here."

"You need to be here," Brun said angrily. "Shut up and pay attention!"

"I don't want to be here. I want to be with my friends. We planned to spend the afternoon sipping the purple mushroom juice. Much more fun than this."

"Purple mushroom is bad for you! Addles your brain! You need to stay away from it." Amelia snorted. Brun continued, "You are just like your brother, Brunder. Too headstrong. Too impulsive. You only think about your pleasures of the moment. Purple mushroom!" He snorted. "I wish you were more like your younger brother. Brar is sensible. He doesn't go cavorting around like a silly bounder, like you do." Alec could hear the older man spit.

"Your mother raised you to be better than this. She would come back from her departing ceremony if she knew what you were doing! I wish she were still alive – she'd give you a scolding and knock some sense into that petulant little face of yours."

"Mother! Everyone knows you poisoned her so that you could consort with Queen T, so stop acting like you want her to be alive," snapped Amelia.

"I did not do anything like that; she died of 'the flux.' Besides," he lowered his voice significantly; Alec strained to hear. "Poisoning is an offense that can get you beheaded, so only fools openly speak of such things," said Brun. "But you need to be prepared. You may become Queen sooner than you think. Our Queen would have died of 'the flux' recently if the Princess' new 'Wizard' had not saved her. The Little Princess wants to be a Big Warrior and warriors often suffer terrible accidents in battle. Then she would not be around to become Queen. And, sometime when her Consort is not nearby, the Queen might have another bout of 'the flux.' Your time may come sooner than you think."

"Well, if I am Queen, I will not go through all of this foolishness with that stupid stone. If I think that someone needs to be beheaded, I will order it and not force people to waste their precious time sitting in the cold watching a silly spectacle."

Amelia rose with a great rustling of her plentiful robes and stomped out. Brun followed, still talking in a low voice. Alec did not hear any more of their conversation. What he had heard was upsetting enough.

≈ ≈ ≈ ≈

Erin and Alec decided to celebrate their consorting as part of the Queen's annual spring festival. Erin was eager to have a public celebration of their union and decided that would be the ideal time. By the time of the spring festival, the mountain snow would have melted and the fields would be green with new promise. The Queen liked to have an event to celebrate as part of the festivities.

"In my country, we would have what we call a 'wedding,' a ceremony where the bride and groom – the woman and the man – appear before their elders and family and friends, and pledge to love and honor each other," Alec said. "Sometimes they are very small affairs, but the bigger ones are fun – a formal ceremony, lots of flowers, and music, and dancing, and fancy clothes."

"A 'welding'?" asked Erin. "That sounds onerous."

"No, no," said Alec, laughing. "A 'wedding'! A coming-together. Do you have any ceremony like that here?"

"Not really. Sometimes we have a grand dinner when people consort, to introduce their families to each other. But not a big ceremony. 'Music and dancing' sounds like something they would do in Gott, not here. But … a feast, and new clothes …" Erin's eyes darted back and forth as she began to warm to the idea and felt Alec's desire to celebrate. "We could have a big event as a part of the spring festival, right here in the gardens of the Residence. We could invite the cream of the town society – they would like that. I could have a new dress made, and new clothing for you! And for Mother! She will like this idea!" And so, with the excitement of a bride, she began making plans.

The word quickly spread that there would be a consorting celebration between the Princess and her man. Everyone wanted to be a part of the party since it was the chance of the year to hob-nob with Theland royalty and cognoscenti. Alec wanted this to be a spectacle to showcase Erin. Alec insisted that some of his country's customs be included alongside the local traditions and the Queen readily agreed.

When the day came, they set up a formal receiving area with white tents in the center of the Residence gardens. A central pathway led from the Residence to an open pavilion in the center of the area, flanked by mounds of white flowers on either side. The guests, those few hundred townspeople fortunate enough to be graced with an invitation, stood on either side of this aisle.

Normally at a formal event of this type, the two would have walked in together, hand in hand; but for this occasion, Alec had other ideas. Two royal whistle-bearers heralded the beginning of the ceremony. First Erin's brother Colin walked towards the center of the pavilion. Then Alec walked alone down the aisle, resplendent in his new suit made in the highest style of Theland by its finest tailor. Erin appeared next, at the garden doorway, wearing a simple long white gown. Two young flower girls walked down the center aisle in front of Erin, throwing out pale scented flower petals. Erin paused for a moment for effect before walking with a slow, stately step towards Alec. As Erin walked by, each of the flower petals glowed gently with its own light. Erin walked to Alec looking like a Greek goddess of old legends, highlighted in fire and light.

She looks stunning, Alec thought. *As a bride should.*

When she reached the front, she took Alec's hand, but Alec wasn't finished with his special effects.

"The crown, please," he said. Colin stepped forward holding a pillow in his outstretched hands, a small tiara nestled atop. Alec took the tiara in both hands and put it on Erin's head. Then he focused a little dark energy, and the tiara lit up, bathing Erin in a soft light.

Alec took her hand and held it up high in the traditional sign that Theland couples used to show they were consorted. Both wedding rings that Alec had made lit up and glowed in soft light, wrapping their hands together in a symbolic joining. Gasps and coos of amazement rose from the crowd, and then the guests cheered and applauded the couple. With that, Alec and the glowing Princess joined the rest of the guests in a long receiving line. All looked at Erin with amazement as she glimmered softly in the evening sun, with two moons setting behind the couple to frame the scene.

Erin and Alec had one more trick to regale their guests. As the sun went down, Alec focused dark energy, and two dozen light globes awoke to brighten the feast area. Again, there were gasps and murmurs of pleasure and delight. The feasting and revelry went long into the night, winding down only when the 'magic' lights started to dim in the early morning.

15 – Touring Theland

Ever since Erin had brought Alec to her homeland, they had talked about taking a trip through her mother's realm so that Alec could see the rest of Theland. One spring afternoon, Erin came out to the corner of the stable that Alec had claimed as his work area. "It is chilly in the Residence, but it is warm out here. No wonder you spend so much time in the stables!"

Alec smiled, and pulled her close. "I'm not trying to get away from you! No, I spend a lot of time out here working, because there is so much that needs to be done. Everything is so hard to do when you have to create everything from scratch and have no one to help you."

She smiled and retuned his squeeze. "Well, you will be spending more time with me. I have good news.

"Mother has agreed to us traveling around the country. She thinks it is a good idea for you to see more of the Theland, and for the people to become better acquainted with me, as the future Queen, and you, as my devoted Consort. She also thinks it would be good for us to get out and away from Brun for a while." Erin wrinkled her nose as if smelling a foul odor. "She thinks he is up to something underhanded. Mother says it would be unseemly and unsafe for the future Queen to travel alone, even if accompanied by a Great Wizard. So, she thinks we should go with a proper royal escort."

"Well, okay," Alec said. "I'm glad that she finally decided to let us go, but I was rather hoping it would just be … you and me."

Erin kissed his nose. "Welcome to the life of a Royal Consort. We have to act royal."

"When can we leave?" he asked.

"I think we could leave any time after the mountain snows have finished melting in the uplands and the roads are clear, but I think it would be best to wait until after the spring planting. Then the villages will not be as busy. We don't want to disrupt their well-being too much."

Alec had envisioned a quiet trip through the countryside for just the two of them, sort of like the more pleasant parts of their earlier travels, but saw the Queen's point of view. The people needed to see their next ruler, and she needed to look like a Royal Princess, not like some vacationing college-kid hitch-hiker.

And there was the issue of safety. Although neither Alec nor Erin had told the story of their travails to many people, Alec suspected that Erin had shared the details with her mother – she had probably told her mother more about the horrors she had experienced in the nomad camp than she had even told Alec. The Queen would not want to risk the safety her daughter, even in her own land.

≈ ≈ ≈ ≈

Finally, after a few short weeks of planning, packing, and preparations, they were off, leaving Freeland City with little fanfare. Twenty riders accompanied them, as well as two supply wagons and a royal wagon for Erin and Alec. The riders were a typical Theland mix of twelve men and eight women. They were expecting to be gone at least a month, possibly a bit longer, and would resupply along the way as needed. From Alec's study of the scholars' maps, he knew Theland was a long valley nestled between two mountain ranges – the Elf Mountains and the Evening Mountains. A central river, the Ryn, ran the length of the valley. He figured that the valley was probably about one hundred els wide and about four hundred els from one end to the other. If they needed to communicate with the Queen or others in her court, a message could be sent from one end of Theland to the other in about four days' time.

They planned a leisurely trip along the Evening Mountains of Theland, then crossing the Ryn and coming back towards Freeland City along the foothills of the Elf Mountains on the other side of the country. Alec knew from the scholars and cartographers that the realm's boundaries in the mountains were ill-defined. The mountain range on the evening side separated Theland from the Grasslands and was settled by no one. The mountains on the morning side were a part of the elven lands – only elves were permanent residents of those mountains, since the winters were so harsh. The sections of the mountains within Theland were mostly used for summer pastures and hunting.

The upper, moonward, edge of Theland was better defined. The kingdom of Gott bordered Theland to the moonward side, where the two mountain ranges came together.

"Gott has been our ally for over a generation now," Erin explained to Alec. "Mother said that she owes the Gott a state visit – she will probably do that in the fall, and we will probably go with her. That would be after the harvest. I don't think we need to visit Gott on this trip, and Mother agreed with that. We need to show you Theland before we venture too far afield. "

Alec was interested in the Elf Mountains. Erin had told him that it was in those mountains where she had seen a dragon and heard it sing.

"Are we going to go near the Theland boundary in the Elf Mountains?" he asked. The elves intrigued Alec because they sounded like they might be people with technical skills that exceeded others around, perhaps even involving dark energy.

"I don't think so," she answered. "We will just stay in the foothills and visit our own villages. There are few roads leading into the mountains in that area and sometimes it is hard to tell where the boundary is. And we don't want to cross into their land by mistake."

"Why not?"

"The elves are very secretive. They do not like intruders and allow visits by invitation only. The last time we had a state visit with them was when Grandmother was a little girl; Mother said that Grandmother told her that she accompanied her mother and father on a formal trip of some sort. She told Mother that she didn't remember much about it but that the elves were handsome people and their city was very beautiful."

The first day they traveled through the pleasant green countryside and newly-planted fields near Freeland City. Alec had seen some of this part of Theland before, during short jaunts with Erin. The landscape was dotted with small farms interspersed with large expanses of forest. The first evening they reached a village at the edge of the Evening Mountains. They were treated with fanfare and a celebration. This was the chance for the village people to see and to impress their future ruler and her consort; rumors of the Great Wizard's abilities had spread like wildfire. Not the quiet trip that Alec wanted.

Two more days, two more towns. Then three more after that. Alec felt almost like a circus performer. They had the routine down. In each town, after they were formally greeted Alec would show off by lighting the town square for an evening of entertainment and socializing. He occasionally would fix some glaring problem in the town. In one town the water supply to the well had broken, and the water had to come from outside. Alec created an underground pipe so that the water could flow from a spring directly into the town center. In another place, Alec coated the steep roadway into the town with cobblestones so that it would have easier access during rain and snow.

As they moved further upriver, the villages became smaller and further apart.

"There will be no villages over the next two days," the lead rider advised them one morning. "We will be making camp for the next three nights."

They soon were approaching the moonward end of the valley, where the two mountain ranges came together. In the last place they visited, they were told of strange booms in the mountains – 'something to do with dragons' was the presumption. The booms were different from late-winter avalanches, the town elders said.

When they reached the end of the valley they camped along the edge of the mountains by a mountain stream. Alec and Erin sat by the edge of the stream as they ate – the cook had outdone herself in preparing their meal.

"Excellent," said Alec and Erin agreed. The cook beamed.

They slept well that night.

≈ ≈ ≈ ≈

The next morning their company broke camp in an orderly fashion and again made their way along the well-traveled road. About mid-day they were startled by a loud boom echoing through the mountains.

"What is that?!" said Erin.

"I don't know," said Alec. "It sounds like how blasting would sound in my country." He knew Erin did not know what 'blasting' was, or how it would sound, but he didn't explain. Instead, they stopped their wagon and listened. A short while later there was a second boom.

"We need to investigate," said Erin. "This isn't normal."

"I agree," said Alec.

"We can take a troop of – say – ten of our riders with us and leave the others here. It's a good spot to make camp," said Erin. "We've lost over half of the daylight this day, anyway, so we can camp here and ride off early on the morrow to investigate."

They halted their company, and Erin explained the change in plans to Thom, the lead rider. By the time they had finished setting up camp, they had heard two more of the strange booms in the mountains.

The next morning they were off early, with Erin leading her small band of riders into the mountains. They rode for the better part of an hour, making good progress up the slopes. The mountains soon became too steep for the trogus; although the trogus could lope for hours across an even plain, they were ill-suited for climbing.

"Let's leave our mounts here, with two riders to guard them, and hike on from here," Alec suggested. They dismounted, grabbed packs and weapons, and started making their way up the steep, rocky mountainside. By mid-day they came to a ridge that one of the guards estimated was about a quarter of the way into the range. So far that morning, they had heard only one boom. It was more distinct than the sounds from yesterday, but with all the echoes from the mountain peaks, it was very hard to pinpoint. They stopped to observe.

"Let me try to pull some dark energy to see if I can feel anything," Alec muttered to Erin. "There might be something in the distance." *Focus.* Nothing.

"Erin, you're better at this kind of stuff than I am. Use your ring and see if you can feel anything around us."

Erin felt for her ring. She pulled on its strength, as Alec had shown her. She could sense others around her – the aura of Alec and the eight guards blazed out at her. She could feel the other two guards and the trogus in the distance. Ahead she felt something. Erin frowned in concentration. She could feel a bear in her den with cubs. She felt a wild drung hiding under the ridgeline. She could feel the hyra in their caves waiting for night. Over the next ridge, she could also sense a large congregation of disturbances. *Those are people,* she thought. Also, she felt a single disturbance further along the ridgeline.

"I can feel a large collection of people," she said to Alec. "They are on the far side of the next ridge." She paused, still sensing. "Also, there is a single person just down the ridge from us. I think he is spying on us."

"We should go talk to him and ask what is going on, I would think," said Alec. Erin agreed.

They developed a simple plan. The main group would start forward while Erin and Alec would hide and wait. Erin could sense the observer and see his movements. They hoped the observer would not have counted the group size and would think everyone in the party was still together. The main group would continue to make noise and not try to cover their location at all. Then Erin and Alec could sneak up close to the spy and find out what was going on.

"No, my Princess, we cannot leave you unprotected," Thom said to her.

"I understand your concern, Thom, but if some of you stay with us, it will defeat our purpose. Go. Go on ahead as I have instructed you." The man looked uncertain. Erin laid her hand on his arm. "We'll whistle if we need you. Go!" The riders and Erin all used a series of whistles for battle communication, and each knew them well.

Alec was clueless about whistling but assumed that between his abilities and Erin's abilities they could take care of themselves, whistling or not.

The main group took off as planned and the two of them remained, crouched motionless behind a rock. Erin sensed the position of the lone individual.

"He is moving down," she said. "He is following our main group. We can move in behind him if we are quiet." They moved along the path that Erin indicated. She would occasionally stop to pinpoint the man's new location. "Shhh," she hissed at Alec. Erin was cat-quiet. Alec was trying hard but was somewhere around elephant-quiet.

After several minutes, Erin stopped, perplexed. "I think he knows we're following him. He may have heard us. He is trying to double back on us. We can cut him off if we move across his path." She considered their next moves. "There is no more advantage to silence." With that, she whistled a shrill blast. Sounds came from below as her riders reversed their course and started rapidly working their way toward the whistle.

"He's running," Erin said. "He suspects the whistle meant he was detected." Erin had the advantage of sensing his position. "He will come out in the draw below us in a bit." They waited.

As Erin had predicted, a man soon emerged from behind a rock outcrop and started to cross the little draw in front of them. He was dressed in a blue uniform; he wore a sword at his side and was carrying a short spear, the weapon of choice in these mountains.

"An Alderman!" Alec said softly to Erin. "That's the same uniform that the slavers wore."

"Stop," shouted Erin, as the man crossed the draw. The two of them stood up, and the man saw that he could not continue in the same direction without crossing their path. He started to turn the other direction but heard the riders coming from below. With both paths of escape blocked, he stopped, then drew his spear and charged towards Erin.

Since his first encounters with armed combat, when he rescued Erin by inventing maneuvers on the spot, Alec had thought a lot about how to handle this kind of situation. He let the lone man continue to charge toward Erin. Erin had drawn her sword, and it was shining in readiness.

The man closed half the distance to Erin. *Now!* thought Alec. *Focus.* Dark energy swirled, and the ground under the man's feet changed from rock to porous sand. He immediately slipped up to his knees into the sand and almost fell over with the change in momentum. But he held his balance and tried to pull his feet out. The sand was too deep for that. He pulled back his spear to throw it at Erin.

Focus, thought Alec.

The middle part of the spear transformed into a burst of smoke that dissipated into the air. The lone man lost his balance with the change in his spear, and he fell backward into the soft sand. The point of the spear, now attached to a short piece of shaft, dropped harmlessly near Erin.

"Very clever, oh Great Wizard," said Erin, knowing that she was pulling his leg.

The rest of Erin's riders arrived just as the man rolled over in the sand and was trying to draw his sword. Two of the women riders quickly secured him, pulled him from the sandy area, and drug him before Erin.

The captive snarled. "Let me free, and we won't be too harsh on you!"

Erin looked at him. "These are <u>my</u> lands, so being harsh on others is <u>my</u> chore, not yours." She spat in his direction. "Who are you and why are you here?"

"I am a fighter for the people of Alder! I am an Alderman," he said proudly. "Now let me go."

"He speaks truth," Erin muttered to Alec.

"Why are you here?" Alec asked, as brusquely as he could manage.

"None of your business. Let me go!"

"Who sent you?"

No answer.

"We aren't getting anywhere," said Alec to Erin. "In my country, torture is discouraged, but here anything seems to be allowed.

"Tell us the truth, or you will suffer," he said to the man.

"I can handle anything you can do," the Alderman said, sneering.

Focus. The little fingernail on the man's right hand caught fire and burned its way out. They could see the pain was intense for him. Erin's riders were impressed. They had never seen anything like this.

"I am going to do that to each one of your fingernails, one by one, if you don't tell the Princess what she wants to know," Alec told the man.

The intruder could see they were serious, and his expression dropped from hostility to resignation.

"That is better," said Erin. She could sense that he had mentally given up and was going to tell them whatever they wanted. "Why are you here?"

"Two of us were sent out this morning to scout ahead to make sure no one interrupted our work," the man grunted. "We saw you this morning as you started up the ridge. My partner went back to the main camp to tell the Captain. I stayed to watch you." He surreptitiously stuck his little finger in his mouth to ease the pain.

"What work are you doing in your camp?" Alec asked.

"We are building a road through the mountain."

"Why?"

"For our soldiers. Our military."

"For what?"

"I don't know."

"He speaks truth," said Erin.

Alec decided to try another line of questioning. "Where is Alder?"

"We have a base in the moonward part of the Grasslands."

"You are from there?"

"No, no; there is just a base there. No one is from there. I am from a land far away."

"How did you get from your land to the Grasslands?"

"I don't know – we just marched through a tunnel, and we were there."

Alec frowned. "That doesn't make any sense," he said.

"He speaks truth," said Erin, looking at Alec and shrugging her shoulders.

"How many of you are up here? At your camp here in the mountains?"

"About thirty soldiers and maybe two hundred slaves."

"Where is your camp?"

"It is about five els away, over the next ridge."

"Show us your camp," said Alec.

"That will take most of the remaining light today to get to their camp. Maybe we should go back and return tomorrow," said one of Erin's riders.

"No," said Erin. "It will take the same amount of time tomorrow to get there. Let's press on, at least to the top of the next ridge. Then we can decide what to do. I don't like being outnumbered three to one, so I am reluctant to go all the way to their camp, but we need to have a view of what is happening." Then she sent one of the riders back to relay the status to her base camp and bring some additional help tomorrow.

"Since they know we are here we don't need to be stealthy. Our friend can lead us to the top of the ridge," Alec said.

The riders started off toward the Alder camp, led by their captured soldier. They quickly moved up the next ridge, but as they reached the ridgetop, they heard a low growl and a dog emerged from the bushes – the kind that the Aldermen used to herd their captive slaves. The dog snarled at them and let out a high-pitched bark.

"It is calling the rest of the pack. We must wait," said their captive, clearly nervous. "Only its handler will give it permission to let us pass." He turned and glared at Erin's riders. "A dog pack can kill even this many armed men if you don't behave."

Erin looked at Alec with disgust. She remembered the role of the dogs in the slave camp, and knew that Alec did too.

"We aren't waiting," said Alec, and with that, the dog's eyes popped out and it flopped down in death. "Let's proceed." Startled, their captive moved on, not sure what Alec had done to the dog.

They walked now wary of other dogs coming for them. They encountered one other dog before the top of the ridge, but Alec quickly dispatched it. At the top of the ridge, they looked down at the valley below.

"Whew," exclaimed Alec, softly. The scene looked like a major highway construction project back in the U.S., but with no heavy equipment, only hand labor. "They are cutting quite a path through the mountains." There was a contingent of a few hundred slaves and some number of blue-uniformed troops. Alec could see where the rock face had been removed and the workers were using the loose rocks to build a berm across a small gulley. *They blasted the rock out,* thought Alec. *But how? These people are primitive – they don't have the explosives, equipment, or knowledge to do that!*

They could see that there was a general hubbub going on in the camp below, with Alder soldiers and slaves running about. Apparently the camp was preparing for their arrival.

Erin pointed to the next hill. "Two other people are hiding on that little rise," she told Alec. "Do you sense any death rods?"

Alec let his senses roam over the camp.

"No, I don't think they have any ammunition here. I can sense the blasting material they use to clear away the rock. That's what is making the big 'booms,'" he explained. "It's possible they have death rod ammunition close to it – I can't tell the difference between blasting supplies and ammunition – but that seems very unlikely. It would be dangerous for them to store the two that close together."

"I don't think it is smart to tackle them with this big an imbalance in troops, even with what we can do with your magic," said Erin.

Alec agreed with her. He had noticed that Erin was unconsciously assuming her natural role as head of the fighting force. Alec was happy to have her command her troops and make battle plans. He was content to be her Chief Wizard – he knew nothing about leading people or conducting warfare, and he could see Erin was good at it.

"Maybe there is something I can do to slow them a little," said Alec.

"What is that?" said Erin.

"They are using blasting material to cut their way through the rocks. I can sense it in that wagon." Alec pointed to a wagon parked on the edge of the camp. "It makes sense for it to be stored out away from everything else. I can set the wagon on fire. That will destroy the blasting material and keep them all busy for the night."

"Do it," said Erin.

Focus. Alec felt the dark energy. Within seconds a fire sprang up on the canvas top of the wagon.

After a few minutes, as smoke began to billow from the wagon, someone noticed the fire and started shouting. First, a couple of the soldiers ran towards the fire. Then they saw that the fire was beyond their ability to control and realized the consequences. Soldiers and slaves started scurrying to move everything to safety away from the burning wagon.

One of the soldiers whipped five slaves to start hauling water and throwing it on the fire. Then the soldier got out of the way. The slaves were doing a hopeless task, Alec thought. He had a terrible feeling about their fate. Then the first of the blasting material ignited, throwing burning brands and lighting fires throughout the camp. Four of the five slaves were consumed as the blasting material burned. Alec saw the fifth thrown across the camp from the force of a small blast, and lay on fire, burning. He felt sick.

"Let's pull back," said Erin. "You have slowed them for now. Tomorrow we will get reinforcements and see what we can do."

They pulled back to the first ridge and found a protected area for a camp. Erin sensed there were no watchers close to them. In the distance over the far ridgeline, they could see a dull orange glow from the burning Alder camp.

16 – The Alder Road

With the first light, Erin stirred. Erin had slept curled in Alec's arms – not nearly as comfortable as in their bed, but his body was comforting and warm. The group ate most of the remaining travel supplies they had packed yesterday, feeding some of the scraps to their captive. Erin could feel the rest of her riders working their way up the ridge. She sent a scout to meet them and bring them to her location.

We have eighteen riders plus Alec, thought Erin, *with more on the way.* Thom, her lead rider, had informed her the night before that he had the Queen's authorization to send for reinforcements if need be, and he had taken the liberty of sending for help to come as quickly as possible. Since the Queen hadn't mentioned this to Erin, she thought to herself, *Mother must think I have a knack for getting in trouble.* Then she added a postscript to her thought: *She might be right.*

"Do you detect anyone in our path?" Alec asked Erin.

"No, not between us and the next ridge."

They climbed the second ridge and returned to yesterday's observation point. The camp was a buzz of activity. Most of the wreckage from last night's fire had been cleaned up and work on the road had resumed. The bodies of the fallen slaves had been shoved to one side for scavengers to pick clean. The Alder soldiers were standing guard, on obvious alert.

"There is a person on the next ridge and two others in the woods below us," Erin said, after assessing the situation. "They are probably spying on us. The rest of the Alder soldiers and slaves are down at the camp.

"There is a big pack of dogs assembled by the camp," she added. "There may be twenty dogs in the pack." Erin crossed her arms and mulled over her options.

"This force is on our land and has only bad intentions. We need to destroy it, but I don't think we are in any hurry. We could wait for more help if we want."

Their bound captive stood nearby and overheard her comments. "The Aldermen will have help arrive before you can," he said. "We have a large force only a day's ride from here. Our Captain would have sent for reinforcements last night after you started the fire in our camp. Our soldiers will want to quash your annoyance, like swatting a small gnat." He puffed out his chest, boasting. "They can have more than a hundred men with several dog packs as well as many death rods here by tomorrow." He looked at Erin, calculating. He had slowly figured out that she was in charge, not Alec.

"Let me go," he said in an oily voice, "and I will put in a good word for you. Our Captain just might let you live, if you surrender now." He looked at Erin. When she ignored him, he added, "Our soldiers do not leave opposing fighters alive, so tomorrow your fate will be sealed. You will be dead. We didn't realize we were that close to pushing all the way through these mountains. When reinforcements arrive, they will put a death-rod post up here, and it won't matter how many troops you try to bring."

"He is speaking the truth as he sees it," said Erin to Alec. "If that is the truth, then this is our best time to fight. If we wait for more help, we will just be more outnumbered. We need a plan to split them, and then take them on piece by piece, so that we will have the advantage."

Neither Alec nor Erin said anything aloud about what Alec could do with gunpowder. That was a secret they wanted to keep in order to shield their advantage. Once the Aldermen leaders figured out what they could do, Alec knew they would develop some strategy to thwart future explosions.

Neither Erin, Alec, nor Thom could come up with a plan that would force the Alderman Captain to split his force. They decided instead that a direct approach was their best chance. Theland was not engaged in active hostilities with these people, so Erin decided to act inquisitively and use that as an excuse to allow her force to get closer to the camp. Erin and Alec discussed potential options; they had practiced different tactics during their respite in Theland in case a combat situation occurred sometime in their future — they just didn't expect that it would happen so soon.

Erin's riders tied their captive to a tree on the ridge and started down the slope. Since the opponents already knew of their presence, they hailed the Aldermen from the top of the ridge and descended noisily. They came to the bottom of the ridge and formed up to march into the Alder camp. Erin led the group with her riders arrayed in six rows behind her. Alec had wanted to be in front with Erin, but she insisted that Alec be strategically placed in the middle of the group where he could react to any surprise without being pressed for survival.

Erin could feel the enemies' disposition. All the enemy troops were arrayed in front of them. The Alder Captain was counting on his dogs for his initial attack. The dogs were deployed on both sides of them in four packs of five dogs each. Erin relayed the information to Alec and Alec was able to quietly relay the situation to the rest of the troops from his strategic location.

Good call putting me here in the middle, he thought to Erin. *If we didn't know about the dogs, we could have been surprised and distracted by the dogs and then totally dismantled with a frontal assault.*

Erin and her force marched up to where the Alder Captain and his troops were arrayed. She noticed they were armed with long swords as well as pikes and shields. Those were potent weapons when used by trained teams on open ground. The pike was not good in mountainous terrain or by mounted troops, but it was the superior weapon for the terrain here. Her people were not as heavily armed as the Aldermen. They all carried the short sword because it was more suited for use while riding trogus, as well as short spears. They did not have any shields. In an even fight, they would be at a disadvantage, and the Alder soldiers knew that. Erin could see that essentially all work had stopped in the camp. There were a lot of ragged-looking workers – slaves – and all of them were watching Erin's approach with trepidation. They knew that they were expendable if a fight broke out.

Erin came five paces in front of the Alder Captain.

"I am Princess Erin of Theland," she announced. "This is my land. What are you doing in my land?"

"Your land. Pah! This land was empty!" retorted the Captain. "This land has been claimed by the great Lord Alder as his land! We are making a trail through it for the benefit of our Lordship."

Lots of deception in that, thought Erin.

"You may agree to be servants of Lord Alder," the Captain continued, "and we will allow you the privilege of serving his needs. Otherwise, I must ask you to depart our land; although you may not survive, as you are intruders in Lord Alder's realm." The Captain looked menacingly at Erin.

"You may start serving Lord Alder by providing us with workers for our road," he said. "We use up about fifty workers a week, so you can provide us with replacements until our road is finished. Mostly men please. We use them a lot faster than women. But we will take some women," he said looking at Erin. She could sense his thoughts about her, and why he wanted some women.

"This is my land," Erin repeated, without wavering. "I command that you stop building your road and leave immediately." Erin could be very imperious when she wanted to be.

Erin had a tactical advantage. She could sense precisely when the Captain decided to quit talking and launch his attack; therefore, she could cue Alec to respond even as the Captain was giving the signal. Alec had called this his 'stealing the snap count' strategy based on some game he knew; Erin thought his game made no sense but understood the meaning of his phrase.

Now. Erin felt the Captain's decision and cued Alec, who went into action just as the dogs were being released.

Focus, and he created three small golden spheres about ten feet above the heads of the Aldermen. Alec carefully spaced the three spheres in a triangular array over the middle of the Alder troops. *Probably don't need such precision,* he thought, *but, oh well, what good is it to be a Wizard if you can't do it right.*

The three spheres scavenged the neutrons and protons from the local air to conserve physical properties, which in turn created a vacuum. Surrounding air flowed into the vacuum from above, gathering speed. The infill air hit the ground and rebounded upward taking a cloud of dust with it. The resulting whirlwind knocked the Aldermen to the ground and then picked them up and tossed them around like sticks.

Alec was pleased with himself. He had tested this back in Theland, and it had taken him many tries before he figured out how big to make the spheres so that he could affect the enemy troops underneath but not Erin's riders. He hadn't been sure it would work in practice. Looking at the results, he could tell it had.

Now, time for Step Two. Alec had no love for the killer dogs. Having seen the levels of savagery that the dogs were trained to pursue he felt no inhibitions about eliminating these animals – these dogs had everything but brutality beaten out of them. *Focus.* All the dogs collapsed, eyes bulging out and boiling blood spattering.

Now it was Erin's turn. He gave her the mental signal. *Go.*

She whistled to her riders. They smoothly broke into three teams and ran towards the disarray of the Aldermen, taking on the now-scattered soldiers with organized precision. In a mass battle, the pike and shield were a better weapon, but a single pike wielded against a trained team was no match. The

Aldermen were fighting singly and ineffectively, and Erin's troops were quickly slaughtering them.

The Alder Captain looked at the disarray about him, saw Erin's riders coming at him, and drew his sword. Erin stepped forward to engage him. He took a soft swing at Erin. *Too bad for him,* thought Alec. *No one fights at anything less than their best and survives against Erin.* He thought of all the extra practice she had put in over the winter months.

Alec's thought snapped back to the present. The Captain's sword stroke snaked towards Erin. She knew that he thought since she was merely a girl, she needn't be taken seriously. Erin's sword flashed as the side lit up, distracting the Captain. His sword hand flinched, and the big blade's trajectory changed slightly – enough to leave Erin an opening. Her blade flicked again and again, and a broad gash appeared across the Captain's throat. With a gurgling sound, he collapsed to the ground.

Good girl, thought Alec, *you used some of the tricks I built into the sword.* They had spent many weeks converting her sword into a perfect weapon. It still glowed when Erin used it and the tiny crystal that lit the blade also continually sharpened the blade so that it always had a razor edge.

Alec watched the battle progress. The last handful of the Aldermen soldiers had regained a semblance of organization and squeezed into a narrow spot between two rocks where the only attack against them would be frontal. Erin and her riders turned towards the soldiers.

Time for the heavy artillery, Alec thought towards Erin. Erin nodded in agreement. That was another of Alec's favorite sayings. Even after Alec had explained it, she still didn't understand what 'artillery' was, or why it was needed, or why it was heavy, but she understood the meaning of the expression.

Focus. Dark energy swirled and acted.

The middle section of the pike of the first soldier turned to smoke, and the point fell to the ground in front of his feet with a soft plop! In rapid succession, the other soldiers' pikes also disintegrated, leaving the men holding stubbed-off sticks. The pike-men discarded their useless weapons and drew their swords. Now the situation had changed. Long swords in a tight setting with shields designed for pike work were poor weapons against the short spear. Erin's riders made quick work of the Alder soldiers. The first five men fell and the last two surrendered.

Erin's troops were victorious. Alec looked with wonder at his Consort. *She truly is a warrior princess! This is what she was born for.*

≈ ≈ ≈ ≈

Erin, Alec, and Thom assessed their situation in the aftermath of the battle. Four of their riders had been killed. Two others were badly injured. Some of the other troops had minor injuries that wouldn't impact their fighting ability.

Alec knew that he didn't have the skill with dark energy to heal serious injuries. Although he suspected that it could be used to heal serious wounds, he had tried and failed on a couple of times, unable to effectively stem the suffering. He knew he could use dark energy to eliminate infections, however, thus saving a lot of lives from complications of minor wounds. He helped the others bandage the injured riders and make them as comfortable as possible.

They had captured two soldiers, four dog-handlers, and ten construction overseers. Additionally, there were about two hundred construction workers – slaves – as well as ten camp staff. Alec thought he recognized a few of the workers as part of the group of captive slaves he had seen on the Grasslands.

They needed as much information as they could accumulate before proceeding further. Alec and Erin decided to interrogate the Aldermen while some of Erin's riders would talk to each of the workers. However, the Alder soldiers didn't add much to what they had already learned. They were troops committed to someone called 'Lord Alder.' Most of them were recruited mercenaries, in it for the money. They had come from different places and then appeared in the Grassland. They did confirm that a significant army had been amassed on the Upper Grasslands – the soldiers thought the army was moving towards the mountain passes into Gott. An Alder side-force was only a day away; the Captain had sent a messenger yesterday to request backup assistance.

Alec felt that they had a better chance of learning about the blasting project if he interrogated the Alderman's construction foreman instead of the soldiers. "What is this project that you are working on?"

"The Aldermen hired us to make a path through the mountains. I really don't know why," the man answered.

Truth, thought Erin to Alec.

"So you don't know what it is to be used for?"

"No," the man answered, clearly concerned that if he didn't give full and complete answers he would be beheaded on the spot. "I have no idea why. It doesn't seem to be a reasonable size – it's not wide enough to move an entire army into your land, if that's what they have in mind. But they are going to a lot of trouble to make it. We supposed that it would be used to either provide a secondary path for some planned attack or resupply for a future battle."

"Where does it start?" asked Erin. "Who wants to build a road into my land?"

"I don't know where it starts. I was brought onto the job after the last foreman was executed, a couple of weeks ago. The Aldermen hired me, for a good price considering the dangers, and I joined them in the Grasslands." The man cowered before Erin.

"The Aldermen are hard taskmasters. The path was supposed to be finished three weeks ago, but the terrain is difficult and the workers got behind. I think that's why they did away with the last foreman. An incentive to the other workers to catch up. Captain drives us unmercifully to speed things along. But we don't have enough workers – we need more slaves. Between them dropping dead from exhaustion, and accidents, we are losing seven or eight workers a day." He looked up at Erin, and at Alec, to see if there was any sympathy for his hard lot.

"Tell me about this blasting material – the stuff that goes 'boom,'" Alec asked. "Where did you get it, and how do you know what to do with it?"

"It is a magic power, and it is forbidden to talk about it," the man said, eager to share his secrets. "There is one Alderman who gives it to us, back at the main camp on the Grasslands, and he said it was magic and to use it only in the way he taught us. He showed us how to use it."

"Where did it come from?" Alec asked.

"I don't know, my lord," the man said, shrugging. "Where it came from, what it is made of, I have no idea. They told us to be careful with it. It must be precious, because they measure it out to us very carefully and we have to account for every pouchful. After seeing what happened yesterday, when our wagon caught afire, I can see why they warned us to be careful." His eyes darted back and forth nervously. "I am sure that the loss of the entire wagon-

191

load of magic powder yesterday will not be viewed favorably. But that was not my fault. There was nothing I could do after the fire started."

"And the Aldermen. Their Captain said they serve Lord Alder. Who is he?"

"I do not know, my lord. They speak of him reverently, but I think that very few have met him. He must have great power."

After they dismissed the foreman, who was very willing to be led away in chains if it meant his life would be spared, Erin's riders reported on the results of their interrogations. As expected, the workers were slaves, captured in some slave roundup or another. They came from lots of places; many were from villages on the Grasslands. They feared to stay in the Alder camp, and they feared to flee. Their backgrounds ranged from farmers to laborers to merchants to an itinerant peddler bard.

The last one interested Alec and he asked them to bring him to talk to them.

"Were you at a little village called Cantin when you were captured?" Alec asked.

"No," the peddler said. "Do you know of Cantin? I was at Cantin when the slavers came, but I escaped their notice and made it back to my peddler-wagon, camped outside the village. But," he stopped and spread his hands. "My companion, my lady friend, was not there. I guess the slavers took her or she ran away. The next day she had not returned, so I headed down the road to the next village. By pure bad luck the very next day I encountered another raid – they captured my wagon, absconded with my wares, and took me as a slave."

"Was your consort named Lily?" Alec asked.

"Yes, that was her name," the peddler said with surprise, "but she wasn't my consort. Do you know her? She was some country girl who wanted to leave home, so she linked up with me to get away from her village. She was good in bed and useful around camp, but it was just a passing affair. Why do you ask? Have you seen her?"

"Yes," Alec said, "we ran into her in our travels."

"Was she all right? I hope she is doing okay. She was a nice enough girl. I needed someone to fill my bed, and she was willing."

"She is doing well," Alec answered.

"Well, that's a relief. Now," the peddler said with a sly grin, "I have in mind seeing if that chunky little kitchen girl in this camp will come with me." He looked at Erin. "You are going to let us go, aren't you?"

Erin nodded in affirmation.

The peddler continued, without prompting, "That little kitchen girl seemed to have always made the soldiers happy, and I need some of that right now. You know they kept the best girls for themselves and just had two or three girls for us slaves. There was such a long line, and the girls always seemed so tired and beat-up that it was hard to get much satisfaction."

"I think Lily will do just fine without you," chimed in Erin, dismissing the peddler.

With a bow and a mumbled word of appreciation, the peddler backed away from Erin and headed over towards the woman he had mentioned.

17 – Winding Pass

The next morning Erin and Alec met with their team to make plans.

"First, we need to close off this new road, before more of these Aldermen see fit to invade our country," Erin said. "Is there a way you can do that, my Great Wizard?"

From where they were sitting, they could see a large rock overhanging the new roadway, a few hundred paces away. Alec created several holes underneath the rock; finally, it came loose and slowly started moving down the slope. It picked up speed as it tumbled, releasing more rocks in an avalanche of boulders and dust pouring over the roadway. By the time the dust cleared they could see that much of the mountainside had tumbled down and created a rubble field across several hundred arns of the trail.

"I think that will make that road unusable for some time," said Alec.

"Yes, I think we have kept them from using this trail," said Erin, nodding in agreement. "It will be weeks before they can clear this blockage. By then we can put some savvy foresters in the mountains. They will be able to harass and stop any crew if they decide to try again. Even if the Aldermen bring their death rods, in this rocky terrain they will be of limited use and our people should be able to keep them from rebuilding their road."

"They don't seem to have a large supply of guns ... death rods ... and they seem to be using them sparingly. But – I wonder what else they have in mind," Alec said thoughtfully. It was apparent to both Alec and Erin that some major battle was brewing, and they would be drawn into it.

"For now," Erin said, "our immediate task is to determine what to do with all these people here in this camp. We can't take them with us. There are too many of them. We haven't enough supplies, and the nearby villages won't be able to handle this many people." After some discussion, they decided that they would let the slaves go free and take the others back to Freeland City as prisoners. They gathered the Aldermen, their camp staff, and their slaves to tell them their decision.

"You are on my land illegally, working for a power that is hostile to my people," said Erin to the slaves, "but I believe that it is not your fault. You did not have control over the actions that brought you here. I am going to allow you your freedom." A low murmur rippled through the crowd. "We will divide the available food and distribute it among you. We will also let you have any extra weapons that are here. When that is done, before this evening falls, you are free to choose whatever path you want. If you want to leave, leave before the sun has set. You will have free passage for the next week. After that, you will be arrested for trespass. If you decide to stay in my land, you must tell my lead rider Thom of your choice before sundown; you must then report to the authorities in the village nearest to this spot and show you have useful skills. If you do not report, you will be arrested for trespass. If any of you cause any trouble, you will be punished severely. This is my word as the Princess of Theland."

The meeting slid into details like when the slaves would get their ration of food and who would get the weapons. Erin let her riders address those issues.

Erin could sense that about half of the freed slaves were happy to be released, and the rest were fearful that they were being left in the wilderness to die. She could do nothing about those fears. They had been brought here by the Aldermen with the expectation they would all die working on the road. It was likely that some had outdoor skills and could survive the trek through the mountains to their homes, but others not so skilled would have a harder time and might succumb before they escaped the mountains. However, Erin was giving all of them a chance for life that they would not otherwise have.

Thom warned the departing slaves there probably would be another force of Aldermen coming up the road from the Grasslands and they should exit through the woods. About half, including the peddler and his new woman friend, seemed to take their advice. The rest chose to use the road for their escape.

Thom was bothered by their choice to cling to the roadway. "The Aldermen will capture them, and then the Aldermen will know what happened. We need to round them up and kill them if they don't go through the mountains."

Erin thought for a second.

"No," she said. "The slaves won't know anything more than the obvious — a force came out of the mountains, destroyed the camp, and left with prisoners. Besides, if the Aldermen do recapture them, it will give them more people to feed and take care of, and it will slow them down while they recapture the fools."

Erin's riders tied the captured soldiers and staff together to walk them over the mountain. There was a sense of urgency to it all since they knew the Alderman reinforcement force would probably arrive early the next day, and they wanted to be well away from the area before then. They gave the freed people three hours to receive their supplies; then Alec set all the Aldermen's wagons ablaze. The freed slaves were very unhappy about this event, but Erin didn't want anything useful left in the camp, or tempt the freed slaves to hang around and use the wagons for shelter.

Late in the day, Erin's band started back towards their base camp at the bottom of the mountain. Just before dark, they came to the place where they had left the Alder scout. The scout was no longer tied where they had left him; blood was spattered everywhere. They found his body about fifty arns away, half eaten.

"It looks like the hyra got him," said one of the riders.

Alec was bothered by the fact that he had left a man tied up and defenseless against the threats of the wilderness. "They ate him," he said to Erin, shaking. "He was alive, and they ate him."

Erin took it in stride. "He was our enemy. This way we won't have to feed another prisoner or guard him." She shrugged her shoulders.

They spent the night on the ridge away from the man's body.

It was slow going the next day with the string of captive Aldermen. It took until almost evening before they reached their base camp and their trogus and wagons. A force of another twenty riders had arrived earlier in the day at their camp and had been making plans to enter the mountains in the morning. They were relieved to see Erin and her returning riders. Thom welcomed the replacement riders: the fresh faces brought news from home, replaced some of the battle-weary people, cared for the wounded, provided appropriate departing ceremonies for the fallen, and replenished equipment and supplies.

≈ ≈ ≈ ≈

"What do we do now?" said Erin. "We have discovered a formidable intruder, the Alder, building a road in our mountains from the Grasslands, leading towards the center of our country. We hear a rumor that there is a large army massing in the Grasslands on the other side of the Evening Mountains, heading towards the mountain passes into Gott. We don't know how big the army is, what its intentions would be, or even where it is heading."

"How many passes are there through the Evening Mountains?" Alec asked Thom. "Is it easy to cross them?"

"No; the Evening Mountains are very rugged, and largely uninhabited. There are very few ways across them," the lead rider answered. "The best pass is the distant one in Gott, Raner Pass. There is also a small pass just across our border that both lands use, called Winding Pass. The road through the mountains is very steep and narrow; it is acceptable for small merchant wagons, but would be difficult to move an army through. But merchants and mercenaries like it because it is a week shorter travel into Gott than Raner pass."

"Would the Alder death rods and explosives change the conditions?" asked Alec.

No one knew.

"Then it seems like we need to take a little trip to Winding Pass to understand what the Alder forces are doing," Erin said. "Thom, I will need a force to accompany me, with you as lead rider, of course."

That evening Erin prepared an accounting of the events for the Queen, and sent a night rider to carry it back to Freeland City by fast dispatch. She also requested the Queen to provide a force to keep the mountains clear of the Alder and to send additional riders to the border to be ready in the likely case that they were needed at one of the passes. Erin knew that given her group's slow pace, they wouldn't hear back from the Queen until they reached the Gott border.

In the morning, Thom directed a wagon contingent to accompany the wounded back to Freeland City. The Alder prisoners would be taken to the nearest village jail before transport to the City to mete justice. With the deaths in the battle and the injuries, they were back to their original number of twenty riders.

A small number for a big battle, Alec thought, but then decided it might be right-sized for their scouting mission.

Erin led them moonward, toward the Winding Pass just over the Gott border. At each town, the people turned out to greet the Princess, just like the beginning of their trip; the battle with the Alder seemed a world away from the gay festivities. After the third village, the main road took a large turn towards the direction of morning. A smaller road branched off and turned back in the direction of the Evening Mountains. A signpost with a weathered board pointed towards the smaller road, with a single glyph in Theland's runes.

"What does it say?" asked Alec.

"It says, 'Winding Pass, this way,'" answered Thom. "People around here call this 'Winding Pass Road.'"

"Originally, I intended that for our tour of Theland, we would follow the main road and start down the other side of our realm," explained Erin. "However, if we go investigate Winding Pass, we need to take this road. The mountains on this side of Winding Pass are a day's ride. Then it is another day to the pass." She turned to her lead rider. "We used to have a small garrison on our border on this side of the pass. I assume the garrison is still there."

"I have not heard anything that would indicate it is not, my Lady."

Alec and Erin had both agreed they had no other choice but to continue with their mission, dangerous as it seemed. They knew it would pain the Queen for Erin to again be in harm's way, but they had to discover if there was a real threat to Theland. If they waited for someone else to do the scouting and return with reports, weeks could pass, and it might be too late.

However, it took two days to reach the border garrison. There had been recent rains and the path was in bad shape. Alec had been forced to use dark energy to improve the way in two places to be able to get the wagons through. Two of the wagons broke down on the rough rocky terrain; both were readily fixed but caused delays. They discussed leaving the wagons and moving ahead, but they didn't have enough drungs to carry their food and supplies. They arrived at the mountain garrison late in the afternoon. Messengers had gone ahead to announce their arrival.

The garrison was smaller than Alec was expecting. It was a crude stone structure built on the steep side of the mountain and was more a way-station than a fort. A crusty officer, Sergeant Urgan, ran the garrison. He had been there for ten years. Since this was a quiet and out-of-the-way spot, he hadn't expected any military action for the rest of his career and was intending to retire soon to the nearby village. The garrison was staffed with twenty people. Ten of them were riders, and the other ten were clerks that monitored the traffic through the pass. Alec thought that the ten that could ride looked like they were out of shape and hadn't practiced with a weapon for months.

Sergeant Urgan came forward and greeted them when they reached the garrison.

"Welcome Princess Erin," he said with a flowery bow. "This is a rare honor. We welcome you to our humble quarters. Our accommodations are minimal, and our food is worse."

"Thank you for your kind words and loyal service to Theland," said Erin. "But we do not mean to intrude upon your hospitality. We will use our wagons for lodging. We have food and cooks, but they would like to use your kitchens instead of our field setup."

"That would be fine," said the Sergeant, with some relief showing in his voice. They set up camp, and Erin's cooks fed everyone, including the garrison staff. After eating, they sat down with the Sergeant.

Sergeant Urgan cleared his throat.

"Princess, we are most honored to have you here, but I am sure that your visit comes with a reason. All I know is that a messenger came yesterday and said you would be arriving. He gave no details about the purpose of your visit."

"Good," said Erin. "We are trying to keep our intentions quiet." She briefly described what she knew of the hostile situation with the Aldermen in the mountains and their reconnaissance mission.

"That might explain some things," said Sergeant Urgan. "It has been unusually quiet here this year. We haven't had any traffic for almost a month. Usually this time of year we get several wagons a day – merchants and whatnot. We were wondering if something had happened in the pass that blocked it, like a rockfall or wash-out."

"Did you send a scout out to check?" asked Alec.

"No, no, keeping the pass clear is not our role. The pass is on the Gott side of the border. Keeping it open is their job. Our job is to monitor people that come in or go out of Theland."

"Do you have anyone that is familiar with the pass area?" asked Erin.

"Yes, two of my men are very familiar with Winding Pass. They grew up near these mountains and know every rock in them."

"How are the roads beyond here?" asked Alec.

"They stay about the same – they can be difficult but passable for wagons like yours. The border is a half a day away, and the pass is another day. Once you are through the pass, and down the other side, the land opens quickly into the Gott side of the Grasslands."

"We want to investigate what is happening at Winding Pass. We will be leaving in the morning to head there. If possible, we would like to take your two men who know the mountains and understand the conditions."

"I don't know if I can authorize that, Princess," said the older man, rubbing his fingers on the side of his nose.

"Our Princess has Queen Therin's writ of authorization," Thom assured him.

"Well, then. If you want them under the Queen's authorization, I will gladly do it." He turned to an aide to have the news relayed to his mountain men. He continued, "There is a Gott fortress just beyond the pass. Sometimes they can get upset if our people show up uninvited. Should I send a messenger to inform them you are coming?"

"That would be a good idea," said Erin. "Also, I will need you to send one of your riders with a message for the Queen to advise her of our progress. And of your able assistance." Sergeant Urgan smiled, pleased to receive royal recognition.

≈ ≈ ≈ ≈

The next morning they were off towards Winding Pass. The garrison had been a disappointment to Alec. He had been hoping for more support regarding both personnel and organization than was there. This part of Theland was secluded from the remainder of the realm and had been at peace for a long time; even though Theland was a war-like society, it did not have a large, organized military force.

By mid-day, they reached the edge of Theland. "We are now in Gott," Erin said to Alec, pointing to the low stone boundary cairn.

They had spent the morning in the last village in Theland talking with the locals to get a better feel for the countryside. The more people they conversed with, the more concerned they became. Normally this was a busy trade route, but not now. The locals could not remember a year with so little traffic at this season. The inn-keeper was most upset; his income depended on travelers stopping at his establishment.

About mid-morning the next day they reached a fork in the road. One way led towards the heartland of Gott, and the other towards Winding Pass and the Gott fortress. They turned moonward towards the pass.

Erin would periodically stop and use her ring to sense ahead as they approached the pass. At one stop she motioned to Alec.

"I sense something. There are many people not far ahead of us. They seem distraught."

Erin called her lead rider. "Thom! Put up the banner of Theland. We don't want to approach them unannounced." Thom unfurled the Princess' banner, and one of the riders carried it in front.

Alec also checked to see if he could sense any gunpowder; he didn't detect any.

They came around the next bend and encountered a lone sentry. "Halt!" he said. "Who are you?"

The lead rider rode forward, holding the banner. "We ride with Princess Erin of Theland. We are a contingent from Queen Therin of Theland."

"And what is your purpose?"

"We have come to check on our trade routes with Gott. We want to see how much traffic is entering our country through this pass."

The sentry laughed. "There is no traffic through the pass! We have lost it to the Alders!"

Erin rode forward to the front of their party.

"We wish to confer with one of your magistrates, or officers, regarding the situation befalling our trade routes. Who is in charge here?"

"Captain Levor is in charge."

"Where is he?"

"He is at our temporary base. It is about two els forward."

"May we have passage to go to him?"

The sentry thought about it. "I have no orders to stop those who would help us. Are you here to help?"

We don't know, thought Erin. "We are not here to oppose," she said.

The sentry pondered this for a few moments. "I guess that is good enough reason. I will escort you to our Captain."

They followed the sentry until they came to a wide place in the road where the Gott captain had set up his base. The sentry turned them over to a lieutenant who escorted Erin, Alec, and Thom to the Captain.

Captain Levor, a slender middle-aged man with a worried frown, strode quickly from his quarters to address Alec.

"If you are here to help, I fear you are too late," he said, with none of the usual Gott pleasantries.

Alec was not used to being identified as the person in charge.

"No," he blurted, "we aren't here to help – we came to investigate the lack of traffic through the pass." Sensing that the Captain was on a different wavelength, he continued. "We also heard a rumor of a hostile army on the Grasslands."

The Captain slammed his fist into his other hand in frustration. "It is no longer on the plains! That wretched army is here in Winding Pass! We lost our fortress three days ago. We are retreating! We have no way to slow them down, so as they advance we retreat."

Then the Captain remembered his place and his customary manners.

"Greetings from the People of Gott. I am Captain Levor. You must pardon my lack of courtesy, but we are under great stress," the Captain said. "And to whom do I have the pleasure of addressing?"

Erin took her place by Alec's side under the banner of Theland.

"Greetings, my friend and ally, Captain Levor," she said in her formal style. "I am Princess Erin of Theland, Heir Presumptive, and this is my Consort, Alec. We come in peace. We carry a message of goodwill from my mother, Queen Therin, and hope to continue our friendship with your people."

"And your purpose here in Gott?"

"As my Consort said, we have come on a mission to assess the situation regarding our trade routes from your land to our land, through this mountain pass. My party includes twenty riders, three wagons, and our support staff."

"Welcome, Princess Erin, and your most esteemed Consort. Unfortunately, my hospitality is limited."

"Tell us what happened," said Alec, tired of the formalities.

"It has been a disaster," Captain Levor said, frowning. "Last winter we learned of an army from a new people, called 'The Alder,' forming on the Upper Grasslands. Since that time, they have been advancing through the Grasslands, sweeping through villages and raiding our merchants. We understand that the main army is heading toward Raner Pass. A small force was deployed toward this pass. They probably intend to seal off Winding Pass to prevent a flanking attack.

"We sent forces to defend both passes. Major Debor was dispatched to defend this pass. He had two companies under him. I led one company, and Captain Smink led the other. We made it to our Winding Pass Fortress without a problem. The Aldermen were in the Grasslands. We had two hundred troops, and they had around the same number." Captain Levor looked down at his dusty boots and shook his head. Alec sensed the officer's dismay at the events he was recounting.

"The Alder were camped out on the Grasslands," the Captain continued, again looking at Alec. "Our instructions were to hold the fortress, but the Major wanted to make a name for himself. He thought we were better equipped than any motley group from the Grasslands. Major Debor decided we would assemble and attack the Alder at dawn with a cavalry charge. Our numbers were about equal, and our training should have carried the day for us. We were ready at dawn. Everything was going right. We charged them. The sun was at our back. They didn't look prepared for us. It looked like we would ride through them, break them, and rout them.

"Then their death rods started. We didn't know of death rods before that skirmish. Now we have learned what other unfortunate men have learned before us. Have you heard of the death rods? They are the curse of the dragon's breath, and no one can escape their deadly teeth! The Aldermen had many death rods that they used on our troops. We lost almost half of our force, and both Major Debor and Captain Smink died in the charge." The Captain spit in disgust. "We retreated with our surviving men in disarray."

"Then what happened?" asked Alec.

"I tried to form defensive positions in the pass," the Captain answered. "I thought we could retreat to our fortress at the pass. But they found high places on the hills on both sides of the fortress. Anytime we went outside, even into the fortress courtyard, their death rods would kill. They can kill from a great distance – further than our most experienced men can hurl a spear."

"Did they move upon your soldiers? How did they engage your men?" asked Thom.

"They have a simple but effective strategy," the Captain answered. "They find a high point and position their death rods there. Then they move their troops forward. When we come out to fight they use their death rods to destroy us.

"After we retreated to the Winding Pass Fortress, they attacked the fortress gate. As we tried to defend the gate, the death rods would kill us. We retreated from the fortress three days ago. Every position we take, they position their death rods such that we cannot defend. Now all I can do is pull back every time they move forward." Captain Levor ended his recounting of their fight. Everyone was silent for a few moments, absorbing the information.

"So," Captain Levor said, breaking the silence, looking at Alec. "Can you help us?"

"My Consort can destroy the death rods," said Erin, trying to assert herself as the leader of her troops.

"How?" asked the Captain, warily, eyeing Alec.

"He is a Great Wizard," said Erin.

The Captain almost laughed. "Hah! There are no Great Wizards," he said, and then realized Alec was her Consort. He turned back to Alec.

"How can you destroy death rods?"

"In my land, they are called 'rifles,'" Alec said. "They are a mechanical object, not magical. They require special fuel to do their job. I can destroy that fuel from a distance," Alec said evenly.

The Captain looked skeptical.

He is not convinced, Alec thought to himself. He had discovered that special-effects made him seem more credible, so he snapped his fingers and his staff lit with the brightness of the sun. With a second snap, he put the light out.

The Captain gasped, and some of his men stepped back in fright. The demonstration convinced the Captain that Alec was more than he seemed.

"Can you show us how to defeat the death rods? Or help us?"

"Those decisions are up to my Consort, Princess Erin," said Alec. The Captain turned to look at Erin.

"We are not prepared to do battle on behalf of Gott," Erin said carefully. "But, these trade routes are important for our country. We agree that they must be protected." She weighed the situation before her. "Although we are sympathetic to the distress of our long-time ally, the Gott, your battles are not our battles. But in this situation, I understand that if we do not help you, the Aldermen will have an entryway into our country through yours. We will do what we can. But we don't have a great force of riders with us."

Good girl, thought Alec. *You sound like a Queen.* Then he spoke to the Captain.

"If we can get them to bring their death rods out of hiding, I can destroy the death rods."

"How do we get them to do that?" the Captain asked.

"We need to set a trap for them," Alec said. "Can you set up a defensive position where they have an obvious high point to use to shoot at us?"

"Yes, about an el ahead there is a good defensive position. We haven't used it because it is open on one side, and we knew that the Aldermen could scale a peak on that side and use their death rods against us. We would be open to the death rods if we tried to fight there. But if we use that to set your … trap … what is the risk to my men?"

"Of course, there is a risk to your men," said Alec, "but what is the risk to your men, and your country, if we do not stop the Alder? Isn't it worth the lesser risk to try?"

Captain Levor considered this and finally agreed to try Alec's plan. The next morning, the Captain moved his forces forward to the defensive position to implement the plan and bait the trap.

Leaving their mounts behind, Alec and Erin took five of their riders and began hiking towards the highest crag. They looked for a point where Alec could see the death rod position. Alec had determined that a line-of-sight was essential in order to use dark energy to disable the rifles' ammunition. If he couldn't see the general locale of an object, he couldn't ignite it.

They reached the crag after a short climb. They could see the Captain's troops on the road below. Captain Levor was expecting the Aldermen to advance towards the point later in the day, and had arrayed his troops such that the Aldermen would have a bitter fight taking the narrow point. The Captain planned to hold the point but knew if the Aldermen deployed their death rods he would have to quickly pull back his troops.

Erin used her ring to sense the locations of the Alder troops. She could feel that they had started to move and that a small group was making its way up the slope.

"They will come out on the rocks just ahead of our position," said Erin quietly. "Are you ready?"

Alec nodded his head.

They saw blue-uniformed soldiers emerge from the rocks and walk towards the overlook. Two of the men carried the death rods. Two others carried boxes of ammunition. The others were wary guards with hands on their spears and swords.

Alec motioned for everyone to get down.

Focus.

Suddenly one of the ammunition boxes burst open in a frenzy of explosions. The wooden sides of the box were shattered into splinters and thrown in every direction. Alec and Erin peered over the edge of their rock hiding place.

Four of the Aldermen appeared to be down, including one of the death rod bearers. Two others were nursing bleeding wounds.

"Go!" said Alec. This was Erin's part.

Erin and her five riders quickly reached the Aldermen. The soldiers saw them coming and drew their weapons. Erin made quick work of the first Alder with a couple of quick slashes. Her troops engaged two of the others. The last Alder soldier decided to run and started down the slope. He made it around the first rock before Erin saw him escaping and followed down the slope.

The man saw he was being pursued and turned to fight Erin. They traded sword blows back and forth for a few moments. Then Erin twisted to his right side. The Alderman turned to counter her move. She stepped back to the other side, and the man tripped on a rock as he tried to again counter Erin's attack. She seized the opportunity and finished him off with a quick slash, her sword glowing.

Erin rejoined the others. Her troops had finished off the other fighters.

"That takes care of that," she said, sheathing her sword.

Alec looked around the site where the Aldermen had dropped their weapons until he found both rifles. One had been damaged in the explosion, but the other was intact.

"Look," he said in wonder. "This gun was made in my homeland. This writing is English."

"Wizard runes," said Erin softly, tentatively touching the rifle with an outstretched finger. Her riders stayed well away from the piece.

One of the riders looked down at the pass. "The enemy is starting to engage the Gott troops," she reported with urgency.

They could see that a contingent of Alder troops was starting into the narrows. A few men peered upwards at the rock overlook, obviously expecting help from their death rod team any time.

"Let's show them something," said Alec. He examined the rifle in his hand, a high-caliber gun with a scope. He opened the remaining ammo box and took out a shell, put the shell into the magazine of the rifle, aimed it at the Alder forces, and pulled the trigger. The rifle recoiled, and there was a splash of dust and rock at the feet of the advancing Alder forces. Erin and her troops had never seen a death rod before; Erin gasped and held her hand over her ears, and two of her riders hit the ground in fear.

"I didn't know you could do that!" she exclaimed. "You made the death rod speak!"

"Missed," said Alec. "Give me another shell!" The second try was a success, and one of the Alder soldiers collapsed with a grunt. Erin continued to take bullets from the ammunition box, one by one, and cautiously hand them to Alec, quickly putting her hands over her ears after each one. After the first shot, Alec was routinely hitting the Alder guards, who were now swarming about trying to figure out why the death rod was mowing them down. *Just like shooting prairie dogs back home,* Alec thought.

At the sound of the first shot, Captain Levor started to pull back his troops. However, by the fourth shot, he realized that something was different – all the death rod shots were landing among the Alder troops and taking them down.

"Hold," he shouted to his men.

Three more bullets tore into the Alder force, and the Alder soldiers decided they had enough. A few broke and ran in panic. Seeing some of his soldiers fleeing, the Alder leader ordered a pullback of the remaining soldiers.

Alec slung the rifle over his shoulder. One of the riders carried the ammunition box, as they made their way back to the Captain Levor.

≈ ≈ ≈ ≈

By evening the Gott soldiers and Erin's riders were back at the base, and after their dinner reviewed what each had done in the afternoon's battle.

"To protect our land – and yours – we need to retake the pass," said Captain Levor. "And to do that we need to retake our fortress." He cleared his throat. "I hear you captured the death rod," he said to Alec. "May we see it?"

"Is it alive?" asked one of the Gott soldiers, with some trepidation. "Will it kill us?"

"Is it true that it is of the dragon's magic?" asked another. "And that you feed it sharp rocks?"

"And will we go blind, or deaf, if we see it?" asked a third, uncertainly.

Thom and a few others of Erin's riders also leaned forward, anxious to see the magic thing that their Princess' Consort had defeated.

"I will show it to you," said Alec, chuckling. "It will not hurt you while I hold it. It is just made of metal and wood. No, it is not magic, and has nothing to do with dragons." The Gott soldiers all looked at Alec with disbelieving expressions. They knew that something that powerful had to have used dragon blood.

Alec fetched the rifle from its sling and held it out before them, the lantern light reflecting off its barrel and scope. Some of the braver troops edged forward for a closer look, and some of the timider retreated to the corners. Alec did not explain how the rifle worked other than to explain that it used a special magic pellet and could kill over a long distance and did indeed make a loud noise that could temporarily deafen a person if they were not careful.

The next morning, they talked with Captain Levor about the tactical situation. "The Aldermen probably have about twice as many troops as we do," the Captain estimated. "I have enough men for defending our position, but not enough for retaking ground. They still have several death rods with their force. Any time they deploy a death rod from a strategic position we can lose men rapidly." He looked at Alec. "I don't see how we can retake our fortress as long as they have their death rods. I don't even see how we can stay here. Our camp here is not a defensible position. If they put a death rod on one of the surrounding hills, we will be lost. The fortress, also, is not a defensible position. Even if we retake it, they can put death rods on the hills above it and force us to leave."

"Then where is a defensible position?" asked Alec.

"About half-way between here and the fortress, Winding Road goes over the top of the pass. That would give us the high ground in every direction. In my estimation, it would have been the best place to put the fortress."

"Why wasn't it put there?" asked Erin.

The Captain was beginning to get used to speaking to her directly, instead of addressing all his remarks to Alec.

"I think it was because of the wind," he answered. "The winter wind here is fierce on the mountaintop. They put the fortress in a location that is protected from the winter wind." He sighed. "And that location worked fine until the death rods."

"Then let's retake that position and build a new base there," said Erin. "If we can battle them on this side of the pass until reinforcements arrive, we will have done the best we can. You can worry about winter winds when winter arrives."

"Reasonable plan," said the Captain grudgingly, "but how do we do it? Can you destroy their death rods before we start the attack?" he asked Alec.

Alec had been reluctant to share the limitations of his abilities with anyone other than Erin. The less anyone knew, the less chance of the wrong information escaping. *Should I tell the Captain the limits of my abilities?* He thought to Erin. *I may need to.* She agreed – they were going to have to explain the extent of Alec's abilities to do effective planning.

"There are limitations on what I can do," Alec told Captain Levor. "I need to be able to see the death rod fuel to destroy it." Alec pulled two rifle cartridges from his pocket. "This is the death rod fuel," he said. The Captain shrank back from the small metal objects. "One of these little cartridges is one death rod shot. Then the death rod needs another for its next shot." *I sound like I'm telling him how to feed a puppy,* Alec thought to himself. "After it has been used, it looks like this," and he showed a spent cartridge. "I cannot destroy them if I do not know where they are. If I can roughly find them, like if I know that they are in a wagon or an ammunition box, I can destroy them. But if they keep their death rods in the fort where I cannot see them, I cannot destroy them."

"I see," said the Captain. Alec suspected that he didn't.

"What do we know about how many death rods the Aldermen have?" Alec asked. "We have reduced their number by two."

The captain thought a moment. "They had four positions that used their death rods in their engagements with us," the Captain mused. "So they had at least four death rods. I think they are too precious a weapon for them not to use all the ones they have."

"I think the Aldermen also will be protecting their death rods. If I were them, I would leave them at the fort for protection and bring them out only when they plan an attack. For this engagement, I suspect they only brought the two we encountered," Alec said.

"That makes sense," agreed Erin.

"We can't retake our fortress," Captain Levor said, thoughtfully, "but perhaps we could retake the top of the pass. I have sent scouts out to see what the Alder troop disposition is. We should know that status later today. It takes about two hours for a messenger to reach the fort from the top of the pass. So, we can have a half-day lead time before they bring their death rods."

≈ ≈ ≈ ≈

Alec and Erin went back to their camp to make sure everything was in working order. Erin inspected her troops and mounts, and sent an update to her mother. Alec had stored the rifle in a container fastened with a stout lock that he had created. Now he extracted the rifle and the bullets and spent some time inspecting them. When Erin returned, he was still looking at them.

"Oh, Great Wizard," Erin said, poking him. "I can see you are developing a plan." He looked at her and smiled.

"Yes, I am developing a plan." He beckoned to her. "Come over here. I want you to look at this." Then he turned over one of the bullets and showed her the bottom.

"Tiny runes?" she said, squinting, at the very small imprint on the bottom of the bullet. "I have never seen such fine detail," she said, turning the bullet in his hand to better catch the light. "Are these runes of power?"

"No," he said patiently. "The runes don't add power, but they do say 'Remington Arms.' That is a company that makes rifle shells back in my homeland. I don't know why they are here." He paused. "It just seems like me being here and other things from my homeland being here cannot be a coincidence."

Then they talked about various things they could do and the strategic advantages of each. After a while, Erin started talking about other things they could do, and they retired to their wagon. They would worry about tomorrow when tomorrow came.

18 – Gott

Late in the afternoon, Captain Levor sent word that his scouts had returned. "Our scouts were able to travel almost to the Winding Pass Fortress," the Captain told Erin. "It is about one hour by trogus to the fortress or two hours by foot. The Aldermen are holding the top of the pass with about twenty men. The rest are at the fortress, just beyond the pass. Our scouts thought that the Alder troops at the fortress seem to be preparing for moving forward, but they look like they are waiting for something. Maybe reinforcements." He looked at Alec. "We could retake the top tomorrow if that will help. Can you destroy their death rods?"

As they talked, a plan emerged. Erin, Alec, and a small team of Erin's riders would move into the Alder-held territory, sneaking by the Aldermen situated at the top of the pass. Since there were no death rods with the Alder forces stationed there, the Captain could retake the area with great fanfare. Recapturing the top of the pass by the Gott soldiers would force a response from the Aldermen in the fortress; they would have to send out a reinforcement column from the fortress, with their additional death rods – if any were there. Once the death rods were brought out into the open, even if they were in an armored wagon, Alec would have a chance to destroy them. The only question was when the Alder reinforcement column would arrive. The Captain cautioned that it might be the next day – Erin's band would have to be prepared to spend the night out on the mountain.

Erin's people were up long before dawn to execute the first part of the plan. They took five riders with them plus one of the Captain's most experienced scouts and a man to handle their mounts. As daylight broke, they quietly rode into the territory held by the Aldermen, coming as near to the soldiers camped at the pass as they could without being detected. Then they dismounted and the handler took the animals back to the Gott base camp. Erin and her band left the main road and followed the Gott scout along an old game trail that ran roughly parallel. Occasionally they could see Winding Road through the trees – it was quiet with little activity. Erin periodically felt ahead to see if she could sense any hidden guard posts. Near mid-morning, they took a short break from their trek.

"We are almost to the top of the slope above Winding Pass," the Gott scout told them. "After that we will be on the other side of the mountain, on the far side of the pass."

Just before they reached the crest Erin stopped, and motioned for them all to be quiet. "There is a hidden lookout post in the woods ahead. It has three soldiers in it, and they appear to be awake, but not concerned or attentive. Time for the next part of our plan."

Alec nodded. "Time to bend the light. The risk of doing this is that I can't bend the light on all sides. There are some angles where we could be seen, even if it is only as a fuzzy reflection. We must stay close together."

The guard post overlooked a small meadow they would have to cross. Alec felt for his medallion and used the dark energy to create a lens to bend light around them. Then they walked slowly and quietly across the meadow. Erin continued to sense the guard post and detected no increased anxiety from the soldiers. After what seemed forever, they reached the far side of the meadow and Alec released the dark lens as they re-entered the forest. The scene around them changed from blurry to crisp.

Erin sensed forward.

"There are no soldiers in the woods ahead. It looks like the only Alder force on this side of the mountain is around the pass. There is some motion on the road, but it appears to be normal travel." They quietly proceeded for another hour through the woods before the Gott scout stopped them at an opening where the game trail overlooked the main road.

"This is the place we talked about," said the scout.

"We wait here," Erin told her riders. "Be patient."

"It's almost high noon," Alec agreed. "The Captain's attack at the pass should start soon."

An occasional figure could be spotted on the road, but there was no sign of a uniformed Alder reinforcement column. It was another half-hour before they heard sounds in the distance – battle horns trumpeting, shouts, and the sound of clashing weapons.

"The attack has started," Erin said. Activity on the road picked up. Messengers were riding rapidly toward the fortress, and there were more people on the road, scurrying into action.

"The plan is for Captain Levor to retake the pass, but not push forward," Erin explained to her riders. "He shouldn't have a problem taking it. The

Alder have a relatively small force there, and the Captain can bring a larger force to bear. The next portion of our plan depends on the Alder reaction. They will probably regroup, and then either stage a counter-offensive or go into a retreat. If they regroup, the logical place would be a clearing along the road between us and Winding Pass, probably that clearing we can see, an el or so moonward. If they choose that position, then reinforcements will pass by us along the road below, probably later this afternoon. If the Alder do something else, then we will have to change our plans accordingly."

Eventually, the sounds of fighting quieted down.

"The Gott have taken the peak," Erin said, sensing the outcome.

As expected, a handful of Alder troops came back from the pass along the road below, with little semblance of order, some obviously wounded. When they reached the clearing several slumped to the ground, exhausted. The Alder officers were working hard to keep their men organized and in fighting array; it looked like they were trying to set up a new defensive position, facing back towards the pass they had just fled. Several messengers left the main group, heading rapidly in the direction of the Winding Pass Fortress.

"Look," Erin said, pointing out a mounted rider. "That is the first messenger coming this way, from the direction of fortress." However, this messenger seemed to be responding to an earlier status report – there would not have been enough time for the soldiers in the fortress to be sending a response back regarding the current tactical situation and the rout on the mountaintop. More than at any other point since his arrival in this world, Alec missed his cell phone. The lack of instant communications on their battlefield was maddening. The time delay necessitated by messengers riding hours to carry information made decision-making fraught with the potential for wrong actions.

"What can you sense, Erin?" Alec asked.

"The Alder commander seems satisfied with the messenger's response. He's back to organizing his troops." She watched a moment longer. "He was anxious earlier. Now he seems calmer and more confident."

"That sounds like he knows reinforcements are on the way," Alec said.

"Seems consistent," she said.

Erin's riders fidgeted as they continued to wait, trying to stay quiet and unobtrusive. The afternoon proceeded slowly. Finally, late in the afternoon under the crossing moons, the first column of Alder reinforcements came along the road, jogging in a rapid cadence. Eventually, more columns of reinforcements streamed past. Then a baggage train came in sight, looking heavily-protected. There were five wagons in the train. The first four wagons looked like standard food and supply wagons. The fifth wagon was built with much heavier sides and a locked door on the back; a squad of ten soldiers were deployed in front of the wagon and about the same number behind.

Alec pointed to the fifth wagon. "That is our target," he said, simultaneously feeling relief that their afternoon had unfolded according to plan, and tension that he might have to kill somebody. "What can you sense, Erin?"

She let her feelings roam out.

"They feel arrogant and confident. This is your fish." That was another saying of Alec's that had no literal meaning to her, but she liked it and could sense that he knew exactly what she meant.

Here goes nothing, thought Alec.

"Get down, everyone. Cover your ears." He reached for dark energy. *Focus.* He felt the death rod ammunition and let go of the dark energy. There was a huge explosion followed by a long string of sharp blasts. They heard bullets zinging all around, including into the trees behind them.

Alec stuck his head up and looked at where the baggage train had been. The secured wagon was in fragments – riddled with holes, it lay on its side. Several of the Alder soldiers and their mounts lay on the ground, dead or moaning and bleeding profusely. Others were struggling with their animals. Two pulling teams of drungs were on the ground and bleating, at least one in mortal agony. The third team had run off the road in fright, and that wagon was stuck on the side of the road with a broken axle; the drungs continued to bleat and chafe in panic. The team on the front wagon had bolted; their driver had let the team run until he regained control, but the wagon appeared to have mowed over several riders and foot soldiers before the drungs calmed down.

"What do you sense, Erin?" Alec was grinning despite himself.

"They are in disbelief! They have no idea what happened." Erin took her consort's arm and smiled at him. "I think that we have finished all we can do here. It is time to try to return before the Aldermen mount an effective perimeter guard."

The small band worked their way quickly back along the game path with Erin sensing ahead. Stealth was no longer needed, and they could move with deliberate speed. They arrived at the Gott troops' new location at the top of the pass just as dark was taking over. Captain Levor wanted a debrief immediately, and both groups went through the events of the day.

"Do you think that the Aldermen have more death rods?" Captain Levor asked Alec.

"I do not know. However, the loss of this many weapons should make them reluctant to bring out more any time soon. They will probably leave them in the fortress in case they have to defend it. They probably wouldn't bring any weapons forward until they receive reinforcement weapons. That would probably take at least a week … maybe longer."

"I am confident that my men can defend the mountaintop, at least that long," Captain Levor said. "We suffered only marginal casualties during our battle this afternoon."

"Congratulations, Captain, on a fight well-won," Erin said, and the two clasped arms.

≈ ≈ ≈ ≈

Alec and Erin decided that they had accomplished more than they had originally started out to do during their side venture into Gott, and felt it was time to head back down the mountain into Theland to continue their original journey: to show Alec around Theland. The Captain was disappointed but not surprised.

In the morning, Erin, Alec, their riders, and staff were up early. Erin was very disturbed by the discovery that the death rod that Alec had recovered was missing.

"Princess, someone broke the lock and took the magic death rod!" one of the riders reported. "We found the broken box behind our wagons." Alec and Erin followed the rider to the location of the discovery.

"Well, without any ammunition, it's not going to do them much good," Alec said, inspecting the wooden box, and noticing the small pile of cartridges left behind. "It'll just be a heavy club, and not a very good one at that."

"Ah," the rider said in understanding. "Without it's dragon's food, it will not have its magic and cannot throw its teeth."

"Um ... yes," Alec replied. The rider smiled with pride that she now understood the source of the death rod's power.

"I suspect that one of the Captain's men took it as a prize of war," Erin muttered to Alec. "Or maybe even the Captain himself."

With no proof, there was nothing they could do, so they moved on towards the border and the Theland garrison. The day was uneventful; they encountered only one messenger heading towards the pass. By midafternoon the next day they reached the garrison. Sergeant Urgan greeted them as they arrived. They spent the afternoon briefing the Sergeant, cleaning up equipment, feeding their animals, and tending to the few wounded riders.

The next morning as they were preparing to leave, while they were saying their good-byes to Sergeant Urgan a messenger arrived. He had been riding hard through the night.

"A message for the Princess," he said breathlessly, "from Queen Therin."

Erin opened the capsule and read the message aloud to Alec.

"'Greetings, My Daughter. Congratulations on your victory.' Blah blah blah. Oh – here's the main part of Mother's message.

"'We have received some very distressing news. Our friend and ally, Gott, is under attack by an invading army. There is a War Council of Gott and its allies in the capital city of Gott. The Council will convene at mid-day on Seft the last. I must attend the war council. I am taking Brun, as head of our Council, and two hundred members of my royal guard. I need for you to join us.'

"Seft the last is in four days!" said Erin in dismay. "Can we get to Gott City in time?"

"Not if you go through Theland," Sergeant Urgan answered. "It is six days if you go down to the Ryn River and then back into Gott. You can only get there in time if you go back up towards Winding Pass, the way you came, and then at the fork, take the other road into the Gott heartland. Even with that, you will have to hurry – but if good fortune and good weather is yours, you should be able to succeed."

Erin and Alec changed their plans to head back in the direction they had just come. They dispatched a messenger to inform the Queen of their plans.

They had an unremarkable trip over the next three days. They experienced the normal wagon breakdowns and logistic delays but were able to get underway again quickly. As they passed through the towns and villages in the

Gott countryside they could feel an underlying tension in the land. It had been a long time since Gott had been at war or fought a significant battle. The mountains ringing their land on three sides protected them; Theland was their ally, the elves never came out of the Elf Mountains, and because generations of anarchy on the Grasslands had left the area without a leader, the only concern from that direction had been occasional marauding bands of nomads or bandits, not armed troops. Now they were facing a dangerous and unknown enemy – an enemy with death rods.

≈ ≈ ≈ ≈

On the fourth day, Erin halted her group as they arrived at the walls of Gott City, the capital of Gott. Queen Therin had arrived the day before; her camp, with its many tents and pavilions, was already set up. Erin and Alec immediately went to the Queen's pavilion, with instructions to their party to set up camp alongside the Queen's camp.

"Mother!" cried Erin, ignoring all formalities and rushing to the Queen.

"Daughter!" the Queen said, hugging Erin. "I am glad you are here."

"Mother, I can sense that things are not right."

"You are correct, as always, my Daughter." She stroked Erin's hair. "I don't know all that is happening, but it is not good. It is not good for Gott, and it is not good for Theland."

"What is the threat to Theland?" asked Erin.

"Things are not good in our land right now," the Queen answered. "Before we left, in anticipation that this unknown blue-uniformed army might threaten our land, Brun talked the Council into giving him complete control of the country and my government for the duration of the war in Gott, however long it should last."

"That sounds like a coup," said Alec, frowning, as he took the Queen's hand in greeting.

"I do not know your word, dear Son-in-law," the Queen said, squeezing his hand in return, "but I sense the meaning – and yes, it does. The Council claims it can make extraordinary decisions in times of war. They claim they can take away my power and authority to rule and grant it to the head of the Council. And of course, the Council head is my Consort, dear Brun. All the Councilors respond to Brun's every desire; he has an uncanny ability to sway them. I am sure that this attempt to usurp my power is all his doing." The

Queen let out an exasperated sigh. "I wish I had never been so stupid as to agree to consort with him, but at the time it looked like the best thing for Theland."

"Where is Brun?" asked Erin.

"He is at a preliminary gathering that is meeting before the formal War Council convenes," the Queen answered. "The formal Council starts at midday. After the opening ceremonies, the first formal meeting of the heads of the gathered lands is this afternoon, and the final meeting will be in three or four days. Over the next couple of days, all parties will meet in negotiating sessions. The final commitments will be made and sworn to at the final meeting. I fear that Brun intends to abandon Gott as our ally, although he will try to do it cleverly."

"What do you need from us?" asked Erin.

"Brun said you two are expected at the meeting this afternoon, you as the Princess and your Consort as a member of the Council. He feels that your riders should be integrated with the riders of my royal guard.

"The royal guard will support me. That is probably the only reason that Brun hasn't taken complete control – they are loyal to me and our line. But – beware. Brun brought about twenty of his men. I don't like their looks."

Erin looked at her mother, searching her eyes.

"Mother, has Brun mistreated you on this trip?" she asked softly.

"Goodness no!" said the Queen. "We lead our separate lives. We travel in our separate wagons. He isn't interested in me." She paused. "So that you know, he has brought two little maids who attend to his every need and do whatever he wants."

"How can we help you?" asked Alec.

Queen Therin smiled at him weakly. "You are a loyal and good son-in-law, and a steadfast Consort for my daughter. You two have already helped me, merely by being here. And now I again must warn you: beware. Beware of Brun. He may be more dangerous than any other foe you will meet."

19 – Treachery

That afternoon Alec found himself alongside Erin in the first of the War Council meetings, which seemed to consist of long and boring introductions. *Worse than meeting with the Chancellor's Office back at the Institute,* Alec thought to himself. Erin had warned him that Gott was much more formal then Theland. Bowing, formal introductions, and lots of flourishes were expected.

A formal reception was planned for the evening. Prior to their arrival, Captain Levor had sent to his superiors in Gott City a detailed accounting of the events at the pass – Alec and Erin were now minor celebrities and would probably be the center of attention at the reception.

Erin tried to describe the Gott protocol to Alec; there seemed to be a lot of rules, including small details as to how to position one's hands or point one's feet.

"Why can't I just let you cue me on what to do?" he asked.

"Because we will be on different sides of the room. The men will be on one side and the women on the other side. We women are expected to parade around and strut. Most of the women – except for Mother, of course – have little to do with affairs of business or government, so we are for decoration and shown off like expensive cattle." She wrinkled her nose and sniffed.

Alec could tell that Erin wasn't happy with the Gott social structure, but it wasn't her land and not a problem she could fix. After that he tried harder to learn Gott protocol and when to bow and how deeply and how often.

"But what if I do something wrong?" he fretted. "Will that be an embarrassment to your Mother?"

"If you know you made a mistake, just apologize and claim it was a 'newcomer mistake.' Your reputation from the Battle at Winding Pass – and as a Great Wizard – will keep anyone from seriously challenging your manners. Or lack of them."

≈ ≈ ≈ ≈

The Queen, her consort Brun, Erin, and Alec rode together in the Queen's wagon to attend the evening reception at the Gott palace, accompanied by the Queen's personal guard, her lead rider Ferd. Most of the Gott dignitaries had elegant carriages; even some of the outsiders had brought (or rented) formal carriages. The Theland wagon looked second-rate in comparison. Brun was clearly upset over this.

"We are good as any of these others! Why don't we look as good as them?" he grumbled.

They entered the palace reception hall and the formal introductions started. Gott was a much larger country than Theland and often held formal events. The palace hall was decorated with artwork, statues, fine objects, and fresh flowers and herbs, all beautifully displayed and lit with the glow of thousands of candles. In one corner some musicians played; it was oddly haunting music on instruments that Alec had never seen before. Apparently, dancing was unknown here, but the music had a strange beat and would have been difficult to dance to, Alec decided.

After the Gott doorman ushered them in, a uniformed butler formally and loudly presented them to the assemblage. "Her majesty, Queen Therin of Theland! And her royal and most esteemed Consort, Brun!" There was a round of polite applause, and then Erin and Alec were introduced, both with their official Theland titles and as "the Heroes of the recent Battle at Winding Pass!" Alec noted that this round of applause seemed more sincere. Then Alec and Brun were ushered to the men's side of the reception hall and Erin and the Queen to the gaggle of ladies on the other side.

As he knew no one and had nothing to discuss, Alec stood quietly against the wall in the back of the men's area and observed the people. The men were all a similar age – there were no elderly men and no young men – and were dressed in similar fashion, although the officials from Gott tended to have sashes and ribbons and medals over their robes or tunics and some wore soft hats. The officials from the various realms gathered in small knots making polite conversation, and, Alec suspected, sizing up each other. Brun immediately started working the crowd, moving from one group of men to another, paying no attention to Alec. He was soon lost to view.

Across the large hall, Alec could see Erin and the Queen amid the other women. The Queen knew many of the noble women of Gott and the other realms and was introducing Erin to them as her Princess and heir. Most of the other women were dressed in fabulous gowns of fine fabrics, designed with ruffles, flounces, ribbons, slits and low necklines, all designed to show off their best features. As in Theland, the young women seemed quite plump to Alec, with pronounced rounded bosoms and backsides, and moved in a stilted, halting way. *Rather like a hobbled horse,* thought Alec. He noticed that a few wore decorative mitts over their hands, and one walked with a very decided limp.

Queen Therin was dressed in elegant fashion, with a regal silver robe flowing from her shoulders — Alec was sure that Brun had insisted that she represent them well, and the Queen was a striking woman for her age. Erin was outfitted in a much simpler dress, since she hadn't planned on a formal event this trip — a long gown of pale peach, with draped bell-like sleeves. Alec noticed that some of the serving girls wore fancier dresses than Erin, but he thought she was the most beautiful of any of them. He never tired of watching her as she moved through the throng of fawning women, her natural cat-like grace in contrast to their measured steps.

≈ ≈ ≈ ≈

The night wore on. It was late in the evening and Alec found himself in one of the never-ending receiving lines that seemed to characterize Gott affairs. After greeting several dignitaries with unpronounceable names, he reached to shake the outstretched of the next person, a short dark-haired man, when he suddenly sensed Erin shout in his mind.

Danger! Watch out!

His instincts took over and he reared back, twisting away from the receiving line. He saw the concealed knife in the short man's hand dart towards him. He tried to pull away, but the man was holding his other hand tightly — his reflexive motion was enough to change the knife's path but not enough to stop it. The knife sliced through his shirt and along the side of his ribs. Without Erin's warning it would have pierced his heart. Alec pulled away and felt everything going black.

This is more than a knife wound. Have I been poisoned? he thought. He reached for his medallion but was losing consciousness too quickly to focus. He fell to the floor with a thud.

The stranger pulled back and started to run.

"Assassin!" someone shouted. The crowd closed in on the short man. He looked around, pulled out his knife, and sliced deep into his own arm. He collapsed and almost immediately started convulsing.

≈ ≈ ≈ ≈

Ever alert at a gathering such as this, Erin sensed the malevolent intentions of the assassin an instant before his knife struck. With all her mental strength, she sent out an urgent thought to Alec even before she sensed where the danger might be.

Then as she turned in his direction, she saw Alec collapse and felt his mind go black. Immediately a cluster of men surrounded Alec and his assailant, either from curiosity or in assistance; she couldn't tell which. Erin pushed her way through the crowded hall towards Alec. Women she could easily shove out of the way but the men did not readily step aside for her, and some clucked that she should go back to her place with the other women. Finally she was close enough to see that both Alec and the short man were turning white from lack of blood, and convulsing.

"Get help!" she screamed. She could see Ferd rushing forward from the servants' area, some distance away; too far away to be of immediate help. A couple of men stepped away – to find help? – and she dropped down to her knees alongside Alec's body, which was still wracked by spasmodic jerks from the convulsions.

"Alec," she moaned. "My Dear Consort!" She could tell he was slipping away. As his convulsions stopped she reached inside his torn, blood-soaked shirt to reach for his medallion to see if she could feel any dark energy. Erin couldn't grasp dark energy like Alec could, but she did feel a little bit as she touched the medallion. She tuned out the voices and music and movements of the Gott guests milling about and, focusing best she could, fed dark energy into Alec, like she had seen him do with her and her mother. She knew that Alec could reach a flood of energy and overpower things, where she could reach only a little energy, but maybe it would be enough. She lay both of her hands on his chest, his red blood seeping into the delicate peach sleeves of her dress.

Slowly she could feel her attempts to feed dark energy into his now-still form working, but only weakly. She could sense she wasn't helping enough – her limited ability wasn't turning the poison around. She tried harder, but she couldn't reach any more energy. Alec was fading fast. Behind her she could feel the assassin's life-force ebb from his body, then felt him die – just as Alec would unless the dark energy took hold.

No Alec! Don't be next! Erin knew that she was slowing the rate at which Alec was fading, but she wasn't succeeding in overcoming the effects of the stabbing and the poison. There had to be something she could do.

Watching Alec over the past few months, with her finely-tuned senses she had always felt that he was wasting a lot of his dark energy in useless swirls and eddies. That worked for Alec because he could find so much energy, but it wasn't working for her because her ability to pull dark energy was not as strong as his. In her mind she felt a wrongness in what she was doing. Could she focus her power on sensing this misdirected flow, and redirect the dark energy in the right way? She tried to move her focus on the energy and the wrongness increased; then she tried to change it differently and the wrongness decreased. She kept trying until she reduced as much of the wrongness as she could, making best use of the energy she could control. Finally, she could see that Alec had stabilized and didn't appear to be declining anymore.

Three people with a stretcher eventually arrived.

"We have lots of stretchers available for these events," one of the porters said to the throng of men near Alec. "There is always some royal getting drunk and passing out." They put the stretcher alongside Alec and Erin helped move him onto it. As they stood with his still body on the stretcher, the porters tried to push her out of the way, but Erin refused to let go.

Then she was aware of the bulky figure of her step-father, Brun, stepping forward and peering at Alec's ashen face.

"Let her go with you," said Brun to the porters. "She might as well use the night to mourn him." He chuckled. "No one survives blue thorn poison. Take him to the morgue and she can watch him die if she wants."

Blue thorn poison? Erin thought. Then Alec <u>was</u> poisoned, and Brun knows it.

Erin went with the porters, holding Alec's hand all the while. They took Alec to the morgue, a nearby stone structure with small slit-like windows, and laid him on a stone slab. Then they left, and Erin was alone with Alec in the dark room, lit only by the faint light of a waning moon and a few stars shining through the cold night sky, tracing the edges of the narrow windows.

Alec. My Alec. My Great Warrior. Erin could feel that he wasn't getting any worse. As the night wore on she kept trying to reduce the wrongness with the little energy she could impart. She could sense the fog slowly clear from his being, and late in the night she felt his mind had cleared enough that she could communicate with him.

Alec, my love, you are poisoned. She let this sink into his consciousness. *I am barely able to keep you alive. I need you to find your focus and pull enough energy so that we can beat this.* Responding faintly to her summons, Alec tried, and failed. *Rest a bit, my Dear Wizard, and then try again.* For the next hour, as his mind cleared, Alec kept trying and finally found a little energy. It coursed out in his usual undirected stream.

Alec, you must listen to me, Erin thought earnestly. *Feel with me, and start directing the energy to where I tell you it feels right.* Alec nodded weakly. He tried to shape the flow of energy as she directed, and slowly the two started to have a little success. The energy started to feel right.

≈ ≈ ≈ ≈

By morning when the sun rose, Alec was alive and conscious. He had beaten the poison but was very weak.

"You did it, Erin," he said. "You saved me."

"No, <u>we</u> did it," she said, fingering his hand and his rings. "It took us both, but you are alive."

They sat together for a long while. Finally, a figure entered the morgue. Erin looked up; Alec was still too weak to move much.

"Mother!" said Erin, surprised to see the Queen at this dismal place. "I sense that things are not right with you."

"Everything is wrong," the Queen said sadly. "Brun sent me here to fetch you. He said that you had all night to mourn your Consort, and that was more than enough time."

"Mother!"

"Six of Brun's henchmen are waiting outside to take us back – you must come with me, or things won't go well for either of us, I fear. He sent Ferd off on some task, so my royal guard wasn't around this morning to protect me. I asked for a few moments alone with you and your Consort before we leave his dead body here."

"They only got one thing wrong," said Alec.

The Queen jumped, startled, and looked at her son-in-law.

"You live!" she exclaimed.

"It seems that way," Alec rejoined, with a faint grin.

"Quiet!" whispered the Queen. "If Brun's men know you are still alive they will finish you off!"

"Mother, what is going on? How did Brun know Alec had been poisoned? Or was it he who ..."

The Queen nodded, and cut her off with a wave of her hand.

"Yes, of course, it was Brun. I wonder now if this whole 'War Council' was just a charade to get us away from Theland. Brun has some sort of arrangement with the ruling Gott nobles." The Queen rubbed her neck, shaking her head.

"Brun gloated over your 'death,'" the Queen said to Alec. "He insisted in telling me all about it, and how clever he was. But he said he was disappointed in the assassin. He said he thought he had paid for the best, and the fool botched the job.

"I wonder how much he paid? And did it come from <u>my</u> royal coffers?"

"Assassin," moaned Erin. "I should have known."

"The assassination was supposed to happen later last night in a quiet moment, away from the crowds, so that people would think you were drunk and died in a fall or something. But that's not what the cur did – I guess he got excited at the prospect of killing you in a big moment, so he jumped you during the height of the festivities. But, Brun said it didn't really matter that it happened where everyone could see, because now all would know you were dead. And, he said, no one ever survives blue thorn poison." She looked at Alec fondly. "Except you, apparently."

"What do we do now?" asked Erin, shaking her head. The Queen arched her eyebrows and reached for her daughter.

"We must go with them," she said. "And quickly. If they think I have taken too long, and come in here and find Alec alive, he will be killed outright. I sense malice and treachery in Brun, but not murderous intentions toward you, my daughter."

"I will need your help, my love," said Erin to Alec, kissing his forehead. "Try to recover as much strength as you can."

"Okay," said Alec. "Will do." Then as an afterthought, "Can you get them to bring my staff here?" *Coffee would be nice, too.*

"Yes," said the Queen, thinking quickly. "I can tell the mortician on the way out that Erin's request is to have your staff laid beside your dead body. He will do that."

Queen Therin and Erin walked out of the morgue to the waiting thugs.

Alec lay on the cold hard morgue slab drawing as much healing dark energy as he could. He could no longer feel the rightness that Erin could sense, but he could flood himself with energy in his own way.

≈ ≈ ≈ ≈

The Queen and Erin were escorted by Brun's men to a small building some distance away from the palace. Brun waited inside. The guardsmen brought the Queen and Erin to him, roughly shoving them through the door of Brun's chamber.

"Take her away," he said to his men, pointing at his Queen. "You know the plan." Two of the men took the Queen by the arms and half drug, half pulled, her across the floor and out the door.

Mother! Erin mentally cried in anguish, as the Queen was taken away.

Erin was left with Brun and his remaining henchmen. Erin thought about trying to fight them, even though she was still wearing her blood-stained gown and had no weapons with her.

It would be close, she thought, *but they will be ready and expecting me to try something. Unarmed, I probably can't take four of them. They are also probably better trained in unarmed fighting than me. I wish I had worked harder to master unarmed combat.*

Brun interrupted her thought. "We are at war, Little Princess, so your mourning time is over," he sneered. "Time for action. First, we need to get your fate settled.

"Understand that if you don't do exactly what I command, your mother, Queen Therin, and your brother, the esteemed Colin, will be dead. However, if you behave, and do as I tell you to do, then I will let them live."

Erin could sense the truth of his statement.

"I have two choices," Brun said, stroking his beard. "When you returned to Theland last year when you were supposed to be dead, you messed up my plans. And you coming up with your 'Wizard' Consort didn't help, either. But, now that your Consort is dead, things are a little easier." He stepped forward and put one hand under her chin, tilting her face towards his.

"Choice Number One, I can kill your mother, the Queen, and then consort with you. I don't really like that choice because it means I would have to ride you enough times to have a handful of whelps and then wait for them to grow up." He took his hand from her face, seemingly bemused by her dismay at this first choice.

"But, I don't like hard skinny girls like you, although it would be the ultimate insult to your father to ride you a few times." He snickered.

"You killed my father, didn't you?" Erin shot back, her dark eyes blazing.

"Of course." Brun smiled. "A good slow-acting poison works wonders! I would have done the same with your mother if your Consort hadn't shown up and saved her. A few more days and my little Amelia would have been Queen, and things would have been fine."

"You killed Leonder, also, didn't you," Erin accused, remembering the questionable circumstances surrounding the death of her lost love.

"No," Brun replied, returning to his chair. "That was totally Brunder's dumb idea. I had better plans, but my son Brunder, he always did stupid things." He looked at Erin, clearly enjoying recounting her former lover's fate. "Brunder told me that he and some of his friends 'borrowed' your little plaything one afternoon and took him out into the woods. They dropped him into a pit with a wild boar. Then they goaded the boar with their spears until it was angry enough to attack your sweet boyfriend and gore him." Brun smiled. "Brunder said the first time around, the boar only injured Leonder, so they had to poke the boar a few more times to make him mad enough to go after your little friend and finish him off." Brun pressed his fingertips together, eyeing Erin, looking for her reaction. She remained stone-faced.

"But that was Brunder's way. Brash. Stupid. That is not my style. I would have been much more clever. Much. My spies knew of you and your mother's plans, and the sneaky way you were going to announce your intent to consort with Leonder while Brunder was away. Since you wouldn't play fair about consorting, it made it harder to get you consorted to Brunder," Brun continued, eager to show how clever he would have been.

"I would have taken Brunder on our hunt. Then you would have announced your asinine consort decision. Brunder and I would have made an unexpected return to town the next day, in time to challenge your proposed consort arrangement. When Brunder won the challenge against your little weakling, you would have been legally consorted to Brunder. Then, I would have worked with you until you were obeying my directions. If you turned out to be too stubborn, after you had your girl-pup, I would have poisoned you off." He stood up.

"But enough about your foolishness in the past. Back to business. Time is wasting." He strode towards Erin.

"Choice Number Two. Let me remind you that your mother's life is at stake, depending on how you answer. Your second choice is to abdicate to my daughter Amelia." Erin struggled to show no emotion. "We will write your abdication note here, today, now," said Brun.

"And if I choose neither option?"

Brun shrugged.

"Then your mother – our dear Queen – is dead. Simple." He crossed his arms and glared at Erin.

"You have only a few moments to decide, because I told them to take your mother to the woods and poison her if they didn't hear from me by the time the tower's shadow crosses the front path. It is already half-way there. We will blame your mother's poisoning on the same rogue assassins who poisoned your Consort."

Erin could feel the sincerity in his statement. She glared at Brun, then sighed deeply. She knew she was defeated.

I can't let Mother die.

"All right," she said, tossing her head back. "You win. I will write the abdication note."

She wrote in her hand what he dictated:

"'After the death of my Consort, I will no longer rule. I thereby renounce all rights to be Queen of Theland, and abdicate from all other positions of responsibility.'"

"Is that all?" she asked.

"No, a little more. I don't want you hanging around the Residence in Theland." Brun smiled at her, or leered.

"'I will remain in Gott for some time with my True Love. Signed: Erin, Princess of Theland.' Got that?"

Erin nodded.

"Good. You have one minute to spare." He handed the signed note to one of his men. "Get the scribes to make a copy for me, and then take the Queen away as we planned."

"Take her away? You said you would let her go free!" Erin exclaimed.

"Free? No, I said I wouldn't kill her – just now, anyway." Brun laughed.

"Now what? What are you going to do with me?" Erin asked. "You know you can't get away with this."

Her step-father chuckled.

"I'm going to make sure you are happy for the rest of a nice long life, my dear Princess. I have just the thing arranged for you, while you are still of breeding age." Her leaned in, close to her face. "And no, I don't want to kill you. The Queen would discover the truth. If I have you safely stashed away where only I can find you, then I can use you as a hostage to ensure the Queen's good behavior." He stepped back. "Besides, your premature death might place in question the legitimacy of Amelia's rule, at least in the minds of any of your mother's loyalists who still remain in Theland."

Erin clenched her fists, keeping her arms by her side.

"Take her away," Brun said to two of the men, wheeling away from Erin. Brun's guardsmen grabbed Erin by her arms and forced her down the hall and into a dingy room; they shoved her into the dark space, slammed the door behind her, and locked it with a loud 'click!' She sat on a small stool, in the half-light of the cell, and cradled her head in her arms, her sleeves still stained with Alec's blood.

20 – Lord Rawl

Oh, my darling Alec. Maybe he was close enough to sense her thoughts. She fingered her diamond band that Alec called her 'wedding ring.' *Things keep getting worse,* Erin thought.

She sat in the room for most of the day. A lone ray of sunlight from the sole high window filtered through the dust and cobwebs. A man came once and slid some food in; she was hungry, so she ate even though the food was cold and stale. *I hope I'm not eating poison,* she thought dully. She slept fitfully off and on. Late in the afternoon two guardsmen came to get her. They grabbed her by the arms, slashed the bloody sleeves off her dress, attached one set of manacles to her wrists, and a second set to her ankles. Then they escorted her across an open commons towards a different building.

"Where are we going? What is happening?" Erin said, grimacing from their rough hold on her arms.

"We are just following orders," one said. "They said to take you over there. We don't know why."

"Now be quiet," said the other thug, shaking her.

They stopped in front of a small building with arched doorways and old tapestries hanging in its entry foyer. For a moment, Erin thought she caught a glimpse of someone leaning on a staff in the archway shadows, but it might merely have been a statue or a carved column, she realized.

"Good afternoon, Princess," Brun said to her with a carefully posed gesture of goodwill and a toothy smile. An older man stood near him, dressed in the robes and floppy hat of a Gott noble. At Brun's command, Erin was pulled into the small room, with Brun and the nobleman following. The two guardsmen shoved Erin to the front of the room, and turned her to face the nobleman, continuing to hold her. Brun awkwardly arranged Erin's dress, pulling it more tightly across her torso and hiding the soiled spots in the folds of her skirt. He looked back at the older man, smiling.

What a phony, thought Erin, sneering at him.

"This? This is what you are offering me?" the older gentleman said, looking Erin up and down.

"Princess, this is Lord Rawl," Brun said, still smiling through his clenched teeth. "He lives in the far reaches of Gott, and needs a young consort. He is a man of wealth and high status. I have offered you to him to ensure your safety and comfort. We are working a deal. You will be pleased."

"I will never agree," said Erin, her eyes flashing. In the nick of time, she stopped herself from spitting at his feet.

"Ah, my Little Princess, but you don't have to," Brun said, menacingly. "In the fair land of Gott, the maiden's father can agree to the consort arrangement. As your step-father I have that right. And, I may say, duty." He stepped back, regaining his false smile, and gestured around the room, with its elaborate carvings, statues, and tapestries. "This is a consorting temple. Nice idea; we don't have anything like this in Theland. Potential consorts come here, look each other over, and then agree to the arrangement." He stepped back towards Erin and took her arm with a paternal stroke. "All we will need, my dear 'daughter,' is a drop of your blood, my blood, and the Lord's blood on the final seal, and then everything will be legal." He smiled triumphantly.

Lord Rawl looked her over, appraising this piece of merchandise.

"This is what you are giving me?" he said in a rasping, squeaky voice. "I was expecting more." He ran his hand up the back of her leg under her dress, grabbed her rear, and squeezed. Erin flinched but the two guards held her steady.

"She is taller than me. Too tall." He felt her hair, her arms, her back. "She is so skinny and hard." He sniffed. "I was expecting something shorter and softer, more curves. Prettier."

"She is a Princess," Brun said, impatiently, "and I am paying you a fortune to take her."

Lord Rawl walked around to Erin's face, grabbed her jaw, forced her mouth open, and peered at her teeth. Erin tried to kick the older man, but Brun stepped on her leg manacles, preventing her leg from moving. If the Lord noticed her disrespect, he made no notice of it.

"Good teeth at least."

Lord Rawl ran his hand over her breasts and squeezed each roughly.

"She is so flat!" He stepped back for Erin and turned to Brun. "You aren't paying enough for me to take her. I need more!"

"All right – how about another ten pieces of gold?" said Brun.

"I need at least another thirty," said the Lord. The two men continued to dicker for a few minutes.

"What do you think I am – a prize cow?" said Erin in disgust.

"You think of yourself too highly if you think you rate with his prize cows," Brun growled. She could see Lord Rawl nodding in agreement.

"She is too impertinent. I fear she will try to run away," said Lord Rawl. "What happens if she runs home to you?"

"If you discipline her properly she will not run," Brun said. "But if she does, we will follow Gott laws since she is your consort and consorted in Gott. Here, runaway consorts are supposed to be returned," he said for Erin's benefit. "I promise that I will return her if she runs away to us. However, I might try her a few times before I send her back," Brun added, leering at Erin.

"I might have to just hobble her up front, you know – but that will cost me more money," the Lord whined.

Brun looked at Erin.

"My 'daughter,' you might not know the customs in Gott. Here, they know how to make their women behave.

"Women consorts are the man's property, of course. A man has the right to use reasonable force to make you women behave. In the countryside, where you will be living with Lord Rawl, they follow local customs. If a woman tries to run away she can be hobbled – usually by cutting the Achilles' tendon in the rear of one leg, right above the heel. Some women wear a leather boot to hobble around, after they heal, but they can't go very far. I know that you are fleet of foot. I'm sure that you wouldn't want that to happen to you." Brun took her hand. "Just so you know, if a woman tries to fight her man, all her fingers will be crushed. I'm sure that would hurt." He looked directly into her eyes. "And of course, Gott women do not carry weapons.

"If you behave well, and do as Lord Rawl tells you, then you will have a good life. A little songbird in a golden cage, as it were." Brun dropped her hand. "But if you don't … if you disobey him, I'm sure that Lord Rawl will do what it takes to make you behave. His interest in you is for breeding, not your charming personality. He is buying the fact that the pups you spit out for him will have a royal bloodline."

Lord Rawl nodded. "Yes. I need royal children to protect my interests."

"If you do misbehave," Brun added, "don't expect help. The people of Gott do not know you, and are not interested in your kind. All the riders loyal to your Queen are back at our camp. Those manacles you are wearing are the kind used here on runaway consorts, so no one here in Gott City will be surprised to see that you are wearing chains. Even if you are recognized, if the Gott authorities check, they will see that with the Consorting Agreement the Lord will be well within his rights to carry you back to his home." Brun shrugged and smiled at her. "And, if you make a fuss, people here will expect him to give you a public whipping."

"Yes," Lord Rawl said, nodding in agreement. "I did have to thrash my second consort many times. She was brazen and would not obey." He wiped his nose. "But that's why I need a new consort. She died after her last thrashing."

"You beat her to death?!" said Erin, astonished.

"Not only are you giving me a skinny one, but you are also giving me a stupid one," said Lord Rawl to Brun. Then to Erin, "No, I didn't beat her to death. I thrashed her, and her constitution wasn't strong enough to handle the discipline." He again gave Erin an appraising look. "Is she good in bed?" he asked Brun.

"I have no idea. Ask her," Brun said.

"Are you good in bed?" Lord Rawl asked Erin.

"You'll never know," she hissed.

"Oh good – a little spirit when we speak of sex," Lord Rawl said with a bit of enthusiasm. "The spirited ones can be trained to be good in bed." He gave a faint leer. "If they're not too impertinent." He turned back to Brun. Erin sensed that the Lord was ready to complete the deal. "If you throw in another ten gold so that I can get her out of these peasant rags and two gold for the cost of hobbling, I guess I will take her. Let's finish the Consort Agreement."

"Aren't you forgetting something?" a voice in the back of the room said. All turned to see who had entered; the guardsmen snapped to attention, horrified that they had not noticed an intruder entering the chamber.

"Who are you and why are you intruding on my private consorting ceremony?" Lord Rawls said with annoyance.

"I am Princess Erin's true Consort, and where I come from there cannot be a new consort while the current one is standing here," the figure said, stepping forward where they could all see him.

It was all Erin could do to keep from squealing in delight.

Lord Rawls looked at the tall man and recognized him from last night's festivities.

"You … You are Lord Alec! The Great Wizard Demon who destroyed the Alder enemy troops with one fire-breath, and ate their entrails for breakfast!" The nobleman cringed backwards, jaw agape, eyes wide open in mortal terror. Alec could see that his reputation was growing faster than a fish story.

"That's correct. I am Alec. Royal Consort. But I did not eat the breakfast entrails raw."

"I am so sorry, my Great Lord Alec! My humblest apologies!" The short man bowed deeply to Alec, doffing his hat in a show of humility and respect – and fear.

"My Lord Alec – I was told you were dead! I would never have bargained for your Consort – your Princess – knowing that you are alive." Lord Rawls looked at Alec nervously, then at Brun, then back at Alec. "Actually, I did not want your Consort at all, but I needed the coins, and Brun offered a goodly sum for her, even though she is not so pretty … I mean, she is beautiful, of course, and of a lovely disposition, I am sure, but I really did not want to consort with your Consort, as you can see …" the Lord babbled. "But times are hard here in Gott, and I have fallen on a string of bad luck, and I needed some coins and Brun offered her … Please excuse my actions! I am so very sorry, Prince Alec! So very sorry …" he muttered, as he backed out of the consorting chamber in obvious fright. As soon as the nobleman reached the entry, Alec could hear him turn and run, clattering down the entry hall.

"Alec," said Brun, showing his teeth.

Is that supposed to be a smile? wondered Alec.

"What a surprise. So glad to see you. So sorry for this … misunderstanding. We all heard that you were dead." Brun spread his arms amicably.

"You poisoned me," said Alec flatly.

"Of course, I did, but I suspected it wouldn't work. I was just … testing you. I thought you might be tougher than the Gott lords anticipated."

"You tried to kill me," Alec said.

Brun looked a little nervous, but made no answer to the accusation. He clearly had not anticipated this turn of events.

"If you hurt Erin, I will make sure you suffer for a <u>long</u> time," Alec said, prominently grasping his staff. Brun's eyes darted from Alec's face to the staff, and back again. Brun did not know the source of Alec's power. Was the staff-that-glowed the source of his magic?

"I know you will," Brun said, still smiling, "as a good Consort would, and I have no intention of hurting her." He gestured over his shoulder at his men, never taking eyes off of Alec. "Let her go, boys."

One of the guardsmen unlocked the manacles, released Erin, and backed away. Erin scrambled beside Alec and slipped her hand on his arm.

"Also," continued Brun, still assessing Alec, "I have no intention of trying to harm you. If the blue thorn poison couldn't do it, I assume you are ready to stop anything <u>I</u> might try! Such a Great Wizard!"

Alec nodded in affirmation.

"I am willing to negotiate," said Brun, licking his lips.

For what? thought Alec, slightly surprised.

"I don't see you have much to bargain with," he said.

"Oooh, but you are wrong! I have much that Erin wants, that I can use to bargain." Brun's eyes narrowed, and his false smile disappeared. "We both know that you could take my life right now if you wanted – but if you do – both the Queen and Erin's brother will die!"

He speaks truth, Erin thought softly.

"So. What is this 'bargain'?" Alec asked.

"Simple," said Brun, sensing that he was regaining control of the situation. "I will not hurt the Queen and Prince Colin if you agree to leave me alone."

"Why should we trust you?"

"Because I have every reason to keep them healthy." Brun smiled broadly. "If they are alive and well you won't hurt me. If they die, then I have no protection. I suspect all the soldiers in Theland couldn't keep you away from me if you really wanted to harm me!"

"True," said Alec. Then, "I guess we will deal."

"Ahh. There is one more little detail to the deal," said Brun. "I was going to announce tomorrow morning that Queen Therin had fallen ill and had to be taken home to Theland. Then I was going to tell Gott and our allies that we support them, but only the Queen has the power to pick the exact support level, and I would get back to them with how many troops and the other details."

"And eventually send none," said Alec.

"No, no, I would have sent a few. The troublemakers and the Queen's loyalists who I wanted to get rid of." Brun beamed, pleased at his own cleverness. "Now I have a better answer!

"I will tell everyone here that we are fully supportive of Gott's war! So supportive that we will immediately commit our Grand Wizard, Alec, who has great powers in battle, along with our Princess and the two hundred or so riders we have here, as a show of our good faith. Then, I will tell them, we will send another thousand riders as soon as we can get them ready!

"I will say that the Queen is so concerned, that she is already hurrying home to her Residence to start the process! To top it off, I will say we have left Princess Erin, our Little Warrior, here in Gott to lead our riders to the battle, and that she thinks the war is so important that she has abdicated her place in the Theland succession line to her dear sister, Amelia," Brun reached into his pouch and pulled out a scroll, dangling it in front of Alec.

"Here is a copy of the agreement that makes the abdication official, signed in blood this very morning by our favorite Princess!" Brun's smile disappeared. "Oh – and the final part of the bargain is that the whole deal is off if you ever return to Theland."

Alec looked at the document and almost said something, but held his tongue.

Is he correct? he thought to Erin. *Did you sign an abdication?*

I had to do it to save Mother and Colin, she thought back to him.

Alec patted Erin's hand and nodded in understanding, compassion, and agreement.

"When will you send the other thousand riders?" he asked Brun.

"As soon as they are ready, of course – but, our mounts are limited. We might have to raise more trogus before our riders would be ready."

"So – you will never send them?"

"I didn't say that," Brun shrugged, "but the war might have been over for years before we are ready."

We have little choice, thought Erin.

I know, thought Alec, *but I don't have to like it.*

"We will take your deal," Erin said to her step-father. "Your life for the other two."

With that, Brun motioned to his henchmen and they quickly departed the chapel.

≈ ≈ ≈ ≈

Alec sagged, leaning his weight against Erin.

"Are you all right?" she said.

"No," he sighed. "I can hardly stand. I don't think I could have done anything if Brun or his buddies had tried to cause trouble. Fortunately, my reputation as a giant-killer has gotten big enough that they didn't want to test me. Let's get back to our wagon – but you're going to have to control me. I don't know if I can keep from killing Brun if I see him in camp."

They walked outside into the bright sunlight and fresh air, with Alec using his staff for support on one side and Erin for support on the other side. It was a long way back to camp; Erin tried to hail a carriage to give them a ride. The first two refused to take them without payment in advance; the promise of coins at the camp was a common ruse that had been used to stiff drivers many times in the past few days. Finally, Alec relented and diverted some of the energy he was using for healing to create a few coins. That was enough to persuade the third driver to give them a ride back to camp.

By the time they arrived at their camp, things were in an uproar. Ferd, the Queen's lead rider, came up to them, breathless.

"Princess! I am so glad to see you! Consort Brun came through here a little while ago, packed up his belongings, and the Queen's, and said he was heading back home with Queen Therin. He said you would be here shortly, and would explain everything."

"How is my Mother?" asked Erin.

"We never saw the Queen." Ferd handed a message to Erin. "Brun left this message for you."

"The seal is broken," she said, examining the capsule.

"Yes," Ferd said. "As you know, I have been with your family for many years, and your father, Consort Derrin, often told me he did not trust Chief Councilman Brun. Even though Brun is now Consort, with all the strangeness going on in Gott, I took the liberty to read the message in case I needed to act for my Queen to protect her against her Consort."

The message was simple.

"'I have departed from Gott, for Theland.'" Erin read aloud to Alec. "'I left a sealed message at the Gott Palace to be read tomorrow. I am with the Queen. Honor our deal and she will be fine.'"

21 – Raner Pass

The next day Erin, Alec, and Ferd went to the War Council. The abrupt departure of Queen Therin and her Consort Brun had stirred up a lot of concerns. The riders from Theland were widely acknowledged as the best cavalry forces among the allies, and if they were not participating in the battle, it would severely limit the ability of the allied mounted troops.

The Head Scribe read the order of events to the assembly. The message from Brun and the Queen would be the first topic after the introductions and opening comments. Alec thought it was an interminable time before the opening portion was complete, but he could see from the reactions around him that the other delegates were surprised at the brevity of the opening.

Brun's message brought no surprises, although Alec half-expected that Brun would announce something different than he had promised Erin. Brun's commitment of the two hundred riders already in Gott was expected by the War Council, although some leaders grumbled that it was really a commitment of one hundred and twenty riders because eighty of the original number were women. The promise of another thousand riders was a heartening surprise to the War Council, as was the commitment of royalty to lead the riders. However, even though Alec's prowess as a fearsome wizard had spread through Gott City, the war-hardened leaders were not as superstitious as their people and viewed 'wizards' as quacks. They had never seen a wizard change the outcome of a battle, and Alec's performance the other night, now rumored to be a drunken fight did not raise their confidence. Brun's comments on the internal governing affairs of Theland – Erin's abdication and Amelia's rise to Heiress Presumptive – were of little interest to the allies and not even noted. Overall, however, Theland's commitment was well-received and the War Council leaders nodded approvingly.

The next order of business was to ascertain the commitments from Gott's other allies. Some were better than expected, and others were worse. On balance, Gott and its allies had a reasonable force to contest the Alder army, even after discounting for the inevitable under-delivering of promises.

No lord at the War Council was willing to cede control of his troops to another lord; consequently, the allied fighting force was organized with seven different divisions, one for each of the supporting allies. The difficulty of running this type of organization was apparent from the first. The only real decision arising from the War Council meeting was that any forces that were present and ready should immediately start the trip to Ramen Pass to engage with the Alder. A column of Gott troops, the force from Theland, and one other band were ready. It was decided that this joint force would leave in two days.

All the next day was spent in obtaining supplies, checking equipment, and preparing for the trip. Alec spent his time helping as he could. Fixing a broken yoke on one of Theland's wagons was one chore he took on. Usually, a replacement yoke could be obtained from the stable. With this many wagons in town, all the replacements had been used and there was a four-week waiting list. Alec circumvented the process and created a replacement part using dark energy and watched as it was installed.

Erin was consumed with the details of her new command. The Queen's lead rider, Ferd, and Erin's lead rider, Thom, were both a great help to her, organizing the Theland force and providing experience and insights. On schedule, and with great fanfare, the massed troops left Gott City, headed moonward to Raner Pass. It took the better part of a week to reach the mountains around the pass. After two days on the road, Alec decided that they were lucky to be an early group. It was already difficult to obtain sufficient feed and supplies during their passage, and it was going to be increasingly difficult for the later groups.

Alec and Erin spent the evenings talking about how they could use their unique abilities to change the outcome of the battle. One evening as they sat by their little campfire, Alec mused about these societies, and how different they were from his homeland.

"So here we are, possibly riding into a battle that will see our death," he said to Erin, tracing scribbles in the ashes on the firestones with a stick. "We are part of a force that is defending the way of life in Gott – a society that mistreats people and heavily oppresses women."

"Yes," agreed Erin. "The only thing that seems worse than Gott is the behavior of the Aldermen. We are helping to defend the bad against the worst." She stared into the dying flames. "We have a better life in Theland. But, if Gott loses to the Alder, we will eventually lose Theland, so we are defending our way of life also. The good against the worst." With that, Alec felt a little more satisfied with their participation.

The land around Raner Pass was not like the other passes Alec had seen. On either side of the pass were high peaks, but the pass area was a rolling vale between the peaks, a little over two els wide. There was a well-traveled road along the center of the pass, but troops and wagons could make their way across much of the broad area.

The Gott fort at Raner Pass was not the walled fortress that Alec had been envisioning. Instead it was a collection of run-down buildings and stables with open areas for maneuvers. The fort was not located on the pass itself – it had been built as a staging area for troops and was never intended to be a defensible fortress. "The pass here is too wide for a hardened fortress," Ferd explained. "Any invading army could skirt around the edge of a fortress built up there."

The Raner Pass Fort was quite old, probably built several hundred years ago, Alec estimated. Originally it had been designed to handle about five hundred people, counting both soldiers and the support staff, but in recent years it had never seen more than a hundred troops and their main role had dwindled from military exercises to pursuing bandits and escorting convoys. The last major battle in this region had been fought on the Grasslands a generation ago, and in that battle, apparently the fort served merely as a staging and logistical base.

When they arrived, Raner Fort was already overflowing. The base commander had decided to stage the additional troops in camps located some distance from the main area of the fort. Erin received their camp assignment and directed Ferd to set things up. It took some time to get the camp established. Since they were anticipating that it would be semi-permanent, there were lots of issues to resolve, such as ensuring their water source was upstream of other troops' latrines and that they had adequate space for tethering, feeding, and exercising their animals.

They went to meet the Gott General late in the afternoon.

"General, I am Erin, Princess of Theland, and this is my Consort, Alec. I have also with me Ferd, the Queen's lead rider."

"General Mawn," the older man said, glaring from under bushy eyebrows. He looked at Erin, then at Alec, then back at Erin. Finally he extended his hand, palm forward, in greeting, but did not reach for Erin's hand. Or Alec's. "I have not previously beheld a woman in command of a fighting force," he said brusquely, "Princess though you may be."

"Then let this time be your first, General Mawn," Erin said evenly, head held high.

The General cleared his throat.

After a hesitation, he spoke again. "There will be a status review in the morning. First thing. If you can rouse yourself from the comforts of your bed."

"I will be there," said Erin.

"I understand that a lot of your riders are women," he said gruffly. "I do not like women in my camp and do not want women riders here."

"My women riders are as good as my men," said Erin.

"That is not the point," the General said. "We know of the fame of your riders, and if your women are even half as good as your men, they would still be better riders than most others among our allies. But, women are weak-willed and scatterbrained, given to lustful emotions, and a distraction! Women destroy discipline among fighting men! The only women I want in camp are ones that are willing to sleep with my men." Erin looked slightly horrified. "And I can see from your reaction that yours aren't."

"Prostitutes," said Alec, helpfully. Erin hissed at him under her breath.

"No, no," said General Mawn. "Working women. I prefer cooks and seamstresses, and even armorers, if they are willing to be available at night. The prostitutes have too much spare time during the day and tend to make trouble. The women who work don't have idle time." He looked at Erin and pointed in the direction of her camp. "Your troops are posted out of the way, so keep your women riders out there. I don't mind your women fighting and dying for our cause, but I don't want them destroying my men's discipline!"

Erin and Alec were walking back to their encampment, Erin mumbling under her breath about the Gott General, when they crossed paths with another set of allied soldiers, from Lashon. The leader of the Lashon forces had arrived three days ago. Ferd whispered to Alec that the Lashon leader had lodged complaints about their camp location, his status in the allied army, quality of food, as well as many other items; the rumor was that the Lashon man was going to bring his complaints directly to General Mawn.

The Lashon lord marched down the center of the path, an entourage of highly-costumed men surrounding him. Their path blocked that of Erin, Alec, and Ferd. As they approached, a walker in front of the Lashon leader waved his hands to shoo the other people out of the way.

"Make way, make way," the walker said in a shrill voice. "The Grand Lord Leader of Lashon is coming through. Make way!"

Erin's group politely moved out of the way, but Erin could not help laughing at the spectacle. One of the Lashon lord's men turned and peered at Erin from under the floppy brim of his large hat.

"You laugh," he said to Erin with a haughty tone.

"I meant no harm," said Erin.

"We do not suffer any disrespect," the man said. "You do not laugh at His Lordship!" He casually pulled his ornate sword and swung it towards Erin. Erin's sword was out like lightning and caught the approaching sword. She twisted, and the man's sword came loose from his bejeweled hand. Erin caught the sword on her sword, spun it, and propelled it across the path into the brush on the other side.

Two other Lashon men pulled their swords.

"Women shouldn't play with swords," one man said, "or they might get hurt!"

"Send her with us for the night, and we will show her what to play with," another man in the Lord's group cat-called.

Alec wasn't particularly happy with this turn of events. He wanted to end it, convincingly. Now. He felt for dark energy. He held his staff aloft and lit it with a glow so bright that it was blinding to anyone who looked at it. Then he lit Erin's sword equally brightly. He heated the sneering attendant's sword until it glowed red. The man quickly dropped it, shaking his burning hand; some of the ornate scrolls splintered from its hilt as it hit the ground.

Alec took one step forward and waved his glowing staff.

"Make way," he said, imitating the Lashon man's shrill tone. "Make way for Her Royal Highness, Princess Erin of Theland! She is coming through! Make way!"

Erin also held her gleaming sword out in front of her, like a torch. The Lashon men couldn't look at Alec's brilliantly glowing staff or her sword; covering their eyes, they decided it would be best to grab their lord and step off the path to get out of Erin's way. However, one of the last men in the group decided it would be cute to harass a princess and started to slap Erin's rear as she passed. Alec had been expecting something like that. Before Erin could react, the cad's clothes erupted in flame. He fell on the ground and started rolling to put the fire out. Alec didn't even look at him – he continued to direct the people on the path to make way for the princess.

"Make way, make way for the Princess," Alec continued to say, well past the Lashon group. Then both he and Erin burst out in laughter.

"If we weren't in a war, this would be funny," said Erin.

≈ ≈ ≈ ≈

The next morning, Erin, Alec, and Ferd were at the General's briefing early. The leaders of other contingents came into the room, milling about. The Lashon group was last to arrive. They stayed as far from Erin as they could.

General Mawn started his briefing with an update on the situation.

"The Alder have assembled a significant number of soldiers on the Grasslands with the clear intent of moving through our Raner Pass this season. The Alder have the terrible death rods that can kill anything within sight and have established death rod posts around their camps to prevent attacks. Right now, we have a slight numerical advantage, but even that may go away if the Alder continue to receive reinforcements at the same rate they have been.

"The Alder use a simple strategy to advance. First, they establish and defend a death rod post. Then, they attack our positions within the range of their death rods. We cannot send reinforcements to stop their attack because of the death rods – the teeth of the death rods kill our men before they can reach our defensive positions. So far, over the past several weeks the Alder have made a slow but steady advance, and we have not been able to stop them.

"The Alder strategy works well on the plains and the edge of the mountains, but I believe that the rocky terrain in the pass will limit their use of death rods and provide some defendable points. Our observers tell us that the Alder do not seem to be able to use their death rods unless they have a clear view; they do not seem to be able to throw the teeth of their death rods over rocks as we do with our spears."

After taking a few questions from senior officers, General Mawn started giving out battle assignments. After ignoring her throughout his briefing, and after conferring duty stations and tactical advice on all the other leaders, he finally came to Erin and frowned. He clearly did not want this woman commander in his camp.

"All know how fierce the riders of Theland are," he said grudgingly. "I want you to take your riders onto the Grasslands and attack the Alder's supply caravans. If you can disrupt enough supply caravans, you may slow their ability to feed and supply their troops. Also, you can serve as bait, and force them to divert soldiers to hunt you down. That should give us more time to prepare for the assault here.

"Your riders will have no trouble entering Alder territory, but you will not be able to take any of your wagons with you. The Alder have not devoted the troops to seal off the pass on their side. A trogus force can still get onto the Grasslands, especially at night, but not with a supply train." He looked at Erin to see if she understood the assignment.

"By the way, most of the Alder supply caravans carry death rods with them."

He's setting us up, thought Alec.

Erin could tell what Alec was thinking but readily agreed to the assignment. She was much happier with an active role than hanging around a camp with a hostile General to provide a static defense of a piece of Raner Pass. She and Alec turned to leave the briefing tent.

"Hmmph. Serves that 'Princess' right to be sent on a suicide mission," Alec overheard one of the Lashon men say. His companion laughed in agreement.

≈ ≈ ≈ ≈

Erin and Ferd decided to send half of the riders onto the Grasslands for their first attempt at disrupting the caravans, with Erin and Alec leading them. Thom would accompany them, and Ferd would stay with the other riders in the Gott base camp; Erin would send for them when they had worked out the most effective strategies for overcoming the Aldermen.

"We might as well leave now," Erin said. "We have no reason to wait around here cooling our heels for another day."

By dusk, the Theland riders were mounted and ready with all the supplies they could carry, and a train of spare trogus for replacement mounts. In the dwindling light, they carefully made their way through Raner Pass. Every el,

Erin would stop and sense in front of them. They moved over the top of the pass easily and towards the Grasslands.

"Something isn't right," Erin said to Alec just before they reached the Grasslands on the far side of the pass. "I sense a group of people only a half-an-el ahead."

"We should probably leave the others and scout," Alec replied.

The two of them left their mounts and slipped forward. At night it was easy for Alec to obscure them. They slunk across the open meadow that was the transition between the pass and the beginning of the Grasslands. Halfway through the meadow, they could see that General Mawn had not known the true situation. An Alder guard post was positioned in the meadow to prevent entrance to the Grasslands. Alec could feel the presence of gunpowder in the Alder post.

They have death rods, he thought to Erin. *I'll wait here, and you go back for the riders. When you get close, I'll make some mischief.*

Erin turned and vanished into the night. Alec found a convenient tree to climb; this gave him a good vantage point to view the Alder fortification. He waited impatiently for Erin's return. Once an Alder patrol walked right under him, oblivious to his shrouded position in the tree. He thought about attacking the patrol but decided that any noise might alert the guard post. Finally, he decided enough time had passed, and he felt for the dark energy. The crack of exploding shells echoed through the fortification and flashes of light scratched the night sky. As soon as the reverberations died down, Alec heard trogus paws beating on the ground behind him. The element of surprise should give Erin the upper hand now.

Even in the dark, Alec could see Aldermen scrambling around their fortification, trying to figure out what had just happened. Then he noticed a couple of Alder running out of the base to a smaller bunker. He could sense that they had retrieved a second death rod. Alec focused dark energy, and the bullets exploded in loud flashes. The man holding the death rod dropped, wounded by stray bullets and flying shrapnel, and screamed and thrashed. Then he was still. The death rod lay in pieces underneath him.

By now the Aldermen at the guard post were rushing to defend themselves from the approaching trogus force. The trogus topped the wall of the fortification, their riders expertly leaning into their leaps, and landed in the middle of the Alder defenders. Erin wanted no survivors, to provide a warning to other Alder enclaves, so the fight was brief but bloody. Alec carefully climbed down from his observation tree after confirming that no one had escaped and reclaimed his trogus.

After the Alder guard post, they encountered no further obstacles before they reached the Grasslands. They moved several els onto the plain until Erin was comfortable that they would not be observed and then established a camp for the night.

The next day, luck was with them. They were still less than twenty els from the pass, and on one of the likely caravan paths. Erin had sent out scouts an el apart across the plains. One of the scouts returned within the hour with a sighting of a caravan. Erin assembled her riders. The traditional tactic that most raiders used to destroy caravans was to attack from the side. They would try something different. They brought their force across the line of travel. The caravan, seeing a large hostile force, stopped and formed up in a defensive circle. Alec could feel two wagons with death rods, one on each side. The caravan also had some armed guards protected by the wagon ring – the armed guards alone would not be a formidable defense without the other lethal weapons.

The more Alec used dark energy, the easier it seemed to become. He could sense the high-explosive material and focused dark energy. Two satisfying explosions resulted. Then Alec focused on one of the center wagons. A blaze started, and people within the caravan left their defensive positions to rush to extinguish it. Next, Alec focused on another wagon and a second blaze started. The two fires were more than the wagon crew could handle – the fires rapidly began to spread to other wagons. A few of the wagons and some mounted men left the caravan to escape the fires and confusion. Erin sent out her riders in small teams to intercept and destroy them. For two hours the caravan was ablaze. Those who had tried to stay were consumed in the central inferno, and those who left were intercepted and destroyed by Erin's troops. A huge column of smoke rose steadily into the upper air, easily seen by the soldiers at the pass.

Erin assembled her riders after the destruction of the caravan. Their losses had been light considering that they had destroyed a large caravan. Erin led them away from the burning caravan, and soon they stopped for the night.

Erin and Alec evolved several strategies for destroying the Alder caravans. Erin spaced her scouts to sweep across the plains until they found a caravan, usually by spotting the billows of dust that the animals and wagons produced. Over time, Alec had improved his ability to create a dark lens to blur large areas – their preferred strategy was to blur all of Erin's riders and position them along the track of an approaching caravan. When the caravan was alongside the riders, Alec would release the dark lens, surprise the caravan leaders, destroy any death rod wagons, and set fire to the front and back wagons. In the resulting confusion, Erin and her riders could mop up the disorganized caravan with ease.

After three weeks on the plains, Erin decided it was time to head back to their base camp near the Gott Ramen Pass Fort, collect the remainder of her riders and supplies, and leave the wounded to be treated. However, when they were less than a day from the pass, they could see large columns of smoke and hear the occasional snap of the death rods.

"It seems that the enemy has engaged the Gott allies and is starting the attack earlier than expected," Erin mused. "I wonder if us cutting off their supply line forced their hand."

"Maybe this is a chance to do a little more damage," suggested Alec. "If we could get in close, and unnoticed, we could eliminate many more of their supplies."

With a bold plan in mind, Erin and her riders approached the back of the enemy camp, which was located in the Grasslands before the pass. The supply wagons were parked at the rear of the camp in what the Alder thought was a safe location. Alec blurred Erin's riders as they proceeded toward the camp. He had found that the easiest places to obscure were open areas with lots of nondescript field and sky for a background, and the open meadows before the pass were ideal.

They proceeded towards the Alder camp along a wide path about a hundred paces across. The path had been stomped clean by the passage of many trogus, drungs, and foot soldiers. A few Alder soldiers were along the edges of the path where patches of low brush could hide an intruder, but no Aldermen were wasting their time guarding the middle of the path. The noise made by Erin's mounts was obscured by the general battle noises from the fight in the pass. Erin kept the pace slow so that their dust mixed with the slight breeze and could only be distinguished by someone keenly peering in their direction. However, most eyes were on the battle ahead of them – not on the path in their midst.

When they were almost on top of the first Alder wagon, Erin gave the signal. Her riders moved in three waves: the first wave was to eliminate any armed opposition before it could become organized, the second wave was to set on fire as many wagons as possible, and the third wave was to protect Alec while he destroyed as much of the ammunition as he could find.

Erin led the first wave and was among the Alder wagons before any alarm was raised. By the time the second wave had started setting fires, Alec was already destroying ammunition wagons. In only a few minutes Alec had destroyed all the ammunition he could locate. The resulting explosions had wreaked havoc. Most of the wagons and their contents were on fire, and most of the animals had escaped the corrals and were running loose in a panic, trying to escape the fires and explosions.

Erin could see a contingent of Alderman soldiers were forming up to defend the supply camp. It was time to retreat. With a shrill whistle, Erin sounded the call to end the engagement. With practiced skill, her riders broke away and started towards the rendezvous point.

A group of mounted Alder riders had returned from the main battle and were bearing down on them as they reassembled. "A large mounted force is assembling to engage us," Thom announced breathlessly. "They have about twice as many trogus as us. Should we retreat into the Grasslands?" He looked over his shoulder at the advancing animals. "It will be close, but we might be able to outrun them."

"No, I think it is time to stand our ground and fight," Erin answered.

The opposing force came towards them at full gallop with every intention of overrunning them. Erin positioned her riders in battle formation, ready for the fight. The Alder trogus were not in a tight fighting formation, but the sheer number of them would make for a bloody fight. The stomping beasts came closer and closer. The trogus were close enough that Alec could sense the sweat boiling off the animals and hear their labored breathing.

Focus, he thought.

Flames erupted on the trogus' tails. Alec had learned from trying this maneuver before that the tail was the most sensitive part of the animal, and any trogus tended to go mad with any disturbance to its tail. After a few seconds, the first trogus broke and stampeded; by the time the approaching riders had halved the distance, two-thirds of the trogus were braying and bucking wildly, throwing riders and rolling on the ground. All that remained was a ragged line of upset yowling animals. Erin ordered her riders to convert from defense to offense and led the charge herself. Her riders charged into the broken Alder line and destroyed any organized opposition. After that it became small group fights – the superior skills and organization of the Theland warriors easily carried the battle. The remaining Alder riders retreated, and Erin did not attempt to follow and pursue her advantage. The battle over, the Theland riders returned to the Gott allies' lines.

22 – Battle

When Erin arrived back at the Gott base camp, Ferd and the other Theland riders let out a cheer – overjoyed to see their commander and their comrades after three weeks. Except for occasional use as messengers they had not yet participated in the battle. They had heard rumors of Erin's successes on the Grasslands and were ready for action themselves. Erin spent some time settling the injured, debriefing Ferd and her field commanders, hearing stories of how things had gone in her absence, and generally stalling before she decided to bite the bullet, as she had heard Alec say, and meet with the General Mawn.

Erin, Alec, Thom, and Ferd rode to General Mawn's new command area, now located closer to the battlefront so that he could exercise control over the disposition of allied forces. They waited about a half hour before they were escorted in to see the General, Erin growing more impatient by the minute. General Mawn sat at a long table with many of his command staff. Erin gave a brief summary of their actions and successes and asked the General if he wanted a more detailed account.

"Thank you, your most Gracious Highness Princess Erin," the General said, resorting to the Gott style of formal speaking, "It seems as though you have had a most successful venture. However, I don't have time to go into a great deal of detail just now, while I am busy directing these important battle operations. I will ask you all to meet this afternoon with one of my orderlies to depose a full detailed description of your exploits for the record." Then the old General looked at Erin with appreciation in his eyes.

"I thought that a woman would drag down my operations, but I must commend you. Your actions have given us a chance. The lack of supplies had forced the Aldermen to attack before they were ready, and your raids diverted a significant portion of their mounted riders to searching the grasslands for you. Talk to Major Voy, and he will give you a detailed status of the battlefield. He will also give you orders on where I need you next on the field." Then General Mawn nodded a dismissal and went on to other concerns.

Well, a Major is better than an orderly, Alec thought to Erin. She smiled grimly; Alec could tell she was annoyed.

Major Voy was all business and did not seem to be concerned that he was addressing a woman. He escorted them to a side tent and began a description of the situation.

"About two days ago the Alder began their advance into our pass. Their plan seems to be simple but effective. They seize a local high point with a good field of view and fortify and strengthen that point. Then they position several death rods on the fortified location. They find our weak point within the death rods' field of view and then attack in force. If we try to reinforce the weak point, they rain teeth of death down on our men. Rarely are we successful in getting enough reinforcements to the weak point in time to keep them from breaching it! Then they encircle our troops. If our troops retreat, they are killed by the death rods. If they fight, they are surrounded, outnumbered, and killed. If they surrender, they are chained and taken away as slaves."

Ferd asked a few questions about details of the locations, and then the Major went on.

"We have to eliminate the death rod positions to have a chance to stop the assault. Yesterday, our allied forces made three attempts to storm death rod positions using mass assaults. In two cases, all our men were killed before they reached the position. In the third, however, we were more successful. We reached the death rod position, killed all the defending Alders, and captured several death rods. It required the death of essentially all the Lashon troops to capture one death rod position, so we cannot repeat that many times." He looked at Alec. "This is the first time our men have seen death rods. We do not know the wizardry that makes the death rods function." Alec sensed a bit of fear in the Majors' demeanor.

"Earlier in the battle the Alder were using three death rod positions, and their fields of death were linked. Now they are down to only two positions – and using them less often. We don't know why – but we hope it is a good sign."

They must be running low on ammo, thought Alec. *Our caravan escapades must have worked.*

"One of their death rod positions endangers our defenders at the top of Raner Pass," the Major continued. "The Aldermen appear to be preparing for an assault – we think it will occur tomorrow morning, probably soon after dawn. We have noticed that the Aldermen use the death rods most often during the daylight hours. We think that perhaps their magic does not work as well at night when it is dark."

Thank goodness, no night vision scopes, thought Alec.

Major Voy leaned forward and looked intently at the three.

"The General has given you this assignment. Your task is to make a mass charge and take out the death rod position before midnight."

Erin looked surprised.

"Today? This afternoon? But Major Voy, we have only just returned from our engagements on the Grasslands!"

"I realize that this is in short order," the Major said, not unsympathetically. "But our need is urgent. Yours is the only allied contingent with great success at eliminating death rod positions. If you cannot clear out the death rod position before the third moon rises, then the General will have to evacuate all of our troops tonight – or face the loss of the core of the entire Allied Army."

Another 'suicide mission,' Erin thought to Alec.

They seem to think that you ... that we ... are expendable, Alec thought back.

I wonder how many trogus we could expect to make it all the way to the emplacement alive, thought Erin.

"Can we see the emplacement before we must attack?" asked Alec.

"No," said Major Voy. "Although it is close enough to threaten our position here, it is too far to send a scouting party, do reconnaissance, and return before you must assemble your riders. The best I can do is to show you our detailed battlefield map." He led them to the map tent.

Alec studied the map. It was a large detailed rendition of Raner Pass showing topography, structures, and trails. Both allied and Alder troop dispositions and locations were marked on the map. Alec was impressed by the cartographic skill and accuracy of the map; the details of the areas he had seen matched his recollection. Alec could see why the situation was desperate. The Alder had captured a bluff that overlooked the top of the pass. From there, they would have unobstructed use of death rods against anyone on the pass.

Erin was not as accustomed to reading maps as was Alec, but she could see the allies' multiple defensive positions marked on it. With the ability to move troops and reinforce those positions, the Gott force would be very hard to defeat. However, with the death rods preventing allied reinforcements, those positions were susceptible to mass attack. As the Major had indicated, the map showed that there was no convenient place to get a good view of the Alder death rod emplacement.

"Erin, without a good view of the death rods, I am going to have to destroy them as they bring the death rods out," Alec said, planning his moves against the Alder. "That puts a lot of our riders at risk – but I have an idea to save the riders <u>and</u> take their death rod position." He slapped his hand down on the map.

"Let's go! Get your riders ready. I will need two light wagons also."

Erin nodded and thought to him, *I trust your ideas, my Great Wizard.*

≈ ≈ ≈ ≈

Erin's fresh riders were ready. Erin and Ferd assembled the riders, briefed the leads, and moved out of the base camp, all before mid-afternoon. Within the hour they had advanced to the edge of the open area in front of the death rod emplacement. The Alder soldiers in the emplacement were watching their every move.

While Erin and Ferd readied the riders, Alec went to work – *Lots to do in a very short time,* he thought. He selected ten riders for each of the two light wagons. They stripped the wagons, and with a lot of dark energy, Alec repositioned many of the planks on the front to form a crude shield. Then Alec positioned the riders. Now it was time to move the wagons towards the death rod position.

At the edge of the open area, the riders unhitched the drungs from the two wagons and proceeded to push the wagons across the open field towards the emplacement. The pushers flinched as several loud bangs came from the death rod posts, followed by a cascade of splinters puffing off the boards on the front of the wagon. However, none of the troops were hurt, even though they were on foot.

Not a bad approximation of a wooden tank, thought Alec, pleased with himself.

After the third shot, Alec spotted one of the death rods.

Focus.

A rapid series of bangs occurred, and a death rod spun high into the air from the recoil. Alec's riders cheered and continued to push towards the Alder emplacement. In the excitement, one the riders craned his head out from the wooden 'tank' for a better look. Promptly, the Aldermen fired a shot in his direction. Bang! He quickly ducked back under the wagon.

"I said, keep covered!" Alec shouted. "You're lucky you weren't killed!" *But that lets me know where the next rifle is,* he thought, and was able to destroy it.

Alec's riders continued to push the modified wagons towards the emplacement. The plan had been for riders under cover to shout directions to the advancing riders or use their battle whistle codes. However, as they approached the emplacement, it was too noisy to hear, so they improvised by looking back and using hand signals to keep the wagons moving in the correct direction. Alec could see a third death rod as it came out. He felt for the ammunition but could not sense any.

Time for Plan B, he thought, and the death rod's barrel glowed red and started to slump. The Alder gunman looked at it with shock and dropped the weapon.

By now the two converted wagons had reached the Alder emplacement, and the riders stormed around the sides to engage the Alder. There were at least twice as many defenders as Erin's troops – even without the death rods, the emplacement troops had the advantage.

At Alec's signal, Erin quickly ordered a charge. The sight of three dozen charging trogus was formidable; the Alder defenders were overwhelmed in no time. In the midst, the conflict Alec saw several Aldermen retreating across the bluff with two more death rods, but they were out of sight before he could focus.

"We did it," Erin said to her consort. "And the sun has not yet set."

Erin consolidated their position near the bluff and settled in to wait. After what seemed like an eternity, a column of Gott infantry arrived at dusk and marveled at their quick success. The Gott infantry relieved the Theland riders and secured the Alder emplacement. Erin and Alec took their weary, but exuberant, troops back to camp; a team of drungs would come in the morning to retrieve the wagons. Ferd went ahead of the riders to settle the camp for the night.

As soon as Erin and Alec arrived back at their camp, a messenger was waiting for them with instructions to report to General Mawn immediately. The two weary people rode towards the command tent.

Inside the tent was a hubbub of activity. As soon as they arrived, they were promptly escorted to General Mawn. He asked for an immediate debriefing. Erin went through the battle describing the modified wagons they had used to approach the death rod emplacement and the resulting battle, including Alec's destruction of the death rods.

"Very good, very good," said General Mawn. Erin knew that they were not there solely to debrief the General and his officers.

Here it comes, she thought to Alec. He nodded.

"We have new information from two of our scouts, who have just now made it back to safety through the enemy lines. They tell us that the Alder are massing great numbers of soldiers, including reinforcements that seem to have come from far away," General Mawn said.

"We have reason to believe that they will attack in the morning. We will need to call upon all our allies for this great effort. We need to be able to respond quickly and adroitly to any crisis that occurs on the battlefield. I am assigning you and your men ... er, people ... to serve as the first line rider reserve."

Erin gave her assent, and the General dismissed them. It took far into the night to prepare for the coming engagement before they finally settled, exhausted, into each other's arms.

≈ ≈ ≈ ≈

Long before first light, they were up and preparing the troops.

"I don't know what today will bring," Erin exhorted her troops, "but we will fight valiantly for victory over the Alder. I know that the day will bring its share of battle wounds, injuries, and death. Fight well, my riders. Fight for our Queen, for our people, and for our land."

"We will, Princess," shouted Ferd, and Thom and the other riders responded in kind.

They were in position behind the front by dawn. As soon as the sky was light, before the sun rose over the mountain peaks, the first wave of Alder attacks started. Not surprisingly the first attack was against the newly-fortified position closest to the captured death rod emplacement. The attack would have successfully overrun the troops at the fortification, but General Mawn was able to move reinforcements up unopposed. When it was apparent that point was well defended, the Alder leader pulled his forces back and redirected his attack on a second strong point. Again, the General's reinforcements saved the day. By now the Alder strategy was clear: continue prodding different fortified points to force General Mawn to commit troops until the Alder found a weak point that couldn't be reinforced. If they still had their death rods, the Alder tactic would have easily succeeded to make the General's movements impossible, but with no death rods, they were not able to decimate the General's troops as they moved.

In late morning the Alder made a second assault towards the initial fortification. General Mawn again moved allied forces to reinforce the point. Suddenly, a ring of fire broke out, encircling the Gott reinforcing troops. The flames were not high, but they frightened the troops and their animals. Then the men in the allied force started falling, one by one, and died with horrendous screams of pain.

"What is going on!" exclaimed Erin.

Alec thought to Erin, *I sense dark energy swirling. I think someone is using dark energy on the other side.*

I sense it too. What can we do? Erin thought back.

I don't know. Alec felt for the swirls of dark energy and tried to smooth the lines. Abruptly, the other user sensed the resistance from Alec and stopped the flow of dark energy. But by then, the Gott reinforcing column had broken, and the men were running away from the ring of fire, in a panic of retreat. The shouts of the allied officers could not pull their troops back into obedience. The Alder ground troops penetrated the Gott-held fortifications.

"This is us," said Erin, and started to lead her riders. "Forward! For Theland!"

Send the troops forward, Alec thought to her, *but you need to stay. We need to defend against this dark user, and I fear I cannot succeed without your help!*

My place must be with our riders in battle! Erin shot back.

Erin! I need you here! Alec answered her.

Erin was torn. She thought of her mother and tried to calm her thinking. Then she decided her mother would have said her place was where she could win with the fewest casualties, and that was with Alec.

"Ride on!" she commanded her troops, and Ferd lead their charge. Erin wheeled her mount and came back to Alec's side.

The Theland riders charged forth towards the Alder infantrymen who had penetrated the Gott front line. But, as with General Mawn's first line of forces, fire spurted up around them, and the front riders started falling. Erin's riders were well-trained, and they stalwartly rode through the deaths of their brothers and sisters, but their comrades were falling quickly.

Alec could feel the massing of dark energy. He saw the flames sprout, and he could feel something forming inside of the riders' bodies before they fell. He tried to smooth the energy lines, but from a distance, it was easier to clump them than smooth them. He watched in agony as more riders fell.

Erin saw her role. She pulled up close beside Alec, took his hand, and opened her senses. Now Alec could feel the forces on the field. He could feel where the dark energy was forming – with Erin's assistance he could sense the subtleties of the flow and instead of bluntly trying to overpower the other user, could move the implementation point with finesse. Minor whooshes of air started to swirl on the battlefield, and the death blows to the fallen riders stopped. Alec could feel that the energy fields continued to pulse and mass, but their effectiveness was gone.

After what seemed like an eternity of fighting the masses of dark energy, Erin's front line of trogus crashed into the Alder infantry line. The beasts wreaked havoc on the enemy in the pitched battle that ensued. General Mawn was quick to find a second reserve column to add to Erin's force. However, as soon as the reserve column approached the battle, the massed dark energy started to occur again, and again the troops fell in death. With Erin's help, Alec again nudged the implementation point, and the deaths stopped. When the reserve column reached the Alder infantry the massing of dark energy stopped. It appeared the enemy user could not distinguish between friend and foe in close combat.

The second reserve column turned the tide of the battle, and the Alder force pulled back. It had been close, but the fortification had held. The battle was done for the day. Gott and her allies were not yet defeated.

Erin could stand by no longer; she led Alec onto the battlefield. Bodies of riders, Alder soldiers, Gott allies, and trogus lay sprawled across the open area; singed grass sent a pungent smell across the field.

"My Princess," a man moaned, crawling from under a fallen trogus.

"Ferd!" Alec shouted. "Are you ... okay?"

"Yes, just winded from falling under my mount. She is gone, but she saved me from a worse fate."

Erin and Alec stayed on the battlefield with Ferd, attending to the dead. The cost of the charge had been high. The enemy dark energy user had taken more lives in a few minutes than Erin had lost in the rest of the campaign. If Alec and Erin had not been able to counter the dark energy foe, they would have lost most, if not all, of their force.

"Look," said Alec, turning over one of the dead bodies. The dark energy user had created a fist-sized rock that had punched through the man's heart. "Very effective and a very quick death."

Probably much easier than my approach, he mused. If the killer missed their aim slightly, then the rock they created would smash some other organ, or the ribs, and would probably disable any person they didn't kill.

Erin stared at the gaping hole in the dead man's chest.

"They have a Black Wizard," she said solemnly. "A Black Wizard of death and destruction."

"Only our combined ability to move the dark energy's focus outside the body saved our other riders," Alec said, reaching for her hand.

≈ ≈ ≈ ≈

That afternoon General Mawn called all the allied officers together.

"We are going to take the war to the enemy tomorrow," he pronounced. "Our carpenters have made four more attack wagons like the ones from Theland. We will use them tomorrow to neutralize the Alder's other death rod encampment. Then we will mount a general attack up the center of the pass. I don't think the enemy believes we will counterattack so we might be able to break their lines." The old General motioned towards his aides. "Get your assignments from my orderlies."

Major Voy was waiting for Erin and Alec with their assignment.

"The General wants you to be available if needed in the assault on the death rod emplacement, but he wants it led by the first Gott battalion. He thinks they need to learn how to counter this threat without your wizardry." He cleared his throat and glanced at Alec nervously.

"As soon as the emplacement is down he wants you to circle behind the enemy and attack them from the rear. The General thinks if this goes well we may break the Alder tomorrow. He thinks the Alder are too cocky and too dependent on the death rods. Without the death rods, their soldiers are not as good a fighting force as we are. If the death rods are taken away, they will not be much of a threat."

A cockerel sounded at the first light of day – Erin already had her riders moving. They rode silently to an assembly point several hundred arns behind the death rod emplacement. The Gott troops pushed their four wagons forward. A few bangs! rang out, splintering wood on the wagons. Alec took advantage of his vantage point to destroy two death rods. The wagons pushed up to the Alder emplacement. General Mawn had sent Gott's finest troops; they poured out around the wagons with precision and took the fortification. There were no signs of additional death rods. Even Erin was impressed with the discipline and the effectiveness of these troops.

Erin had her riders quickly on the move. The Alder guard post at the bottom of the pass was almost deserted. Only four troopers with no death rods remained at the post. Erin watched the quick fight between her riders and the guards with studied interest. The four guards appeared to have been assigned guard duty because of their limited fighting skills. The riders quickly dispatched the guards and secured the post. They rode past the guard post into the Grasslands at an easy pace, preserving their strength. Alec and Erin kept their thoughts to themselves. They would probably encounter one or more dark energy users, and they needed to be ready. The sounds of battle continued all around with unabated fury. The riders moved into position with what seemed to Erin to be an agonizing slowness.

Erin ordered her troops to advance towards the Alder camp. They could see the reserve columns of Alder troops waiting to be thrown into battle. Erin decided they would be her target and her riders charged towards them. The sounds of paws beating the ground was the first warning the Aldermen received. They attempted to turn to face the charge, but the trogus were among them before they could prepare, and death was on all sides. Teeth, claws, and spears all did their damage.

Now that Erin's riders were through the first reserve column they headed towards a second Alder column. This group had more warning time and had put up a partial pike line to stop the charging animals. Erin's riders raced towards the line, and then at the last second swerved right and left and entered the Alder ranks from the sides. Again claws, teeth and spears served their purpose.

With the Alder reinforcements scrambling to defend themselves against Erin's riders, the unreinforced main line of the Alder broke into small-scale fights as the troops started to fall into disarray. The Alder commander needed his reinforcements to support his main line; he sent a smaller, determined-looking contingent toward Erin's riders.

As the Alder contingent neared, Alec could feel dark energy swirl and start to coalesce as a rock inside one of the front riders. He smoothed the energy lines. Now proximity was on his side. Several more times dark energy clumped, and he smoothed it. Now the Alder force was only arns away, and the riders defending Alec and Erin engaged the approaching Alder soldiers. The dark energy lines twisted again, and a fire broke out around Alec's bresta. Alec straightened the lines, and the fire turned to white puffs of steam blowing into the air. Erin could see that the Alder weren't going to win the fight against the riders if Alec could continue to negate the Black Wizard.

Alec felt an intense clumping of energy and knew the focus was on him. He tried to smooth the fields, but the amount of energy kept increasing faster than he could work.

Help me, his thoughts cried out to Erin.

Erin could feel his mental struggle and took his hand. Alec could now sense the dark energy field but couldn't feel any way to unclump it without creating an unstable point and destroying both himself and Erin. With Erin's ability assisting him, he could sense a little further along the swirl of dark energy. The energy kept increasing – it felt like a silent roar within his head.

"Focus!" Erin exhorted.

"I can't. It's not working." Alec grimaced with the effort.

If I can't stop it, maybe I can dam it up, he thought to himself. He let the dark energy continue to build and then pushed the focus point to where Erin's senses told him the origin was. He fed his energy into the coalescing dark energy and let it continue to build.

And, with a sudden explosion, Alec could feel the snapping of the dark energy lines. His arm flew back involuntarily, losing the grip on Erin's hand. He felt the Black Wizard's medallion overload with the addition of his energy and felt it burst into fragments. A huge rock appeared a few paces from them and settled into the soft ground with a dull thud.

That was meant for us! he thought.

Air whipped around in a brief windstorm that knocked Alec from his mount and caused Erin to almost lose her balance. Erin slipped off her trogus and ran to Alec.

"Are you all right?" she asked breathlessly.

"Help me up! I must be ready for the next fight," Alec answered.

"We have succeeded, Great Wizard!" Erin exclaimed. "We have beaten the Black Wizard!"

The field suddenly seemed eerily quiet. Although a few of Erin's riders were still actively engaged with Aldermen, they seemed far away. Most of the Alder troops were retreating into the Grassland.

Alec could sense which body was that of the other wizard, sprawled on the ground along with the dead and dying Alder soldiers. Alec walked towards the body, Erin a few steps behind him. The wizard lay face down; Alec reached the figure and stopped, Erin right behind him.

"The Black Wizard is a woman!" Erin exclaimed in surprise.

23 – The Black Wizard

Alec was stunned. The Black Wizard was a woman. *But – somehow – maybe I knew that…*

The woman was dressed differently from the other Alder soldiers: instead of their coarse dark blue uniforms, she wore a form-fitting black garment with blue reflective stripes. *Almost like the runner's tights I used to wear back home,* Alec thought.

The Dark Wizard stirred, and then rolled over. He could see blood and a ragged hole in her chest where her medallion must have been. One of her arms was bent at a broken angle, obscuring her face.

She doesn't have long to live, Alec thought, kneeling beside her.

"Alec?" she said.

He gasped, taken aback. Her voice was one he hadn't heard in a long, long time, but yet so familiar, even through her pain. He rocked back on his heels, in shock and disbelief.

"Alec – I should have known … Alder always suspected you survived." Wincing, she moved her broken arm from her face. The snub nose, the cropped hair, the fulsome mouth, came into view.

"Sarah," Alec whispered.

"I should have known that the rogue user would turn out to be you."

"Sarah." He gently touched her face – the face that he had once held so close, that he had once loved. She looked older than he remembered; even though it had only been – what? – A year or so since he had arrived in this strange place. Older, and somehow, harder.

"Sarah – what are you … how … how are you here?"

"I am here to assist our colony, of course."

"Your colony … you mean, the Aldermen?"

"Yes! Alder's men!" Her face twisted in pain.

Alder's men?

"Dr. Alder? At the Institute?" *What?*

"Yes, Dr. Alder. His colony here."

"Colony? What colony? How can he have a colony …"

"Of course he has this colony. He's worked on this for years, to establish a foothold on this planet."

Alec shook his head. Of all the things that he might have expected, this was a total befuddling mystery.

"You are dying Sarah. We need to stabilize you." Alec took her hand and coursed a small thread of dark energy through her. "Erin and I can probably heal you," Alec said, wondering if he was truthful, given the enormity of her wound.

Sarah looked at Erin for the first time.

"So that's how you beat me," she said bitterly. "You had help from a cross-breed! Keep away from her! The Elders warned us that cross-breeds are as evil as the elves!"

Erin looked at Alec, her dark eyes filling with tears, and backed away from Sarah.

"You are one of us! Stay away from the cross-breeds!" Sarah gasped, her breath becoming shallow. Her eyes rolled up, then closed.

Alec kept pushing dark energy into Sarah to keep her alive, at least until she could accept help.

≈ ≈ ≈ ≈

After some time, Sarah seemed to stabilize. It could have been a few moments or a few hours: Alec couldn't tell the difference. Some color came back into her face, despite the hole in her chest, and she opened her eyes.

"Sarah ... Sarah, can you tell me what is going on?" Alec said softly. "How did you get here?"

"I came through the transporter, of course. Alder sent me. I am surprised to see you, Alec. You still look ... young. On Earth, it has been over four years since you left; time flows more quickly there than here, since Earth does not have as much dark energy."

Four years? "What portal?"

"In your time with Alder, did you ever know that this was his project – his purpose – or hear anything about setting up a dipole on another world?" Her eyes searched his face.

"No! I never heard of any ... project. I came to work with Dr. Alder because he was a renowned expert in the field of dark energy! I was lucky that he chose me to work with him!" Alec replied, surprised at how much he suddenly missed his former mentor.

"Huh," she said, "Did you really think it was an accident – luck – that he picked you? It was because of your work – your brilliance, really – in understanding how to use dark energy. He thought you could be useful to the project."

"But you say he kept secrets from me."

"Alder never really trusted you; he always felt like something wasn't quite right about you. You always had some sense of ... wanting to help people too much. Wanting to do what you thought was 'right.' That's why he had me get close to you. Date you. To see what you were really made of." She smiled at him, grimly, through her pain. "But I was always Alder's girl; even when I was with you, I was Alder's."

"You and Dr. Alder? Really?"

"Yes, long before you came along, Alder and I were together. But you were my little assignment – to get to know you better, to make sure that you could be one of us. Alder didn't like it when I started sleeping with you, but I told him it was part of getting close." She let out a little laugh. "You were the better lover, and I didn't want to break up with you. I have always been very fond of you – I did love you, you know; I loved you, Alec." She tried to reach out, to touch him, but her broken body failed her and she couldn't. Alec squeezed her hand tightly, bringing it briefly to his lips. Then he fell silent, again feeding a pulse of dark energy into her body, keenly aware of Erin, standing behind him.

"All I wanted, all through grad school, was to work at the Institute, with Dr. Alder. Now you're telling me that my work there was for a hidden purpose, and your interest in me was only to get information for Dr. Alder." His mind was spinning. "But you said you needed to know that I was okay, that you could trust me to be part of your secret project. You said 'one of us.'" She nodded slightly.

"What do you mean, 'one of us?'" he asked, genuinely puzzled.

"Oh Alec, there is so much you don't know!" Sara sounded exasperated, even though she was very weak. "Our world and Nevia – this world here – are part of a million-years-long battle between the elves and the orb. The war has been going on across the multiverse since before anyone can remember."

"What are you talking about?" Alec wondered if Sarah was going mad from pain.

"The Elders explained it to me, like they explained it to Alder. Long ago, millions of our years ago, the elves were the only race in the multiverse. Then the elves created another race: the 'orb,' as the elves called them. They needed to have another class of people – beings – to take care of work tasks and be expendable. The orb look like elves but do not have all the mental powers that elves have.

"The elves turn some of the orbs into compliant drones. Drones have no self-will: their only desire is to please their masters, the elves. The elves use the drones to do everything for them and run all aspects of their society. They treat all their drones and the orbs like expendable, inferior animals. But, since the elves created the orbs and drones in their own image, they sometimes cross-breed and create creatures like your girlfriend here." Sarah paused to catch her breath.

"A million years ago some of the orbs escaped and established their own societies on other worlds. Many of the outposts became isolated from the homeworlds; they went rogue and lost all knowledge of their past. Then after awhile the elves realized that the orbs were competitors. The elves started a campaign to eradicate the orbs, and a war between the two has raged across the multiverse ever since. Many worlds have active hostilities, but most of the multiverse consists of outposts and guard stations."

"How do you know all of this?" asked Alec.

"Because the orb Elders told us! They came to our world and contacted us. How do you think Alder found out about dark energy? Did you think that he just magically 'discovered' dark energy one day in such a dark energy back-water as Earth? How do you think anyone made the first tricrystals? Our world is just an isolated orb outpost."

"So you are saying that there are ... 'orbs' ... on Earth?" Alec asked, incredulously.

"Yes, Alec. Yes. There are orbs on Earth. You are one of them. I am one of them. We are all orbs! All humans are orbs – part of the great orb culture that spans thousands of worlds across the multiverse!"

Alec looked at her in total disbelief.

"We are orbs," Sarah repeated, earnestly. "You need to understand that. About ten thousand years ago the people on Earth lost touch with the orb culture. Our unstable civilization is the result. And now, things are getting worse."

"How?" asked Alec, still not choosing to grasp that he was something called an 'orb.'

"The elves are active on earth and plan to domesticate us and eventually turn us into their drones. They always need more drones and Earth would be a good source. Twenty years ago, an orb scouting party reconnected with Earth and discovered the elf plan. They looked around for people who would be able to understand how dark energy works, and found our Dr. Alder. Alder is a key contact for them. He is a part of a secret organization on Earth that works with the orb to oppose the elves. They showed us about dark energy; but Earth is a low field for dark energy. We don't have much of it. Not like here, on Nevia. It is strong here.

"Because we don't have much of a natural background of dark energy on Earth, our orb Elders do not think that the elves can be defeated when they rise up against us and that time may be coming sooner than we thought. The Elders think that Earth has no chance to win against the elves. They recommend taking our best ideas and people and flee to another world before the elf domestication starts and all the humans on Earth are turned into drones, or worse.

"You've got to understand. Alder doesn't like the idea of being turned into a drone. Neither do I. Neither would you. He has been trying to figure out a way to defend the Earth. With our technology, we understand some things about dark energy better than the orb Elders. Your mathematics opened the door to figure out how to link our world with a zero-point world, which would provide us with an adequate background of dark energy. That is what Alder was trying to do. He hired you because he eventually wanted to use your mathematics to calculate the effects of linking Earth with a zero-point world. Until you were cleared to learn of the orb, he couldn't tell you any of this."

"So Alder is trying to save the world. Earth."

"Yes."

"Um, okay. What is a 'zero-point world'?"

"A place where dark energy is strongest. The orb Elders told us of this world, 'Nevia,' or 'the Land of the Five Moons.' Nevia is a valuable world and is what they call a 'zero-point world.' Nevia has a focal point for maximum dark energy, called a 'zero-point.' Alder plans to link Nevia and

Earth. He has calculated that the link has to be made at the focal point, the zero-point. If it works, it will allow Earth to resist the elves."

"Are the … 'Elders' … going to tell him how to do this?"

"The Elders are not scientists and are not able to figure this out. They want to make use of the high level of technology we have on Earth. They're sort of like parasites," she sighed. "Even though both elves and the orb Elders treat technology-worlds like the plague, they need us. Orbs count on finding rogue high-tech worlds like ours and then using us to make stuff for them in exchange for valuable knowledge. That's why they sent a scouting party to Earth, twenty years ago when Alder was just starting his research. But technology always creates run-away worlds. If technology gets beyond the level that you see here on this world, it goes unstable and destroys civilization. It's happened untold times and will happen on our Earth eventually."

"So they consider this – this medieval society where people go around hacking up each other with swords – to be the ideal world?" Alec blurted. "There is no technology here! Don't they want high-tech things? Don't they see the value?"

"The elves dislike technology, but they often use the technology that benefits them. With the right technology, dark energy can be used to transport people and things between worlds and even between universes. Over time, with the use of orb- and drone-developed technology, the elves have expanded across the multiverse. They use their high-tech tools to control people, as well as use it for ordinary things. The elves use negative dark energy to mentally control orbs and their drones.

"The elves can manipulate negative dark energy – you know, anti-dark-energy – but cannot use positive dark energy. Orbs can manipulate positive dark energy, but not negative dark energy. Negative dark energy is what allows cross-breeds – like your girlfriend – to sense emotions, among other things."

She's in pain, and beginning to ramble, thought Alec. *I'm losing the flow of feeding dark energy into her.* He tried to reach for higher levels of dark energy; tried to feel the 'rightness' of the energy entering her body.

"Tell me more," Alec said. *If I can keep her talking, maybe I can keep her mind off her pain.*

269

"Like I said, the elves have some kind of things that they use to control their 'orb herds.' The Elders told us about them – some kind of finger ring and some kind of neck collar that they make the drones wear. The Elders also showed Alder a medallion, and how to make them. The Elders said that the elf rings and medallions were invented a million years ago on high-tech worlds.

"The elves have many weapons that were invented on high-tech worlds. They dislike the weapons but will use them when they need them. The drone collars came from a high-tech world only a hundred thousand years ago. For a while, the orb thought it would be a weapon that would turn the war against them. Then another high-tech world showed them how it had a flaw and was straightforward for captives to negate. Since then, the war has returned to a stalemate. It is mostly a low-tech war with extremely high-tech medallions, rings, collars, and other things fought across millions of semi-feudal worlds."

Alec interrupted Sarah's rambling as a thought occurred to him. "I did calculations about linked worlds in graduate school."

"You never published your information or told anyone?" asked Sarah, surprised.

"I never told anyone because the calculations never produced anything useful," said Alec. "They create an unbalanced solution and always result in a singularity. It's as if some missing forces should balance and produce a stable solution. Otherwise, your 'multiverse' couldn't exist. Anyways, a link like you described would create a black hole. It would suck everything into itself."

"You mean Alder is in the process of creating a black hole?"

"That's correct," said Alec.

"You must stop him!" For the first time, Sarah began to cry. "For my Celeste!"

"Celeste?"

"I have a child at home. My Celeste. I want my daughter to grow up, and have a chance to live, even if the elves may eventually take over our civilization."

"What is Alder trying to do?" asked Alec.

"Alder intends to set up a dipole. At this end the dipole needs to be on the actual zero point, somewhere over in that second mountain chain. Alder thinks an elf outpost might be at the site. He suspects that this bunch of elves may also have gone rogue, and that they may also have lost contact with the multiverse. The orb scouts felt like elves were dangerous vipers that should be avoided at all costs, but Alder thinks he could handle elves with high-tech weapons. The transfer point he opened on this world is behind me, back on those grassy plains. Alder needs to capture the actual zero-point site and move some equipment there. It is hard to move things from Earth to here because we must collect so much dark energy before each move. At first, he thought we could move a few tanks into this world and dominate it. That turned out to be too difficult, so he settled for trying to conquer everything with the use of a few rifles as weapons. You foiled that.

"Alder can't come himself because he can't be away from Earth for very long. He didn't trust sending anyone else because he feared they would go rogue and establish their own little kingdom instead of doing his bidding. So, he sent me. He is taking care of my Celeste, and he knows that while he has my daughter, I'll do what he wants. He also sent along a few weak medallions so that I could recruit and train some locals to help run the portals at the transfer site." Sarah closed her eyes and winced. It was getting harder for her to breathe.

"You know, you made all this possible," she continued, again looking at his face. "Alder would have failed that night if you hadn't been there and done whatever you did to help him. Alder first created a gate – transporter – to this world about ten years ago. The gate was unstable and very unreliable. He still doesn't understand what you did, but it stabilized the gate. The gate will stay open and stable as long as your medallion is in this world. If you send your medallion back, the gate will close. It was a lucky accident that allowed him to find this world. I don't know if he would ever be able to find it again." She closed her eyes and gritted her teeth; pain was overcoming her resolve.

"If he knew about it, Alder would never believe your math – your theory about creating a black hole – and he will never quit on his own, so we must stop him. Let's go to the gate and send your medallion back and close it. Then Celeste would have a world to live in. We would still have my medallion so that we could rule the world. I would let you use one of the other weak medallions. You know my new medallion is stronger than the old ones and individually coded so only I can use it. Your medallion would be a lot weaker than mine, but at least you would have a medallion. I have missed you. We could rule together."

Alec shook his head. "One problem with your plan is your medallion was destroyed in our fight," he said. Alec did not mention the fact that his original medallion was lost in the Grasslands or that he had figured out how to make additional medallions.

"It can't be. I can feel dark energy flowing through me," Sara protested.

"I am doing that," said Alec. "I am giving you strength. Let me try to heal you."

She felt her chest with her good hand – the gory mess and the ragged hole. She could feel her heart beating weakly. She could feel that there was no medallion on her being.

"No, no," she said. "Leave me alone and let me die. I'm nothing without my medallion." She rolled away from him, her breath increasingly ragged.

"Please Alec," she whispered. "Save my child. Celeste was born eight months after you left, and might be your daughter. Alder thinks she is his child, but I feel that she is not. Please save her. If you promise to save my daughter, I will tell you one more important thing."

"I will try," he said.

"The elves have a dark energy concentrator near the zero point. I think it masks the location of this planet from the orb. Somehow it was set up so that it even masks Nevia from the other elf planets. The elf concentrator is going out of phase. Alder told me his transfer point might have accelerated the shift out of phase. If it isn't put back in phase, it will go high-order unstable and destroy all of the elf kingdom on Nevia as well as all the surrounding land. If you manage to avoid the blast and don't fix the concentrator, both elves and orbs in the multiverse will quickly notice a new zero-point world. They both loathe cross-breeds – they will move quickly to terminate any cross-breeds, and then fight each other for dominance of this world – Nevia. If you want your girlfriend, or her children, to live, someone needs to stabilize the concentrator. The elves probably can't fix it, or they already would have."

"Please, don't let my daughter die. Please Alec."

He squeezed her hand; he could feel that the life-force was ebbing from her limbs.

"Oh, there are passwords at the transfer point that I can use to get in. The answer to the password questions are 'diamonds' and 'pfzzz ...'"

"What? I didn't understand the second word," Alec said, but knew he was too late.

Sarah's jaw dropped open, her head slumped back, and her eyes went glassy. Alec could feel his dark energy wilt.

"She's gone," he said softly. "Sarah, I loved you."

Erin had heard the exchange between them. She came to Alec, still kneeling by Sarah's body, wrapped her arms around him and held him. After a long time, she spoke.

"I could sense that about half of what the Lady Wizard said was true; the rest was partially true but filled with self-serving deceptions."

"What about … what about the part when she said she had a child?"

"That was truth, my Dear Wizard."

"And … that it … that she … could be my child."

"Truth."

He let this sink in, still staring at Sarah's body.

"I am with you, my Great Wizard," Erin said. "I know you loved her." She kissed the top of his head as a tear rolled slowly down his cheek and into his red beard.

24 – Decisions

Alec and Erin slowly and silently walked, hand in hand, back to their trogus and rode away from the battlefield. Although the battle was won, they could see a few skirmishes continuing along the margins of the victory; the Alder troops were clearly in a rout. They rode back towards the main Gott camp, crossing the pass. Alec pondered the multitude of things that Sara had told him – wars across the millennia, human orbs, Dr. Alder's ability to create interplanetary travel, and the uncertain role of Alder's men. And the potential of having a daughter on earth was almost unfathomable.

But, all in all, the day was a victory. The allied Gott forces had won the battle and regained Raner Pass, and the Alder were driven back to the Grasslands to regroup. Ferd arrived at their camp shortly after they did, and Ferd, Thom, and the other riders crowded around, wanting to hear about the unusual battle, the rings of fire, and the Black Wizard.

Having secured the pass, the next morning General Mawn sent an infantry company to attack the main Alder camp on the Grasslands. Unfortunately, the Gott allies were soundly defeated by a reinvigorated Alder force that used death rods to augment their troops. That evening at the General's council, the excitement was muted and feelings were mixed. Gott and her allies had removed the Alder force from Raner Pass and had developed tactics for reducing the threats from the death rods. However, the large Alder army on the Grasslands could be re-equipped with death rods and resupplied, thereby continuing to pose a threat to the Gott forces. Because the open Grasslands were an ideal setting for the death rods, it would be very difficult to successfully attack the Alder forces as long as they remained at that location.

General Mawn directed Erin to resume her previous mission of harassing the Alder supply caravans while the General reinforced the pass based on his new understanding of how death rods could be circumvented. That assignment fit well with Alec's and Erin's plans, and she readily agreed.

≈ ≈ ≈ ≈

The next morning, Major Voy unexpectedly arrived at the Theland camp breakfast tent, unannounced.

"A messenger arrived early this morning. He rode through the night with an urgent message for you, Princess."

"A messenger?"

A weary man was ushered to their table. Spattered with mud and smelling of trogus, it was evident that he had ridden long and hard.

"A message for Her Highness, Princess Erin of Theland," the man intoned.

"I am Princess Erin," she replied, and the messenger gave her the capsule and retreated respectfully. Erin opened the pouch and read the message. "Oh no," she gasped, and her eyes immediately filled with tears.

"What is it?" Alec asked.

"My Mother!" Erin began to sob. "My Mother has died! My Mother, our Queen!" The Theland riders eating nearby overheard, and immediately all breakfast chatter stopped. "But she couldn't have died! I would have known when she died. I would have felt her death."

Erin turned to the messenger, "Are you sure of this?"

"The story was all over Freeland City when I left, that the Queen was dead. I am sorry to be the one to bring the news."

"My Mother has died, and ..." She swallowed hard as she continued to read. "And now Amelia has claimed the throne!" There was a ripple of surprised gasps.

"But, My Lady, should not the throne of Theland descend to you?" one of the riders asked. Erin looked at her. This was not the time to cause a disturbance within her fighting force.

"The Council has decided to invest the Queenship on Amelia," Erin said, trying to regain her composure, although she wanted to scream. Then, turning from her riders, she said: "Please excuse me." Clutching the message tightly to her chest, she quickly left the tent.

"Thank you, my dear man, for your kind service and expeditious delivery," Alec said to the messenger, trying to remember the words that Erin always used to thank, and dismiss, couriers. He marked the messenger's slate, signifying that the message had been received and read. Then he followed Erin to their wagon, not surprised to find her sobbing.

"Brun," Erin choked out. "Brun did this." Alec could only nod in agreement and watch his princess cry.

≈ ≈ ≈ ≈

General Mawn understood Erin's wish to delay her mission. "I must give my Mother, the Queen, a proper departure ceremony," Erin said, certain that Brun would not honor his consort in the traditional custom.

Even though they did not have the Queen's body, Erin took a day to go through the ancient ritual, Alec by her side and the Theland riders in attendance. By the end of the ritual, Erin had regained her composure, and Alec could sense an unwavering determination to avenge the wrongs that Brun and Amelia had vested upon her mother.

The next day they were off, following General Mawn's orders. Erin would continue to mourn the loss of her mother, but she was a true rider. There would be time for additional mourning, but now she needed to lead her people. Erin took her entire force with her, as well as a few supply wagons. Their progress would be slower, but they would be better able to support themselves. The trip through Raner Pass and onto the Grasslands was uneventful. Once on the Grasslands, they found that the Alder caravans were much more heavily guarded than before; the first caravan they encountered required more fighting to subdue than earlier ones.

They planned to take their riders evening-ward. Alec knew that the war between Alder and Gott would not end until either the transfer gate to the other world was closed, or they lost.

"Sarah told us how to close the gate, once we find it," Alec said, explaining the intricacies of the matter to Erin. "The first step is to try to find my lost medallion, while we are out here on the Grasslands carrying out General Mawn's mission."

"We must tread carefully," Erin cautioned. "These Grasslands are dotted with bands of Alder scouts, just waiting to find us. And if they do find us, they will tail us, out of our sight, until they can bring together enough of their soldiers to attack us."

Under Ferd's able guidance, they were able to avoid the Alder scouts and their nomad spies. After two weeks of traversing the Grasslands and destroying caravans, they recognized a small village as the place where they had broken free of the Alder slavers many months before. They saw no need to stop, but now they had their bearings. The next step was to retrace their path and attempt to find the area where they had been captured. It took them three days to find the small village where Alec had rescued Ilave. Alec wanted to see how Ilave had fared, but they had to wait for most of a day to avoid an Alder scout patrol that Erin had sensed.

They approached the village cautiously. The village had been re-populated in the year since Alec had last seen it, and the gates and fortifications along the outer wall had been repaired. But as soon as the village sentries saw their force, the residents pulled the gates closed and moved inside the walls. Alec didn't blame them. A large trogus force on the plains in times of war did not bode well for a small village. Erin directed her riders to make camp for the night half an el from the gate. Only Erin, Alec and a few riders approached the gate.

"Halloo," Alec shouted.

No answer.

"We come in greeting, with no harm intended for your village," Erin called out.

"Go away," shouted a booming voice from within the walls. "We are poor, and we have nothing to offer you, weary travelers though you may be. Leave us alone!"

"What of hospitality? Do you have none to offer travelers in these lands?" Erin cried.

"We wish you well, but we cannot open our gates for anyone," the voice answered.

"Wait, I know that voice!" Alec said to Erin.

"Harl, my friend, is that you?" he called.

There was a brief silence, then a bit of scuffling noises, and then a head popped cautiously over the village wall and looked out at them.

"Alec, Erin, my friends – do my eyes deceive me?" the man shouted in delight. "It is indeed I, Harl, your friend and servant! What brings you to these forsaken plains?" He looked past Erin's small party to the riders making camp in the distance. "And with such an impressive force," he added.

"Our mission is not one to be bandied over fences, but we come in peace to your town," Erin answered.

With that, the village gate slid open, and Harl trotted out to greet them.

"Welcome! Welcome, my friends!" There were bear hugs and back slaps all around, and then Harl hustled them through the gate into the safety of the village walls. "Welcome to our humble village! I'm sorry for the reception but times are so troubled now that we are afraid of our shadows. We will gladly offer you our hospitality!" Harl gestured towards the Theland riders setting up camp on the open plain. "But I am afraid that we cannot accommodate a large force such as yours."

"That is all right," said Erin. "My riders are set for the evening. But let us hear your tale since we parted, and then we will be on our way." They entered the village, crossing the square where Alec had seen such carnage. It was now in good repair – no signs of the past bloodshed – and the village looked prosperous.

Alec looked about for a certain inquisitive youngster and soon spotted him.

"Ilave! Come here!" said Alec. The boy approached hesitantly until he recognized Alec, and then came with a bound.

"You came back!" he said, joyfully, and jumped onto Alec in greeting.

"I did, and I see you carried out my instructions to keep the village safe until your people returned!" Alec set the boy back on his feet and tousled his hair playfully. With that, Ilave beamed.

Ilave took them to meet his parents and his older brother. Alec remembered his conversation with them after he had rescued them from the slavers, and was pleased to see that the older boy also had survived the raid. Now they offered the hospitality of their humble home, but Harl interrupted and insisted that they eat with Lily and him.

Erin and Alec shared a simple dinner with Harl and Lily in their cottage. Erin was especially glad to see Lily; they had become close friends during their time traveling together.

"You've taken up with Harl, I see," Erin said to her out of earshot of the men.

Lily giggled. "I'm still with him," she said. "Not ready yet to make a permanent commitment and consort with him, but that may come soon." Erin could see that they clearly were compatible, and Lily was happy. Erin shared the details of her consorting with Alec as they bustled about setting food and drink on the small table.

"After you left us, many of the good folks that you freed chose to stay here, and the remaining villagers took us all in," Harl told Alec. "Then they asked me to stay on as the Village Marshal. Of course, I had to agree! I was the best choice around!" Harl roared with cheerful laughter, and Alec soon joined in. "Me and my Lieutenant, my sweet Lily, we've been here ever since.

This is home now." Harl looked at Lily and winked at her, and she smiled back. "Life is difficult out there on the Grasslands," Harl continued, "because of all the marauding bands. Besides the Gryg, and the other nomad tribes, we have to contend with the Aldermen."

"Are they still taking slaves?" Alec asked.

"Well, if they catch you, they'll make you into a slave, if they don't just kill you first. But," he added, spreading his hands expansively, "they haven't sent another slaver force through this country since you were here. That's a good thing! I guess they got enough folks to carry out whatever they are doing." He stabbed his bread into the gravy on his plate. "But, every once in a while an Alder scout patrol comes around. You have to avoid them because they either capture or kill any folks they encounter." He filled Alec's cup.

"And you? What brings you back out here?" he asked, turning to his guest.

Erin gave an abbreviated version of their story, mentioning only that they were disrupting Alder caravans at the behest of General Mawn. Neither Alec nor Erin mentioned their encounter with the peddler-man to Lily. After dinner and more conversation, they thanked Harl and Lily for their hospitality and after hugs and promises to come back; they returned to their troops' camp for the night.

≈ ≈ ≈ ≈

Erin and Alec had reached a decision point. Although they were on the Grasslands to carry out General Mawn's assignment, Erin's riders did not know that their leaders were using this as a cover for their true mission: to search for Alec's lost medallion. Erin and Alec had decided that the search for the missing medallion could best be carried out by the two of them without the encumbrance of the full complement of riders. They felt that they could sense and avoid the Alder scout patrols and defend themselves if necessary.

They discussed their plan to split up with Ferd and Thom.

"It will be easier for us to find what we need to defeat the Aldermen," Erin told her lead riders. "The Wizard can better use his wizardry if there are not so many riders around."

"This is a bad idea, My Princess," Ferd said. "You are placing yourselves in grave peril."

"There are still many caravans crossing these plains, supplying the Alder," Erin calmly replied. "I need you to continue as you have been: find the caravans and raid them." *You also will be pulling the Alder scouts away from us,* Erin thought.

Erin and Alec separated from the Theland riders and made their way around the rises and falls of the undulating grasslands, an extra trogus to carry supplies in tow. Backtracking from Ilave's village, they were certain they were in the correct general area. With a little work and some help from Erin's ring, they found the ragged path they had been traversing when the Alder first captured them. Unfortunately, there were many els along the trail where the encounter could have taken place.

Alec knew he could not feel a second medallion if he wore his medallion or carried his staff, but he would be able to feel a medallion from about seven or eight paces away if all other medallions were more than fifty arns from him. They previously had developed a search strategy and Alec practiced the skills he would need. Erin would hide Alec's medallion, and he would practice sensing the medallion in order to find it. Now they perfected their routine. First Erin would feel for Alder riders. Then she would take Alec's medallion, his staff, both their trogus and the pack trogus away from the search area. Alec would crisscross the area in a search pattern to try to sense his old medallion.

On the afternoon of the third day, they were covering their last search area for the afternoon. Erin could sense that there were two groups of Alder scout patrols within a couple of els, but neither was heading in their direction. They decided it would be safe to complete their search while Erin continued to sense the groups.

Alec left his medallion and staff with Erin and started to walk the area. It was a relatively large area; Erin couldn't tell if it was right or not. It looked like what she remembered, but everything looked similar on these plains. In their days of searching they had not found any remains of their ruined clothing or other debris from their capture to give them a lead.

Alec had walked to the far side of the search area when Erin became concerned. A group of about a dozen Alder riders had changed directions and were moving towards Alec's position. Erin started to edge her animals towards Alec in case they needed to regroup.

Then disaster struck. One of the distant trogus stepped on a prairie-skarn. The skarn hissed and spooked the trogus; the animal threw its rider and bolted in the direction of Alec. Two of the Aldermen took off at full gallop after the beast.

Alec, we have a problem! Erin thought. *They are going to top that far ridge in a few moments and see you.* A lone walker on the Grasslands would be an easy target for mounted riders.

Alec ducked down in the tall grass hoping to cover his location. Erin had the animals in a little draw; they would be hard to spot.

That crazed trogus is heading straight toward Alec, she thought. *If it doesn't kill him, the riders certainly will.*

If Alec had either his medallion or his staff, it wouldn't be a problem, but without them, he had little chance. The Alder would assume a lone figure was a deserter and wouldn't give him a second look if they found him. They would aim their trogus towards him and let them chomp him in two. Erin had to do something.

"I am leaving your staff here! Make your way here and get it, and then come to help me. I am going to distract them!" she called out to Alec.

She mounted her trogus and rode out toward the approaching trio. The spooked trogus saw her and steered to the right. She turned to the right also. The two riders saw her and headed toward her, calling the other scouts to join them. Erin took her animal another hundred arns away from Alec. She drew her sword and slowed slightly so the two riders could start to catch her. They gained on her until they were almost abreast of her. She jerked her animal around, startling the riders. The first one tried to pull up, and that gave Erin time to bring her sword around and slash a deep gash in his side. She turned her mount and didn't see the rider fall off in pain.

She wheeled her trogus towards the second rider. He was coming straight at her. She angled her animal to one side. The two heavy trogus crashed into each other in a mass of teeth and claws. Erin jumped clear of the melee. The two trogus locked in mortal combat for dominance. They would fight until one was victorious and the other dead. The Alder rider was caught in the struggle between the two beasts and shredded as an incidental casualty of the fight.

Erin turned and sprinted towards the third trogus. It had stopped about one hundred arns away. She was less than a third of the way to the animal when she could tell she wouldn't make it in time. The other Alder riders were galloping down on her and would reach the animal before her. She looked around to find Alec. She could see him running as fast as he could in the tall grass.

Too far away to help me, she thought. *I am on my own for this one.*

She headed for a slight draw that would give her some cover from the galloping beasts. The first Alderman came charging down on her. She sidestepped his pike and raked her sword across the back leg of his trogus. It reacted in anger and bolted upright. The Alder came sliding down; as he fell she slashed his throat.

Three down, she thought.

Then she backed into the draw. The other Alder scouts came up to the top of the draw and looked down at her. They dismounted from their beasts. *Nine more,* she thought. Five drew swords. Four of them held catch-pole pikes, and one also held a net.

They think to capture me, she thought. *We will see.* She looked at the catch-pole pikes. They were very effective weapons for team fighting. They looked roughly like Alec's staff with a sharp point on one end and a large curved hook on the other end that could be used to catch a foot or an arm and bring a fleeing slave under control.

One of the Aldermen stepped down into the draw. Erin launched toward him with fury. He raised his sword and parried her, but she was too quick, and he lay on the ground, blood freeing flowing. The others were warier now that she had taken out one of their comrades.

The other Aldermen came into the draw on all sides of her. She could see that they planned to surround her and approach from her blind side. She launched an attack in one direction. The fighter retreated to let the others close in behind her. She kept launching attacks in different directions to keep them at bay. It was working, but it was tiring her and not stressing them at all.

When I am exhausted they will take me at their leisure, she realized. She tried to change her plan and flank them. They just let their circle flow with her changing direction.

She heard a swoosh from behind and saw something descend over her head.

That accursed net, she thought, remembering how she had been captured in one before. She slashed at it, but it came down over her. *Not again!* she despaired. Then she felt a hot spot on her breast: *Alec's medallion!*

Despite repeated tries under Alec's tutelage, she was not proficient in using dark energy; but she could do a few rudimentary things.

Focus. The net changed to a collection of loose fibers raining down on her. The net-thrower's rope flopped toward her. She grabbed the rope and pulled. The net-man was not expecting that and lost his balance, crashing into the swordsman beside him. Erin jumped towards the men, slashing with her sword – and the two were down. Now she was outside of their ring. She cut across the hamstring of one of the catch-pole holders. Then she was one-on-one with a swordsman. The others were struggling to come around the bodies of the downed scouts and surround her again. The swordsman tried to back away but was blocked by the edge of the draw. He decided his only choice was to engage Erin. He was competent, she thought, but she couldn't afford to take much time with him. He repositioned his sword just a hair too low after blocking one of her thrusts. Erin took advantage of his error to ram her sword into his side. The fight was over.

Now Erin turned. She was soaked with sweat and panting for breath. There were four Aldermen left: one swordsman and three catch-pole carriers. She stood facing them, her chest heaving. The four spread out and approached her. One swung his pole at her. Erin had spent a lot of time working with Alec in fights between swords and staff. She had done it to improve his ability to defend himself, but it had left her very familiar with how to work against the staff. She twisted, deflected the blow, and left a slash across his arm.

Not fatal, but it will slow him, she thought. Then she felt one of the catch-poles loop around her ankle. She jumped and slashed at the wounded fighter. She caught him, but not a mortal wound.

Then Erin was engaged with the remaining sword fighter. She felt another catch-pole hook around her feet. She jumped the same way again, as a fundamental lesson from her combat instructor crossed her mind: 'Never do the same thing twice.' The wounded fighter was ready and anticipated her landing. The pole was around her foot, and he was jerking to pull her onto the ground where he could control her. Instead of resisting, she turned and fell onto the pole, rolling, and grabbed it. If the fighter hadn't been wounded, he would have been able to twist his pole and capture her; but he was hurt and didn't have enough strength to twist. The two of them rolled together onto the ground. Erin managed to get free of him and back on her feet. She was starting to hurt from a collection of cuts and bruises and was wearing out – after pushing her body as hard as physically possible; she was reaching her limits. The remaining two pole holders and swordsman eyed her warily.

Go time, she thought, *before they get organized.* She attacked the remaining swordsman. They engaged in a furious display of flashing swords. It went on for longer than Erin wanted before she saw an opening and jabbed her sword into his stomach. The sword penetrated deeply and came out reluctantly. If Erin hadn't been exhausted, she could have jerked the sword out with no problems. But the stuck sword gave the other two the time they needed. Erin was still pulling on her sword when she felt the crack of a pole across the back of her legs. She collapsed from the blow. She fell one way and the dead scout's body, with her sword still stuck in his midsection, fell in the other direction.

Her leg was searing with pain, but she rolled over onto her back looking for a weapon. The sharp end of a pike was thrust towards her chest. She arched her back and bucked to one side, just enough to make the pike miss a killing blow – but it impaled her upper arm. She felt the pike pull out and she felt her arm shear and saw her blood start to spit out profusely. She saw a pole coming straight down towards her head in what she knew would be a skull-cracking, neck-breaking, death blow. Her legs wouldn't respond quickly enough to get her out of the way.

Down to two, she thought, *and to be beaten by a stupid pole.* The pole continued its rapid descent toward her head, and she flinched in anticipation of the pain. Then the end of the pole turned to dust, and powdery ash fell onto her head. The pole man looked at his weapon with astonishment. Erin didn't wait. She forced her aching legs to respond and tried to move towards her sword. Her leg collapsed and wouldn't support her weight, so she rolled towards her sword. She could see that the remaining pole man was pulling her sword from the scout's body.

No, you don't, she thought and remembered the trick that Alec had built into her sword. The sword handle became red-hot, and the Alderman dropped it in surprise, looking at the badly burned spot on his hand. Erin rolled to where her sword now lay. She grabbed it and tried to come to her feet. Her leg wouldn't respond, and she collapsed onto her back, sword in front of her.

Alec came over the top of the draw and saw her in the carnage below. He saw the two remaining soldiers and blood spurting from Erin. The two soldiers looked at him with no fear in their eyes.

Anger raged within him.

In an instant, one soldier was gone with bursting eyes and boiling blood, and then the second was gone, his heart turned to stone. Alec slid down the draw and took Erin in his arms. Blood was gushing out of the pierced artery in her arm and she was fading from consciousness.

"Erin don't leave me," he whispered. Then he tried to apply pressure to her arm, but it wasn't doing much good. He called on dark energy and let it course through her body. He could feel it was helping her, but not enough.

Help me, Erin, he thought. *Show me what is right.* With the last flicker of consciousness remaining, Erin opened her mind to him. Alec could feel that what he was doing wasn't wrong; it just wasn't right. He moved the dark energy focus around and could feel more rightness in her arm. The blood stopped spurting out. Alec grabbed the skin of her arm and pulled the flesh together with his hands until he felt the rightness from Erin; then he could feel the torn muscles and skin bind back together.

Then he looked at her leg. The lower leg had a compound fracture – the sharp ends of one bone poking through her skin – and was twisted in an unnatural angle. The sight made him sick.

"Erin," he said, trying not to gag, "we need to fix your leg. Can you help?"

She nodded weakly. "If you keep the energy flowing I don't feel any pain. I can sense the pain is there, but I don't feel it."

Alec gingerly took hold of her leg and started to gently twist it around, with Erin sensing where it should be. It took him some time to get it correct. When finally both bones were properly in place, and he released the dark energy, her leg looked normal, although bruised.

Then Alec held her tightly for a long time, wetting her hair with his tears.

Finally, he whispered, "I need to move you. We don't want to be close if they discover this fight." She nodded weakly, her eyes still closed.

"Are you strong enough to feel around? Can you sense if there are any others?" Alec asked.

Erin sensed the surroundings. "The other group is still a good two els south of us and doesn't seem to be aware of our fight here," she said.

"Good! Let's collect our stuff, and my staff, and get out of here. I'll find a safe place to see if we can heal you."

Erin looked down at her body. She was covered with splattered blood, she could feel multiple cuts and bruises all over, she had deep red marks from her partially-healed arm and leg wounds, but she was alive.

You saved me, she thought to her consort. *Again.* She could sense his love, wrapping her like a cloak.

"Alec, I left your staff, so you could get it and have a weapon," she said. "How did you manage to turn the spear to dust without it?"

"Because," Alec said with a slight chuckle, "I did the stupidest thing possible! When I saw what a predicament you were in, I ran straight over here to help you instead of going to get my staff. And, do you know, about half-way here something caught my eye. And there it was! My old medallion, stuck in a thick clump of grass!" He took her hand in his. "I grabbed it and came on over here. Good thing, too – if I had gone to get my staff, the fight would have been long over when I arrived."

And I would have lost you.

≈ ≈ ≈ ≈

Alec collected their gear, helped Erin get on his trogus, and grabbed the lead of their pack trogus. They traveled slowly for a couple of els. They were hopeful that the Alder soldiers wouldn't notice the scene with their fallen comrades for a few days, but Alec wanted to get far enough away that they wouldn't be easily found.

Erin was in shock and pain by the time they stopped. Alec found a strong hummock of brush and grass and created a recess in the side for Erin to lay. *This seems like the first few weeks that we were together, fleeing the nomads and camping out on these plains,* he thought. Then he hobbled the animals. Next, he carefully undressed Erin, looking sadly at the mass of cuts and bruises that covered her body.

"Impressive," he said, trying to make her smile. He felt her legs. They looked badly bruised but no longer broken. Alec felt for the dark energy. As the night wore on and the moons came out, he wrapped his arms around Erin and let the dark energy flow. He bathed Erin in it, again letting her body show him the rightness, soaking it in. He could feel when she quietly slid into sleep. Her ragged breathing became more regular and her sleep deeper. Towards morning, he released the dark energy and closed his eyes.

≈ ≈ ≈ ≈

Erin woke heavily. She was very sore but was alive. She saw Alec lying beside her and knew he had spent the night helping her heal. With her movement, he woke up.

"You look much better this morning," he said, tracing the outline of her cheek with the back of his hand.

Erin looked at him, wordlessly, and hugged him. The two held each other for a long time, aware that they had almost lost each other. Then Alec went to make something for the two of them to eat.

His cooking has not improved, Erin thought, as he proudly fed her some gritty mush.

"It is a good thing that you are a Great Wizard and that you perform your other consortly duties well," she said. "You would never make it as a royal cook." She held up her spoon, letting the glob of mush drip off. They both laughed.

They stayed at the camp for three more days, giving Erin time to recover from her injuries. Alec hunted several times to give them fresh meat. He also captured one of the Alder trogus to replace Erin's lost mount. Water was not a problem since Alec had learned to use dark energy to create it. After the mush incident, Erin insisted on doing the cooking. By the third day, Erin was tired of being camp-bound and ready to move. They decided that they would start the next part of their journey in the morning.

Alec wanted to give Erin a treat. First, he created a lined depression and then created enough water to fill it. Next, he heated the water and created a hot bath for Erin. She relaxed in the warm water and let it soak into her aching body. It felt delightful to her, and she purred "Thank you!" to Alec. Alec could feel that it would be a good last night at the camp.

25 – Transporter

How are we going to find the Alder transporter? thought Erin, late in the night, not sure if Alec was still awake.

"I have been thinking about that," Alec replied softly; he, too, was awake. "I can feel a pulsing in the dark energy fields. Initially, I thought it was just a natural variation in the field, but now I think the pulses are tied to the elf device on one end and the transporter on the other. I can sense and follow the field lines and lead us to the device."

The next morning, Erin felt well enough to travel, and they started off in the general direction towards the evening sun. Erin would periodically feel for Alder patrols, and Alec would sense the direction of the field lines. When Erin felt a patrol, they would hide, let it pass, and then continue. Twice, patrols came close enough that Alec needed to produce a blurring field to obscure the view. In one case they could tell that the Alder trogus smelled their animals, but the Alder riders just spurred them on.

The passing Alder patrols became more frequent. On one day, after they had been traveling for a week, they spent most of the time waiting for a clear spot between patrols.

"That probably means we are getting close to the transporter," Alec said, thinking aloud.

"Then we probably need a new plan," Erin answered. "We can't just keep hiding from all these patrols." After discussing their options, and weighing the possibilities of failure, they decided on the direct approach.

"There have to be supply caravans going in and out of the transfer area. We can join one and pretend that we are traders."

"Yes," Alec agreed. "That will allow us to move forward, at a reasonable speed, and not spend time hiding."

So far, they had been avoiding towns as they traveled. Their best tack to find a caravan would be to enter a village, look for a caravan, and join it. Erin began feeling for collections of people. They were wearing the typical loose clothing worn by Grassland villagers, so they were not concerned about anyone recognizing them as part of the Gott forces. They also had a few local coins, collected from the destroyed Alder caravans, and Alec could make more if they needed them.

Within a day Erin sensed a small village, and they entered it confidently. The village inn had only four sleeping rooms, but fortunately, one of the rooms was vacant, and they took it for the night. After settling in they went to the common room to eat. As the evening went on, the common room filled with locals who came to have a meal and an ale; Erin and Alec sat to one side listening to the local gossip.

"Any caravans going through these parts?" Alec asked after a while, striking up a conversation with a group of the local villagers. Erin sat meekly behind him, as a Grasslands woman would.

"Well, there's a town about a half-day away," a friendly-looking man at the next table said. "It's where most of the caravans stop. They have a larger inn than this one – the food's not as good as here, but they have more rooms." A couple of other locals joined in, advising Alec of where to find caravans, which ones might be headed in the right direction, and what they might be carrying.

The next morning, they walked over to the stable to collect their mounts. Four young men were looking at their trogus.

Seedy characters, thought Alec to himself.

"Good-looking animals you have," one of the men said.

"You don't look like the type of people who should have such good-looking animals," said the second. "We have a couple of animals that that would be better for you, and we'd be willing to trade you even, fair and square," he continued, pointing at two old and worn drungs tied up on the other side of the stable.

"I don't think we would want to take advantage of you," said Alec, "but thanks for the offer. We will keep our current animals."

The four started to surround them.

Alec raised his hand.

"That is a bad idea," Alec said calmly. "Leave peacefully, and you will be fine. Otherwise, if you bother us, you may regret it."

One of the young men laughed, and the four continued to move around them, drawing closer. One of them lunged towards Erin. In a blinding flash, her sword was out, poking the young tough in the chest. A few specks of blood spurted from the contact point and stained his shirt. He gasped in surprise, more startled than hurt. The other three backed off, and all four of them headed for the door and ran from the stable.

"We should move on," said Alec in a low voice. "I fear this is not over."

Erin sheathed her sword, and they went to collect their trogus. The stable had fed and brushed the animals; they quickly saddled their mounts, harnessed their pack animal, and led them towards the stable doors. Then they heard a slight commotion outside. Erin looked through the stable window.

"Ten individuals are coming our way, including our previous four," she said.

Bring your trogus back even with mine, Alec thought to her, *and then hold them quiet and still.*

The men in the courtyard turned the corner and looked through the stable doors, prepared to stop the travelers. The stable appeared empty.

"They've already left," one said.

"They had to go the other way, or we would have seen them!" another exclaimed. The men turned and ran off in the other direction.

Alec dropped the obscuring lens, and the dark energy no longer bent the light. They were once again visible.

That was close, he thought to Erin. *Let's get out of here before they come back.*

Erin had trained their mounts to move quietly when needed, and she gave them the signal to hold still as she and Alec swung into the saddles. They were able to leave the stable without making too much noise. However, before they had crossed the far side of the courtyard they heard a yell from behind as one of their intruders spotted them. They urged their mounts to move out quickly. Erin used her senses to look behind but did not detect anyone following them.

They rode for most of the day, finally arriving at the larger town late in the afternoon. The town was large enough to boast three inns; they had no trouble finding lodging and stabled their trogus. That evening at dinner they sat next to an Alder soldier.

"I see you are a fighting man," Alec said, trying to sound admiring. "You must have an exciting life! What would it take to join your force?"

Having started on his second ale, the Alderman looked at Alec, appraising him.

"Well, it is a good life. You are tall: with your size, if you can swing a sword at all my group would be glad to have you."

"I know my way around a blade a little bit," Alec answered. "Who would I need to see to join up?"

"Talk to my Captain in the inn down the street," the Alder soldier said. "Our force will give you a week's training and then send you off for a few weeks to protect one of our supply caravans. After that, they will assign you to a unit in the battle zone. The pay is good, the food is good, and the women are freely available," he said, and then looked at Erin. Alec could tell that the soldier was eyeing Erin's sword, still attached to her waist.

"And my consort, here," Alec said, "she knows a little bit about handling a sword."

"Bah! There are no women in the Alder troops! Even if she could swing a sword with the best of them, and I'm sure that's not the case, we don't want her as a soldier. Hah!" He eyed Erin closely, his eyes squinting slightly. "But we can always use extra camp girls." Then, looking at Alec, he said, "If you are willing to let her work two nights out of three they will let you have her every third night." He smiled. Obviously he thought that was a good offer.

"Well," said Alec, a little put off by this exchange, "it sounds like a great opportunity. We will ... uh ... we'll sleep on it, and maybe look for your Captain tomorrow."

Alec and Erin left and went to their room.

"'Great opportunity?'" Erin said, giving him a dig in the ribs. "'Every third night?'" They both burst out laughing.

"Well, looks like our plan to join the Alder isn't going to work," Alec said, still laughing. "Time for 'Plan B.'"

"'Plan B?'"

"You know, our other plan. We'll purchase another wagon, and then take it on the road towards the Alder camp, and look like we are 'for hire,' looking for a load to haul. You know – like peddlers, sort of, but not."

The next morning, they started looking for a wagon. At the first place, they told a simple story of how they had come from out of the area and needed to move an aging aunt.

"So our aunt ... I mean, her aunt ... Aunt Perrin ... has a lot of ... stuff, and we can't carry it all, and so we need to buy a wagon." Alec smiled disarmingly. The ostler just laughed.

"All our wagons are being taken to haul supplies for the Alder. I don't think there is a free wagon in town! But I guess you could try the junkyard and see if they have anything. It seems like several of the Alder wagons broke down recently – seems like they had a lot of problems with fires and such – and they might have something you could get and repair."

"Fires?' "said Erin. "How unusual, out on these plains! Who would have thought that would happen!" Alec bit his lip to keep from grinning and kicked her ankle. The ostler just looked at her.

They went to a few other likely places and heard the same story – no wagons, the Alder had taken them all. Finally, they went to the junkyard and told their story. The yardman listened sympathetically.

"Your old aunt? Yes, I had a similar situation myself. It was really hard to get her to move – her eyesight was gone, and she had so many pots and pans. So sad when they get like that. It was so hard to move all her things. We had to get a wagon ourselves – none for hire, you know, and do it all for her."

"And so, we need a wagon," Erin piped up, cutting off his tale.

"I'm afraid that all my useable ones are long gone," the yardman said, shrugging his shoulders. "All I've got is one broken wreck – I don't know what happened to it. Some of the wood is all splintered and broken, and it has some holes in it. No axles. It must have rolled over and crashed down a gully!"

"Let's take a look," Alec said. The yardman led them around heaps of discarded items and broken bits of this and that, to a pile of shattered wood in the back of the lot.

"Woof!" whistled Alec. "It's a lot worse than I thought it would be!"

"Can you fix it?" asked Erin.

"I don't know," Alec said, rubbing his chin. *Sure,* he thought to her.

"Well, I can let you use the shop here and my tools, if you can refurbish it, if you want to buy it."

Alec studied it for a long time, conversing mentally with Erin.

"Well," he said finally. "It's going to be a challenge, but I would hate to disappoint Aunt Marrin."

"'Parrin,'" corrected Erin.

"How much for the wagon?"

"Thirty large golds coins," said the yardman.

They both gasped.

"That wagon … that pile of wood … wouldn't be worth five small gold coins in brand new condition!" Alec said.

The owner smiled. He knew they had few other choices and his business nose told him they were hooked. He shrugged his shoulders and spread his hands.

"What can I do?" he said. "Times change. The Aldermen, they buy up everything as fast as we can supply it! It is all that I have," he gestured towards the broken wagon, "and demand is high for wagons."

After a long negotiation, they finally agreed on fifteen gold coins, including three drungs and all the materials to repair and outfit the wagon. Alec promised to return in the morning with the coins. That night, after their supper at the inn, Alec brought a pouch-full of dirt into their room. He pulled out a gold coin and studied it intensely. Then he made gold coins, one by one, until all the dirt was used up.

The next morning they went out to close the deal. The junkyard dealer was pleased to see them. He had insisted on coins in advance and was surprised that they carried that many coins. Fifteen gold coins were more than many Grasslanders saw in a lifetime. He checked each coin to verify it was real, biting into the soft gold.

"She's all yours," the yardman said to Alec. Then he quickly left to secure his new fortune.

Alec went to work. They pulled the wagon into the shop with the three drungs. His previous experience with wagons had taught him how to repair almost any piece. One of the first things he did was to make a winch and pulley system so that he could do most of the heavy work himself. Occasionally he would borrow one of the yard hands to assist him. Erin could see that he was enjoying himself with the work; this was more interesting to him than strategizing how to fight a battle. By late afternoon, with liberal applications of dark energy, Alec had repaired the main beams and replaced the broken wheels. Erin's chore was to stand guard and sense for any danger. With their experience at the previous town, they were worried about town toughs.

On the third afternoon, Alec was completing the work that needed to be done on the wagon when two grubby men walked into the shop.

Watch out! Erin alerted. Alec looked up and noticed that yard hands had left the shop and it had gotten very quiet.

The two men stared at the wagon and walked all around it. Then they looked at Erin, gave her a leering look. One gestured towards her sword and smirked.

"That's our wagon," one of the men said, spitting sideways.

"I don't think so," said Alec, casually picking up his staff and leaning on it. "I bought this wagon just the other day and have been fixing the entire thing."

"That couldn't be," said the other man. "You have only been here three days. It takes weeks to do a complete repair job. It is our wagon that we left here to have a little work done. Now get your hands off our wagon, or we will treat you as a thief and punish you appropriately."

"We might be willing to sell you our wagon," the first man said, cagily. "I think a nice wagon like this is probably worth at least forty gold."

"The punishment for wagon thievery is death, you know," the second man said. He grasped his sword and looked at Alec. They could see that Alec did not have a sword or knife with him.

Erin slid smoothly beside Alec from where she had been watching. The two looked at her and her sword and again smirked.

"Pretty little toy that you have there, little girl," the first man said, pointing at Erin's sword.

"We will give you until tomorrow to find the coins to buy our wagon," the other man said, grinning gape-mouthed at Erin. "And while you are looking, we will let your little friend here entertain us" He licked his lips. "If she isn't good enough to earn her keep, we may have to charge you another five gold to cover our efforts."

"I don't think we are interested," said Alec, still leaning on his staff. "Now, why don't you leave us alone and go pick on someone else."

The two men snarled and drew their swords. Erin's sword was out and slashing before theirs were fully drawn. The two engaged Erin.

"Little girl thinks she can do swordplay! We'll teach you a little lesson, dearie."

Erin's sword moved with blinding speed as she engaged the two fighters. Alec stepped back ready to help. Both men considered themselves excellent fighters and knew how to fight together, but they were no match for Erin's sword – it moved faster than the eye could follow. In only a few moments both men lay on the ground dead.

The yardman appeared out of nowhere. He looked at Alec as Erin wiped the blood from her sword on the shirt of one of the dead men.

"What happened here?" the yardman said with utter innocence.

"Why I don't know," Alec said, with equal innocence, staring at the dead men as if he had just noticed them. "These two came in here while I was working and seem to have had a disagreement. They must have fought with each other and ended up on the floor." He peered quizzically at the two bodies. "They seem to be dead! Since this is your shop, I would suggest you clean it up, so that I can finish working."

The junk man looked at Erin and then looked at Alec. Then he looked at the two bodies on the floor, then back at Alec.

"I will take care of it," he said, with a discreet cough. "We wouldn't want their friends to know about this because they might come and take their anger out on my shop."

"We won't say a word," said Alec. "Now clear them out and let me go back to work. We want to leave tomorrow."

Erin sat down, back on her perch, alert to any more intrusions.

What you taught me worked, Erin thought to him. *I used the dark energy crystal, and could sense everything they were going to do before they did it. I felt like they were moving in slow motion. It almost makes fighting unfair.*

Alec came to her perch and hugged her.

Anything that keeps you alive, and in my arms, seems fair to me.

≈ ≈ ≈ ≈

The day started with a trip to the town stables. They paid the stable master to board their trogus for a month and took their three drungs with them to the junkyard shop. They harnessed two of the drungs to their wagon and tied the third to the back. They were happy to get out of town, heading in the direction of the convulsing energy field lines.

In the afternoon they encountered a caravan of empty wagons heading in the same direction. They met with the Caravan Master.

"We hear that fortunes can be made hauling supplies for the Aldermen," Alec said. The Caravan Master looked at them slightly suspiciously. "We are down on our luck, and we borrowed her father's wagon to see if we, too, can make a bit of coin."

"Are you an experienced hauler?"

"Well, we both know how to load and drive a wagon, but we've never hauled cargo for others before," Alec admitted.

The Caravan Master looked over their wagon with a skeptical eye. He needed every wagon he could get, and theirs looked reasonably sturdy. Then he looked at Erin. She looked too good to be a typical camp follower. He suspected she was a run-away rich kid. Perhaps she would garner a hefty ransom; perhaps he could collect it. Accidents could happen to her companion on the way, and she would require someone to console her. He would make sure that he filled that role.

"I need experienced drivers," he said, "and you have a good wagon. I will let you join up with us; to compensate for our service, I will require one coin in four of your profits."

"Yes, of course; that will be an acceptable arrangement," Alec said, and they were members of the caravan.

The caravan was stopped three times over the next two days as they moved along the road. Each time the Caravan Master showed his seal, and after a cursory inspection of the wagons, the caravan was allowed to move forward. Several times during the day, they heard a low rumble coming from ahead of them. *What is that?* thought Alec.

I don't know, but it is the same sound that I heard when you first appeared in the Grasslands, Erin thought back to him. *Except yours was much louder.*

Late on the second day, they reached their destination, the large Alder camp in the Grasslands. The camp appeared to extend for several els in each direction. There was only one gate into the camp and it was heavily guarded. The camp boundary was protected by two rows of what looked to Alec like concertina wire, separated by about twenty arns, with dogs patrolling the open area between the rows of wire. Every fifty arns or so was a watch tower, and Alec could sense ammunition in each. The caravan moved to a staging area and parked with a number of other wagons.

The Caravan Master went off to check with the camp's loadmaster. He soon returned and told all the caravan drivers there was a three-day backup before they could load. He gave them directions to the stable for their animals and told them they could do anything they wanted, but he exhorted them to not get in trouble.

Alec had been sensing the oscillating dark energy fields as they moved towards the Alder enclave. It was apparent they were close to the source of the oscillations. After eating they sat in their sleeping hut and thought to each other.

This is it, Alec thought. *This is the place we have been searching for.*

Then we should use tonight to scout out the situation, Erin thought back.

It may be dangerous. I don't know what we might encounter. I could go scout alone, and you stay here in the sleeping hut until we know what is here, Alec suggested.

Absolutely not! Erin responded. *I am with you, and this is a place where you will need me.*

After dark, they carefully made their way toward the source of the dark energy oscillations. Alec had both his medallions with him as well as his staff. They moved stealthily towards a central area. As they approached, a large boom! rang out. The surrounding air shimmered and a whirlwind raised dust. Lightening flashed from projections on a large building in the center of the area, illuminating a large gray building in the middle of a field of packed dirt.

That building seems to be the source of the oscillations, Alec thought to Erin.

It looked to Alec like a prefabricated metal warehouse, of the type that was so common on Earth. It looked to Erin like the largest building she had ever seen. Erin could sense the presence of roving guards. Alec created an obscuring field and they easily crossed the open field. The two of them came to a side door of the gray building, lit by a dim light bulb. Erin stopped and looked at the light bulb with amazement. "Keep moving," hissed Alec.

Erin could sense that no guards were close as they crept up to the door. Alec tried the knob, but the door was locked. Then he noticed a cipher lock on the door, like those used at the Institute and other secure facilities back home.

Let's see what happens, he thought to Erin. He pushed the pad on the lock.

"Please enter your password," a computerized female voice said in English.

English! Alec wavered, startled by the sound.

Your Wizard language? Erin thought to him, uncertainly, slightly taken aback by a talking door.

Yes! It had been so long since he had heard something in English that he almost didn't recognize it.

"Please enter your password," the monotone repeated. Then after a two-second pause, "Press one for keypad entry or press two for password entry."

Alec pressed '2.' A long pause followed. Then the voice asked, "What is a girl's best friend?"

Alec thought he knew the answer but reflected on what Sarah had told him as she lay dying in his arms.

"Diamonds," he said. Green blips crossed the keypad screen. Alec waited nervously.

Did I get it right? he thought to himself. Then there was a faint whir.

"What kind are her boyfriend's best friend?" the monotone voice asked.

This was the part he hadn't understood, the word that Sarah was trying to tell him as she died. The first password was a pun – a line from a song that only English-speaking Americans would understand. Then the answer came to him: the second password was a pun that would only make sense to English-speaking dark energy users. There could only be one answer.

"Artificial," Alec said.

The computer whirred softly for a few seconds, and then the door lock clicked.

"Please enter," the computerized voice said.

Thank you, Sarah, Alec thought to himself.

Alec reached down and turned the knob. The heavy door slowly opened. He grabbed Erin's hand, and they stepped inside and closed the door behind them. The room was dark, but Alec had prepared a light globe for this situation. He pulled out the small globe and lit it with dark energy. They were standing inside a large room with an elevated platform in the center. There were two smaller platforms on the other side. Pallets were stacked around each of the platforms. A large roll-up garage door was on the far end of the room. Alec could feel dark energy pulsing through the platform in the middle of the room and from the smaller platforms on the side of the room. The far side of the room was stacked with more pallets of equipment that looked ready to be deployed. Alec pointed them out: supplies ready to be taken to the Alder's war.

"What do we do now?" Erin whispered.

"We have to figure out how we can stop this thing," he answered. "Do you sense anything?"

Erin felt the energy.

"The answer feels like it is on the platform in the middle," she said. They walked together onto the platform. They held hands and Alec felt the dark energy while Erin felt for the rightness of what he was doing.

Alec looked at Erin.

"I think I must go to the other side and leave my medallion there to fix the problem. Do you want to wait for me here?"

Erin looked at him.

"I go where you go. You are my Great and Good Wizard, and I will stand with you wherever you are."

Alec felt the dark energy and used his original medallion to begin feeding energy into it. Erin sensed the rightness of what he was doing. The platform pulsed and throbbed. Multicolor flashes filled his eyes. Light and dark, dark and light; the flashes slowed, and a wave of nausea began. He felt the change and squeezed Erin's hand tightly. He could feel an intense dark energy field being generated by a concentrator but could no longer feel the dark energy background. His ears popped, then cleared.

"We are on my homeworld now," he told Erin. "Can you feel anything different?"

Erin let her senses roam. They were in a well-lit room, brighter than the glow that Alec's light globes could provide. There were more supplies stacked high on pallets, supplies that she did not recognize. The pallets looked ready to be moved through the transfer point. She flinched – to one side of the other pallets were several stacks of death rods.

"My senses are clearer here than at home." She grabbed his arm. "Someone is watching us from the little room," she said.

Alec looked at the control room window and saw a slight figure within. The figure looked up, saw them, and raised his hand; then flipped a large switch. Alec felt the dark energy concentrator stop and the room became quiet. Then the person stepped out of the control room and walked towards them: a thin man with grizzled graying hair and beard, wearing wire-rimmed glasses and a ring like theirs.

"So!" the man said. "You have returned! I was wondering if you were still alive."

Alec looked at the man.

"Dr. Alder," he said.

"Alec," he said, chuckling, and extended his hand in greeting.

26 – Portals

"I am glad that you have returned, Alec," Dr. Alder said, smiling. "We need your help." He turned towards Erin. "And who is this with you?"

Alec looked at his former mentor. "This is my Consort, Her Highness Erin, Princess of Theland."

Alder looked at Erin for a long moment. "Pleased to meet you," he said.

Untruth, Erin thought to Alec.

"Come with me. We have a lot to do, and not much time to do it," Dr. Alder said.

"I can't stay here," Alec interjected. "I didn't come here to help you. I came to shut down the transfer point before it destroys both worlds. Then I'm going back to Theland with Erin." Hearing and speaking English seemed odd; the language sounded flat compared to the lilting tones of Theland.

"I'm afraid it is too late for her planet – for Nevia. Our transfer point has unbalanced a local dark energy device at the planet's focus zero-point. Based on our measurements we can't count on more than six weeks before it goes unstable." Then, eyes darting towards Alec's neck, "Now that you have brought your medallion back, we can decouple from Nevia and keep the instability from reaching us." He gestured towards a doorway, "Let's get out of the concentrator room."

"We don't intend to stay," Alec said again.

"We can figure that out later," Alder replied. "Anyways, it will take at least a day before the concentrator is recharged enough that we can use it again."

He is lying, Erin thought to Alec. Alec nodded to signify he understood.

Dr. Alder motioned for them to follow him. The three walked to the entry door. Alder stopped.

"The process hasn't changed, Alec. Or have you forgotten? All medallions have to stay in this room."

Without a word, Alec took his old medallion from around his neck and handed it to Dr. Alder. The older man took off his own medallion as well and put both medallions into a safe. Alec noted that the protocol was much different from the simple locker he used to use at the Institute. Alder spun the safe's combination lock, securing both medallions.

Dr. Alder ushered them through the entry door and down a long hallway. Armed guards stood at intervals along the hall. They walked past a large gate with a set of heavy steel bars.

"Where are we?" asked Alec. "This isn't the Institute."

"No, we've moved our operations," answered Dr. Alder, continuing to hustle them down the hallway. "We needed greater security than they could provide at the Institute." He gestured to the hallway. "This is the only way in or out of the concentrator room," he said. "We need to ensure our safety. The guards check everyone and everything that comes in or goes out." They stopped at a small windowless side room. Alder motioned them inside and flicked on the lights. The room was sparsely furnished with a small office table and a couple of folding chairs.

"Not quite the friendly research atmosphere that I recall," said Alec.

"Yes, we are on a more warlike footing than when you left," Dr. Alder said. "The elves are trying to stop our efforts." Then he looked again at Erin. "I see she's wearing an elf ring. I hope <u>she's</u> not an elf. If she is, we are going to have to kill her."

"Elf ring?" asked Alec.

"Nevia has many elves," Alder replied. "The Elders have a test device. Tomorrow they will verify what she is." Then Alder spoke directly to Erin: "Please don't try to touch any of our guards. They have instructions to shoot any woman who tries to touch them, lest she is an elf."

"Well, we encountered Sarah before we came back here, and she told us that Erin is a 'cross-breed.' Not an elf." Alec carefully did not mention that he had fought Sarah as an opposing foe, or that Sarah had died.

"I'm glad you saw Sarah," Alder said. "But it's too bad that she is still on Nevia. I was hoping she would come home before now. If she is with my troops, there is no way to get her back here before the device fails." A sad look crossed Alder's face. "I dread telling our daughter Celeste that her mommy won't be coming home. But, it was Sarah's choice. Sarah knows it is important to link the worlds."

Not much remorse there, thought Alec.

"Why do you need to link the worlds?" he asked.

"It requires a little history for you to understand the reason," Dr. Alder said, resuming his customary role as a teacher. "The elves established a herd of orbs – that would be us, humans – here on Earth some tens of thousands of years ago. A small elf population has always been on Earth to watch over the orb herds, but that elf population is only large enough to exert minimal control. About thirty years ago, the elf population started significantly increasing. Soon there will be enough elves on Earth that they can take control of the world! They will rule us if we don't oppose them.

"The elves think the orb herd – human population – on Earth is ripe to be culled and domesticated. That makes us a high-interest world for the elves. Over the millennia, elves have domesticated many orb herds and have developed a lot of ways to minimize resistance – domesticating equipment, mind control, things of that sort."

"So, we're 'orbs'?" Alec asked.

Alder nodded.

"About twenty years ago, when I was just starting my research into energy fields, orb resistance leaders on a sister world sent some of their Elders to Earth. They sought me out, and taught me about dark energy, in order to help us resist the elves here on Earth," Alder continued. "Orb populations, like us, resist being domesticated by the elves, if we can figure out how to resist. The Elders work with a small cadre of us in secret to keep the elves unaware. The Elders told us that with so little background dark energy on Earth the elves have an advantage and will take control of our world.

"My solution to oppose the elves, and defeat them, is to couple Earth to a powerful dark energy source – another planet. That's why I found Nevia; it is a powerful source. If I can couple the two worlds at the focal point, enough dark energy will seep through so that we can use it directly here on Earth. From your time on Nevia, you probably understand what using dark energy directly allows. It lets us do extraordinary things!"

Dr. Alder fell silent for several minutes.

"But now, we have a problem, a 'situation' if you will," Alder continued. "The elf device on Nevia is about to become unstable. We can tell that from our measurements of the changes in the available energy. When that happens, it will destroy everything around the device. We no longer have time to win our war on Nevia and link to the zero-point before then. We must let Nevia go. I will have to find another version of Nevia in the multiverse that has a zero-point, and try again to link the different focal point between the worlds. You should be able to help me do that."

"So you plan to just let Theland – Nevia – be destroyed?" said Alec, incredulously. "Your soldiers there – the Aldermen – everything?"

"That is my plan. Unless the elves find us here in this fortress and destroy us first."

"Is that the reason for all of the guards?" asked Alec.

"Yes," replied Dr. Alder. "This facility is in a secret location. Even I don't know the exact location. A heavily guarded portal is the only way to reach this place. The elves have tried several times to shut down all dark energy facilities, especially here on Earth. At first, they tried to shut them down by manipulating human systems – our politicians, governments, rulers, the like – to do things like discredit our science, or eliminate all our science funding, or watering down the quality of our science teaching in our universities. Things like that. But we now make enough gold, platinum, diamonds, and other precious materials, and sell them on the open market, to pay for ourselves, and we don't need government money. When they saw that influencing our politicians was no longer effective, the elves tried a more direct route and began to attack and destroy our facilities. Our concentrator at the Institute, that you knew, is long gone. Some 'arsonist' set it on fire. That is why we relocated to this secret facility."

"So are other science institutions involved?" Alec asked.

"Not really," Dr. Alder replied. "The orb resistance on Earth – and most of it is in the United States – has never tried to link worlds like I am doing, although some of my colleagues know about my work.

"Our orb Elders recommend that we abandon Earth and move key people – like you and me – to another world with a better dark energy background. They figure that the elves will be so busy converting the people who remain on Earth into compliant drones that they will not notice or pursue the lucky ones who escape." Alder shook his head. "That is the traditional orb strategy. Run to a different world whenever possible and only fight when there is no alternative.

"But I don't like the orb strategy. This is _my_ world. I don't want to let the elves have _my_ world. I want to fight for Earth." He looked at Alec, his small eyes glinting behind the lenses of his glasses.

Has Dr. Alder lost his mind?

"The Elders have taught me so much since you left!" Alder continued excitedly. "On this attempt, when I opened the portal to Nevia, I didn't know

303

that I had to balance the fields that create time as well as the fields that create space. You were very good at figuring out these sorts of things. That's why I recruited you into our work in the first place, and that is why I need you now. Your ability will give us a chance to correctly link to a focal point the next time we try, on our next zero-point world. Your theoretical knowledge should allow us to balance the fields correctly next time, and not create this unstable mess!" Dr. Alder chuckled.

"The next time we will easily win any battle to capture the focal point! I have learned many lessons from this fight – looking back; I know how I could have fought."

"Who are the elves on Earth?" Alec asked.

"You never know; they walk among us, and look like us," Dr. Alder said, clearly avoiding the issue.

"How did you develop the transfer portals?" asked Alec.

"I haven't figured out how to make the portals," Alder answered. "The Elders gave them to me. We have several. Besides my transfer point in the warehouse on Nevia that you used, there are two other portals connected to another continent on Nevia. We were using all three to transport the troops we recruited and trained."

Another continent on Nevia? Alec thought.

What does he mean by that? Erin thought back to him, then realized he could not explain it to her at that moment.

"How did you figure out how to use the portals?" Alec asked. "It must not be too difficult, since you are moving a lot of men and equipment."

"You probably saw the portal and the portal generator before you came here. They are easy to use. You take it to the sites at both end points and infuse it with dark energy at both places to move back and forth. When I try again, I will have the Elders give me more portals. Then I can supply my soldiers on the battlefront without needing a long supply line of wagons and things like that. If I do that I should be able to win any fight easily." Dr. Alder looked at Alec.

"But enough of this discussion for the night! You two will be my guests – but you are going to have to stay here in the compound for the night. We are not really set up for overnight visitors. The best I can do is let you sleep in this room, on the floor. I will have the janitor bring you some bedding. I can't allow you to leave this secure area until the orbs verify she is not an elf."

Then he spoke directly to Erin. "Please don't try to leave, because the guards are trained to shoot to kill. Tomorrow, we will bring in some orb advisors and hear your whole story. They will be able to verify that you are not an elf – if that is the case. Then we can find you both a more permanent place." Alder left the room, shutting the door behind him. They could hear his footsteps receding down the hall.

Alec looked at Erin and thought, *What do you sense?*

What he tells us is true, but he has bad intentions towards us, Erin answered.

Yes, thought Alec back. *I sense that Alder's accommodations for the night are closer to a jail than a hotel!*

What do you think he will do to us? Erin asked. Alec could sense that she was frightened, here in his strange world. He stroked her arm, trying to be reassuring.

I think Alder's 'more permanent place for us' may involve locking us up. Alec spent a few moments considering their predicament. *Right now may be our best opportunity to get out of here. I think they intend to use me – us – for their purpose, and not let us go.*

"This is your home world, don't you want us to stay?" asked Erin, aloud.

Alec thought briefly, weighing the options before him. If they stayed, he would be back home here on Earth and have Erin with him. He could do his research with the aid of a computer, and he would have a cell phone. The best of both worlds. But if he stayed, Erin's people would die. And if they all died, he would never be able to explain either to Erin or himself why he let them die. On the other hand, if they went back to Erin's world – Nevia – both of them might die before they could stabilize the elf device, if it existed, and if it could be stabilized – and if they could find it.

He turned to Erin.

"What do you think?"

"I want to be with you," Erin answered. "I will stay with you. Whatever you want, whichever world you want to live in, I will do, too."

That answered Alec's question.

"Let's see if we can get out of here, then." *We have people and lives to save.*

The two of them stepped into the hallway. The guards looked up.

They are not going to allow us to leave, Erin thought.

Alec spoke to the closest guard.

"Is the bathroom that way?" he asked, pointing to his left, down the hallway.

What is a 'bathroom?' Erin wondered.

The guard nodded.

"Yes, there are bathrooms in either direction, both men's and women's." Then the guard returned his attention to his post, watching several video monitors with blurry images of doors and hallways.

"Here, I will show you where it is," Alec said loudly to Erin. Then he took her arm and walked with her down the hall. The guard paid no more attention to them. The two of them walked past the bathroom and to the door leading to the concentrator room. Alec pushed on the door, and it opened. An alarm went off and started beeping loudly.

They control access by locking up the medallions, he thought to Erin. *Good thing that Alder didn't know I have a second medallion.* He pulled her into the noisy room. *We need to be quick before they respond to that alarm.*

Alec walked into the little control room where they had first seen Alder. The control panel was unfamiliar to Alec, but he understood the function of the controls. It had been a long time since he had operated a concentrator control panel so he was tentative initially, but gained confidence as the system responded to his commands. He felt the concentrator restart and felt dark energy pulse through the room. Slowly the dark energy strength increased until the field was at full power.

Come this way, Alec thought to Erin. The two of them walked to the spot in Dr. Alder's laboratory where they had first appeared from the Grasslands after their journey through time and space.

Alec felt the rich dark energy from the concentrator surround him. *Focus.* He was satisfied when he felt the control panel fuse and melt. Sparks flicked onto the control room window. The concentrator coasted to a stop, and the dark energy started to decrease rapidly. *Focus.* Alec pushed the remaining dark energy into the platform. Erin placed her hand on his arm and showed him the rightness of what he was doing. The platform pulsed and throbbed. Multicolor flashes filled his eyes. Light and dark, dark and light, the flashes slowed. This time the nausea was noticeably less. He could feel the background dark energy field.

"We are home," Alec said, and it did feel like home.

"And I am with you," Erin said, squeezing his arm. He smiled at her.

≈ ≈ ≈ ≈

Alec could feel a change in the pulsing of the transfer point.

"The transfer point is shutting down," he said. "We have solved this end of the problem – Alder can't use this as a conduit from Earth anymore."

"Does that mean that the Aldermen cannot receive any more supplies or death rods from your world?" asked Erin.

"That's right," said Alec. "They can't get any more stuff from Earth. Not through this portal, anyway. The Alder will soon run out of ammunition, and whatever else they've been getting, and then they will have to fight on an even footing."

"So, their death rods will not be fed," Erin said, quickly grasping the import of what she was hearing. "Without more fuel, the death rods will go hungry, and without the death rods, this war will be the same as the usual battles between two lords." He nodded.

"Let's find the portal generators and then get ourselves out of here," Alec said. "We are still in danger of being caught."

Alec found his light globe still lying where he had left it and relit it. They looked around the warehouse. They saw two identical looking platforms on the other side of the warehouse.

"I think those are portals," whispered Alec to Erin, pointing at the platforms. Stacked by one platform were several hundred bars that looked like gold. *Payment for services* thought Alec. Alec felt for dark energy, and the gold bars turned into a pile of sand.

On the side of one platform was a stand with a six-inch-long hexagonal rod on top. Alec pulled in dark energy and felt the rod. He could sense the rod willingly take his energy and feed it into the surrounding area. Alec sensed the area start to fade. He quit feeding energy into the rod, and the fading stopped. The area returned to normal.

"Oops!" Alec said. "I almost ported us to somewhere else!" He took a closer look around the platforms. "It looks like they use one of these to go each direction. They must have trained several locals to use dark energy to run the platforms." He picked up the rod. "Let's take this and get out of here. That will limit their operations! They won't be able to go anywhere without it!"

"If there are two platforms, won't there be two of those things?" asked Erin. Alec looked around.

"The hex rod for the other platform must be on the other end. It's not worth the risk for us to try to find it right now. They will still be able to use one platform, and get here, but it will limit their effectiveness because they can't get <u>there</u>, wherever 'there' is."

Near the platform chamber was a small screened shop. The door was locked, but it was a simple task for Alec to convert the deadbolt to sand and swing the door open.

Erin could see that Alec was in toy-land. *My Wizard sometimes acts like a large boy,* she thought fondly.

Alec poked around on the shop benches, examining the assortment of tools and gadgets, and picked up two small spheres.

"These are dark energy storage devices," he said in amazement. He put them both in his pocket.

Erin could see that he wanted to explore further but could feel that Alec knew it was a bad idea. Alec pulled himself away.

"I guess we'd better get out of here," he said reluctantly. "Someone might come by on patrol soon."

They crossed the Alder warehouse to the door with the electronic keypad, where they had entered. Erin sensed the outside surroundings.

Several guards outside, she warned.

After a long wait, Erin sensed that the guards had left. They opened the door and stepped out.

"Unauthorized opening," the computer's monotone announced, and an alarm started to sound. Alec closed the door.

Several guards approaching, Erin sensed.

Stay here in the light, Alec indicated. Then he created an obscuring field as they stood together under the door's security light. Four guards came running up in response to the alarm. Two of them carried torches and searched the dark area near the warehouse door, but none of them bothered to search the apparently-vacant area under the light. Eventually, the alarm stopped.

"Just another false alarm," one of the guards said in disgust. They gave one last cursory look around and then left.

It is clear now. With Erin sensing ahead, they crept slowly and carefully back to their wagon undetected and climbed into their sleeping area. They were both exhausted and slept deeply through the night.

≈ ≈ ≈ ≈

"Now we must find the elf device before it becomes unstable," said Alec the next morning. "There will be no more supplies delivered through this transfer point, but it will probably take them at least a week or so before they notice. We don't want to get stuck here for a couple of weeks while they figure it out – we need to leave this caravan."

"But now that we have signed on, it will be hard to leave," Erin said. "The Caravan Master will want his share of our 'earnings.' And we will need his seal to show we have permission to cross the Grasslands."

"Let's see if we can play on the Caravan Master's sympathies to get out," Alec said. "People do this all the time at home. You will have to do some acting – you will have to 'pretend.' Let me explain to you what we need to do."

Alec and Erin went to see the Caravan Master later that morning. Alec was holding Erin tightly by one arm, almost dragging her along. Erin looked like she was in tears.

"Caravan Master," said Alec, "can you help me? My girl here is homesick. Such a bother! She's tired of me and wants to go home." Erin managed to squeeze out a few tears. "She is screaming at me, always in tears, and angry," Alec continued. "I can't stand it anymore. Can you help me, please? I need a break!"

"No," said the Caravan Master, looking at Erin. "Sorry, son, but there's not much I can do until we have a load. We are so short of wagons – the Aldermen won't let an empty wagon go back."

Erin, in tears, jerked free of Alec and ran to the Caravan Master, tripping and ending on her knees in front of him.

"Please Sir, help me!" she sniveled. "He is just awful! He wanted me to sweep the wagon. He makes me wear these dirty clothes because he won't hire a wash girl or buy me new clothes." Erin looked up at the Caravan Master. "You look like you would be so much nicer," she said, wiping her eyes.

Maybe this will work, the Caravan Master thought. If this rich girl wanted to leave the tall man, and come to his wagon, he wouldn't even have to dispose of a rival. He drooled at the thought of a new conquest in bed this afternoon. It had been at least a week since he had enjoyed a woman.

"And he didn't provide me any food this morning. I am so hungry."

"We don't have any coins left for food!" Alec said, feigning anger. "You spent all the coins you brought!"

"Oh! Please help me," said Erin to the Caravan Master. "He won't prepare my food. He wants me to cook! Even after I let him touch me and do his thing, he still wants me to cook! Please take care of me." Erin crawled closer to the Caravan Master and grabbed the leg of his loose trousers. "I will be good for you," she said coyly. Then she sniffed his trousers and wrinkled her nose. "But you must take a bath first. And I hope you are not like him because he smells like a drung and sweats all over me."

The Caravan Master looked down at Erin and helped her to her feet.

"Take her if you want," said Alec, "but I am keeping the wagon." He tried to spit on the dust like he had seen so many men do, but his 'insult' was ineffective. He discreetly wiped his chin on the back of his sleeve. "She was okay when she had her father's coins and could buy me food, and new clothes, but now that she has spent all the coins, all she does is complain. You can have her!" Alec turned on his heel. "She can come to pick up her clothes anytime," he said, over his shoulder.

"I don't care about the wagon!" Erin screamed. "You can have it!" She took the Caravan Master's arm and glared at Alec. "He is a good man, a wealthy man, a Caravan Master, and will buy me a new wagon when I need it. And my clothes – there are too many for me to carry! He will send a girl to get them for me." Then she wrinkled her nose again. "But they are so dirty and old." She leaned on the Caravan Master's shoulder and looked up at him adoringly. "Throw those old rags away. I am about to get all new clothes."

By now the Caravan Master was having second thoughts. The last thing he wanted was a whinny, expensive woman. Why would he want a lazy woman who wouldn't do any work, when there were half-a-dozen compliant camp followers who would do anything to get in bed with him?

"You will miss me," Erin said pouting at Alec. He turned to face her, hands on his hips.

"Hah!" Alec said. "That little girl who serves breakfast at the meal tent is a little cutie. She has looked at me. Maybe I will go talk to her."

Erin burst into tears again.

"He keeps telling me I am ugly – not round and plump enough. It's not my fault that I am skinny! I try to eat more, but I can't get any good food. There is no good cook to make me breakfast or serve it to me in my wagon."

The Caravan Master looked at Erin. Maybe she wasn't as attractive as he first thought. She <u>was</u> skinny. And hard. He knew exactly the camp follower that Alec was talking about. She was cute and had been in his bed a few times and would do anything to be in his bed permanently. She didn't whine, and she was plumper, and she would cook and clean.

"Just a minute," the Caravan Master said to Alec, disentangling Erin's arm from his. "You can't just leave her. She is your responsibility."

"She wants you, not me," Alec said, turning again to walk away. Erin rolled her eyes longingly at the Caravan Master and tried to take his arm again.

"She's your problem! You must take her!" said the Caravan Master, shoving Erin towards Alec.

"And if I don't?"

"Then the wagon stays with me! I won't let you keep her wagon without taking her." The Caravan Master looked at Alec smugly. He could see that he had Alec in an awkward position.

Alec let out an exasperated sigh. "Ok, I'll take her – but only until I get to where I can send her home."

"Then take her and wait until we have a load for you."

Erin grabbed the Caravan Master' sleeve.

"Don't make me go with him," she wailed. "I know you will like me if you take me. I know – I will come to your wagon and recite the old poems of our people! My father likes that – he says it calms him so that he can sleep!" Erin launched into a loud chant-like monologue. "'In the beginning of time, when the time was mine, we learned this rhyme …' No, wait. That's not right. 'In the beginning of time, when …' Are you listening? I will speak louder. 'In the beginning of night, when might was right …'" Erin kept stumbling on the words, repeating herself, getting louder with each iteration.

The Caravan Master thought quickly, again pushing Erin away from him.

"Maybe I can find you a load," he said to Alec, speaking loudly over Erin's 'chant.' "I need a load of scrap lumber hauled back the way we came. It doesn't pay very well, so no one wants to haul it. You have three drungs, so you should be able to pull the load." Alec came back to the Caravan Master, ready to bargain, as Erin continued to try to remember the words in her poem.

"I will let you do this as a favor; given your situation, I will require only three coins of four of your profits as my caravan fee."

"That is too much," said Alec loudly, over the chanting. "I will have to give the wagon back to her father when I drop her off, and then I won't have any coins left for me." He again turned away. "I will just suffer – I will leave her with you and wait for the regular load."

"Well, just because I want to help her, pretty thing though she is, I will only charge you two coins of four," the Caravan Master offered, desperately wanting Erin to shut up.

"Oh ... I guess I will do it," said Alec.

"Take her and go load your wagon. Come by after you are loaded – but make sure you come without her! Then I will give you your passes and seals." With that, he paddled Erin several times on her rear, gave her a shove towards Alec, and said, "And at least make her sweep and do your wash!"

"Lazy drung," he muttered to himself.

Alec grabbed a reluctant Erin's arm and pulled her angrily along with him. Erin looked back imploringly at the Caravan Master, who studiously refused to look at Erin.

They made it half-way back to their wagon before they broke out in laughter.

"So, you call that 'acting,'" said Erin.

"Yes, and you did it quite well!"

"My people do not do anything like that – but it is fun to pretend to be someone you are not! It is easy to do when you can sense the other person's feelings." Then with a serious expression, Erin added, "You know I can chant better than that. And I do remember the words."

27 – Through the Grasslands

"All loaded?" Erin asked.

"Yep, every last board and scrap!" Alec replied. "Time to be off!"

Only a few other wagons were carrying shipments from the Alder warehouse, headed back in the direction they had come from. The reduced number of shipments didn't seem unusual to the people around the warehouse since often there were days when the transfer point could not operate. Only Erin and Alec knew that no new supplies would ever again come through the transfer point.

The main gate of the Alder camp was an intimidating arrangement of death rods and guards but the guards at the main gate allowed them to proceed after a perfunctory check of their load and their seal from the Caravan Master.

By the next afternoon, they had returned to the village where they had purchased their wagon. They had been stopped three times by Alder patrols, but their credentials satisfied the Aldermen. At one stop, one of the patrolmen looked leeringly at Erin but did not attempt to approach her.

They delivered the load of scrap wood as required, and then, having no further use for the wagon, looked for a buyer. They took it to the wagon dealer they had talked to before; he offered them five gold coins for the wagon. They weren't concerned about the price but haggled until they received fifteen large gold coins for the wagon and three drungs. They collected their trogus from the stables and were on the road, heading into the Grasslands.

Their first concern was to avoid Alder patrols as they tried to reconnect with the Theland riders waiting for them on the Grasslands. As they moved away from the transfer point, the Alder patrols became widely spaced; evading them became easier.

Alec couldn't resist playing with the new device he had taken from the Alder warehouse. He laid out two circular areas about a hundred paces apart. Then he took his hex rod to both locations and created a portal at the two ends. First, he started by moving a rock between the two locations and bringing it back. Then he moved a trogus back and forth; the animal brayed in consternation when it realized it had moved through no action of its own and shook its head and mane mightily until it regained its senses. Finally, he felt that he understood the mechanics of moving objects between portals.

"Ready for some fun?" he asked Erin.

The two of them stood in the center of one of the marked circular areas. Alec fed dark energy into the hex rod. The world started to dim, went momentarily black, and then lightened back to normal.

They were at the other portal.

"Presto!" crowed Alec, thinking he sounded like a Wizard – a pleased Wizard at that. "Much easier to use a portal than to transport across dimensions."

"I could have walked between these two circles faster than that!" Erin exclaimed.

"Well, yeah, but if the two portals were farther apart, then you couldn't," Alec said, slightly crestfallen.

"I do see that it could be useful," Erin said, trying to mollify him. "It could be used to link Freeland City in Theland with our villages on the outskirts. They always complain about being out of touch."

With Alec's experimenting finished for the day, it was time for supper. Alec offered to cook, but Erin steadfastly refused.

"That Caravan Master told you that you should make me cook for you," Erin said, teasing him. "Besides, no one at home will let a Princess cook," She tested the hot rocks that Alec had prepared for her. "Besides," she added slyly, "we want the food to be edible." And it was.

The next morning, they were up early and riding again, making their way across the sea of gray-green grass at a good pace. About mid-morning they saw a plume of smoke on the horizon.

"What's that?" Alec asked, pointing at the smoke. "Is that our boys?"

"It does look like a burning caravan to me," said Erin. "But we are too far away to tell – by the time we get closer, everyone on the Grasslands will be headed there to see what is going on. Plus, our riders will not stay around, if it is a burning wagon, and if our riders were the ones who set it on fire." She stiffened and looked around, suddenly wary of the waving clumps of grass.

"Besides, I think we have a tail." She paused to get a better bearing on what her senses were telling her. "A group is about four or five els behind us, probably on our tracks."

"You know this business," said Alec. "What do you suggest?"

"I think we need to ditch our pursuers and see if we can figure out where our riders are," she answered.

Alec agreed.

"Every Alder soldier within sight will be heading towards that smoke column. Let's change directions and see if the bunch behind us is trying to follow us."

After about a half hour, Erin stopped again.

"They changed directions at the same point that we did. They have a good tracker if they can follow us and not lose speed in the process. "

"How many are there?" asked Alec.

"I think there are only five of them, so we shouldn't have too much of a problem if they want to take us on. Let's see what we have."

"If they are still a few els behind us, we should have time to lay out a good observation post."

They picked out a place that would suit their needs. Then they rode a few hundred arns past the spot before they made a wide arc and circled back to the new observation point. Alec obscured them from view. They did not have long to wait until the five riders came along. They looked more like a band of ragged hoodlums than Alder soldiers – they were not in uniform, wore old and torn clothing, and had little sense of organization. One of them was clearly an excellent tracker and was leading the way, following their trail from his small Grasslands drunglet.

The ragged band passed within thirty arns of the observation point. Alec's obscuring lens kept them from noticing Alec and Erin.

Following us, Alec thought, *and not Aldermen. Or Gryg.*

Then we should confront them, Erin thought back. *They have no business following us.*

Alec dropped the obscuring lens and they rode forward, their hungry trogus making slight growling noises at the sight of the men and their animals.

"Hello, strangers! Are you looking for us?" Alec called out.

The five saw them with a start. The lead tracker forced a smile. The nearest man turned towards them.

"We are poor men riding through the Grasslands, in search of animals to trap for their hides. We mean no one any harm," the man said, shifting uncomfortably on his little spotted drunglet.

"And why are you following us?" Alec demanded.

"Following? You? Why no. Just an unfortunate accident of direction," he said. "We will be going about our business now if you don't mind."

"I don't want any hint that you are trying to follow us," Alec said sternly.

The lead tracker was starting to get worked up.

"A lone bloke out here on the grasslands with a lass, and you are telling us what to do." He ran his tongue over his ample lower lip. "If you don't watch your words, we may have to teach you a lesson or two."

Alec let his trogus paw the ground; it emitted its low, guttural growl.

"You think you could take us on, mounted?" Alec said. "Maybe at midnight you could do some damage if you slunk up and stabbed us in the back under cover of darkness. But not out here in the full light of day." Alec tried to look as menacing as he could. "You don't look like much. Now be gone! Or I will have my lady teach you some manners." He motioned towards Erin. The five men knew they were being insulted but weren't sure which way to take the conversation.

"We will be off and leave you be," the lead tracker finally said. He kicked his little drunglet, and it trotted off, the other men following.

"Jackals!" spat Erin. "If they could, they would sneak up on us to rob and kill us, but they won't try to tackle us directly."

"We will have to watch carefully to make sure they don't continue to follow us," Alec said.

≈ ≈ ≈ ≈

About an hour later, Erin stopped.

"They are back on our track again. This time they are staying a little further back and seem warier."

"I guess we will have to have a second conversation," Alec said.

They found a good spot to pull the same maneuver again. This time they had to wait several minutes before the five men came into view, looking in every direction as they shambled along the trail. Again, the obscuring lens served its purpose. As soon as the men passed, Alec dropped the lens, and he and Erin moved forward where they could be seen.

"It doesn't look like you follow directions well," Alec said. "Why don't you dismount."

The five just looked at them; one of them laughed, drew out his spear, and spurred his drunglet towards Erin.

Erin goaded her trogus forward. The trogus charged, taking the little spotted drunglet down with its claws. The rider was thrown from his mount in front of Erin; he grabbed his spear and tried to lunge at her trogus' throat. Erin caught the spear with her sword, breaking it into two pieces. Her trogus reached out and grabbed the man's arm with its teeth – there was a sound of cracking bones and shredding flesh. Erin pulled her trogus back and spun it around to make sure there were no more threats.

"I said, dismount!" The men slid off their mounts. Alec herded the men into a little group, their small drunglets hovering nearby, nervously eyeing the two trogus.

"Now – why are you following us?" he asked.

The tracker, standing on the ground, looked up at him.

"You know the truth, so why do you ask?" the tracker said.

"I guess just politeness," said Alec. "My mother always told me to be nice. She would have told me that I shouldn't kill anyone without their permission. Now, what are you trying to do?"

The tracker stepped forward, "Look," he said, nervously eyeing the growling trogus. "The Alder hired ten of us – all of us are expert trackers. Our job is to find a marauding gang of trogus riders that are terrorizing the caravans out here on the Grasslands. We found their trail two days ago. Three of my companions are staying on their trail, along with a tailing Alder force. They will keep an eye on the marauders until the Alder collects enough soldiers and death rods to destroy them."

Our riders, thought Erin to Alec.

"When is that going to happen?" Alec asked.

"I think they plan to corner them a half a day from here along the Aleinte Escarpment. The rest of us were sent to look for stray riders who might be part of the gang. We are just doing a job." The tracker shrugged his shoulders and eyed Alec. "We found your tracks this morning and were following you."

"If you aren't part of the marauding gang and you haven't done anything wrong, then come with us to any Alder camp, and they will pay us and let you go," another man chimed in.

Erin and Alec looked at each other with concern.

We need to see if we can meet up with our riders quickly, Erin thought to Alec.

Erin looked at the men standing nervously on the ground.

"We have no real fight with you," Alec said, "but we can't let you get back to the Alder. We will leave you alive, but we are going to take your animals with us."

"Mercy, sir, have pity on us. Leave us our food and water, or we will die," one said.

Erin pulled her trogus and rode over to each drunglet. She cut the saddles and packs off, letting the tack fall to the ground.

"You have what you need," she said. Then she took the halter rope of each drunglet and attached them to the back of her trogus. She started off through the Grasslands towards the escarpment. Alec quickly followed her. After a couple of els, she turned to Alec.

"The drunglets are slowing us down; I am going to release them. I will just keep one to feed our trogus here. The trackers will find them, but that party will never be a concern to us." Alec nodded in agreement.

As soon as their trogus were fed, they released the other drunglets. Then they urged their trogus forward, and they rode the plains rapidly. Late afternoon brought them in sight of the Aleinte Escarpment.

$$\approx \ \approx \ \approx \ \approx$$

Near the escarpment, they stopped for Erin to feel the surroundings.

"There is lots of activity swirling around us," she said. "I think we must be close to our riders." She continued to sense the situation. "There is so much activity that it feels like a battle is brewing. There is a large concentration of riders and animals close to the escarpment – that is probably our people."

"I suggest we head for them," Alec said.

"There are several other large concentrations of people around, but the direct route between us and our riders is only lightly covered. Do you sense any death rods?"

Alec next let his senses roam.

"I don't feel any death rod ammunition close around. Let's do it."

They paced the animals as they rode – they wanted the mounts to be fresh if they needed to fight or to sprint. Every few minutes they stopped, and Erin sensed around them.

318

After about two els Erin thought to Alec, *The large group is about another el ahead of us. Between them and us is a picket line. Can you do something?*

I can blur us, but it won't work when they get close to us because the trogus will smell each other, Alec thought back to her. *But it will let us get closer before they start converging on us. Might reduce how many we must fight our way through.* He created a blurring lens. The two of them slowly rode forward towards the picket line.

We are as close as we are going to get without the other trogus smelling us. We are about a half el from the outer lines of the other group. There are two Alder between them and us. I think it is time for the direct approach, thought Erin. *We will leave our pack animal here.*

Alec nodded in agreement and dropped the lens. Both prodded their trogus and headed towards the troops. Two Alder riders in front of them looked up in surprise and pulled out their short spears. They turned their animals with obvious skill. Erin slanted to the left. Both riders ignored her and moved to intercept the tall man.

The two Alder riders closed quickly on Alec. Alec's only obvious weapon was his staff. The Aldermen knew it would not be an effective weapon against their spears and they rode forward quickly and confidently.

Focus. The first Alderman's trogus flopped onto the ground. Alec turned to the right and the second trogus was delayed as it maneuvered around the downed animal. The Alder rider accelerated his animal and started to gain on Alec.

Focus. The Alder rider collapsed, but his trogus kept sprinting forward. Erin rode in from the side, and her trogus pushed the Alder trogus out of the path.

Then the two of them rode rapidly towards the mass of riders assembled before them. Five riders with spears started riding out to intercept them. For a second Alec felt they were heading into disaster – then one of the oncoming riders recognized them and let out a whoop of joy.

"Princess!" He whistled a signal to his comrades, and the others immediately separated to allow Erin and Alec to ride through the Theland line. They had found their riders.

They collected their pack animal and rode quickly to where the Theland lead rider had established his base.

"Ferd!" Alec cried out.

"Welcome, my Queen," Ferd said to the two of them, grinning broadly. "Your Highness, Queen Erin, I stand before you as your most humble servant. Welcome, Consort Alec."

"'Princess,'" Erin corrected him. "I remain 'Princess.'"

"Princess, we are glad to see you, but would not want to put you in such danger!" Ferd said. "Three days ago, one of the Alder patrols found our track, and they have been following us ever since. They tried to attack us twice, but both times we defeated them. They have determined they can't fight us with even numbers – unless they have death rods, of course. The Aldermen have been slowly amassing more and more riders. For the last day they have been shadowing us, adding a few more riders periodically. I think that either when they have a two-to-one superiority, or when they get some more death rods, they will try to attack." The lead rider looked at his Princess. "I didn't try to retreat because I wanted to stay here in the Grasslands and wait for your return. Now they have backed us up against Aleinte Escarpment. We can't take the wagons up it. We can ride our trogus up the escarpment and away, but we have about twenty wounded riders in our wagons that we would have to abandon, and I have been reluctant to do that."

"I think we have another problem," said Alec. "I sense that the Alder have gunpowder stores located on the top of that escarpment. I think they must have found a death rod or two and placed them up there. They appear to be well back from the edge of the escarpment, and I can't get to them. If we go up the slope, they will be able to destroy us as we come over the top. It would be deadly to go up. They would get a lot of us before I could destroy them."

"That only leaves the direct route out the front," Ferd said. "I think we can punch through their lines and get most of our riders out. It will be another day before they have enough riders to stop us – but the wagons with our wounded wouldn't make it."

"Not a good set of alternatives," said Erin. Then a gleam came into her eyes, and she looked at Alec. "How about your new toy, my Great Wizard? Can we use it?"

Alec started to say 'no,' because he needed two points for portals, and would have to go to the other point to set it up. Then he realized that he already had an end-point.

"If we are willing to move our people and wagons to the plot where we tested it, that should work," he said. Ferd looked at him quizzically, not understanding what Alec was talking about, but not about to interrupt his Princess nor question her Consort.

"That place will be fine," Erin said. "Let's get out of here tonight before anything else happens."

Alec described to Ferd what they would do and asked him to ready the riders for a little 'wizard magic.' At the edge of the Theland troops' encampment, in the evening twilight Alec marked out a circle the same size as the circles he had made on the Grasslands where he had tested his newfound equipment. After some quick calculations, he determined that each circle was big enough to fit either ten riders on trogus or one wagon. Erin designated Thom and eight other riders as the initial group. Alec would go to the other portal with the first set of riders to ensure everything worked, and then return to transport the remainder.

The nine riders lined up inside the circle, looking somewhat unsure of what was about to happen next. Alec joined them and fed dark energy into the hex rod. The world faded and returned. Suddenly, the nine riders and Alec were in an undulating field of grass instead of the dusty camp by the escarpment.

"Move quickly," Alec exhorted them, shooing the awed people and their mounts out of the marked circle. "Get out of this circle and fan out to ensure the area remains clear. Otherwise, you will be in the way of the next wave of riders." He looked around at the sea of grass. There did not appear to be anyone within sight.

Alec strode back to the center of the circle, and everything faded again; then he was back at the escarpment. Erin had already lined up the second wave of ten riders. That wave disappeared. Then they began to cycle the wagons through, one at a time.

Alec had timed how long it took to remove everyone from the portal, and established a time allowance for each cycle. The riders had strict instructions to clear the portal circle within their time allowance, no matter what it took. The next group would be sent after the agreed interval.

Alec wanted to send Erin in one of the early waves, but she refused, saying she would go in the last group with him or not at all. The wagons and the wounded riders all cycled through the circle with no problem and over half the riders had been ported when trouble struck. A Theland scout came riding up rapidly.

"Princess, the Alder are mounting an attack on us. They have a sortie of thirty riders coming this way to see what we are doing. They must have heard the noise and commotion of moving our wagons and trogus into the magic circle."

"Then we need to pick up our pace," Alec said, "so that we can all be gone before they get here." By this time, all that remained were several riders and their mounts. "The original time allowance was set for the wagons, so now we should be able to move twice as fast. This next wave can tell the troops on the other end to move out of the way more quickly."

As the Alder riders started galloping forward, they saw their enemy vanish into the air, ten at a time. The Alder were close enough for the Theland troops to hear the heavy breathing from the charging trogus when Alec, Erin, Ferd, and the last three Theland riders moved onto the ring. Alec looked at the approaching Aldermen and then fed dark energy into the hex rod. The world faded, and then they were on the other side.

A cheer went up from Erin's riders when she stepped out onto the Grasslands.

"We made it!" she said, in relief.

There was still enough daylight for the Theland riders and their wagons to regroup and travel. The Theland riders were afraid of the portal circle and wanted to get as far away from the 'magic ring' as they could, and as quickly as possible. It was dark when they finally stopped for the night, setting up camp by the light of the five moons.

The next morning the Theland contingent prepared for their long trek out of the Grasslands. On the second day, the scouts returned saying they had sighted a caravan. Erin decided they should take out the caravan. It would be a good way to resupply themselves.

"We should use your new trick, the magic circle, to capture this caravan," Erin said. "Call upon your magic, oh my Great Wizard."

Erin, Ferd, and Thom plotted the path of the caravan, and then Alec and a couple of riders went ahead to create a portal point that would be large enough for twenty riders at a time. They watched as the caravan moved along the route. When the middle of the caravan was abreast the portal point, they sent the first twenty riders through and quickly sent a second twenty through.

Forty snarling trogus suddenly showing up in the middle of the caravan were enough to disrupt things. The caravan guards were unprepared and quickly disarmed. The caravan was stopped, and the drivers and other personnel escorted into the center. The caravan drungs were released and sent scurrying into the Grasslands. The Theland riders then came alongside the wagons and extracted any supplies they could use, taking two of the wagons to carry the extra supplies. Then they burned the rest of the wagons. They left the caravan people wagon-less to fend for themselves.

Four days later they reached Raner Pass. Erin been sensing ahead for troops or another enemy; however, the Alder had repositioned their army back into the Grasslands where they could use their remaining death rods to good effect to defend their forces from attack.

"It seems that the Alder General is waiting for significant reinforcements before he tries to assault Raner Pass again," the lead scout reported.

He may have a long wait, Alec thought. Erin smiled at that.

Erin's forces crossed through the pass and triumphantly rode into their old camp near the Gott fortress before the sun set behind the mountains.

PART THREE

28 – Elf Mountains

The next morning, Erin dispatched a messenger with a request for a meeting with General Mawn. By late afternoon no meeting had been set up. That was not particularly concerning since her people needed a couple of days to repair damaged gear, attend to the wounded, and resupply. Alec and Erin put the time to good use by applying healing to their injured riders, and other warriors, where they could. The next day they still had not heard from the General. Erin dispatched a second messenger with a repeat of her initial request. By noon of the third day, when they had still not received any reply, Erin was becoming annoyed.

"It's time for a ride," Erin said. "The General is deliberately ignoring us, probably because of Amelia."

The two of them rode to the General's headquarters with Ferd and an escort of twenty riders, as was befitting a princess of Theland. They tied their mounts to the posts in front of the General's headquarters and walked in.

"Her Highness Erin, Princess of Theland, to see His Excellency General Mawn," Erin's courier announced.

They waited.

No response.

Finally, Major Voy came out, looking a bit sheepish.

"Greetings. We have heard of your success on the Grasslands. We appreciate your esteemed efforts. General Mawn is very busy today. He might be able to meet with you tomorrow, but he has permitted me to debrief you today."

"No," said Erin, regally, to Major Voy. "The Princess of Theland wishes to speak to the General, and he will see me. It is that simple." The major looked uncertain. "I don't make threats, but I promise you that I will act if he cannot find time to see me."

Major Voy went back into General Mawn's headquarters. After several minutes he returned.

"The General wants you to know that he has pressing business that takes precedence over you. He also wants you to know that you are not recognized as a Princess of Theland by Queen Amelia of Theland, or as the leader of her troops. Therefore, Gott adheres to the instructions of our gracious ally, Queen Amelia of Theland." The major cleared his throat slightly, looking quite uncomfortable.

"Queen Amelia has sent directions that you are to be detained here at the fortress. She is sending a new leader for the riders of Theland to replace you. General Mawn says that if you relinquish your command and promise not to flee, we will not put you in chains but let you remain with your riders.

"However, in appreciation of your contributions to Gott in the war against the Alder, the General will make time in his busy schedule for you. He will see you personally, one week from today." Major Voy tried unsuccessfully to give her a stern look.

"That will not be acceptable," said Erin. Motioning for her retinue to follow, she marched to the front of General Mawn's command center.

"General Mawn! Erin, Princess of Theland and Leader of the Theland Riders, is here to see you!" she yelled. She repeated herself a second time and stood waiting. When nothing happened, she said loudly, "Oh Great Wizard, the good General appears to be yet asleep. Will you awaken him?"

"With pleasure."

A great clap of thunder rang out, and then a second clap, followed by a small whirlwind.

The General burst out of his command tent and looked angrily at Erin. A company of Gott guardsmen appeared, armed with swords and spears. The guards looked nervous. They knew the reputation of the Theland riders, and of Erin's reputation as a great Warrior Princess.

Erin looked at the Gotts and smiled, a determined gleam in her eyes.

"You have made me angry, General. You only have three times as many guards here as I have riders. If you want to fight my Wizard and me instead of talk, that is your choice, but I like my odds."

The General spent a long moment looking at Erin. He motioned for his guardsmen to stand down.

"General Mawn, I have things to do that are important, and I am not interested in you wasting my time. I have fulfilled the obligations of assistance to Gott that my mother, Queen Therin of Theland, proffered to you. I have lost skilled riders of Theland to back your cause, and return to Gott with many wounded, noble riders who have suffered greatly in support of your feeble troops. Without us, you would not have won the battle here at Raner Pass. Also, we have disrupted the enemy caravan chain as you ordered us to do, and we have dispatched many Alder soldiers who no longer stand as a threat to you.

"Now, I am going to take my riders and return to Theland. I have urgent matters to attend to in my homeland. I request that you provide us with a seal granting us free access through the allied lines and Gott for our trip home."

General Mawn nodded, with a slight smile. "Come back tomorrow, and I will see what can be done," he said.

"No!" said Erin. "We will wait here."

The General shifted uneasily.

"The longer you stall, the longer it will be before you can return to your 'pressing business,'" Erin said. "Have you seen what happens when angry trogus rampage through a camp? I would suggest that you don't try to do anything that might be inopportune."

General Mawn rubbed his jaw and then beckoned to Major Voy.

"I do not want to be a part of the internal politics of Theland. Issue them a free passage instruction over my mark and seal. Please debrief them. I would like to know more about the situation deep in the Grasslands."

"I am sorry, General. I have 'pressing business' to attend to and do not have time to debrief the good Major." As soon as she received the seal of passage, Erin did not wait. Before sunset, she had her entire force of riders and wagons traveling away from the General's camp and into Gott.

≈ ≈ ≈ ≈

Several issues weighed heavily on Erin. The first was finding the truth about her mother's death and punishing those responsible. The second was resolving the succession to the Theland throne, after Brun used the extorted abdication document and her absence to install Amelia as Queen. Overriding all these problems was the potential destruction of Theland and all her people if the elf concentrator destroyed itself. Because Alec could feel the increasing oscillations in the dark energy from the unstable concentrator, he kept impressing upon her the need to go quickly to the focus point in the Elf Mountains. In Erin's mind, saving her people was more important than resolving her status or avenging her mother.

Erin was certain that Amelia would not allow them to move unimpeded once they reached Theland. She decided the best strategy would be to split her riders. Her large force would not be able to travel rapidly with their wounded riders and supply wagons, but a small group of riders should be able to travel rapidly before Amelia could assemble a force to stop them.

With Ferd in command, most of Erin's troops continued at a slow trek across Gott towards the center of Theland through the main route along the River Ryn. Ferd would make sure his progress was well-known so that the information could quickly reach Brun and Amelia.

Erin, Alec, Thom, and forty riders split off from the main group to head through Gott; they would enter Theland near the Elf Mountains. It would require at least six days of hard riding to reach the Elf Mountains but if they moved quickly they should not encounter any of Amelia's riders.

On the fourth day, they safely passed out of Gott and into Theland and in another day they came to the edge of the Elf Mountains and made camp. The next morning, they rode into the mountains. About mid-morning they came to a narrow passageway through the rock.

"This is the only way I know to enter the Elf Land, and this is as far as we can take the trogus," said Erin.

"What next?" asked Alec.

"From here we need to go on foot. We don't want to take a large group, or they will think we have hostile intentions. Just the two of us, Thom, and four riders will go the rest of the way." She turned to her riders. "Thom, Cryl, Nikka, Rhor, and Bon – you five will come with us. We will need food for three days.

"The rest of you, make camp here. Take care of the trogus. If you don't hear from us in two weeks, assume we need help and send a rescue column."

The seven left the others and started their walk into the Elf Mountains. The passageway ran through the side of a cliff, and they walked for about an hour before it opened into a high meadow. They started across the meadow and walked for another hour.

"Stop!" said Erin abruptly, looking at the ground. "Look at that track! I would recognize it anywhere." She pointed at a scuff mark. "That is the mark of Alec's staff! We must have gone in a circle." Her riders looked chagrined. Except for Alec, they were experienced trackers and should have caught the significance of the mark.

They walked for two more hours through the meadow when Bon stopped.

"Look," she said. "That is my mark. I have been marking our trail since we encountered Consort Alec's track. We are still doubling back on ourselves." Erin sighed in exasperation.

"We are getting nowhere. We might as well make camp here for the night and try again in the morning."

Few of Erin's riders had ever encountered elves, and the five riders accompanying their group were not even sure what an elf would look like. There was a lot of apprehension and concern in the camp that night, but the night passed uneventfully.

Alec took Erin aside in the morning.

"I have been thinking about what is going on. I think the elves have created an optical distortion region to protect their land. I have an idea." He had the riders cut about a hundred stakes, each about an arn long. He hammered the first one into the ground where they had camped; then, he walked backwards towards where the passageway first came out of the mountain side and hammered in a second stake. As they walked, every thirty paces he hammered in another stake. It was a slow process, and he could hear Cryl and Rhor muttering that this was a waste of time.

After five stakes they looked back. Alec pointed out how their seemingly-straight path had curved distinctly to the right.

"Move back to the left," Alec said and fixed the next stake. They fixed the stake so that they were in a straight line with two of the earlier stakes. After that, they stopped and checked their path by lining up with the previous stakes. Every time they stopped, they could see that their straight march had drifted offline. Finally, when they were almost out of stakes, the line of stakes and their line of march agreed with each other.

"I think we are through the distorting region," said Alec. Because of the delay it had taken to check and correct the stakes, they had made slow progress that day. It was time to camp for the night.

They reached the far side of the meadow by late morning on the next day and found a path that led further into the mountain. The path took them along the side of the mountain and then turned to follow a narrow, deep ravine formed by a small rill of water. Halfway into the ravine, they heard a voice.

"Who intrudes in our land?" the voice said, in a reasonably good rendition of the Theland language.

Erin stepped forward, looking for the source of the voice.

"I am Erin – Princess of Theland and descendent of the Elf Lian. I travel with my Consort, Alec, and my personal guard. We come to your land to meet with your leaders to discuss a matter of great common importance."

There was no response, so they waited.

After fifteen minutes Erin was becoming restless and thinking of moving on when five people stepped out of the front edge of the ravine: a tall woman with four men standing behind her. The woman acted like the leader. The four men were armed with short spears and swords.

So, these are elves, Alec thought. *No pointy ears.* The woman looked very much like Erin, tall and lean, with black hair pulled back in a knot, and was wearing a ring like Erin's. Even though she was apparently on patrol, she wore a long over-cloak of brightly-colored material over her trousers and tunic – these fit more closely to her form compared to the loose-fitting wear of the Grasslands, and were much more colorful, with an iridescent pattern.

"You enter our land uninvited," said the elf woman.

Erin repeated her statement.

"I am Erin – Princess of Theland and descendent of the Elf Lian. I travel with my Consort, Alec, and my personal guard. We come to your land to meet with your leaders to discuss a matter of great common importance."

The elf woman motioned to the accompanying elf men. The men spread out and walked towards Erin's group. Erin motioned to her riders to remain still.

"Don't draw any weapons," she whispered. "We need to make this a peaceful encounter."

The elves continued to advance until they were positioned on either side of the seven. Alec felt very defenseless – but knew that Erin was right. If they acted in a hostile manner towards the elves, they were guaranteed to get a poor reception.

When the elves were in place, the elf woman spoke.

"Any who come to our land uninvited, forfeit all rights." She raised her hand, and Cryl slumped to the ground.

Alec thought to Erin, *I can feel she is using her ring to twist the lines of force. Can you untwist them?*

Now that Alec pointed it out, Erin realized that she could use her ring to manipulate the twisted lines of force from the elf woman. Every time Erin had worn her ring, she had always sensed the force lines, but never realized that she could manipulate them. Now she worked to sense the lines and mentally try to untwist them. After a second or so, she could sense them straighten. The elf woman sensed Erin's actions and increased her intensity. Erin could feel that she and the elf woman were linked into a mental struggle through their rings. The lines started twisting again, and two more of Erin's riders slumped to the ground. Then the elf twisted the lines in a way that Erin did not expect. Before Erin could respond, she felt her mind becoming unfocused and confused. The elf woman looked at her and sneered, then twisted the lines of force differently. Erin was thrown off-balance mentally and could not respond quickly; her mind became fogged, and she lost control of her body, slumping towards the ground as her knees gave way.

Alec was concerned by the force lines. He could feel that Erin and the elf woman were engaged in a mental battle and that somehow his ring was protecting him. He started to focus to draw dark energy in case they needed it. Then, as Erin lost consciousness and started to fall, Alec broke his focus and grabbed her.

The elf woman looked at him and twisted her force-lines again. The force slid past him. *Focus.* Just as Alec started to gather dark energy, the blunt end of a spear hit him on the head. He collapsed unconscious to the ground with Erin in his arms.

≈ ≈ ≈ ≈

When they came back to consciousness, the seven members of Erin's party found themselves lying in a row, shoulder to shoulder, at the side of the ravine, next to the flowing trickle of a stream. Their weapons had been removed, but Alec's medallion still hung from his neck, and he and Erin still wore their rings. Alec's head ached from the blow that felled him. As his vision cleared, Alec could see a band around Erin's neck, like the neckpiece she had worn when enslaved by the nomads. He noticed that each of their riders also wore a neckband. His hands went to his neck, and he could feel that he, too, wore a neckband.

The elf woman walked over and looked at them. She said something in a strange language – when she saw that none of them understood, she changed to a heavily-accented version of Erin's language.

"You are now my captive drones. I am Mother Marta. These three are my clutchmen," and nodding at the fourth, "and he is my apprentice. You will show us respect." She strode around the pile of fallen travelers. "I am taking you to our drone pens. The Drone Master will train you and then decide your fate. However, I am going to train you enough to make you compliant on the way there. I want you to feel pain.

"Hurt!" she commanded.

An intense, agonizing pain pulsed through Alec.

"Stop pain!" The pain went away.

What just happened? thought Alec.

"You will not try to speak without permission," the elf woman continued in a commanding voice. "You will answer all my questions fully and address all responses with 'yes, Mother' or 'no, Mother.' If for some reason you need to communicate with us, you will come and crouch at my feet and wait for permission to speak. You will not try to harm us or escape.

"If you do not fully follow directions, I will give you pain until you fully comply." She clapped her hands sharply.

"Line up in front of me! Stay on your knees with your heads down!" After a few zaps of pain, the seven of them complied and were lined up on their knees with their heads down, in front of the Mother.

The Mother stepped up to the first rider, Cryl, touched him, and started asking him questions. He eagerly answered in full and told everything about himself and the rest of them. Then she told him to undress, and he was quickly on his knees in front of her, naked. The same thing happened with the next rider, Bon, and on down the line. Eventually, the Mother came to Alec and touched him. Nothing happened. She looked at his hand and saw the ring. She motioned to one of her clutchmen, and he grabbed Alec's hand and roughly pulled all the rings from his fingers.

Now when the Mother touched him, Alec felt a deep desire to please her. It seemed to him that there was nothing more important in life than pleasing the Mother. He would do anything to please her. The Mother twisted and implanted a version of the elf language in his mind. She started asking questions, and he answered fully, volunteering important information that she hadn't asked. He told her his complete history, about his boyhood growing up in Washington State, about his life in Theland, and about his medallion and staff. He knew she wanted him to remove his medallion, so without being asked, he took it off and handed it to one of her clutchmen. Next, the Mother told him to undress – he almost tore his clothes off as he willingly complied. Then the Mother released him, and the feeling that he had to please her immediately dissipated. His mind returned to normal with a sense of revulsion, at what he had just done, and a feeling of regret that he had voluntarily handed over his medallion.

Erin was next. The Mother touched her, and nothing happened. The Mother reached down and carefully removed Erin's ring. Then, Alec could hear Erin telling the elf everything she asked. Erin held nothing back. Erin also willingly undressed.

Finally, the elf asked, "Is the tall one talented at coupling?" and pointed at Alec.

"Oh yes," said Erin, beaming.

"What about the one beside him?" the Mother asked, pointing to Thom.

"I don't know," said Erin. "I have never coupled with him."

The answer surprised the Mother; then she indicated for Erin to return to her place in line.

The elf apprentice came up to the Mother and stood in front of her respectfully with his head down.

"Speak," said the Mother.

He gestured towards Alec, and continued, "You could make that one you like please you while I use the women and then kill them for you. That won't waste any of your time."

The mother gave the apprentice a withering look and shook her head.

"Although our tradition is to kill all captive women immediately, I think the stories told by these three are important enough that the Disca should hear them," the Mother intoned. "We will not kill them here. We will take all of them with us, not just the males." She looked at her disappointed apprentice, and then her captives. A sly smile crossed her face. "We do have a little time to enjoy them." She eyed the three women.

"I think that one might be a cross-breed," she said, pointing at Erin. "Stay away from her. She might give you trouble. You can have whichever of the other two you want. Leave her alive when you are done."

The elf looked at the two female riders, eagerly licking his lips, and pointed at Nikka. The Mother walked up to her and took her hand.

"Stand up," she said, and the woman stood. "Please him," the Mother said and gave her hand to the elf apprentice.

Nikka tried to resist but was immediately struck by intense pain. Finally, she gave in and stopped resisting. She began helping the elf remove his clothes, and compliantly slithered underneath him, legs spread, in the middle of the wet, muddy path.

Then the Mother walked over to Alec and touched him, gesturing for him to stand. Alec immediately felt a deep desire to please the Mother, to cater to her every want, to satisfy her. He felt himself grow hard. Then the mother touched Thom and gestured for him to stand next to Alec. He had a similar reaction.

"Look up," she said to them both. She looked them both over for a while, stroking their arms and legs, and feeling their bodies. Alec hoped desperately that she would pick him, that he would be the one to satisfy her. Then she took Thom's hand. She didn't say a word, and the rider eagerly followed the Mother to a spot away from the muddy trail. Soon Alec could hear her moans of pleasure – Thom was doing a good job at pleasing her, he figured.

As soon as the Mother left, Alec was released from his deep and urgent desire and felt more than a little embarrassed and ashamed at his obvious physical reaction to her.

Where are we? Alec wondered. Without their rings, he could not communicate with Erin through their thoughts, and suddenly realized how dependent he had become on this method of conversing.

He turned his head to look around the ravine. One of the clutchmen noticed him standing with his head held high.

"Look down!" the clutchman growled. Alec immediately felt intense pain and looked down. The clutchman walked up to him and poked him in the chest with a strong finger.

"You wild orbs are arrogant! You think that you are as good as we are! You fancy that you are like an elf!" He kept jabbing Alec in the chest. "But you'll find your place. We train animals like you naked until you become a bit domesticated. It can be quite uncomfortable, if you know what I mean! But, if you do well and learn your place quickly, we will give you a bit of a reward

– perhaps a few clothes, something to wear." He smiled paternally, then scowled.

"Now! Punish yourself for looking up!" Alec felt intense pain, growing and throbbing until he was bent double with the intensity of it. Alec wasn't sure he could stand it anymore. Then the clutchman seemed to tire of Alec's writhing. "Return to the line," he said, dismissively. The pain quit, and Alec scrambled back to his place in line on his knees with his head down.

Soon Nikka returned to her place in line. She was coated with mud and gravel and was very upset at having willingly participated in being raped. From his head-down position, Alec could see that the clutchmen were enjoying the Mother's tryst, listening to the sounds of sex and sneaking a quick peek now and then. After a while the Mother returned, pushing Thom in front of her.

"You were not good enough," she said. "Punish yourself." Thom flopped on the ground moaning and contorted in pain. The mother looked at the body on the ground and said, "Suffer silently." Thom's body continued writhing silently at her feet. "When the Drone Master finishes training you, you will perform for me again. I expect you to be much better." The elf woman touched Alec. "I should have picked you. Dream about me tonight, because I will have time tomorrow for you to please me." Then she said to the writhing man at her feet, "Return to your place." Thom dutifully got back into line with his head down.

The Mother turned to the seven, still on their knees with their heads down.

"Get up and follow us," she said in her elf language. After a moment Alec realized that they all understood her and were following her. Her apprentice picked up the sack of captured weapons, medallion, and rings; their discarded clothing and packs were left where they had strewn them.

Alec could feel a compulsion deep in his mind that was encouraging him to obey the mother. It did not control him like her touch, but he still felt the desire to cooperate and obey her. He wondered if the others felt this way too. After a few steps, Cryl hesitated and then bent double in agony. Erin started to say, 'this is not the time to resist,' but before she could speak, she felt intense pain. After that, they all followed the elves quietly and compliantly.

Occasionally splashing through the small, muddy creek, they came out of the ravine, walked across a bowl-shaped meadow, and back into a dense forest. Well into the forest, they arrived at a small shack.

"Go in," commanded the Mother. "Stay there. Sit still. Do not talk to each other." All seven of the captives went into the shack, compliantly sat down, and did not talk to each other. The stench in the room from old urine was intense. Erin was in despair – she had been controlled by a neckband once before and had only been released with Alec's medallion; now she was unable to do anything to shield her riders or complete her mission. Her five riders were mortified, and dejected – they had not protected their Princess and had not offered the least resistance to the Mother.

The elves stood outside, mumbling in their language. The Mother communicated with her clutchmen mentally, but spoke aloud to her apprentice. Alec heard them agree to leave the apprentice to watch the captives; the others could continue to patrol in case there were more intruders. The apprentice was further instructed to stay alert, and not dally with the women captives tonight. The elf Mother told him that she would return tomorrow afternoon and take the prisoners to the city when the replacement patrol arrived.

The seven sat in the shack. The Mother opened the door and took one last look at them. She eyed the mud-coated woman who had been victimized by the elf apprentice, and at the man who had displeased her. Then she smiled maliciously.

"Go and please her until morning," she said to Thom, pointing at the muddy woman. "Accept him," she said to Nikka. Then the Mother closed the door and left.

Thom began reluctantly crawling towards the muddy woman, his intentions clear. Nikka retreated until her back hit the corner of the shack. Thom continued to crawl towards her. At first, a look of quiet desperation covered the woman's face. Then it was replaced with a look of hope. She was prohibited from speaking, but she pointed at the mud on her arms. The crawling rider was half on top of her before he understood what she wanted: it would please her for him to clean the mud off her. Thom began to lick her arm, using his tongue to loosen the mud and clean her. Nikka made fake sounds of pleasure as he continued.

Although it was hard to ignore them, Alec sat in the shack, shivering slightly, deep in thought.

We need to get free and recover our rings — and my medallion — before the elf Mother returns, he thought. *If Erin and I aren't wearing our rings, she can make us do anything she wants, whenever she touches us.* He thought about how long they had been on the path through the elf lands, and how long it would take the elf Mother to return. *We have less than a day to escape before she returns. But we can't escape unless we can figure out how to beat these slave-bands around our necks.* He remembered his last conversation with Sarah, as she lay dying on the battlefield. *Sarah said these bands had an easy counter that high-tech worlds discover. It is my puzzle to solve,* he thought.

29 – The Elves

Alec lay awake in the darkness, trying to ignore the sounds of licking and moaning, and the mumbling of Bon, the rider who talked in her sleep. He wanted to hold Erin but was unable to move.

The ability to control others was apparently not a talent that an elf was born with – the elf Mother generated an energy field and used lines of energy to gain control. Alec went over everything he knew about energy fields, and lines of energy, and shielding from fields, and twisting lines. Everything seemed to come to a dead end. *Not right,* he thought. *It doesn't seem right.*

The elf Mother is using something to generate the lines, he thought. *What?* Besides her ring, of course. Then he slapped his hand on his thigh. *The band!*

He was trying to make the problem too hard. The answer to the Mother's ability to control was within the band. How did the band work? How did the band know when to inflict pain? What was it about the band that caused pain? Or pleasure? But – the bands weren't alive, and weren't electronic, like exercise trackers on his home planet. By themselves, the bands couldn't understand the instructions given by the elf Mother. The Mother's ring was just like the one Erin had given him. Alec thought about how he had communicated with Erin when they both wore their rings, or how Erin could sense truth. He thought about the level of technology in this primitive world, or lack thereof compared to his Institute.

Think. He listened to the sounds of the night, of Rhor snoring lightly, and Bon still talking in her sleep. Then the solution came to him, and he chuckled aloud.

Erin looked at him, startled by the sound of his voice. She had been watching him, and even without her ring, knew he was puzzling through this. Now, she could see his elation. She wanted to ask him what he had figured out.

Alec looked at Erin and thought to himself; *I think I know the answer!* Then, he said to himself, aloud, "I think I know the answer." Pleased at the sound of his own voice, he looked at Erin and said to himself, again aloud, "Yes! I know the answer!" Erin looked at him wide-eyed. She tried, but she could not answer him.

Alec continued to talk to himself, aloud. "It is dark, and we can't do much right now. We will see if we can't do something when the morning light comes." Finally, he was able to drift off to sleep.

Alec had nightmares all night about unsuccessfully attempting to please elf ladies.

≈ ≈ ≈ ≈

The elf apprentice was up and fixing himself breakfast. The sounds of licking and moaning had finally ended with the first morning light. The two riders were laying in the corner both exhausted. Alec could see blood coming from Thom's mouth and tongue. Nikka had no speck of mud on her.

The smell of food wafted through the cracks in the shed door, and Alec's stomach started grumbling in response. No one had fed the seven yesterday, and it was clear the apprentice wasn't going to feed them this morning. He had not even left them any water.

Alec had hoped that while the apprentice was preoccupied with preparing breakfast, he could try what he now knew. Unfortunately, the elf was positioned directly in front of the door, utensils clattering against his metal plate. Alec could hear when the elf finished eating and then heard rustling noises. Then the elf opened the door, which squeaked loudly as it opened. The elf stood in the doorway, silhouetted by the morning sun, naked, every hair on his body catching the early light.

He looks furry, thought Alec. He wasn't used to seeing naked elves.

The elf looked at Erin leeringly; then he looked at the two women riders.

"You women," he said, imitating the elf Mother's bark. "Get on your hands and knees! Crawl over here." The three women resisted for a few seconds and then complied, crowding together before the naked elf's feet.

"The Mother told me not to do anything last night, but she didn't forbid anything this morning," he said, grinning. He looked at Erin and said, "Look up at me." She complied. The elf patted her on the head. "Nice hair. Too bad I can't have you." He looked at her another long minute. "Maybe some other time. Crawl over to the corner," he said, and Erin complied. Then he looked at Nikka and Bon.

"I already had you," he said to the freshly-cleaned rider, who was glossy and damp from being licked. "I want to try someone new. Up on your knees!" he said to Bon. She tried to resist; Cryl tried to get up and help her. "No, no!"

338

said the elf to the man. "Stop!" He stopped. "Now, punish yourself until she returns, but do it quietly." Cryl started rolling on the floor in intense pain. By now Bon had lost mental control and had risen to her knees before the elf. "Now," said the elf apprentice, running his tongue across his lips, "crawl over there by the fire and spread yourself out on my sleeping blanket."

He's new at this, thought Alec. *And, his commands are not precise.*

As soon as the woman passed through the doorway, the elf slammed the door behind her, again throwing the shack into darkness. Alec felt that this might be his only chance to act before the elf Mother returned. He looked at Nikka, still on her hands and knees in front of the door.

"Nikka should open the door," Alec said aloud, speaking to himself. Nikka obligingly reached for the latch but recoiled in pain and backed off.

"Now I am going to try to open the door," said Alec, still speaking to himself.

Don't hurt yourself, thought Erin. *I don't want you to be in pain!* – then realized that Alec could not sense her thoughts without the rings, and she couldn't move or talk to him.

Alec stood up, walked over to the door, and opened it without a problem. As before, it squeaked loudly as it opened, and Alec stepped outside cautiously. The elf was occupied with Bon on the blanket, thrusting and grunting, and didn't notice the creaking door. *I need to take care of the elf,* he thought. Alec moved to the other side of the shack, hoping that the sacks with their weapons were still where the apprentice had dropped them the day before. They were. Alec grabbed his staff and started pulling it out, but the bag fell sideways, and the swords and knives clattered out. *Oh no,* thought Alec. He turned just as the elf, still naked, came scrambling around the corner.

"Stop!" shouted the elf.

Alec stopped cold.

The elf reached out to take the staff from Alec. Just then Bon came around the corner, hate and anger in her eyes. The elf turned to look at her.

Okay, I 'stopped' – I have fully complied with his command, thought Alec, *and now I can 'go.'* Alec took hold of his staff, raised it, and bashed the elf apprentice over the head with a very hard blow. The elf collapsed in front of him. Alec ran over to the sacks; one held neckbands and a key. He immediately removed his neckband and snapped it around the elf's neck. Then he ran back inside the shack and removed Erin's neckband and those of the five riders.

They rearmed themselves. Rummaging through the sacks, Alec found a small pouch with their rings and his medallion. The riders found food for their group, and enough clothes to outfit all of them, after commandeering the clothing of the elf apprentice.

Alec looked at Erin, dressed in the brightly colored elf clothing, and smiled. "You look ..."

"Gaudy?" she finished, holding up the corners of the tunic and wrinkling her nose. In turn, she laughed at Alec's outfit, which was too short to cover his legs fully, and tight over his chest.

As they ate, Nikka, Bon, and Erin commiserated with each other over their ill-treatment, and the men listened sympathetically, apologizing for their inability to intercede. The Theland riders had always had a great spirit of camaraderie within their ranks. Thom in particular was ashamed at his own behavior.

Erin walked over to the elf apprentice, still sprawled where Alec had bashed him.

"He is going to die," she said.

"Well," Alec said, "I intended to kill him, not just harm him."

"We need to heal him," said Erin. Alec looked at her. "Yes, he deserves to die for his actions," Erin said, "but a dead elf will make it tougher to get the elves to work with us. My mother taught me that sometimes actions that are the best for my people and Theland must come before personal justice — what you call 'revenge.'" Alec and Erin sat next to the elf, laid their hands on him, and shortly he was healed. He sat up, slowly shaking his head, and buried his face in his hands.

"Lay down," Erin commanded sharply, and the elf apprentice complied. "On your belly. And be quiet." Erin assigned Rhor to be the elf's handler.

Now that they were reunited with their rings, Erin and Alec again were able to communicate by thought.

How did you get free? thought Erin to Alec, not wanting the elf, or the other riders, to hear.

Sarah gave me the clue, he thought back. *I was trying to figure out how the neckbands work. They must be like your rings — the band must be able to sense the victim's feelings. So, if you are wearing a neckband, and you think that you have followed orders —*

you feel that you have done what you were told to do – then there is no pain. You feel good. But, if you think you haven't? Then – boom. You feel pain.

Is that what you were figuring out last night? Erin responded. Alec nodded. *But – how were you able to stand up, and talk, and open the door?*

By this time, they had walked far enough away from the shack that they could not be overheard.

"I changed how I thought, and how I felt," explained Alec. "I decided to interpret the orders very literally so that I would feel that I had complied."

"I don't understand," said Erin.

"In places like my home planet, Earth, there are lots of people who need to use complicated information and actions. Engineers, physicists, chemists, lawyers, accountants, and lots of other people must interpret information in very precise manners. When you're conducting a chemistry experiment, it can make a big difference if you heat something for 'about five minutes' or if you heat it for precisely 'four minutes and forty-five seconds.' And for some things, like physics experiments, you must be more precise than that – you might have to measure something in nano-seconds. That was the clue. Low-tech worlds, like here, tend to process information more broadly. You probably would not need to measure anything in nano-seconds."

"I don't even know what a 'nano-second' is," said Erin, "much less whether I would ever need to use it."

"It's one-billionth of a second," said Alec helpfully.

"I don't know what you are talking about," Erin said, somewhat annoyed by his lapsing into wizard-speak. "What's a 'second'?"

Alec remembered that he was in a world where people did not use clocks and told time by the position of the sun against five moons and the shadows of their hand passing across the ground.

"Well, think about it this way. You could either say that you are in the Land of the Elf, or you could say that you are standing near the elf shack."

"Both are true," said Erin.

"Or you could be even more precise, and say that you are standing right here, next to me."

"Still true."

"So, if somebody back home asked you where you are, all three answers are correct. And if you told one of your soldiers in Theland to 'come here,' he might think you meant the Elf Land in general, or this shack, or right here by us. Your soldier would comply if he did any one of those things.

"When the elf Mother said, 'stay there,' when she had us go inside the shack, at first I assumed that she meant to stay in the shack. If I tried to leave I would feel pain because I would be going against what I felt she meant. But! Then I decided that the world was divided into two places: 'here' and 'there.' Since <u>she</u> said 'stay there,' she meant the spot where <u>she</u> was standing would be 'here,' not 'there.' See? 'X marks the spot,' as they say." Erin looked at him quizzically, and he continued.

"Every place else besides the spot where she was standing would be 'there.' That meant, if I had to stay 'there,' I could be anywhere except 'here' – the precise spot where the Mother was standing when she gave that order. It meant I could go outside the shack if I stayed away from that one place. I was complying with what she commanded me to do, and I <u>felt</u> that I was following her orders. That's why I did not feel pain as long as I felt that I was following her orders."

"That sounds like splitting hairs, my Great Wizard," Erin said.

He laughed. "It is, but since I convinced myself that I had complied with her orders, it worked."

"But you could speak, in the shack, when no one else could."

"Someone else was speaking," Alec replied. "Bon was talking in her sleep."

"But she wasn't talking to anyone, just herself."

"Exactly!" said Alec. "So I figured that as long as I was just talking to myself, out loud, then I was okay. We were told not to talk <u>to</u> each other; but the elf Mother didn't say anything about Bon not talking in her sleep. Or me not talking to myself. Out loud."

It took Erin a moment to digest Alec's explanation.

"How did you overpower the elf apprentice, since the Mother told us not to harm him?"

"She said not to 'harm' them. I think if I had threatened him, or just poked him with my staff, I would have been in pain. But I wasn't trying to 'harm' him; I was trying to 'kill' him!"

"Oh," said Erin.

"And when he told me to 'stop,' I did. Once I had stopped, he didn't tell me I couldn't start again, so I felt that I had complied with his direction.

"That's why this neckband mind-control stuff doesn't work well against people who are used to precise directions and thinking in precise ways. I don't know what would happen if they had a good trainer," Alec mused. "It's possible that with enough time, they could figure out how to be precise enough to make it impossible to disobey."

"We need to go back to the shack," Erin said, pulling his train of thought back to the moment. "What is our next step?"

"I think we just hang tight," Alec said. "Rest, maybe eat a little more and wait for the elves to return. Even if we wanted to get out of here and go back, the elf Mother's patrol is between us and the ravine. We can't outrun them, so we might as well face them here."

Erin shared their plans with her five riders.

"Would it be better to ambush them?" Nikka asked. "The ravine is narrow. We could wait on top and rush them. We would have the advantage of both our weapons and surprise." Erin sensed that the woman badly wanted to avenge the attack against her body.

"No, I don't think so," Erin said gently. "We still need to meet – peacefully – with the elf leaders, and that would be …. difficult … if we kill off this patrol squad."

Erin banished the naked elf apprentice to the confines of the shack and arrayed her five riders to best face the elves when they returned. Erin practiced responding to the energy twists that she had seen. Around midafternoon, Erin sensed the elves before Alec heard them.

The elves had no concern about keeping quiet, and Marta's clutchmen called out to the apprentice to alert him to their return. But when the elves came around the last bend of the path, they could see Erin standing in front of the shack with Alec at her side. They could see the riders, who were strategically deployed in the surrounding woods, but not their apprentice. The elf Mother quickly strode forward.

"What are you doing out here?!" exclaimed Mother Marta, in annoyance and surprise. "And why are you dressed? Take off your clothes and go back inside!" No one moved. "Hurt!" she screamed. "Feel pain!" Again, they just stood and looked.

Erin stepped forward.

"We came here on a mission of peace, and mutual importance – not to be treated like dirt," Erin said. "We came to talk to your leaders. Please take us there."

The elf Mother ignored her.

"Where is my apprentice?" she demanded. "How did you remove your neckbands?" Then she raised her hand and started twisting the force around Erin. Erin started untwisting the force.

Erin and Alec had developed a three-level plan. The first level was to approach the elf Mother and negotiate by talking to her. That clearly wasn't working. The second level was for Erin to out-maneuver the elf Mother's energy lines. Alec could see that the elf Mother was much more experienced than Erin in twisting force bands and that this second level of their strategy was not going well. The third level was for Alec to permanently neutralize the elves if the first two levels didn't work; Alec was confident he could kill them before they knocked him out, if he had to, and was becoming concerned that Erin was not winning her battle. Alec felt that he had one chance to help Erin. He touched her arm and let the dark energy flow. Almost immediately the dark energy opened reservoirs that neither of them knew existed. Now Erin could twist the lines with almost no resistance. She twisted, and the elf woman started to collapse. Without their Mother, her clutchmen were defenseless and fell, whimpering.

Alec released the dark energy from Erin. The two of them looked at each other in amazement.

What was that? Alec wondered. *That power!*

I never felt anything like that before, Erin thought back to him, wide-eyed.

Then Erin called her riders from their positions in the woods.

"Get them banded," she snapped. She removed the elf Mother's ring.

"We are going to treat you as you treated us," Erin said, as the four elves came to. "No better, no worse. Undress." The clutchmen immediately dropped and began to cry in pain, and then the elf Mother began to yowl. "Be quiet," commanded Erin, and the four writhed quietly. The clutchmen were the first to disrobe and groveled at Erin's feet. The Mother was last to comply, but after a minute she obeyed. Rhor brought the elf apprentice out from the stinking shack and positioned all the elves in a line along the path. Alec tied the Mother's hands behind her back and fixed a short rope lead around her waist. He would have the responsibility of watching her; along with Erin, he was not susceptible to her controlling touch if he wore his ring, but the riders did not have that benefit.

Erin exchanged her clothing for the Mother's discarded outfit.

"Now, lead us to your council," Erin commanded, and they started along the path, away from the shack.

≈ ≈ ≈ ≈

After leaving the shack in the woods, they made quick progress through the elf territory. One of the clutchmen lead the way, with Erin right behind. Alec came next and kept control of the elf Mother's leash. The other clutchmen and the apprentice were brought along tied in a line in the back, with Rhor bringing up the rear. Periodically Erin would stop and sense ahead.

"There are six elves coming towards us," said Erin after one stop, just before they entered a clearing in the woodlands. "They will be here in a half hour."

Erin interrogated the elf Mother about this group. She tried to be coy, but between Erin's ability to sense the truth, and the pain that the neck band inflicted when the Mother tried to resist, she soon opened up.

"You are sensing the replacement patrol for our search area" the elf Mother said. "The group will have their Mother, Kara, her three clutchmen, and her two apprentices. Each of us patrol for a week; then we rotate. Even though Kara is the mother of that clutch, she is not as talented as me – I am one of the strongest of the coercers. Until now, I have not been beaten in a single combat, and I don't understand how you beat me."

She tells truth, Erin thought.

"We should meet them here," said Erin. It will take the better part of a half-hour to get ready and strategically, this is a good location." She turned to the riders. "Array our captives in a row on their knees with their heads down. Put the Clutch Mother behind the men, and then you fan out behind them. Make sure our captives do not lift their heads without my permission.

"You and I need to stand in front," Alec told Erin. "Be ready to repeat the performance we put on to capture our Elf Mamma here."

The oncoming elves weren't concerned about intruders this deep in their land, so the elf Mother wasn't sensing the land ahead of her for threats. However, when the elves entered the clearing they stopped short and ceased their banter as they saw the group lined up before them. These elves were trained to stop intruders and they quickly converted from trekking to a combat formation and walked, carefully, towards the waiting group. They approached to within a spears-throw and stopped.

Erin stepped forward.

"I am Erin – Princess of Theland and descendent of the Elf Lian. I wear an elf ring in acknowledgment of my heritage," she said, holding up her hand. "I travel with my Consort, Alec, and my personal guard. We come to your land to meet with your leaders to discuss a matter of great common importance." She gestured to the naked elves behind her, who were on their knees, heads down, neckbands visible. "We have not been well-treated in your land." She stepped slightly to one side to reveal the captive elf Mother, who was in the same submissive posture as her clutchmen. "I expect you to escort me to your leaders with the dignity and honor that an official delegation of a neighboring ruler deserves. If you choose not to treat me appropriately, then I will let you join your friends. It is your choice."

The oncoming elf clutchmen looked at their Mother, waiting to respond to her desires. The elf Mother, Kara, raised her hands and started to twist the force lines around Erin. Alec stepped forward, fed Erin dark energy, and the elf Mother flopped on the ground unconscious.

"Back away from your Mother," Erin said. The five male elves knew they were outclassed and backed away. "Drop your weapons," said Erin. "<u>All</u> of your weapons," she quickly amended, remembering Alec's treatise on precision. There was a muffled clatter as the elves dropped their spears, swords, knives, keys, quills, toothpicks, and walking sticks onto the soft ground of the forest glade.

"Band her," said Alec. Thom snapped a neckband on the woman elf and removed her ring, handing it to Erin. Erin roused the Mother.

"Undress," she said. The Mother fought the compulsion for a long time, writhing and howling and gnashing her teeth. Erin looked on, stony-faced, and did not attempt to quiet her. After what seemed like several minutes, she finally quit resisting and complied, her bright-colored robes forming a small pile next to her. "On your hands and knees! Crawl over there next to the other elf Mother." The Mother did as she was told. Alec tied her hands behind her back and fastened a rope around her waist, attaching her to the first Mother. Alec could see how roping the elves around the neck would give him much better control, but it reminded him too much of his experience with the Alder slavers.

Erin turned to the five male elves.

"We did not come here to cause harm – we came to discuss a matter of great importance with your leaders. Now you have a choice. You may continue to wear your clothes and escort us to your leaders, or we will put a neckband on you and herd you, naked, with our other captives."

The six male elves looked at each other and seemed to try to establish mental communication with their clutch Mother for instructions.

"No, do not communicate with the Mother," said Erin. "She has lost her right to lead."

With pained looks, they quit trying to connect with their Mother. The elves talked among themselves in low voices; they seemed to Alec to be plagued more with uncertainty than disagreement on whether to comply with Erin.

Eventually one of the clutchmen stepped forward.

"We will escort you to the New Haven. What happens there is not our decision."

"Fair enough," said Erin. "I will permit you to send one of your clutch in advance of our party, to announce our arrival to your Council. That will give them enough time to ensure that our delegation is appropriately received." The elves nodded, and one of the clutchmen took off at a quick pace.

30 – New Haven

The trek through the Elf Mountains forest to the elves' central city was uneventful. The four elves lead the way; Erin and Alec came next with their six captives; followed by Erin's riders. Alec mused that if it were not for the gravity of their situation, he would enjoy hiking through this woodland. After a couple of hours, they came to the edge of the forest and crossed through fields with rows of well-tended crops; naked farmhands were diligently working the fields. Most of them did not pay any attention to the little band. Only occasionally did someone glance their way; even though six of the elves were naked, the farmhands didn't seem to care. After crossing the fields the little band reached the outer perimeter of a city; there were few outbuildings, and the rows of crops came all the way up to the walls of the city. The New Haven walls were substantial. Alec thought that they appeared to be about twenty feet high with a recent coat of whitewash on the outside. Their path took them to an ornate metal gate leading into the New Haven.

A small force was arrayed in front of the gate – Alec estimated about twenty people. It seemed to be composed of small teams, each with a lead woman and three men supporting her.

Time to be bold, Erin thought to Alec. They marched up and faced the force arrayed against them. Erin motioned to Alec.

Alec stepped forward.

"Her Highness Erin, Princess of Theland, and descendant of the Elf Lian, has come to consult with your leaders on a matter of great import. Whom may we be addressing?"

A woman and her three men came to the front of the group ahead of them. Mimicking Erin, she motioned to one of the men, and he stepped forward.

"Her Excellency Varra, Clutch Mother, and member of the Disca of the New Haven, stands to hear your plea," he announced, feeding Erin the words the woman telepathed to him.

"Thank you, Clutch Mother Varra, for allowing us the privilege of addressing you," Erin said, taking her place in front of Alec. "We are an official delegation and come to discuss with you and your Council a common issue of great urgency."

The two women stood facing each other, assessing the other. Alec could not feel any energy lines from either of them. *They must have hit the 'mute' button,* he thought.

A long silence ensued as the two women stared at each other. Finally, Erin broke the silence.

"We are sorry we required your scouts to escort us in this manner, but they did not share our urgency," Erin said, pointing to her captives. "Now that we have arrived at your fair city, we will release them to you as a gesture of goodwill and an indication of our peaceful intentions. They have been gracious company on our trip, so I would ask that you reward them for their hospitality. May I turn them over to your authority?"

The elf woman looked with disgust at the naked, banded elves and then, with exaggerated grace said, "We thank you. We will accept their return and promise they will be appropriately handled." At her mental command, her clutchmen came forward to receive the elves. "Come to me!" Varra commanded, and the banded clutchmen and the apprentice immediately walked to her in a single file; the two clutch mothers made a motion towards her, but Erin gave them a command to wait until Alec could obviously and ceremoniously hand over their rope lead to the clutchmen.

"We welcome you and your delegation to our New Haven. We will allow you to appear before the Disca tomorrow," Varra said. "Since you have bested two Mothers, I grant you the privileges of a Mother until the entire Disca can properly determine your status. Until then we will provide you with our hospitality. We will prepare a residence for you, and accommodations for your clutchmen and drones." A banded drone came forward to escort them.

Erin's team was led through the middle of the New Haven. Alec was amazed at the city. All the buildings were constructed of solid white stone. Windows were abundant and covered with panes of glass-like material. The buildings were brightly colored, two and three-story structures with fanciful towers and balconies. Colorful patterns were inlaid on the surface of most outside walls. All the Mother's residences were large with a single entryway and elaborate gate, and appeared to have an interior courtyard.

Erin and her party were taken to a large residence. As Erin stepped into the residence, three banded drones stood respectfully waiting for her to enter. The drone who had escorted them turned and stood with his head down waiting. It took Erin a second to understand that he was waiting for permission to speak. She nodded her head. "Mother, these three will take care of your every need."

The head drone stepped forward and waited patiently. Alec noticed that all three drones' heads were slightly bowed to ensure they didn't look Erin in the eye – they were bowed at the perfect angle to see and respond to facial expressions but not look into the eyes of their masters. Erin nodded. The lead drone very politely asked Erin about her preferences in food.

The drones quickly prepared a meal consistent with Erin's preferences. Alec investigated the food preparation room and was astonished to see that they were preparing the meal on a device that was powered by transmitted dark energy and that there was a food-storage cave that was cooled in the same way. The seven Thelanders were served a multi-course meal complete with a rich dessert. It was the best meal they had eaten since they had left Theland. The lead drone apologized for the simplicity of the meal and promised that tomorrow night the meal would be up to proper standards. As the meal progressed, the sun set and the natural light faded from the large windows. One of the drones touched some globes on the wall and the room filled with light. *Even nicer than my globes,* Alec thought to Erin.

After the meal, and a last quaff of ale, a drone appeared to show the riders to their quarters. The head drone unobtrusively came up to Erin and stood with his head down.

"Yes?" she finally asked him.

"What else does the Mother need?" the drone then asked deferentially.

"A hot bath and some decent clothes would be nice."

Immediately one of the drones scurried off and within five minutes had returned with a tailor at his side. The tailor unfolded several samples of clothes. The first sample looked too much like the loose clothing of the drones or the people of the Grasslands. The second sample was in the garish style of the elves and not to Erin's taste. The third sample was closer to the dress of Theland and Erin asked for things in that style.

"The sets of clothing in this style will be ready for you and your clutch by the time you awaken," he said. Then he sprinted off.

The lead drone approached Erin and waited head down respectfully. Finally, Erin figured out what he wanted.

"You may speak," she said.

"Your warm bath is ready upstairs," he said. "I hope it is the right temperature for you, and of an aroma pleasing to you."

Alec followed Erin upstairs to the sleeping suite. The drone led them through a sleeping room and into an ornate bathing room. Then the lead drone stood carefully to one side, with eyes averted, as Erin undressed and slid into the warm water. Alec sat on a bench of carved stone nearby. The drone collected all of Erin's clothes and discretely folded and stacked them. Erin let the warmth sink into her pores. She had not had a proper hot bath since she left the Residence in Theland.

The drone stood quietly and unobtrusively at the side of the room. Whenever the water temperature started to cool even slightly, the drone would discretely touch a panel on the wall. Alec could feel dark energy flow and reheat the water.

The drone had decided that Alec was closer to a drone than a clutchman – even though Alec did not wear a neckband – so he approached Alec and said, "Will the Mother want me to provide any other services?"

"What is usual – what do others ask of you?"

The drone sighed and looked down at his crotch.

"In my prime, I was known for my ability to provide exquisite pleasure to the Mothers," he said wistfully. "My capability is not what it used to be, but I will give my best if she desires it."

"I think I can take care of those needs," Alec said, smiling wryly.

The drone was relieved.

"Thank you! Thank you! I was hoping you would," the drone said. "I would have given her everything I had, but I am no longer up to the standards the Mothers demand."

"My pleasure," Alec said.

The drone, satisfied that Erin was enjoying her bath, pointed to the wall.

"Do you know how to control the room temperature for the Mother's preference?" he asked Alec.

Alec looked at him in surprise. He had often missed central heating on the cold nights and primitive conditions traveling across the Grasslands, and missed air conditioning on a few hot, muggy days in Theland, but had not realized until this moment that all these rooms were at pleasant temperatures.

"No," he replied.

The drone motioned for him to come into the sleeping room and walked over to a wall. "Place your hand here and you can increase or decrease the wall temperature to make the room more desirable for the Mother." Alec looked closely. The location was indistinguishable from the rest of the wall. "Remember to do it in advance because it takes a few moments for the room to adjust. Many Mothers like to sleep in cool rooms but desire the room warmer when they rise." He looked at Alec. "Do not disappoint the Mother by waiting too long to start the warming," he admonished.

Alec felt the wall.

"Not there. Here," the drone corrected, pointing to the proper spot.

Alec could feel the wall focusing dark energy from the concentrator. He lowered the temperature and felt dark energy cool the wall and a layer of cooler air roll of the wall. He raised the temperature and felt the dark energy heat the wall and a warmer air layer rise from the wall. Alec played with the wall in fascination for a few minutes. This was an application that he had never considered.

Then he noticed the lead drone staring at him as if he were a country bumpkin and stepped away from the wall.

Alec looked around. Only the two of them were in the room. Alec pulled out a key for the drone neckband.

"Do you want me to take your band off?" Alec asked.

The drone recoiled in horror.

"No master! Please no!" he said. "That would displease the Mothers, and I do not want them to be displeased. Their pleasure is much more important than my life."

Not the reaction I was expecting, thought Alec.

The drone touched one of the sleeping room windows, and Alec could feel the dark energy changing the glass to a darker shade, immediately diminishing the glare from the artificial light globes in the courtyard. The two of them walked back into the bathing room. The lead drone noted with quiet horror that the water temperature had dropped while they were gone and quickly raised it. After that Erin dismissed the drone, and the drone collected Erin's folded clothes and quietly left. Alec slid into the hot water with Erin, and they talked about the day's events.

Alec periodically did raise the water temperature.

"They know I am truth reading, so everything they say is the truth," Erin told Alec, "but I sense an undertone of deception. We need to be careful tomorrow."

Just in case of trouble, Erin summoned Rhor to stand guard at the door of their sleeping quarters, but there were no events. Even though the bed was comfortable, and he was with his consort, Alec slept poorly. He sensed dark energy all through the night. It felt as if there were multiple sources of dark energy, and one source appeared to be throbbing and pulsing in erratic patterns.

≈ ≈ ≈ ≈

In the morning, the drones were working long before they were up. Alec could see that one of the drones had been there early because the window was clear, the room was warm, and Erin's purloined travel clothes had been cleaned, stacked, and folded beside her bed. The new clothes from the tailor were also placed beside her bed. The tailor was waiting discretely outside the sleeping room to ensure that the Mother's clothes were perfect and that her clutchman was properly outfitted. The cut was tighter than Alec preferred, but it was due to the style and not to imperfections in the skill of the tailor. Alec thought Erin looked radiant in the outfit that the tailor had made.

"How long did it take you to make the clothes?" Erin asked, twirling before a mirror.

"All night," the tailor replied, bowing his head. "It was no trouble at all. I sent for help from other shops, and we finished just before I brought them here."

"Well, good work," said Erin. "Now you can go get some rest."

"Thank you," the tailor said, beaming at the compliment. Elf Mothers expected perfection, and they never complimented service. The tailor continued, "But, of course, I have others that I must serve today. I will take a short break this evening when I have completed my day's tasks."

A delightful breakfast had been prepared and was carried to Erin's room so that she and her clutchman could eat in bed if she desired. She did. As they were finishing breakfast, a drone announced that she had a visitor. Erin took her time finishing breakfast and preparing herself for the day. Then she came out to meet her visitor: a young woman elf, with three male elves following

"Greetings," the young woman said. She wore a ring like Erin's on her hand. "I am Zera, and I am your host. Welcome to our city! The Disca will see you at mid-afternoon. I have been instructed to show you the New Haven. I understand you know very little of our ways. I will escort you and your clutch. The other three members of your party who are not your clutchmen may remain here at the residence for the day."

Erin summoned her riders and directed Thom and Bon to accompany her and Alec; she gave the other three riders instructions to not stray far from their quarters. Zera looked for a long time at Bon.

"Your clutch choice is strange, but I know of no tradition that forbids it." Then she turned her gaze back to Erin. "The Disca has honored you with all the privileges of a Mother, but no weapons will be allowed at the gathering, so leave your sword."

Erin reluctantly took her sword off and hung it by the door. The other three also removed their swords. Alec looked at his staff and decided it was not a weapon.

"I know little about Mothers or what privileges have been bestowed upon me," said Erin. "Can you explain it to me?"

As they left the residence, Zera explained.

"When a girl acquires her talent we have a solemn ceremony. At the end of the ceremony the girl is granted womanhood and is called a Mother. Every Mother leads a clutch – her clutch would include her, or course, and her three male elves, and their accompanying drones.

"Mothers usually have only one talent, but a few have multiple talents. My talent is as an empath. I can sense feelings. The coercers have the most desired talent and are at the top of the pecking order, even though the empath talent is more important to our society. I don't think that you orbs – or cross-breeds – have anything like that."

"What happens to the boys?" Erin asked. "Do they have a similar ceremony?"

"Oh no!" Zera said, with a touch of contempt. "They are just males. Nothing special. But when they are mature, the Mothers assign the males to a clutch. Once a male enters a clutch, he is under his Clutch Mother's control."

"So you tell them what to do?"

"Yes – we can mentally communicate with our clutchmen over long distances."

"Then all of the … males … become your servants?"

Zera laughed. "No, the male elves serve the clutch. The male <u>drones</u> are our servants – they are orbs that we have domesticated. They do our bidding and perform everything required to maintain our society."

"How do I tell them apart?" Erin asked, feeling slightly confused.

Zera laughed again. "The drones wear the neckbands, of course, and the male elves do not. We use the bands to ensure the drones remain totally compliant."

"I see – the Mothers control the drones through the neckbands," Erin said, remembering her own time wearing a slave neckpiece. "But how do the Mothers control others … the clutchmen? They … you … seem to have a great deal of control."

"We sense the force as if it is lines that move around people. As an empath, I feel the change in the lines to sense truth. A good coercer can twist the lines to influence behavior."

"I have sensed the lines before, but I never understood what they were," said Erin. "What about the apprentices? Are they like clutchmen or like drones?"

Zera looked at her and shrugged her shoulders. "We can only bond with three clutchmen, so often there are more male elves than we can bond. We have apprentices because it cuts down on the number of unclutched males that are loose and causing trouble. A Mother can have up to three apprentices in training to replace her clutchmen."

I guess you are my clutchman, Erin thought to Alec. *Or do you need more training?*
Alec unobtrusively kicked her ankle.

Zera continued to walk them around, pointing out interesting items of commerce or business taking place in the New Haven, always addressing herself directly to Erin.

"That is a special work-training facility. We train some of our drones to use dark energy. They keep the city in repair."

Alec wandered over to get a closer look at one of the drones working in the facility, with Zera frowning at his impudent display of interest. He could feel that a band of dark energy connected the drone's medallion to a structure in the middle of town.

355

Erin, he thought, *they have a projection generator and dark energy receivers. They can use that to generate dark energy in a central location and then transmit it over a distance. They use the dark energy transmitted from the concentrator to support their lifestyle!*

Don't use Wizard-speak on me right now, please, Erin thought back.

They headed up a broad boulevard passing a large ornate building.

"This is our Ministry of Tradition," Zera said proudly. "One of our most important ministries. Very important to guide our everyday events, to make sure we all adhere to the ancient ways. We know that innovation and change will set our society on a path to ruin, so we only allow change if it is approved by all members of the Disca."

"What happens if there is a change?" asked Erin, thinking of her sword with the glowing handle. "If you find a better way?"

"It is hard to imagine that someone would find 'a better way,'" said Zera with a hint of disdain. "To repeat an action that is not a tradition requires approval and incorporation into our lexicon. By design, it is very time-consuming process, and it is challenging to add something to our traditions. Or take something away."

Alec opened his mouth to ask a question, but a thought from Erin stopped him.

Don't anger Zera unnecessarily. Play along with the rules here. Either think the question to me or get permission like a good clutchman.

Alec stepped in front of Zera and stood with his head down. Being taller than the elf, he stared down at the top of her head.

"Ask," said Zera, looking up at him, clearly more satisfied with Alec's behavior.

"I thought it was technology that you feared, but you use a lot of technology in your lifestyle."

"It is not technology that leads to ruin," said Zera. "It is <u>change</u> that opens the path to ruin. Innovation brings about change, so we only allow technological innovation when it is essential. Afterward, we follow the new tradition and not the old one."

This conversation reminded Alec of the new technology – death rods – that Dr. Alder had tried to introduce on Nevia. "You seem to use the sword and spear for your defense. Why don't you use weapons that fire projectiles, like the death rods used on the Grasslands?" he asked.

Zera decided that Alec asking the second question was only a minor breach of protocol.

"All kinds of weapons that use projectiles have been tried by escaped orb herds, on many worlds, but they are easy for our dark energy drones to counter by creating bending fields that divert the projectiles. We have many counter-weapons stored in our armory. Many of them we have never used. We have found that the only weapons that cannot be countered are those that are powered by strength and speed of arms – our swords and spears."

They came to another large building with no windows. "This is our Hatchery," Zera said.

"Hatchery?" questioned Erin.

"For our eggs. I forget that you orbs do not reproduce as we do."

"Eggs?"

"Yes, our eggs. An elf Mother produces two clutches of eggs during her breeding lifetime. The two breeding periods are about three years apart. It is a wonderful time! For four days or so when the eggs ripen, we go into our breeding frenzy! We couple with as many males as possible while in the frenzy." Zera smiled broadly. "About a month after the frenzy, the Mother goes to the hatchery and deposits her eggs. We always have four eggs, three male and one female."

They entered a large room that had rows of cradles; only about a fifth of them seemed to be in use. On one side were small soft nests with groups of eggs the size of a robin's egg, bathed in a warm light; the center of the room held covered cradles with individual leathery eggs; on the far side were eggs the size of a large watermelon, each in its own open cradle. Alec estimated that there were close to a hundred eggs all total.

"Your way is different, is it not?" Zara asked Erin. "I hear that you must grow your eggs inside of your body?"

"Yes, we grow our baby inside, below our heart," Erin replied.

"This is so much easier. A growing egg can become quite heavy; I can only imagine that it would feel dreadful to have such a burden inside of your body. And I can't imagine what it must be like to tear it out of your body when it is finished! Once my eggs are laid, I am done with that business."

Alec saw people moving from cradle to cradle and infusing dark energy into each egg. They were using a device to focus the dark energy that reminded Alec of the crystal that the old Seer had used, back at Erin's city.

"What are they doing?" Alec asked.

Zera looked at Erin. "You have a poorly mannered clutchman. If he were mine, I would severely discipline him for speaking without my permission."

When Erin nodded that it was all right to answer, Zera said to Erin, "They are feeding the eggs. The eggs need to be fed several times a day with dark energy. The special cradles hold the dark energy and allow for fewer feedings a day. The nursemaids do the feeding and watch the eggs until they are hatched."

"It looks mostly empty," said Erin.

"Yes, our numbers are slowly declining. We started out in the New Haven with twenty thousand elves, and now we are down to only about five thousand. Our number of full-elf female births isn't sustaining our population."

"How long does it take … for the eggs … to be done?"

"The Hatchery swaddles the eggs for ten trips of the five moons," Zara said. "Then when the egg is ready, we open it. Much easier on our Mothers than your way," she added slyly.

"Where are the babies?" Erin asked.

"Babies?"

"You know, infants." Erin made a cradling, rocking motion with her arms. Zera looked puzzled. "After they come out of the eggs. What do you do with them? Do they go back to their mothers?"

"Oh! The freshlings? No, of course they don't go back to the Mother! Why would she want them? She is done. The fresh elves are put into the child-pen as soon as they emerge," she said, pointing to a nearby walled area. As they left the room, Alec looked through a viewing window and nudged Erin. An attendant was helping an elf-child out of a newly-opened egg; as the moist creature unfolded, Alec thought to Erin, *That looks like a four-year-old on my world, not a baby!*

Zera led them to a smaller room with no cradles, dominated by a solid crystal panel.

"What is that?" asked Erin.

"It is our freshling panel," Zera answered. "It shows us the true blood. We test all freshlings soon after they emerge. Freshlings that are not pure elf are eliminated." She raised her eyebrows in a slight smirk. "Cross-breeds happen fairly often because we enjoy frolicking with our drones. That is why we do not have enough female elf births. Almost half of the females are cross-breeds."

She led Erin to the panel. "We know that you are a cross-breed – go ahead and touch the panel. You can see how it works."

Erin touched the panel. It glowed red. "Child of Lian," an artificial voice said.

Then Zera touched the panel, and it turned green. "Child of Elia." She smiled, with a palpable sense of superiority.

Zera gestured to Bon, Erin's rider. She touched the panel, and it turned brown.

"Pure orb blood," said Zara, dismissively.

Then Thom touched it. The panel turned red. "Child of Lian," the panel said.

"Try it," Erin said to Alec.

It will just be brown, and that won't help you, he thought to her.

Erin thought back, *Try it, just for fun.*

Alec touched the panel. It turned red. "Child of Siara," the panel showed. Alec pulled his hand back quickly.

What! How can that be? he thought.

Erin was startled at this result as well, but before she could collect her thoughts into a coherent message, Zera took her arm.

"Do you understand about cross-breeds?" she said, looking a little concerned, glancing at Alec. "Male cross-breeds are only a minor concern. If they are useful, we keep them but make sure they are not capable of breeding. We always need male drones." She patted Erin's arm. "But Mothers are a different situation. We hear that some elf societies allow cross-breed Mothers to be a part of their society, but our tradition is to only allow pure elf Mothers to live. Unless the Disca changes our tradition, there will be a problem with you. The Disca has never allowed a female cross-breed to live.

"I fear for you," she said to Erin. "If you go before the Disca, they may not allow you to keep your life – and the fate of the others in your party will depend on your fate."

Erin let this sink in. "We have already decided on our path and don't plan to change it now," she said. "Our reason for being here is so important that maybe the Disca will disregard your ancient traditions. We will not know until we meet." Then she changed the subject.

"According to the history of my people, and as indicated by your sensor, I am a direct descendent of an elf named Lian. She is called the First Mother of my land. Who was she?"

Zera thought for a moment. "I am not familiar with an ancestor of that name, but your land was settled by elves that did not agree with our traditions. One such tradition was that of eliminating cross-breeds." She paused. "The name 'Lian' has a special meaning to us. It was supposedly given to the first girl elf freshling on a newly-settled world. The word means 'First Mother' in an ancient form of our language." She squeezed Erin's arm and led the group from the building.

Alec was still ruminating about the freshling panel. *It must have malfunctioned, he thought to Erin. Probably with their dark energy concentrator becoming unstable, it glitched and said I was a cross-breed.* That had to be it.

≈ ≈ ≈ ≈

After leaving the Hatchery, Zera took them to the Drone Domestication Facility where they met the Drone Master, a stony-faced elf woman.

She welcomed them, somewhat stiffly, Alec thought. "I heard that they tried to band you but that you thwarted them. This is where you would have come if you had remained banded. I would have taken good care of you and domesticated you thoroughly. I train about fifty new drones every month. In the New Haven, we have over ten drones for every elf. Most Mothers have at least one personal drone for both their pleasure and their daily needs.

"It usually takes one trip of the five moons to domesticate a new drone. Once a drone is properly domesticated, its every desire is to please the mothers. After it is domesticated, we send it to specialized apprentice programs. Those with no special skills we use in the fields. Someone like you," she pointed at Alec, "would be perfect for the pleasure houses. Someone like you," she pointed at Erin, "would have been eliminated the first day. We eliminate all captured females. We raise more than enough females in our breeding program to provide all our new breeders."

"Where do your new drones come from?" Erin asked although she figured she knew one source.

"We grow most of our drones in our breeding program. Sometimes we are short of males, so we cull the orb herds in the surrounding lands. Since we use females only for breeding, our breeding programs produce too many of them; we don't need more so we don't have to cull the orb herds for females." She peered at Erin. "We don't like to cull on your land," she added.

"Thank you," said Erin. "I appreciate that."

"Oh, it's nothing personal. It's just that Theland is harder to reach than some of the other surrounding lands. Our yield is much higher in other places, like Gott or the Grasslands, so we only cull on your land when the picking is poor in other places."

"I don't remember any episodes with elves coming to cull us," said Erin.

"Of course not," the Drone Master said. "We send only a few coercer Mothers and their clutches when we do a cull. All of us have total control over an orb if we touch it, but a coercer wearing a ring can additionally influence an orb if it is within her sight. She can mentally encourage an orb in any direction it is inclined to go. Sex is the easiest thing to encourage, but sleep is next easiest – because everyone wants sex and sleep.

"Depending on the orb and the strength of the coercer, it takes from a second to a minute to slide the orb into sleep. When we cull, our coercer will slide all the orbs she encounters into sleep. Then she will take the ones we want and leave before she wakes the others. She and her clutchmen put a neckband on the ones they take, and ankle chains, and then march them here. It is a very simple way to cull our herds on the surrounding lands. We let the herds breed, cull what we need, and leave the others."

Ask how she trains them, Alec thought to Erin.

"How do you train them?" asked Erin.

"As you would any animal," the Drone Master answered. "A simple system of reward and punishment. The neckbands serve to assist me with both. The orbs are wild, but not very clever.

"After I have trained an orb, it will continue to follow my directions. When an orb is fully domesticated, it has released its free will and would die before disobeying. By a single trip of the five moons, almost all orbs are fully domesticated and will obey without requiring continual contact." She was proud of her success as an orb breaker.

They walked along a row of clean pens about one arn wide and twice as deep; they were three-sided, with no gate or barrier on the front.

"These are individual holding pens," the Drone Master explained.

"How do you keep the ... orbs ... from leaving?"

361

"There are no doors – that serves to emphasize to a new capture that it has lost its freedom and cannot escape. We should have a cull crop returning in a few days, and we will put these pens to use, like the ones on the far end."

They walked down the row to the far end where each open pen contained a man. The men were dressed in simple clothes, like the loose-fitting clothes of the Grasslands, Alec thought. As the Drone Master approached, each man moved to the front of his pen and went down on his knees, eyes down. The Drone Master stopped at one pen.

"Come out!" she commanded. The drone came out and kneeled in front of her. She touched him and said, "You were too slow and not respectful enough. Go and punish yourself!" She paid no more attention to the drone as he walked over to a specially marked post in the center of the pens, undressed, and then dropped down in silent agony.

The Drone Master moved to the next pen. "Come out!" she said to the kneeling drone. She touched the drone and said. "Did you fully obey everything yesterday? You may speak."

"No Master," the drone said. "I dreamt of my family and longed to see them again."

"Then punish yourself. You will not do that again." The drone scurried over to the specially marked post, undressed, and was also on the ground in silent agony. Alec saw the first drone complete his punishment, dress, and return compliantly to his open pen.

The Drone Master repeated the process with a third drone. The drone answered, "Yes, Master. I only want to serve you and the Mothers."

"You may return to your pen," the Drone Master said.

Turning to Erin, she said, "I give them pleasure for positive achievements, but obedience is something we expect – we do not consider mere obedience to be a positive achievement. We force them to discipline themselves until there is not a shred of wildness or independent thought remaining. Occasionally one of them will not give up the last little bit of itself, and so I direct it to kill itself with pain while the others watch."

Erin asked a question that had been gnawing on her. "The nomads on the Grasslands have slave neckpieces, but they use them to break people in a very different manner than you do. Why do they do it differently?"

"We know they have a few. They must have stolen some of our neckbands." The Drone Master shrugged. "I do not know why they do what they do. Sometimes we lose a neckband when a cull goes bad and the coercer must leave suddenly. Using the neckband to quickly break an orb into a slave is a very inefficient way to use it. They probably do it because they only have a few bands, and don't know any better. We make our neckbands and have as many as we need. We use them in a much more efficient way to effectively train our orbs to be drones. If you try to break orbs too quickly or too harshly, about half die and most of the rest turn into mindless automatons. Those are useless to us – they can only comprehend simple instructions and rapidly forget their tasks. We would kill them as useless hunks of flesh; I do not know what the nomad slavers do with them."

Erin shuddered at the thought of what had almost happened to her.

"We have used the bands for generations," the Drone Master continued, "and we understand all the weaknesses of the neckbands and the ways some orbs can circumvent them. Marta, the Mother you first bested in the forest, is one of our strong young coercers, but she has not yet been on a cull. If she had been on a cull, she would have known to doubly secure new captives. Not only do we band a new one, but we also chain it for extra security. If she had used chains, your clutchmen would be on the inside of my pens this morning."

Zera touched the Drone Master on the arm.

"We thank you for this informative tour and your answers to our guest Mother's questions. But it is time for us to move on."

As they were leaving, the Drone Master turned to Alec.

"You are tall and look strong. Maybe I will see you again soon."

Alec grimaced.

Zera led them away from the drone domesticating facility. A sense of relief came over Alec as they left. If they had been captured, and taken here, escaping from the mind-numbing drone domestication would have been almost impossible.

And the last statement of the Drone Master stuck in Alec's head.

≈ ≈ ≈ ≈

They approached a brightly colored three-story building.

"And what is this?" asked Erin.

"That is our Pleasure House," Zera answered with a smile. "The best of the drones are sent here. Elf men are committed to their clutch Mother and won't engage in carnal pleasure without their clutch Mother's permission. But Mothers are free to couple or otherwise feed their desires with anyone they want. We like to use newly-domesticated drones. A well-trained one will do exactly as we desire. We can mentally direct them as we want. It can be heavenly!"

Zera walked behind Alec and placed her hand on his rear, giving it a little squeeze. He tried not to flinch.

"We have some time," she said to Erin. "Your tall clutchman could take his ring off, and we could enjoy him in the Pleasure House together. He looks like, even without training, he could be pretty good. I wouldn't couple with him without your permission, of course, but together we could have a little fun with him."

"He's already trained and pretty good," Erin said, a bit sharply. "I don't think he needs any more training and I don't want to share him." She took Alec's arm and Zera dropped her hand.

The next stop was the Education Center.

"Our collective history is stored here," Zera told them. "The archives go back five hundred years or more – since we first arrived on this world."

They don't have paper here, or much of a written language. How are they stored? Alec wondered.

"There's a large, beautiful, crystal structure in the center of the building, with many facets," Zara said as if anticipating his question. "Our story is stored on it. I've never seen another one like it anywhere else."

"Are there any records older than that?" Erin asked, after being mentally prodded by Alec.

"I have heard that the history of the broader elf multiverse also is stored here, but not many are interested in that, so it is rarely accessed. I have never bothered to look.

"We know what is important. Elves settled this world five-hundred-fifty-seven years ago to escape punishment meted out by the false dragon queen. We must wait one thousand years before the punishment will no longer be inflicted upon the descendants. All the orb herds on this world were planted by us five-hundred-fifty-seven years ago except yours. Your herd is descended from a small group of elves that did not like the rules at the New Haven and formed a second community. Then they interbred." She sniffed in disgust.

Nearby was another ornate building

"This is our Harm House," said Zera.

Where they harm people? thought Alec.

"'Harm House'?" asked Erin.

"This is where our elves come if they have been harmed. Injured. We rarely suffer from the diseases of the orbs, but our brave Mothers and their clutchmen do suffer from broken bones or wounds."

"Can you heal them?" asked Alec, momentarily forgetting that he was not supposed to speak.

Zera gave him a withering stare and started to tell him he was an impertinent clutchman; then thought better of it.

"No," Zera answered, still scowling at him. "Currently we have no Mothers who can heal. Healing is a rare skill, and a healer is only born every few generations."

Let's try – it might generate some goodwill, Alec thought to Erin.

Erin then asked Zera if they could go inside. The first Mother they encountered had a compound fracture of her left leg that had been awkwardly set.

"This is Henra. She is one of our coercers. She fell the other day and broke her leg. She will stay here until it heals, but her leg will always be deformed. She will never walk properly again and probably will have to find another occupation. A coercer must be able to go on patrols or culls, and she will not be able to do that with a crooked leg."

Alec walked up to her and touched her. Henra recoiled in shock at being touched without permission, by a clutchman, no less – or was he a drone?

"We can fix this if you want us to," he said.

Henra decided that relieving her pain took precedence over protocol, and nodded agreement.

Alec took Erin's hand and laid his other hand upon Henra's bare leg. He pulsed dark energy through the fallen mother. Then he let Erin guide him until he felt the rightness and moved the leg bones back into position. It was a messy and complex break; it took Alec several motions to get the bone, with its splinters and fragments, back into the right place. Then Alec used dark energy to strengthen it. In the end, Erin showed him the rightness of the job.

"Your leg is back in the right place now," Alec said to Henra. "It will still be sore for a day or so, but the bone and tissues are healed."

Henra gingerly tested the leg and found she could walk, with only a little weakness.

"Thank you," she said. "I will be forever grateful! I have an important engagement this afternoon that I could not miss. My drones were finding a litter to carry me, but now I will be able to get there on my own." She smiled, pleased at her recovery.

Zera led them away.

"Are there others who need healing?" asked Alec. No longer scowling at him, Zera took him to other rooms, and they healed the broken bones and gashes of several more Mothers and clutchmen.

"Are there no drones who need healing?" asked Erin, as Zera showed them back to the boulevard.

"No," said Zera dismissively. "We put down any drones that are injured badly enough to require healing. We have a plentiful supply of drones, so it isn't worthwhile for them to take up time or space here in the Harm House. Besides, even if a drone does manage to heal, most of the time it can no longer perform up to our expectations. Then it is useless."

By this time, it was mid-day. Zera was about to suggest they return to the residence for a meal when a messenger came, bowed, and spoke to Zera.

"They are ready for you," the messenger said, with a sidelong glance towards Erin and her clutch. "They have decided to meet in the Audience Hall instead of the Disca Chambers because it holds more people. They are expecting that many will want to attend."

Zera turned to Erin.

"The Disca is ready. They want me to take you there." Zera's clutchmen fanned out behind them, walking directly behind Erin and her 'clutch.'

So, we can't escape, thought Alec as they headed towards the Audience Hall.

31 – The Disca

Erin had been alert during Zera's tour of the city. Now she was on high alert.

So far there have been no lies, but they know I would notice a lie, she thought to Alec. *I think they are being truthful but deceptive. Be ready for something.*

As they approached the Audience Hall, Erin instinctively stood closer to Alec. *There are a lot of elves inside the Hall, and their anxiety level feels very high,* she thought to him.

Zera ushered them through a gated doorway and into a broad, dark, entry passage. A second large, heavy door opened, and they were shown into the main chamber – a brightly-lit circular room with a high ceiling and two tiers of balconies. The room had space for several hundred people, Alec estimated. The balconies were full of clutchmen. The bottom tier only had mothers. Alec did a quick count: there were fourteen mothers arranged around the central circle.

The elf Mother, Varra, stood in the center of the central circle. Alec noticed a stack of drone neckbands discretely placed by her side. The massive doors closed behind them with a thud.

"Welcome to our Disca," Varra said, and raised her hand as if in greeting. Immediately Erin could feel the lines begin to twist – a massive twisting, more powerful than any she had experienced. A coordinated effort from all the Mothers, she thought.

Erin saw her two 'clutchmen' riders collapse, and saw Alec, even with his ring, stagger from the intense onslaught. She sensed with her ring and tried to untwist the lines, but the lines were two thick for her to do more than slow the twisting. She would soon be overpowered. She changed her effort and tried to untwist the lines around Alec. Her mind started to get foggy.

The untwisting gave Alec a few seconds of clarity. *Focus.* A rush of air came down in a loud whoosh. Elves, both Mothers and clutchmen, were picked up by the whirlwind and thrown all over the hall. In the confined space between the balconies, little secondary vortices formed and the resulting whirlwinds continued to toss bodies around. The Mothers stopped twisting the lines and focused on ridding the vortexes. The lines thinned and smoothed. Erin's mind, on the verge of blacking out, cleared. She looked for

Alec. He was on the ground, knocked over backwards from the force of the downdraft, but moving. She ran to him.

"Thank goodness you are alive!" she said breathlessly.

As the whirlwind subsided, the Mothers, one by one, started another mental attack against Erin and her 'clutch'. Erin could feel the lines starting to twist around her and grow thicker as the mother started coordinating their efforts.

Alec stood and took her hand. "Fight them and I will feed you energy!" he said. He focused and pulled dark energy through his medallion and started feeding it to Erin. She started to smooth the lines. By now all the Mothers had joined in the effort against them. Erin was holding even but wasn't gaining. Alec kept feeding more and more dark energy. She stopped the twisting of the lines but couldn't untwist the lines.

"I need more energy," she grunted to Alec.

Alec tried to pull more dark energy but could feel that his medallion was at its limit and about to fail. He sensed Erin's stamina fading against the combined force of the Mothers. "I need more!" she cried, "or they will win!"

His staff lay at his feet where he had dropped it when his burst had reverberated through the hall. He reached down with his free hand and picked it up. Alec focused through the medallion on his staff and felt the oscillating dark energy from the elves' concentrator. He continued to focus the background dark energy through his medallion and now tried to focus the energy from the concentrator through the second medallion on his staff. He had never tried to focus two medallions at once. One mental lapse and his medallion would explode, killing him for sure.

Focus! Focus! Alec grimaced as his staff linked to the dark energy source. He reached out to the source of pulsing energy through his staff and pulled on it as hard as he could. Erin felt the extra dark energy flow into her. The elf Mothers were coordinating and twisting the lines at full strength and Erin could feel the sweat dripping down her forehead from her exertion. Her mind was starting to get fuzzy when the additional dark energy came from Alec; then with a new sense of clarity she directed all the dark energy that Alec was sending her towards the twisting lines. Slowly the lines started to untwist. The outcome hung in the balance for a long moment. Then Erin gained the upper hand and the lines began to untwist rapidly. The collected elf Mothers resisted her untwisting but couldn't stop her. Erin twisted the lines around the

Mothers. Alec saw one Mother drop to her knees, her head in her hands, sapped by her mental efforts, and then collapse to the floor. Then another dropped out, and within a few moments there was no resistance. The room became eerily quiet.

Erin staggered back a few steps as she quit twisting, and released the dark energy back to Alec. Alec released the background energy and then released the concentrator. He felt a snap in the concentrator and then a ragged pulsing flow in the dark energy from the concentrator.

"That was quite an arm-wrestling match," Alec said, looking around.

Erin had no idea what he was talking about.

They looked around the auditorium. The Audience Hall was strewn with elves, tumbled in every direction. Alec's wind-burst, and Erin's slumber efforts, had knocked down the entire assembly.

Erin turned to her two riders, lying face-down on the floor. She felt Thom's wrist and then Bon's. No pulse.

"They are both dead," she said with a sigh. "They killed them." She shook her head sadly. It was hard to lose any rider, but it was especially hard to lose Thom, her personal assistant.

"Maybe it isn't too late," said Alec. "Let's try a dark energy version of artificial resuscitation."

Erin had no idea what he was talking about but knew to trust her Great Wizard's wild ideas.

Alec grabbed both riders' hands and started feeding dark energy into them. He motioned Erin to help and she put her hands on his shoulders. After a moment Thom's chest began to move as he started to breathe again; coughing and sputtering, he sat up. Bon opened her eyes soon after and Thom helped her up. The two looked at the jumble of bodies in the room in surprise.

≈ ≈ ≈ ≈

Alec walked over to where Varra lay.

"Let's recruit some help to finish what we came to do, and then get out of here. We haven't much time."

Erin looked at him questioningly.

"I am afraid the concentrator may be about to fail," Alec explained. "I had to use a lot of dark energy from it and I think that drove it further out of balance. It doesn't have long before it goes unstable."

He picked up one of the bands and snapped it around Varra's neck and removed Varra's ring. On an impulse, he removed the rings from the other downed Mothers as well – fourteen rings. As he did, he recognized one Mother as Henra, whom they had healed only a few hours ago. *So much for eternal gratitude,* he thought.

Alec tossed a ring to each of the riders. "Wear those rings. They will protect you from some of the elf magic."

"Wake up," Erin commanded, poking Varra with her toe, and the Clutch Mother woke up.

Varra looked around at the fallen elves, then looked at Erin and realized she was banded. She put her hands to her neck and felt the weight of the neckband.

"You will help us willingly, or we will force you," said Erin ominously.

"Yes! I will help you." Varra said.

"Were you trying to trick us?" Erin asked. "We came here on a peaceful mission."

"Yes, of course!" Varra said. "We used Zera to distract you while we prepared to capture you. Zera is an empath, not a coercer. She believed we would treat you fairly when you met with us this afternoon, so you detected no deception." Varra flung her head back and flared her nostrils. "We never had any intention of treating you arrogant, sub-elf animals as equals!"

"Bite your lip," said Alec, annoyed at being called an animal. Varra bit her lip until it bled.

"Continue your account," commanded Erin, giving Alec a stern look.

"We assembled as many strong coercers as were in the city today – including me, there are fourteen of us here. We spent all morning practicing to conduct a coordinated attack. We don't do this very often; we never need to make a coordinated mind onslaught against the locals. If I had imagined you were stronger than fourteen of us, I would have postponed the meeting for a couple of days so that I could have three times as many coercers."

"Why did you want to kill us?" Erin asked.

"Because you are a cross-breed!" Varra exclaimed, as if she were lecturing a not-too-bright child. "You are both cross-breeds! That is why we had Zera test you, to make absolutely sure."

"What is the problem with cross-breeds?" Erin asked.

"You saw! What you did! The two of you together! If you can beat our coordinated attack, there is not much any one of us can personally do to control you. That is why we do not let cross-breeds live. Some like you, can draw both energies and wreak havoc on our way of life."

"If Marta had done her job and killed all the females when she encountered you trespassing on our land, we would not be in this situation. Marta will be severely reprimanded for her violation of traditions."

"So little Zera set us up, did she," Alec said, annoyed at this whole turn of events.

"She followed the direction of the Disca. As I said, she is an empath." Varra continued, "Empaths are not as strong as coercers. We use empaths as herders; you might call them 'spies.' Working with you will help her improve her skills when she is herding."

"Spies? You have spies?" Alec exclaimed.

"Of course! This is our world – and we use herders to watch our herds of wild orbs in many lands. Like your land – Theland. One day we may have enough elves to manage all our herds and direct them, but right now we just watch and discretely influence."

"What … what do you know about the situation in Theland?" Erin asked.

"Your internal squabbles are so boring that we only pay attention when we want to cull our herd. We know of the Gott War and the strange intruders from the Grasslands. We know of your Queen Amelia and her irrational behavior, including her many beheadings. We will continue to encourage her until your people tire of her and start a rebellion against her insane rule. Then the Disca will use the rebellion as an opportunity to clean out you cross-breeds."

"And just how would you do that?" asked Erin, with interest.

Varra obviously did not want to divulge the elves' strategy, but the neckband forced her to answer.

"The rebellion will be bloody and will weaken Theland. Once your riders have killed each other, we will encourage, coerce if we must, Gott to invade. We can control the Gott fairly easily. They have few cross-breeds; they are mostly pure orb. After Gott takes over the Theland, it will be simple to convince them to eliminate the trouble-making cross-breeds in Theland, like you, and resettle it with their excess population from the Gott uplands. Those orbs are useful to us as drones."

"How do you know there will be a rebellion and that it will be bloody?"

Varra's looked at her as if she had asked another stupid question, "Because our empaths will steer the outcome to ensure that it is evenly matched, rebellious, and bloody."

"And what was going to happen when Erin returned?" asked Alec.

"Erin wasn't going to return. Amelia's father was supposed to not allow that to happen."

Alec was growing impatient. "This is all very important stuff," he said to Erin, "but we need to quit dilly-dallying here and find the concentrator and see if we can stabilize it."

"The concentrator! Bah!" said Varra in disgust.

"Why don't you care about fixing it?" asked Alec. "You elves here and your residences depend on it working. Without it you can't survive!"

"That is a drone problem. You are trying to bring a drone issue to a member of the Disca! We are above that! Even if you weren't going to die because you are cross-breeds, insulting the Disca by asking us to address a drone issue should result in your death."

"But it's your power supply!" Alec exclaimed.

"The drones are here to fix problems like that and not bother us about them," Varra said. "So what if they die? Sometimes the drones die trying to repair things. If one dies another will take its place until the problem is fixed. We leave drone problems to the drones."

Alec shook his head at the elf's logic. "Let's hope we're not too late."

"We need to get our riders first," said Erin. "Take us to where we left our riders."

There was no pain in Varra's eyes as she willingly led them from the Audience Hall towards the residence where they had spent the night.

"You are truthfully doing what I asked," said Erin to Varra, "but I detect some deception. What is it?"

"I am taking you to the residence where you left your drones," Varra said, "but I doubt your drones are there – alive, anyway. Our plan was to kill them after you entered the Audience Hall. We let them live until then in case you returned to the residence for some reason. We held council long into the night deciding what to do. You were easy," she pointed at Erin. "We all agreed to kill you immediately. Your other two females we have no use for, and plan to eliminate." Looking at Alec, she said, "Some of the Disca like your looks. We decided we will band you and domesticate you. If you are good, we will keep you and if you are not good we will terminate you. I am looking forward to seeing if you give me pleasure."

"Your other male drones we argued back and forth about. Some wanted to band them and turn them into useful drones. Finally, we decided it was not worth the trouble to keep them alive. They should all be dead by now."

They ran the rest of the way to the residence, dragging Varra along by her arm. When they reached the building, no one appeared to be around.

"You go that way," Erin said to Thom and Bon, pointing to the stairs to the upper chamber where they had been quartered, "and we will go around to the back." The two raiders ran towards the stairs. "Bring weapons," Erin shouted after them.

Erin and Alec, still holding onto Varra, ran through the front courtyard and the central rooms on the first floor. "Hear that?" Alec said, motioning towards the garden courtyard in the back. Erin reached the courtyard first, and screamed at the sight.

Cryl and Rhor were sprawled on the pavement of the courtyard. Both riders were lying face up. Were they dead? or asleep? Alec wondered – but a slight movement of Rhor's chest answered the question. The third rider, Nikka, was kneeling on the ground behind them, howling in pain, her legs covered in blood and a band around her neck. She held a blood-coated knife up above her head with both hands, blade pointed down towards her chest.

A Mother elf, with the three males of her clutch, sat on one of the garden benches under a pergola beside the courtyard, laughing and pointing as they watched the howling rider, obviously gaining great pleasure from the scene. Then the Mother turned, saw Erin, and began twisting field lines around her. Erin and the Mother froze in intense concentration as they twisted the fields around each other. The three clutchmen drew their weapons and started towards the immobile Erin.

Alec, still dragging Varra, saw that Erin was frozen in place. *Focus.* Alec pulled in dark energy to raise the blood temperature of the clutchman, expecting them to fall with popping eyes and bleeding ears. To his amazement, the dark energy swirled around and erupted in a flame in front of the three clutchmen, stunning but not disabling them. The rebound of the energy wave slapped Alec's body, giving him a severe headache. He took a breath. *Focus.* He picked up a decorative statuette and sent it towards one clutchman, his aim bolstered with dark energy. The figurine slowed as it approached and hit the man with just enough force to bruise but not impair.

They are negating dark energy, Alec thought. *I may just have to protect Erin the old-fashioned way.*

He shook Varra's arm.

"Get out of the way, do not try to escape, and do not try to participate in this fight," he said to Varra. Alec turned towards the three clutchmen and swung his staff. The three had only short swords as weapons, since their role today was to escort the Mother, not engage in a fight. Alec's staff was long enough to allow him to hit the first elf and knock him to the ground. Alec tried to hit the second one, but the clutchman backed out of the way. It was a game of cat-and-mouse, with the two remaining clutchmen trying to get on different sides of Alec while staying out of his staff's reach. Alec hoped that Erin was getting the upper hand in her battle; he needed to keep the clutchmen occupied until she won.

≈ ≈ ≈ ≈

Varra followed Alec's instructions precisely. She walked over to the opposite side of the courtyard, out of the way, and sat down by Rhor's sprawled-out form. She grabbed his arm.

"Wake up," she said to him softly. He woke up. Then she said, "You want to please me. You want me. I am ready for you." She looked at him alluringly. Rhor started breathing heavily and his hands started feeling Varra's body. "Not here! it will be so much better over there. Carry me over there." The rider picked her up and walked across the courtyard into the anteroom, oblivious to the ongoing fight. Varra said, "It will be so much better if I don't have to wear this neckband. Take the key from my pocket and remove the neckband." Rhor eagerly removed Varra's band.

Varra now was free.

Varra thought about joining the battle but without a ring she couldn't match Erin. She could see that Erin was about to get the upper hand over the elf Mother, so Varra made a quick decision, slipped through the door, and hurried away, leaving Rhor sitting on the ground, stunned and dismayed at his own behavior.

≈ ≈ ≈ ≈

After several minutes Erin got the upper hand in her mental battle with the Mother. The Mother slumped down. At almost the same time, Alec's staff caught the second clutchman. Erin saw Varra leaving the courtyard, but her first concern was Alec. She twisted the lines, and the last clutchman collapsed.

"Thanks," Alec said to Erin. "They have something that I don't understand, that negates dark energy." He pulled open the shirt of the slumbering clutchman and found a strange amulet around his neck. "This seems to defuse the dark energy around it," Alec muttered. He pulled similar amulets off the other two clutchmen. "Does she have one?" He felt around the Mother's neck, then pulled an amulet from beneath her tunic. He removed her ring and put a neckband on her.

Erin went to Nikka, who was still holding the knife, stopped her pain, and removed the neckband. Nikka collapsed at Erin's feet, now sobbing, tears welling from her clenched eyes.

"My Queen! I am so sorry!" She said. "Forgive me. They came, and we thought they were escorting us to join you. They walked us into this courtyard and put the other two to sleep. Then they banded me," she sobbed. "They handed me a knife and told me to cut my toes off. To resist was to endure unimaginable pain. I resisted and was in pain for what seemed like forever. Finally, I could not stand it anymore and I started cutting my toes off." She buried her face in her bloody hands. "I could tell the elf woman was experiencing intense pleasure from my despicable act. Finally, they tired of playing with me. The elf laughed at me and told me to plunge the knife in my heart. I resisted but the pain was terrible. I was about to end the pain and plunge the knife in when you came!"

"You are saved," said Erin gently. "None can resist these elf devils."

"Let's see what we have," Alec said, and Erin roused the elf Mother from her sleep. The Mother quickly understood she wore a neckband and didn't try to resist.

"Stand up," Erin said, and the woman stood up. Then Nikka rose up on her mutilated and bloody feet and, looking at the Mother with hatred, took two wobbling steps forward and silently thrust her bloody knife into the elf woman's heart.

With her last breath, the Mother grabbed Nikka and hissed, "Stop breathing." With a heart-wrenching cry, Nikka drew her last breath and slumped to the pavement, dead. The Mother had a pleased expression as she fell dead across Nikka's body. Just as she fell, Thom and Bon entered the courtyard. Even the battle-hardened Thom blanched at the sight of Nikka's maimed body and severed toes.

"Another rider lost," he said softly. "She died nobly, in service to her land."

32 – Concentrator

Erin snapped a neckband on the surviving clutchman and woke him up with a sharp kick. "What were you trying to do?" she screamed.

"We were told to come and kill the three drones," the clutchman said, shrugging his shoulders. "No one gave us any instructions concerning <u>how</u> we did it or how long it took, so our Mother thought she would at least have some pleasure from the death of the animals. Mother had your female drone cut off her toes. Your drone did resist for a long time before she complied." Then the elf looked at Nikka's body with obvious glee. "But, the longer she resisted, the more exhilarating it was for the Mother when she finally complied!" He giggled. "Mother was getting bored, so she told your drone to put the knife into her heart. She was still resisting but she wasn't going to hold out much longer! Next, she was probably going to have your other drones butcher themselves before they were allowed to put themselves to death. It gave my Mother much pleasure to watch drones do those acts. You animals will do almost anything to avoid a little pain!"

Should we kill him for his cruelty? Alec thought.

Not yet – we might need him to find the concentrator, Erin thought back. *Let's find the concentrator before the hornet's nest awakens. Varra has escaped, and will soon bring help.*

"What is your name?" Erin asked the elf, glaring at him.

He shrugged. "I am a clutchman, I do not have a name."

"I expect you to cooperate with us." Erin gave him a little burst of pain.

"I will fully cooperate," he said quickly. "I have no more interest in experiencing pain than your drones did."

"Take us to the concentrator building."

"It's on the other side of the city. You will never beat Varra on foot," the clutchman said. "As soon as she reaches help, they will communicate across the city with Mother-to-clutch communications."

What is that? wondered Alec.

Mind reading, Erin thought back.

"What is the best way for us to get there?" Alec asked the elf.

"Take the portal system. That's what we would do. Portals link our city. The nearest portal is around the corner from here. We will have to take three different portals to reach our destination, but it will be much faster than walking."

"Lead us," said Erin, "but first we must honor our departed rider." By now Thom had roused Cryl and Rhor had rejoined the other riders in the courtyard. Erin held a brief departing ceremony before Alec turned Nikka's body into ashes. Thom spat into the dust and recited the ancient curse of the victor.

As they prepared to leave, Thom handed Erin her sword. "My Lady, I took the liberty of removing this from your sleeping chamber," he said, "and we have retrieved our other weapons as well."

"Good thinking," Alec said, and handed out two more rings so that each rider wore one. With the clutchman on a leash, the group left the residence and moved down the main boulevard.

Alec asked about the strange amulets they had been wearing. "We have many tools to subdue you animals. That is a defuser – it doesn't allow the concentration of dark energy to build up around it. We use it when we face dark energy wizards. Dark energy sometimes undoes the domestication process, so occasionally one of the drones assigned to use dark energy reverts; we wear the defuser amulets when we subdue them. Mother was concerned about you cross-breeds, so we were wearing them today."

"What other tools do you have?"

"Our rings, of course," the clutchman said. "Those are the Mothers' most valuable tool."

"Where did they come from?" Alec asked. *Someone must have invented them.*

"It is said that the rings originally started as an orb weapon – that the orbs developed the rings to try to resist the elf Mothers. If an orb has a ring, it is difficult for the Mother to twist the lines to control it. Eventually, our Mothers learned that they could use the rings to twist the lines at a distance. Without the ring, the Mother has to touch an orb to control it."

The conversation ended as they came to the portal. They faced a small platform about five arns in diameter. On one side was a pedestal with a bulky looking controller on top.

"Can you operate this?" Alec asked.

The clutchman gave him a surprised look. "Of course not! Elves cannot feel the dark energy – that is why we have drones. Only drones can control the dark energy! We use drones to control it, even in our residences."

"So how do we operate it? Can any drone run it?" asked Erin, looking up and down the empty street for a drone.

"No, only special drones trained with the dark energy medallions can operate these. If one of the drones is not here, then sometimes you can stand on the platform and wait until someone comes from the other side. The trip will swap us to the other end."

They all stepped onto the platform.

Can you run this thing? Erin thought to Alec.

I don't know. Maybe.

Alec looked around the platform and saw the hex pedestal. *Focus.* He felt the dark energy. He could feel the portal controller on the pedestal. It was like the previous one, back in the Grasslands. He pushed dark energy into the controller and the light around them faded, went black, and then returned. They were in a different place, with drones moving all around them.

I guess the answer is: I can operate it, he thought to Erin.

After being around Alec this long, Erin could occasionally understand sarcasm. She rolled her eyes and thought, *If Zera had a clutchman that behaved like you, she would severely discipline him.*

In spite of their situation, Alec smiled at her.

≈ ≈ ≈ ≈

"Where is the next portal?" asked Erin. The clutchman pointed at the middle one of three circles marked on the ground across the way. They casually walked through the crowd of drones to the next portal. The drones efficiently moved out of the path of the Mother and her clutch, allowing them to move unimpeded. No alarm had been raised and no one was concerned about their presence. A drone operated this portal, and he promptly ported them as soon as they stepped on the device.

They appeared in a location empty of drones and elves. The clutchman led them down a narrow street and through a maze of paths to reach the third portal. This device was empty, so Alec ported them. They emerged at the base of a hill. At the top of the hill was the concentrator building. The building was different than most of the others in New Haven – it was blocky and gray.

"This is the building you want," the clutchman said. "Before you punish me for not being forthright, though, I must tell you that I have never been inside, and I don't know of anyone who has been past the outer room."

"How do we get in?" asked Alec.

"Many of our oldest buildings have stone locks, including this one. You put your hand on the stone and it opens if you are allowed in. Otherwise it will not open. Since it requires dark energy, no elf has ever opened the door. And of course, no drone would ever think about entering without direction from their Mother."

"Let's see what we can do. I may have to use dark energy to open it," said Alec.

They entered the outer chamber. The room was small and cold with no windows. A heavy door was set on one side of the room. A translucent stone panel was beside the door. Alec could feel dark energy oscillating even more strongly than before.

"I may have to break the door," Alec said, examining it. "You try the panel first, Clutch-Man"

The clutchman put his palm on the stone panel. Nothing happened. Alec tried next and put his palm on the lock to see what he could feel. Nothing happened. Then he pushed a little dark energy into the panel. The palm lock seemed to get slightly warmer, but the door did not open. Erin walked up.

"I can feel you are close. Try again," she said, placing her hand on the panel next to his. Alec pushed a little more dark energy into the panel and directed it to where Erin felt the rightness. As if responding to Erin's presence, the heavy door opened with a click.

Erin turned to her riders. "We are going in. Guard him, and protect the door for us." Erin and Alec stepped inside the next room and looked back. The door swung smoothly shut.

Alec looked around. The octagonal room had its own internal light. It was larger than it looked from the outside. Alec estimated the ceiling to be twenty feet high. Conical blocks were mounted about two-thirds of the way up and spaced uniformly around the outer wall. In the middle of the room was a transparent sphere about an arn in diameter. Small points of light moved inside the crystal, forming ever-changing patterns.

"I understand this layout," Alec said, eyes darting around the equipment. "Those cones are transmitters. That ball in the center is a concentrator."

He walked around to the other side of the sphere and stared at the flickering lights for a long time. "Look at this concentrator! It has a million little tricrystals arrayed inside the sphere. It's using a four-dimensional alignment of tricrystals for the focus. The array uses the three standard dimensions and a complex pattern that changes with time to create a fourth dimension. I know how to do that theoretically, but never thought I would actually see it done! It can have ten-thousand-times more power than a three-dimensional concentrator! To use time in the structure, the active tricrystal pattern has to constantly vary."

Erin knew that Alec knew she didn't understand anything he had said.

Alec looked discouraged and turned to Erin. "How am I going to figure out the pattern to decipher it?"

Erin had been looking around the room, more concerned about threats from guardian elves than flashing lights, and figuring out how they could best defend themselves. Trying to be helpful, she took another look around the odd-shaped room.

"There is a square in the corner by the far wall, like the one in the elves' education center. Might it have the same purpose?" she said, pointing.

Alec walked over to the panel and looked at it. "I guess it can't hurt to try it." He put his hand on the stone.

The stone lit up and information seemed to flow directly from the stone to his mind. "Greetings," the voice inside his mind said. "I have enabled the door to open only to a member of the House of Lian. I do not want the enforcer elves to gain access to this concentrator. If the door is forced open, the concentrator will destroy itself and my message will never be heard."

Who are you and why is your voice inside my mind? thought Alec.

"I speak to you from the past. I have encoded this message to be received if, in the future, you need to know of this device. I am a dark energy drone; my Clutch Mother now is Lian, the daughter of Syna.

"Formerly, in her lifetime, I was a dark energy drone of the Clutch Mother Syna, a descendent of the True Dragon Queen and one of the founders of the New Haven, where this concentrator is located. I came to this place with my Mother Syna through the transporter many years ago, at the time of the Founding, when she was fleeing the wrath of the False Dragon Queen and her enforcers.

"To protect those of us here at the New Haven, early on we set up a cloaking device so that the outside worlds could not locate us. I was trained on the original concentrator and the cloaking device. After Mother Syna died, her daughter Lian inherited me and took me with her when she started her free colony in the land away from the New Haven, and I was re-trained.

"However, after Mother Lian left the New Haven, somehow the elves accidentally turned off the cloaking device. The enforcer elves have located the New Haven and this world is now engaged in a pitched battle with the enforcers. If the enforcers win, all the Mothers on this world will be skinned alive to discourage others from trying to do what we have done: find a new world and establish a New Haven to escape the False Dragon Queen.

"Unfortunately, for some reason, early in the battle with the enforcers New Haven's main concentrator disintegrated. That blast not only destroyed the concentrator, it also destroyed the enforcers' transporter site and killed all of New Haven's dark energy drones. Since I am the only living dark energy drone, Mother Lian sent me from her free settlement to help the elves here in New Haven. I found this backup concentrator and started it in an over-power mode. Even though it is small and not really designed for this energy load, it should be adequate for the city power needs and for the cloaking device.

"At this time, the cloaking device is preventing the enforcers from finding us again. But, if it fails, we will be overwhelmed. The False Dragon Queen is vengeful. She has decreed that she will blame our descendants for a thousand years. It will be necessary for the cloaking device to continue to operate for that period of time.

"I am a mere drone and am not an accomplished operator of a concentrator. Sadly, there is no one alive with the skills needed to help me establish the perfect pattern. I believe, however, that the starting pattern I created is adequate, although it is not perfect. It should last for many generations, many centuries.

"In time, however, the pattern may start to oscillate; that could lead to a system failure. If that happens, and you have come to fix the pattern I installed, then you will need to stop the concentrator, establish a new good pattern, and then restart the concentrator.

"If you are here for that purpose I will continue to describe in greater detail how to generate a new pattern." Alec continued to listen in rapt attention to an increasingly detailed technical discussion about the concentrator. He understood what the device did and how it worked. At the end of the description, he backed away from the panel and sat down. He was exhausted.

≈ ≈ ≈ ≈

Erin sat beside him. "You were at the panel a long time. Did you learn anything?"

"I was?" To Alec, it seemed as if only seconds had elapsed.

"It is already dark outside," she pointed out.

"Well, yes, I did learn something. I learned a lot. It was like I was listening to a voice recording inside my head, from a drone of Lian, the elf you are descended from. The first part was a history lesson. He told how the elves here were fighting with other elves for some reason that wasn't explained, and then came here to New Haven to escape. Something about a 'Dragon Queen.' More specifically, a 'False Dragon Queen.' The other elves were looking for these elves, so they set up a cloaking device to help them hide; the outsiders may still be looking for them. The cloaking device is the only thing that keeps them from finding us all and wiping out the elves as well as the rest of us." Alec sighed.

"I guess that answers an important question," he said, stroking his beard.

"What question is that?"

"At first I was thinking that we would shut the concentrator down and not turn it back on. These elves don't deserve for us to restart it just so that they can run their fancy facilities, but if we don't restart it we may be at risk – Theland would be at risk – and we might have even worse elves poking around trying to kill everyone. I know what needs to be done to restart the concentrator, but first I need to rest for a few minutes before I try it."

"We've been in here a long time," Erin assured him. "I can sense elves out there, but they seem to be content to wait us out. No one has tried to attack our riders. Take a nap and then you can try again. We don't have provisions for an overnight stay, but we still have some refreshments from our tour this morning."

Alec slept far longer than he imagined he could. He awoke to Erin watching him with tired eyes.

"Did you get any sleep?"

"I dozed lightly, but I did not want to give the elves an opportunity to exploit. Are you ready to try the device?"

"Sure!" *Just an alien control system on a strange world and the potential to blow up everything around me if I do it wrong.*

Alec took a deep breath and put his hands on the sphere. *Focus.* He started to push dark energy into the sphere. The sphere resisted his effort. He pushed harder and slowly the sphere accepted his energy. As the energy built up, he felt the sphere respond to him – much more easily than he was expecting – but the pattern of energy within the sphere was very complex and continually changing. He pulled the energy out and could feel the concentrator stop focusing dark energy. The sphere shut down.

"Okay. The concentrator is shut down. Now the hard part will be to re-start it with a stable pattern."

Alec pushed dark energy into the sphere and it came back to life. There were so many patterns swirling in the system that his mind couldn't grasp any of them. His head started to throb with the effort required.

Erin, come help me, he thought. She grabbed his arm and felt with him. *Most of the patterns are wrong,* he thought. *Help me feel the wrong ones. There's too many – if I can get down to just a few, then I can work with them.*

Together they could feel the wrongness of some patterns, although neither understood how they knew. They worked with the patterns for a long time, eliminating the obviously wrong ones, until only a few remained.

"I can merge these now to make a workable pattern," Alec said. Erin continued to hold his hand as the remaining patterns flowed together.

"I sense a slight wrongness in one part," Erin said.

"If we had lots of time, I could fix the wrongness, but this pattern will operate the concentrator – and it's the best we can do right now. Time to restore the power." Alec focused dark energy on a different portion of the sphere and the sphere lit and started humming on its own. The dark energy concentrator started operating and dark energy was broadcast to the city. There were no oscillations in the dark energy from the concentrator.

Alec felt the dark energy field. "Success!"

After a few hiccups of light, the cloaking projector resumed operation. "That cloaking device is supposed to make it difficult for the False Dragon Queen, whoever she is, to find this place and transport here from her world, wherever <u>that</u> is. "

"You are indeed a Great wizard," Erin said, smiling at him.

"I couldn't have done it without you. Very nice job," Alec said, as he relaxed his mental control and let the concentrator resume operation on its own. They stepped away from the concentrator and sat down for a few minutes watching the internal patterns glow and evolve, little points of light flashing and moving.

"I wonder if the elf Mothers noticed that they were without power for a little while?" Alec mused. "It would have been terrible if their bath water got cold."

33 – Backtracking

"Time to go home?" Erin asked.

"Let's see if we can get out of here." Alec put his hand on the door panel and nothing happened. "Come over here, Daughter of Lian." Erin placed her hand on the door panel and felt it actuate. The door slid open.

The riders in the outer room instinctively reached for their swords when the heavy door opened. When they saw it was Erin, they relaxed. "No attempt by the elves to do anything," Thom reported. "We had a quiet night, and we all got some rest." Almost unnoticed, the inner door silently closed behind them.

"We are ready to leave, if we can get out of here," Alec said. He pointed at the clutchman. "What do we want to do with him?"

"We don't want to take him with us, that's certain," Erin said. She confronted the man. "Sleep!" she commanded, and the clutchman promptly fell asleep. "I guess we are good to go now," she said to Alec.

The group paused at the entryway and Erin stopped and sensed what was outside. "There are many elves in the street below. They are very confident, so I suspect they are well armed."

"That doesn't sound good," Alec muttered. "I wonder if there is another way out of this place."

Thom pointed to a utility ladder that provided roof access; Alec climbed up to the roof, followed by Erin. The roof provided a panoramic display of the city, sunlight shining off the white walls of the buildings and highlighting the brightly colored panels. At any other time, Alec thought, it would have been a beautiful view. However, now was not that time. On the street below, they could see a crowd of armed elves. "Nice view, but no escape," Alec noted.

"Look," Erin said, pointing at an elf woman walking up the path to the building. It was their guide, Zera, followed by her clutch. Zara hailed them.

"I have been selected by the Mothers to handle your capture," Zera called to them. "May I enter the building?"

"You may enter, but you must leave your ring outside as a sign you don't intend treachery," Erin said. "And leave your clutch outside." Erin scrambled back down the ladder, Alec close behind.

Zera entered the building, alone. "Your behavior in mending our concentrator has been adequate," Zera said. "Therefore, we will acknowledge your contribution and allow you a peaceful death." She pointed out the door. "The Disca has assembled many coercers, waiting outside, to curb you if you do not submit. There are thirty coercers already here and another twenty on their way. Submit to me peacefully and allow yourself to be banded without trouble and we will kill you mercifully. However, if we must subdue you, you will be given a very painful death." She looked at them hopefully. Neither Alec nor Erin moved. The riders scowled at the concept.

"Submit and be banded," she repeated.

"And then what?" said Erin.

"We will allow you and the other female to die on the Determination Tower this afternoon," she said to Erin, smiling. "It is close by. Jumping from the tower is a most painless way of death. It is high, death is immediate, and all the elves may gather to watch you die. It is quite nice." Then pointing to Alec, "We will allow this male to serve in the Pleasure House for a few months before being sent to the Tower to die. The other males we will send to the Drone Master and let her decide their fate."

She smiled expectantly, then seemed somewhat surprised that no one in the group was quick to accept her offer. "We offer you a quick death. If we must curb you, you will suffer for many months before we allow you to die."

Erin laughed. "Your offer will let him die happy, and me die unhappy! That is not a deal that is of interest to us. We ask for peaceful passage from your land. If necessary, we will fight for our freedom, or for our death, but we will not surrender!"

"You seem to think we are negotiating. We are not," Zera said, shaking her head. "Negotiating can only happen among equals. Do not forget your place. You are animals. Animals must be curbed and trained to do their elf's bidding. Your fate is death, either early and quickly, or slowly and painfully. We are offering you the opportunity to submit peacefully to your fate. If you resist and fight like wild animals, we will treat you accordingly. When you are ready to submit, I am here to facilitate the transition," Zera said. She turned her back on them and walked back outside where her clutchmen waited.

"What do we do now?" said Erin. "I can sense them out there waiting for us. She's right – there are at least thirty coercers out there with their clutches.

At the Audience Hall we beat a dozen coercers, and maybe we could beat twice that number, but not the entire population of elfdom!"

Alec sighed. "Also," he said, "fighting that many would require a great deal of dark energy. If we try to draw too much energy we could destroy my medallion and your sword – that could destroy us as well, just like what happened to Sarah! We need to change the equation." He thought a moment. "I have an idea." With that, he climbed back up to the roof, Erin close behind him. He pointed to the Determination Tower nearby and the Hatchery slightly farther away. "Give her a warning," he said to Erin.

"We want to give you fair warning," Erin shouted to Zera. "Clear everyone away from the Tower, because Alec will bring it down before you can run there."

Zera's clutchman relayed the message. As far as Alec could tell, nothing happened – he couldn't see any movement of people away from the tower.

Focus. After a moment, Alec could see a few stones fall from the side of the tower. Focus. Two more tries – a few more chunks fell. Alec looked at it, disappointed. Then as he watched, he could see that one wall started to slowly lean a bit; after an agonizing second, the wall collapsed. Then, as he intended, the tower started to buckle, and then quickly fell, bringing the entire structure down with it. A column of dust rose up from the rubble of the building, and Alec could hear the screams of the injured, crushed beneath the blocks of stone.

"You didn't heed our warning, and now you have lost elves," Erin shouted to Zera. "My Consort, Alec, destroyed your tower to show you that we are serious and that we are angry. We asked for peaceful passage from your land. We ask again and expect everyone to clear away from this building and let us leave."

Zera, replied, "You are mistaken. There were no elves there; you only killed drones."

"Let us leave! If you don't, next we will destroy your Hatchery. When that building goes, not only will all your eggs be crushed, you will also lose your swaddling cradles. That will be the price you pay if you do not let us go!"

Zera's clutchman relayed the message, and shortly returned to her with an answer.

"The Disca does not believe you!" Zera shouted back. "They do not believe that you can hurt what is locked inside the safety of our nursery."

"Then tell them to look at the flames that are rising from the top of your Hatchery," Erin shouted. "My Consort can make a fire big enough, and that burns hot enough, to roast all of your precious eggs, and melt all of your swaddling cradles." From the doorway, she could see smoke rising from the roof of the Hatchery, and she knew that all the elves assembled outside of the building could see it too.

After a long time, a message came back.

"The Disca will allow you free passage to the New Haven gate, but they warn you that you will be painfully punished when you are caught outside the city walls."

≈ ≈ ≈ ≈

"This is our chance," said Erin. "We need to get to the gate as fast as we can, while they are putting out the fire in the Hatchery and tending to those trapped by the fallen tower." As Alec scrambled down from the roof, Erin sensed the outside. "There is a noticeable backing off. Elves are leaving the area." Then shouting to Zera, "Tell them to leave us an open path to the city gate. You will come with us to the gate to ensure compliance." When she felt that the elves had pulled back sufficiently for them to reach the gate, Erin motioned to the others.

"Let's go," Erin said. The six of them took off toward the gate, Zera's clutch following close behind. As they came almost within sight of the city gate, Zera gasped.

"They are betraying their agreement!" she said in surprise. "They are going to trap you, just ahead on the path, in the last turn before you would leave the New Haven." She touched Erin's arm. "For wild cross-breeds, I feel that you have been as honorable as your animal nature allows. I am ashamed that my people do not keep their agreements – but they feel that agreements with animals do not have to be kept."

"Aren't they concerned that we will burn down the Hatchery?" Alec asked.

"They don't fear you will carry out your threat," Zera retorted. "Look around. They have picked this point because there is no view of our Hatchery. They don't think you can hurt it if you can no longer see it."

Alec looked around.

"They may be right. We need a new plan," he said.

"What – die gloriously?" Erin said.

"I wouldn't be your favorite Great Wizard if I didn't have a very desperate idea. It may not work, but we will go out with a bang." Alec started pulling and holding power from the concentrator – he pulled all the power that his medallion and the staff could manage. He could feel them straining.

"Now," he said to Zera, "Tell them that I have pulled the power from the concentrator. If I let go, it will destroy the concentrator, me, and half the city. Tell them to back off, or I will destroy everything. You can sense I am telling the truth. Without the concentrator, you will not be able to support your lifestyle and have hot baths."

Zera relayed the message.

"They will back off," she said, "but they know the precise range of the concentrator's energy field and will be after you when you are out of range."

They reached the ornate gate in the New Haven wall and Zera opened it for them. Erin turned to Zera.

"You and your clutch are free to go," she said. "Thank you for your assistance."

"You have turned out to be more honorable than I thought possible for your kind," Zera said. "When we capture you, again, I will put in a favorable word with the Disca for them to kill you painlessly."

≈ ≈ ≈ ≈

They were off. They suspected there would be elves ahead of them as well as a large force coming after them. They moved quickly but carefully. Time was important, but they needed to conserve their energy in case they had to fight their way out. They planned as they covered ground.

"We spent two nights making the traverse from our camping ground to the city, but we should be able to make it in one twelve-hour transit. We should expect to encounter at least one set of elves between here and the ravine," Alec said.

"We must assume they are communicating with each other and are tracking us. I would expect that their strongest elves were called back to the city to stop us, so we can anticipate accordingly," Erin said to her riders.

Every little while they would stop so that Erin could sense the surroundings. At one stop, Erin detected a party coming from behind, just at the edge of her senses. Alec could feel her apprehension.

They reached the shack where they had been held captive and walked past without stopping. Finally, Erin thought, I feel something ahead. They proceeded carefully. Erin stopped and sensed again.

"It feels like there are three groups ahead. I think they are planning a surprise because they know they aren't strong enough to tackle us head-to-head," she said. Alec agreed. They proceeded carefully.

"I can sense two groups on one side and the third group off to the other side," Erin said. "If these are weak coercers, I should be able to take the first attack, but you need to stay alert for a second attack. Thom, you and the riders need to be ready."

As they came around the next turn, they came upon the first bunch. Eight elves were arrayed on the path in front of them. The two Mothers didn't say a word but immediately started twisting the field lines. Erin used her ring to engage them and started twisting the field lines around them. Alec felt the twisting, but his ring deflected the field lines around him. The four riders aligned themselves around Erin in case the clutchmen attacked, but the clutchmen only seemed interested in protecting the Mothers and not attacking Erin. Alec stood behind Erin warily watching. He could see that Erin was gaining ground on the two Mothers.

Alec felt and heard the movement to his side – then the third Mother and her clutch emerged from the woods. Erin and her riders were consumed in their fight and didn't notice the new threat. Alec stepped up to engage the Mother. He felt the Mother attempt to twist the force around him, but the lines flowed smoothly past him. The Mother realized his ring was protecting him and deployed her clutch. The three clutchmen spread out so that they would engage Alec over a semicircle. They all carried short spears, similar in length to his staff, so he had no advantage in reach.

Focus. Alec tried to create a small rock inside the first clutchman. Nothing happened except a rebound of energy that left his head slightly throbbing. Four to one, he thought. Need better odds than that. A blast of air generated by Alec staggered the three clutchmen, but it also staggered Alec enough that he lost much or his advantage. He recovered just an instant more quickly than the others and attacked the forward clutchman. The clutchman quickly retreated, stumbling backward. Alec could not take advantage of the stumble because the other two clutchmen moved to Alec's side and a blow to take out the first would leave Alec open to a spear thrust.

Alec backed away. The three clutchman regrouped in a semicircle and started to press him. One thrust a spear at him, but Alec pulled in dark energy and the clutchmen's movement appeared to be in slow motion. Alec stepped inside the spear thrust and brought his staff around to hit the clutchman. As the staff approached the clutchman, Alec felt a jarring wrench as the force lines smoothed and time returned to normal. His disabling blow converted to a glancing blow on the clutchman's shoulder.

Alec stumbled back, slightly stunned. The three clutchmen were getting dangerously close, so he attacked vigorously. They retreated in front of his attack and pressed from both sides. Alec tried a combination of gathering dark energy to speed time to get close to his opponents, and then releasing the energy just before attacking. That kept him competitive with his three opponents but didn't give him enough advantage to land a disabling blow. He initiated a furious series of attacks that caused the clutch to retreat slightly.

Alec was tiring rapidly. Mentally he could call up dark energy, but physically his body was wearing from the exertion. His periodic flushes of dark energy provided some relief, but not enough to restore his body. He needed something else, or one of the spear thrusts would soon hit home, and the fight would be over. Alec attacked the clutchman edging closest. Then he realized it had been a feint. The clutchman on the other side thrust his spear towards where Alec was moving. Alec realized too late what they were doing. He drew more dark energy and increased his speed. He was partially successful as he contorted his torso away from the thrust. He felt the spear approaching and then time returned to normal.

Just as the spear was about to strike him, a second spear appeared at his side and diverted it. He glanced to his side and saw Bon. With the rider assisting him, the tables turned. Alec attacked a clutchman with his staff and Bon used the opportunity to thrust her spear through the momentary opening, skewering the man.

Then the fight ended. The Mother and the other two clutchmen collapsed.

"Good timing," Alec groaned, and Bon nodded. Alec remembered to collect the Mothers' rings before they started hiking again.

Erin could feel the elves' pursuit behind them. It was not dangerously close and was not closing the distance. "Something doesn't seem right. They seem to be in no hurry to catch up with us."

They came to the ravine where they had been originally captured. Erin felt ahead and could not sense any opposition.

"It is likely they do not have many clutches out here. They have not anticipated us escaping. But, the number behind us is relatively large." They walked into the ravine past the spot where they had first encountered the elf Mother Marta, and found their packs where they had dropped them. They took the time to change back into their clothes – most appreciated were their boots since the elf tailor had only provided them with decorative thin-soled walking shoes. They rummaged through the packs and found enough food to satisfy their immediate hunger. Then they were out the other side of the ravine, and to the meadow where they had placed the stakes.

"We need to cross this field without getting lost. We cannot afford to take a long-time backtracking, or they will catch us. Hopefully our stakes are still here," said Alec. They looked for a few minutes. They were about to give up and dare the meadow when Alec spotted a stake. "There!" he said, pointing. They ran to the stake and could see several more ahead of them. They were not in a straight line, and there seemed to be at least ten rows of stakes spreading in all directions.

"This is some illusion. I am going to try something." Alec pulled some rope out of his pack. "Here, you hold one end, and I will take the other," he said to Erin. "Stay here at the stake." Then Alec walked to the apparent position of the next stake. There was no stake there. He turned around to look at Erin, and there was ten Erin's spread over the field. He followed the rope back and returned to Erin.

"I can't imagine them taking the time to deliberately move our stakes," said Alec. "This must be another illusion designed to slow us until they can catch us. I wonder – can you can sense the fields here?"

Erin felt for the field lines. She could sense a slight twisting and blurring but could not do anything with it. Alec tried feeding her dark energy, but the lines still did not untwist.

"Let's try the opposite," said Alec. "I am going to create a backward blurring field, an imaging field, and you are going to try to sense when I have the field lines right." Alec created the field, and Erin helped him adjust the focus. The multiple stakes slid together and he could see the next stake. Cryl walked forward carrying the rope. Alec shouted directions. As soon as he quit believing his eyes and followed Alec's directions, Cryl found the next stake and grabbed it. The others followed the rope to the next stake. They kept repeating this process, alternating Cryl, Bon, and Rhor advancing along the line, until they reached the end of their stakes. They recognized their previous camping spot when they passed it.

"We are almost through now. Thank goodness! Because it will be dark shortly," Alec said.

≈ ≈ ≈ ≈

They reached the break in the mountain where they had emerged from their initial climb and scurried down the narrow path towards Theland. They had traveled only a short distance when Erin detected someone ahead. They moved forward until they could see a lone figure sitting on a rock.

Careful, Alec thought to Erin. They crept forward, but Rhor's boots crunched on a buried stick, and the figure stood up, sword in hand.

It was one of Erin's riders of the group left behind just a few days ago.

"Oh!" exclaimed Erin, with a sigh of relief.

The rider turned around with a start.

"Princess!" he said, equally surprised. "I am so very pleased to see that you and your Consort are all right!" He looked behind her to see the four riders behind her. By his expression, Erin knew that he saw one rider was missing.

"We have survived, but sadly, Nikka did not," Erin said gently. The rider bowed his head briefly and Thom stepped forward to clasp his arm.

"Let's get down to the others," Erin said, and they joined the camp where the riders greeted them with smiles and cheers.

"I am so grateful to see your return, My Queen!" said the lead rider, and greeted Thom with gusto. The riders all greeted one another noisily, glad that they would soon be leaving this place.

"What is your wish for our next steps?" Thom asked Erin, after the riders had settled down.

"We need to organize a defense against the elves," Erin said, and gave her riders a quick update on the situation with the elves.

The riders reported on their situation. "We have a problem," the lead rider said. "Amelia's riders found us three days ago. So far, they seem to be staying in the distance."

Erin let her senses roam. "You are right," she said. "There is a group of riders and animals within a couple of els of us, and on our other side, there are elves following us."

"How many?" asked Alec.

"I can't determine exactly," Erin answered. "Only a small group is following our trail. It almost seems like they are in no hurry to engage us."

"Would they follow us here into Theland?" Alec asked.

"The elves do not recognize our borders," Thom explained. "And we have never had a definite border along the elf Mountains. So they might well be following us yet."

"Our first chore is to survive the night. Then tomorrow we will worry about tomorrow," Erin said. She selected nine riders to watch the trail leading from the Elf lands, assigning them in three shifts of three riders. Alec gave one rider in each shift a ring with explicit instructions to call for help and awaken him if the other two fell asleep. Late in the night, one rider cried out.

Alec and Erin woke up and came to assist. They roused two riders from an elf-induced slumber. Erin sensed the surroundings. "A Mother is nearby but backed off when she couldn't take out all of our guards."

"Then I guess they did follow us into Theland," Alec mused. He drifted in and out of sleep, dreaming of eggs and elves.

34 – Dragon

The sun had not yet broken over the top of the peaks, but the morning half-light filtered into camp when Erin woke and sensed their surroundings.

Four elves are lurking in the mountain, watching us, she thought to Alec, waking him. *I don't sense any other elves close. They still seem to be waiting for reinforcements instead of attacking.*

She roused Thom. "We need to be away from here before any elf troops arrive," she said. "There is a group of riders and trogus camped not far from us; I would estimate around one hundred riders. We are in Theland, so they should be our riders."

Erin thought to Alec with a satisfied smirk, *I am learning your wizard-speak. I can use wizard words like 'estimate.'*

While the riders were still eating, Erin walked to the middle of the mess area and spoke forcefully. "There are riders not far from here. If the riders are my sister Amelia's troops, we need to greet them without hostility. They are our Theland brethren. Remember this: you are the Escort of the Princess of Theland, and you are returning from a victorious campaign. You have shown the greatness of the traditions of the Theland riders. Let us greet our fellow riders proudly and peacefully – unless they act otherwise."

A shout went up from the riders, and then in unison, a chant of "Hail to Queen Erin!"

Erin raised her hand and waited for the riders to quiet. "We return as victorious riders and hail our victory. I am the Princess of Theland. I have vowed to find the truth and avenge my mother's death. After that, I will determine my role based on what is best and right for my people. At this time, I am proud to be your Princess and to have you as both my escort and my comrades in arms."

The riders saluted, and a chant went up, repeated over and over, "Hail the Great Warrior Princess, Victor of Theland!"

Erin let them chant for a minute and then again raised her hand. "Finish your breakfast and your duties, and then let us ride. We will show that we are true riders."

Soon they neared the group of people she had sensed. Erin's flag bearer unfurled her banner as they rode towards the other camp; it caught the breeze and snapped taut. Erin had expected to encounter sentries long before, but they were almost upon the camp when the first sentry noticed them and raised an alarm to announce their presence. It was clear that the people in the camp were just starting to rise for the morning; some were still sleeping. She noticed with dismay that the trogus looked poorly-kept, hungry, and were tied in disorganized groups; an underfed trogus served as a threat to other nearby animals and to any person who wandered within reach.

After the sentry raised the alarm, the camp became a whirlwind of undisciplined activity. Erin thought to Alec, *We could have made two passes through their camp and killed most of the riders before they were even out of bed! These are not the kind of riders that Mother would have been proud of.*

Erin motioned, and her riders halted just beyond the edge of the camp. They waited while riders saddled their animals and milled around without any semblance of organization. Finally, four riders tentatively came forward. Erin's flag bearer sounded the royal whistle; Erin could see by the look on their faces that the approaching riders recognized the pattern.

One rider, wearing an ornate sash, came close and said, "Who are you to be in my area and use a royal whistle?"

Erin's flag bearer rode forward and with pride announced, "We escort Her Highness Erin, the Royal Princess of Theland, returning from her victories with our allies, and her Consort, Alec. Who are we addressing?"

Erin sensed surprise and puzzlement at the announcement from the speaker. "I am Commander Kirkdar, under direct orders from Her Royal Highness, Queen Amelia of Theland. I was not told to expect the Princess in my area. Welcome Princess Erin. And Consort."

Erin rode forward. "Greetings, Commander. What are you doing with such a large force in this area?"

"Queen Amelia sent me out with these riders to look for a dragon in this area, and destroy it. Two days ago, we received a report of bandits camping nearby. I asked for reinforcements before I tried to round up the bandits. I am relieved that your riders may be the cause of the rumor of bandits, because I fear that no reinforcements will be coming."

"A dragon. I have not heard of a dragon in this land!" *Nor anywhere else in Theland for decades.*

"Yes, a dragon has been seen in this area. A few days ago, it ravaged a village. Not much remained of the village after the dragon finished."

"Commander, I will let you continue with your search. We are heading towards Freeland City."

"I cannot do that" the Commander said, with a hint of uncertainty. "I cannot allow anyone else to be in my area with any weapons. The Queen has forbidden anyone to possess a weapon without a direct seal from her."

"Commander Kirkdar, you would think to try to impede a Princess?" Erin kicked her trogus and it reared up; Erin looked down on the startled Commander and let the full weight of her displeasure seep through her ring.

The Commander blanched at the mental onslaught. For the first time, he looked at Erin's battle-hardened riders. Then he thought of his riders who were still getting organized. "Princess, if you give up your weapons and let my force escort you back to the City, that would be acceptable."

Erin continued to glare. "No. We are riders. We do not give up our weapons except in death. You may escort us to the City if you would like, but we will have our weapons."

"That would be acceptable," said Commander Kirkdar, relieved that he had an excuse to return early. "Join me for breakfast; it will be a while before my force is ready to ride."

Erin nodded, and they rode into camp. Commander Kirkdar dismounted and motioned for them to join him in his interrupted breakfast, his food now congealed on his plate. The cook threw the cold food on the ground and started to prepare a new meal. Erin, Alec, and Thom joined the Commander at his table.

"Tell us what has happened. As you know, we have been battling in the Grasslands on behalf of our Gott allies, and are just returning."

The Commander started, "Queen Amelia is working very hard in her first months of rule to fix many of the problems caused by the last queen and undo her failed initiatives."

Alec could feel Erin's mental anger rise, but she held her tongue and listened to learn more.

"Assisted by her advisor, Lady Pequa, she has made huge strides in making Theland great again. They are removing the unscrupulous people who used their influence over the queen to line their own pockets, and are no longer coddling them. Our Queen Amelia is beheading any bad people who do not pledge their allegiance, or will not consent to leave. She is making it safe within our land, so no one will need to have a weapon. She has forbidden the ownership of weapons, except by her riders of course, and certain members of her court, and a few others. She says that only villains need a weapon, so anyone who wields a weapon without the Queen's permission is a villain and subject to her punishment. Our former queen allowed too many people to have weapons."

Again, Alec could feel Erin working to control her rage.

"Commander Kirkdar, I thought I knew all of the senior leaders amongst the Theland riders, but you are not familiar to me. What is your background?"

"Yes, the former queen required that all the riders had to demonstrate their ability before they could join the ranks, and other tests of skill before they could rise to leadership. Queen Amelia feels that system was unfair and unfortunately discriminated against the people. Now anyone who is willing to serve our Queen can be a rider, once they pay the entry fee." He smiled. "Of course, the fee is much higher for my position." He stroked his sash.

So that's what Amelia is doing, thought Alec to Erin. *Pay for service. Nice.*

"How is Brun, our esteemed Council Head? That sounds like the kind of 'improvement' he would have come up with," Alec said.

"You are correct, Consort Alec," the Commander said. "That was one of the improvements he instituted. However, he had a disagreement with his daughter, our fair Queen Amelia; we were not told what. Obviously, he was not serving her with the loyalty she deserved. But Lady Pequa advised Queen Amelia to dissolve the Council because it was no longer needed, so she did. I understand that Brun left the City after the Council was dissolved; I do not know where he went. But our Queen Amelia is ruling splendidly without a Council, ably assisted only by the Honorable Pequa."

The cook brought out the steaming food and served it. They were quiet as they ate, Erin and Alec ruminating over what the Commander had told them. Then some of the camp riders started shouting and running. Commander Kirkdar looked annoyed that something might interrupt his breakfast a second time, but the shouting became louder and more intense.

Then Erin sprang to her feet and gasped, "I can sense it! A dragon!" She didn't hesitate but ran from the Commander's tent towards her riders. "To arms! To arms! A dragon approaches!" She looked up and high in the sky could see a large silhouette against the clouds.

Alec also looked up, gaped-mouth in disbelief.

≈ ≈ ≈ ≈

The dragon circled above the camp casting her long shadow across the tents in the early morning sun. Erin sensed fear from her riders and panic from the Commander's riders. Even high in the sky, the creature appeared huge; her leathery wings moving minimally as she floated in the sky.

Erin extended her senses to the dragon. She felt a complex interweaving of thoughts, each line of thought competing with the others. Erin could sense three distinctly different interweaving thought patterns, all stitched together in a rigid pattern held together by a complex web of twisted lines of force.

Erin watched as the dragon circled twice more before landing gracefully in a grassy meadow several hundred els from the rider camp. The dragon slid effortlessly through the grass. Only the marks left by her enormous weight indicated where she had been – the tall meadow grass crushed and torn in her wake. Erin was enthralled with the beast and felt a deep connection with her – for she immediately sensed the dragon was a 'her.'

Riders were scurrying about Erin in frenzied activity as she watched the dragon. She could sense Alec concentrating and analyzing the beast. The dragon's long, sinuous body continued to move effortlessly across the field, her tail flicking back and forth.

The dragon raised her head and looked around; her eyes were higher than the bushes on the edge of the meadow. She opened her mouth and emitted a puff of flame, searing the ground around her. A few bushes blazed briefly and then died out in the morning dew. She opened her mouth and let out a bellow. Her sharp, knife-sized teeth glowed in the morning sun, and her tongue flicked in her mouth. Erin sensed no hate in the dragon, just resignation, and hunger.

The camp was in bedlam. Erin quit sensing the dragon and called for her riders to prepare. Her riders mounted their trogus and formed up around her. She whistled, and the riders organized into a defensive formation to wait for the dragon. Commander Kirkdar's riders were still in frenzied activity caroming in every direction, some on their mounts, some on foot, some merely stumbling about in confusion. A few had panicked and were hiding in the trees; no one was providing direction.

Commander Kirkdar mounted his trogus at the first opportunity and collected ten riders with him. He shouted, "I am going to take the message to the Queen that we have found the dragon. The rest of you stay and fight." The Commander and his followers took off at a rapid pace.

The dragon looked at the fleeing riders. With a hop and a jump, she was in the air. Alec felt an immense pulse of dark energy propel the beast. The dragon's long flowing body seemed to float and accelerate on a cushion of dark energy. She used her wings to steer. The dragon swooped down into the midst of the fleeing riders; her sharp front claws knocked several riders off their trogus and her flicking tail eliminating several others. All but two of the riders fell – Commander Kirkdar and one other continued to flee the scene. The dragon soared past the remaining two riders and wheeled high in the sky.

Then the two remaining riders watched in horror as the dragon started down towards them; they spurred and whipped their trogus and fled in different directions to escape. The dragon soared towards one of the riders, opened her mouth, and plucked the man from the trogus. With rider in mouth, the dragon wheeled high in the sky and turned towards the last fleeing rider, Commander Kirkdar. She opened her mouth, dropping the other rider like a limp doll as she closed the distance to the Commander. He looked over his shoulder at the approaching dragon, screaming in terror, and furiously whipped his mount. The dragon continued to glide as she plucked him from his trogus.

The dragon landed with far more grace than would be expected of a beast her size. She crunched the body in her mouth and tore it apart. The clothes and armor caught on her teeth making it difficult to feed, but she shook her head, spitting out the chunks of metal and leather, and swallowed half of the Commander. His ornate sash, now separated from his body, caught the breeze and billowed briefly high into the air before disappearing into the trees. Erin sensed that one person was not enough to satisfy the dragon's hunger; the dragon slithered to a second body and continued to eat.

≈ ≈ ≈ ≈

Erin held her riders in place while the dragon attacked the fleeing men. Most of the Commander's riders had finally armed themselves and found their mounts, but there was no leadership among their ranks. Erin heard the mumbled conversations.

"Commander Kirkdar got what he deserved."

"If we all make a run for it together, some of us will escape."

That was the last thing Erin could take. "Riders to me," she shouted, and gave a signal on her whistle, her sound amplified by a little dark energy from

Alec. The Commander's riders at first continued to look confused but after another whistle from Erin started to gather before her with a semblance of organization.

"Where are your team leads?" she asked the first group of riders.

One voice finally spoke up, "Most of them fled into the woods. The others tried to escape with Commander Kirkdar. I think that the more they paid to have a job, the less courage they seemed to have."

"I know you, don't I?"

"Yes, Princess. I served your Mother, Queen Therin. My name is Hank; I used to be a Lead Rider. I have been around you since you were a little pup trying to swing a big sword. If I hadn't been on the Elf Mountain patrol when Queen Therin's riders went to Gott, I would have been riding with you. Now, under Queen Amelia, the new leaders don't like me telling them what they are doing wrong, so they have demoted me, but I would be proud to be a rider for you."

"Okay, I give you a battlefield commission, Hank. You are now the lead rider for this group. Pick the other leads you need and get organized. We have a dragon to fight."

Erin addressed the assembled riders. "You are riders of Theland. You have a proud heritage to uphold. Together we are going to fight a dragon. Together we will prevail."

Erin's riders started a chant, "A dragon to fight! A dragon to fight! We go to fight a dragon!" It was infectious, and soon Hank and the Commander's riders joined in, all chanting in unison.

"You have motivated them," said Alec.

Erin turned to Alec. "I can sense that most are adequate riders but need leadership. A few will bolt and run when we face the dragon, but the others will do their job. Now the important issue: How do we fight a dragon?"

Alec thought for a second before answering. "I have been watching it. That dragon is a big biological storage container of dark energy. It seems to manipulate dark energy instinctively. I can sense it focusing and using its stored dark energy. It uses dark energy to fly, and it consumes its stored dark energy at an incredible rate. At the rate it was using dark energy, I think it could only fly for an hour or two before it must stop and recharge.

"I don't think I can create something inside the dragon that would hurt it, like we did against the Aldermen. Anything that I tried to create would give the monster extra dark energy, but if we can wear it down until it is low on dark energy, we might be able to harm it. I don't think the dragon can live without dark energy to keep it alive."

Alec stopped again and thought for a few more seconds. "Your sword might be useful because it has a tricrystal in it. If you can get close enough, I might be able to use the sword as a focus to suck a little dark energy out of the monster. I can treat the dragon as a source and pull dark energy from it. If I could pull enough energy from it, we might be able to stop it." Erin nodded in understanding.

Thom and Hank had organized the riders into formations and sought her attention. Erin turned to them. "Our plan is simple," she said. "We will divide into three groups and attack the beast. Thom, your group will take one side, and Hank, your group the other. My group will take the front. The beast will not die easily so it will take many blows to destroy it. Any group that can safely attack should do so.

"We only have a few lances so make every one of them count. Throw your spears from close enough that they will penetrate the dragon's hide. When the beast turns to face your group, retreat. Let's go!"

"A dragon to kill! A dragon to kill!" rang from the riders, giving them the courage they didn't otherwise feel.

Erin gave the command to advance. The dragon lay on the ground ahead of them half asleep, the bloody remnants of the last rider she had consumed scattered close about. One eye was half-open and nonchalantly watched as Erin approached. Erin sensed the dragon's emotions as they rode closer. The tangle of interwoven thoughts within the dragon's mind made it difficult to understand. There was one chain of thoughts from a reptilian brain that wanted to eat and sleep and survive. There was a second chain that felt magnificent to Erin, but was so alien she could not understand it – she sensed that a soul was crying for help but totally isolated from any sensory input. A third interleaved consciousness controlled the animal's senses and body. That brain appeared to be curious and watching Erin with a detached interest. Then, threaded through all of this was a woven layer of twisted lines, binding the other three parts together.

Erin rode closer. She sensed the dragon was not afraid of her or her riders, nor particularly interested in them. Erin could not sense any hostility from the dragon. For a second, Erin regretted having to fight such a magnificent creature.

Her sensing was interrupted as her riders moved into formation. Erin whistled, and the three groups of riders began to circle the dragon. The dragon did not stir and seemed unconcerned. Their circle complete, several of the riders threw spears at the dragon's side. The spear throws were true, but a dark energy lens swirling around the dragon bent the spear trajectory over her huge body and the spears drove into the ground on the other side. The dragon never flinched.

Erin charged towards the dragon, her sword shining in the sun, glinting into the dragon's eye. The dragon appeared mesmerized. Erin approached the giant beast and then rode to one side; the dragon moved her head to follow Erin's movements. Several of the riders used the distraction to drive their lances into the dragon's side. Alec felt the dark energy of the beast react to the thrusts. Even with the full weight of rider and trogus at full gallop, the lances barely penetrated her outer scales; however, the attacks roused the dragon from her fascination with Erin's sword. The dragon swiveled, breaking the lances. The cuts in her side where the lances had penetrated hardened almost immediately, and dark energy flowed, healing any damage. The dragon turned her head and snapped one of the riders from his trogus, breaking him in half. The dragon's tail lashed out, and two more riders were down. Then the dragon's tail snaked towards Erin.

Instead of trying to flee, Erin goaded her trogus forward towards the beast's tail. At the last instant, she prodded her trogus to jump and the trogus' teeth and claws dug into the skin of the dragon as it clambered up and onto her back. Erin hopped off her mount and slashed the animal's back; her sword glowed with dark energy and interacted with the dark energy in the dragon. Erin was rewarded with a line of fire along her sword cut into the dragon's skin. Blood gushed from the slash and boiled as it touched the dragon's burning outer flesh; the dragon screamed with pain from the flow of dark energy into the sword.

The dragon rolled over to get the annoyance from her back. In the nick of time, Erin jumped and just cleared the rolling beast. She slid to the ground, letting the great tail slide over her sword as its weight pushed her into the soft spongy soil. The dragon roared in pain as the dark energy of the sword cut into her tail and produced another flaming streak. The dragon lifted her tail to stop the pain; then Erin saw the heavy tail flick towards her trogus. Erin sensed the trogus; her trogus recognized her and responded to her senses – it jumped and grabbed the tail with its claws. It rode the tail until the end of its arc and then, responding to Erin's command, lept off. Erin watched in relief. She had grown fond of her trogus.

The dragon turned and faced her. Erin looked into the eyes of the beast. Only her blazing sword separated them. She could sense the dragon's pain, mixed with curiosity about her sword. The dragon opened her mouth and roared; knife-like fangs shone in the sunlight.

Alec was frantic. He had to do something, and every one of his usual tricks wasn't going to work – they would only serve to strengthen the dragon. A radical idea came to him, but he had no time to think it through before the dragon started her lunge towards Erin. *Focus!* The dragon started to snap at Erin when a stone arch appeared, shielding Erin. Erin quickly rolled under the arch. The dragon's teeth crunched into the stone, but the arch held steady, continually renewed from the dragon's internal dark energy. Erin could smell the dragon's putrid breath as she crouched only inches from the fore teeth.

The dragon continued to bite at the stone arch, even as she screamed in pain from dark energy being pulled from her body. Then the dragon reared, pulling the arch into the air with her mouth. Alec released his focus of dark energy, and the stone arch collapsed in the dragon's mouth, scattering pieces to the ground.

Erin sensed anger and pain in the dragon. The rearing beast's torso was now several arns above her, the long neck and giant head looming directly over her. She sprinted towards the dragon's body, ready to slice again with her sword. But before Erin could reach the animal, with a great bellow the dragon launched herself into the air. She flew almost directly over Erin and headed into the sun. Erin watched the magnificent animal as it seemed to levitate effortlessly.

Then she turned to her riders and raised her glowing sword high. A great cheer arose from her riders. They had faced the dragon, and it had fled.

"Riders to me," Erin shouted.

Thom and Hank quickly called their riders, and Alec went to help with the injured while Erin mustered her riders.

"Report in," she said.

"We lost five riders in the battle with the dragon and had another five injured enough that they require treatment," Thom told her. "Ten of the new so-called 'riders' fled in fear during the attack. We will never see them again." He spat in disgust.

Hank gestured towards the Elf Mountains. "There is a village in the direction that the dragon went. I am concerned about its safety."

"Then we shall chase the dragon after we have a proper departing ceremony for our fallen comrades," Erin said. *Brun and my sweet sister will have to wait,* she thought.

She found Alec with the injured. *I could feel the pain you caused the dragon,* she thought to Alec. *It is what saved me. What did you do?*

I was desperate, thought Alec back to her, and slipped his arm around her shoulders. "The dragon was about to eat you," he explained, "and everything that I usually do was only going to add to the dark energy reserve of the dragon. That's when I had an idea. I treated the dragon like a dark energy source. I focused and pulled energy from the dragon. That's where I found enough dark energy to create that stone arch. Pulling energy from the dragon seems to hurt it. If I could pull enough energy out, I think the dragon would die. My medallion is strong enough to pull enough energy to enrage the dragon, but I don't think my medallion is strong enough to kill it. I will have to come up with something else in order for us to defeat the dragon."

≈ ≈ ≈ ≈

Erin could sense the dragon in the distance. She had wanted to ride all night to catch the dragon, but Thom convinced her that the riders would be too tired to fight. She had a few hours of sleep with her riders, but Alec did not sleep. He had taken the opportunity to make a new weapon against the dragon – a barbed javelin, with small tricrystals embedded in its hooked end. He managed to finish making three of them before it was time to ride out.

In the early morning as they approached the small village near the Theland border, Erin could sense intense fear. They soon met scattered groups of villagers fleeing along the path. One group cheered when they saw the armed riders, and Erin called a brief halt to talk to them.

She and Alec dismounted as five frightened people came up to them. One, an older woman, was shivering, either from the cold morning air or from fear, Alec couldn't tell which. He directed enough dark energy to make a warm fire emerge from the ground. The people gasped and looked at the fire suspiciously, then decided that the heat was nice and gathered around it, warming their bare hands and feet. Alec pulled a blanket from his pack and wrapped it around the old woman. She looked at him gratefully.

Erin greeted them. "We are here to help you. What can you tell us?"

The old woman shook her head and said, "Run! No one can fight the dreaded beast! It came in the late afternoon yesterday and wheeled in the sky above us. Then it landed in my son's grain field, just outside the village wall. It was going to be the best crop he ever had! Then the beast landed and crushed it all." Then she stopped, and a tear trickled down her weathered, dirty cheek. "But I guess it won't matter to him now, what the dragon did to his crop."

"I'm sorry," Alec said.

The woman regained her composure and continued. "The dragon slept in the field all night. Then early this morning, it woke and tore a hole in the village wall. Our guardsmen tried to stop it, but there was nothing they could do even to slow it down. The beast wandered through town, knocking things down as it went. It found where we were hiding. Then the dragon broke down the wall of our house. It was as if it could sense where we were! When it approached we fled – but we ran right into it. Then, it killed without compassion. It killed my son. It maimed his consort. I don't know where she is, or even if she lived. The only reason I was spared was that it was busy killing the others as I ran. We have run ever since, until we found you. Please help us!"

Erin had a sick feeling in her stomach. *I'm afraid we are too late,* she thought to Alec. She called to Hank, "Task a few of your riders to collect the fleeing villagers, guide them to safety, and help them. Feed them and try to calm them." Hank nodded. "The rest of us go to fight the beast."

Erin and Alec remounted and Erin led forward in a fast trot. The path ran straight towards the main village gate. They came out of the woods into a field of grain on the edge of the village; the stalks were crushed and broken, the heavy seed heads trampled into the mud. Erin could sense the dragon nearby, and then saw her sleeping in front of a hole in the village wall.

Erin grouped her riders into three groups as before. The other two groups each had several of Alec's new javelins – 'wizard toys,' as the riders called them. Erin led her group towards the sleeping dragon. Her task was to wake the dragon and draw the beast far enough away from the wall that the other groups could attack from the sides. Erin could sense that the dragon was no more interested or concerned about the riders on their mounts than of the beetles that crawled amongst her claws. *Rouse the dragon for me,* she thought to Alec.

Focus. He gritted his teeth, then started pulling dark energy from the dragon. The dragon roared, and Erin could sense that it was in pain.

Keep it up, she thought to Alec. *I can feel her distress when you pull dark energy from her.*

Erin drew her sword. *Focus.* She gripped the hilt tightly. *I'm not as good at this as Alec is,* she thought. Then she gained her focus and her sword began to glow. Erin felt the dragon's interest in her sword. The dragon uncoiled and started lumbering towards Erin.

Erin had been waiting for this and now directed her trogus towards the dragon. The dragon stopped and waited patiently for the trogus and rider to come close enough to catch. Erin sensed and anticipated the dragon's attack – at the last instant, Erin veered her nimble trogus to the side and the giant mouth closed on empty air. The frustrated dragon charged out after Erin, trying to catch her. Erin rode calmly back towards the dragon, waving her sword, luring the beast away from the village wall.

The riders on either side used the opportunity to move in close enough to use Alec's new javelins. A rider goaded his trogus, and the animal scrambled close to the dragon's side. With all his force he launched the javelin over the dragon. The javelin sailed true and flew over the dragon, landing in the field on the far side. The rider attached the rope from the javelin to his saddle, turned his trogus, and pulled the javelin back over the great beast. The barbs on Alec's special hooks grabbed and skidded over the dragon's skin, scratching the surface of her scales, until the hook grabbed. The rope snapped, leaving the hook in the dragon's side. Dark energy pulsed through the dragon to destroy the hook and heal the wound. The wood shaft was destroyed, and the scratch on her skin healed all the way to the hook. Dark energy pulsed into the hook and the tricrystals that Alec had embedded in the hook acted as a focus to concentrate and release the energy. The dragon cried out as the pain in her side increased. The harder she tried to push dark energy to repair the damage, the more dark energy flowed from the hook.

The dragon forgot about chasing Erin and rolled on her back to attempt to dislodge the painful hook.

"Another javelin – get its wing," shouted Alec.

A second javelin-thrower rode close to the rolling dragon and tossed his javelin. It sailed over the dragon. The rider began pulling the rope. The aim had been good and the hook pulled across the dragon's wing, making a furrow in the thick skin, but didn't hold. It popped off the wing and the hook embedded firmly in the dragon's neck. The dragon screamed again as the pain from the second hook throbbed.

The dragon lashed out at the riders, who by now had overcome their terror of the great beast and were careful to stay away from the fangs and claws. The dragon lunged at a few riders before she sprang into the air and flew towards the Elf Mountains.

As the ponderous beast floated out of sight, the riders let out a cheer. They had fought the dragon a second time and won. The dragon had been driven away. They hailed Erin with shouts and whistles as she called them to assemble.

"You have done what no riders have ever done before! You have defeated the dragon, and driven her away! You have spared Theland from this terrible beast! You are Great Riders – the greatest in all our history! I salute you and am honored to have led you in this great fight!"

"The dragon is gone! The dragon is gone! We have conquered the dragon!" the riders shouted, chanting in full voice for several minutes.

Erin raised her hand to quiet the throng. "Now I must return to my original mission. As the Royal Princess of Theland, I am returning to Freeland City. I have several tasks in the City that require my immediate attention. I would be honored to have any who want to accompany me and my Consort as Theland riders to come with us as part of our party – you will be my honor guard and escort. Any who want to stay here, or leave, may do so. It was my honor to have led such renowned riders in this great fight."

Only three of the riders left. The rest remained as part of the Princess's Royal Escort.

35 – Amelia

Erin met with Thom and Hank. "Our first task is to connect with Ferd and the remainder of our riders before we confront Amelia. If everything has gone as planned, Ferd will be traveling on the road that runs alongside the River Ryn. We will proceed in that direction. What do our riders need?"

"Some of our trogus need to be replaced and others need new saddles and tack before we ride. Can we get the village ostler to help?" Hank asked.

"And healing herbs," Thom said. "We have used up our supplies. Would the village have them?" He turned to Hank, and the two men proceeded to enumerate items needed, the probable availability in the nearby village, and other matters of logistics and preparedness.

It was late in the evening before Erin and Alec had a chance to talk to each other. "Your new weapon prevailed against the dragon and carried the day for us. Without it, I don't think the dragon would have fled. I sensed that the lines within the dragon were twisted and almost compelling her to fight."

Alec sighed. "I have been thinking about your dragon. I think that it is being controlled by the elves using some dragon-equivalent of the drone band that they used on us. You should think about whether you can untwist the lines. I fear we will encounter the dragon again."

"You saved me again, my Dear Wizard. What would I do without you?"

"I don't want to know," Alec whispered into her hair. They sank into their bed, concealed from the stars and the rest of their camp, and lay in each other's arms enjoying the peace and freedom they had. Finally, they settled into a deep and contented sleep.

For the next few days, they rode across Theland. At every village and town, Erin's couriers announced her arrival. News of their feats had spread ahead of them, and most of the towns were jubilant to greet them. The sight of the Great Warrior Princess, the Dragon Vanquisher, the Greatest Hero of all times – as well as her Consort, a true Great Wizard – was more than enough reason for a parade and village feast. They rarely encountered any of the sentiments of dissatisfaction against the former queen, Queen Therin, that Commander Kirkdar had expressed. Instead, the people were awed. They were looking at the hero of the Grasslands War; the only person in their memory who had confronted the elves in the elf lands and returned; and, greatest of all, a hero who had single-handedly stood in front of a dragon with her magic sword and driven it away. Never in their lives had there been such a person in their village and everyone wanted to see her.

After her lead riders clattered through on their trogus, Erin's standard-bearer would ride through with her banner. Then Erin would follow, holding aloft her gleaming sword. "I am your Princess Erin, returning from the Grasslands War to avenge the death of my mother, Queen Therin, to reclaim my rightful place, and to mete justice on those who have abused their responsibility during my absence."

Even though Erin was the center of attention, often the real hero turned out to be Alec. In almost every town there was a pressing project that needed to be accomplished, and Alec left each town improved – whether it was providing a water distribution system, fixing a backed-up sewage system, or repairing a washed-out road, Alec gamely tried his best to help each village.

After several days they reached the Ryn River. At the first village along the river road, a group of village councilmen came out to meet them, obviously in a state of high anxiety.

"Welcome, your Highness, Lady Erin. We are so glad that you have arrived, and we beg your help. We have been left without guardsmen since ours were conscripted by Queen Amelia for her forces, and are now we are in a defenseless position here by the Ryn. We fear that we are in great peril!

"Queen Amelia's riders from the highlands have been fleeing down our river road towards Freeland City. We have heard of the disturbances in the Grasslands and near the Elf Mountains, and now the Queen's riders tell us that a large and fearsome force is coming down the river towards our fair village. They told us our only hope is to flee also!

"But we do not wish to leave our fields, so close to the time of early harvest, and we hear that Freeland City is overrun with riders and the Queen's people. We sit here in the face of this great force, without allies, and defenseless. Can you help us? When the marauders come, will you defend us from their wrath?"

Erin smiled at the news of a force on the river road. "It will be my honor to ensure that the approaching force does you no harm. We will ride towards it today and determine its intentions." The councilmen looked at her gratefully.

"Be careful! We have heard you are a Great Warrior, and your Consort a Great Wizard, but the fleeing riders have left tales of horrors too terrible to describe."

Erin nodded in acknowledgment and led her riders along the banks of the Ryn. She cautioned her riders that they were approaching another band of warriors, but they were not to take any hostile actions without her explicit directions. Then she sent out trusted scouts. Within several hours her scouts reported back that they had encountered the scouts of the approaching force.

One of the scouts returned with a smile. "My Princess, I have great news. I met the opposing scout, and she is my cousin! We greeted each other warmly. The approaching force is our comrades, led by Ferd!"

Erin, Alec and Thom rode forward under Erin's banner to greet their long-separated riders. The caravan of Theland riders and their wagons was a welcome sight. Ferd rode out to greet her. The four dismounted and clasped arms in greeting, smiles all around.

"Greetings, my noble rider," Erin said to Ferd. "I see that you have timed your journey well; we meet you as we planned so many days ago. I hope your people have fared well on the journey."

"My Princess, we are so very glad to see you! Our scouts have been looking for word of you for a week or so, and we recently heard of your travel across our uplands and the accomplishments of Consort Alec in improving our people's villages. We delayed our departure from the last town, and spent a few additional days there, hoping to encounter your contingent. We knew we were getting close to you."

"And your mission? Did you encounter my sister's wrath?"

"There have been a few encounters. But you? I hope you accomplished your quest. We have heard stories of great accomplishments! Stories of besting elves, and dragons, and of course the stories of your triumph in the Gott War on the Grasslands have travelled far." Erin smiled in acknowledgement.

"Our exploits have not been as exciting," Ferd continued. "We have had a relatively uneventful and leisurely trip along the Ryn. When we came back into Theland from Gott, some of Amelia's riders thought to stop us at the border, but they were all bluff. I told them I was returning on orders of the Royal Princess and did not want to be impeded. I must report that they did question your authority to command riders. A couple of their riders tried to bully us and attacked. We dispatched them, and the rest ran. They have been running ever since."

"We are happy to see you," Erin said, with more than a touch of relief. "I feared that harm would befall you, where I could not help you, separated as we were." She smiled nonchalantly.

"We have had some adventures, but the stories are more exciting than the truth. Join your force with mine. We have adopted some of the 'riders' impressed by Amelia's commanders. Some of them, like Hank, were riders under my mother's banner, and others seem to have been conscripted. I want you to integrate the new riders into our structure. They are good but lack proper discipline.

"Tonight, we celebrate our reunion, and tomorrow we continue along the river road."

≈ ≈ ≈ ≈

From the hill where they were camped, Erin could see the distant glow of Freeland City as evening turned into night. The evening lights of nearby villages outlined the twisting river as it snaked through the green lowlands. The familiar sight told her that she was home. Erin viewed the road to the city with a feeling of nostalgia. Freeland City was her home, and her family had always been its heart. Queen Therin had ruled Theland wisely – for all of her life, Erin's mother had ruled with truth and compassion for its people.

Erin's thoughts turned to her mother. She had not been able to truly mourn her mother ever since they had received the bitter news of her death. She wished her mother were here. She wasn't ready to rule. There were too many decisions and the lives of too many people hinged on her decisions.

Her thoughts were interrupted by the approach of a rider, "Princess, pardon my intrusion, but there is a man who would like to talk to you."

"Oh?" It seemed odd that a lone man would approach her camp at this time of night.

"He claims he has important information about Amelia," the messenger said. "However, he insists that you must promise you will not harm him until after you hear what he has to say. If you cannot promise, then he will not talk to you, but he says he has much that you will want to hear."

Erin sighed. "Tell him that I will talk to him and promise that I will not harm him until after I give him a chance to speak. We will hear what he has to say. Bring him to my tent, and ask my Consort to join us."

≈ ≈ ≈ ≈

Erin sensed the visitor approaching long before he arrived. She muttered to Alec, "I wish I had not made that promise, but I will honor my word."

A tired, dusty man walked into the light. "Greetings, Princess."

Erin snorted in recognition of the voice, and the large figure.

"Greetings, Brun." The two looked at each other warily.

"If I had known it was you, I would not have made any promise about your well-being. I will hear you out – but know that I fully intend to punish those responsible for my mother's death. Why are you here?"

"Well, my step-daughter, I think you will want to hear what I have to say. I am here because I am escaping from Amelia." He shook his head. "She has become a mad Queen."

"I sense that you speak the truth." Erin continued to glare at the man standing before her. Then her rage boiled over. "Why did you kill my mother?"

Brun raised both hands. "I did not kill her! I did not have anything to do with your mother's demise. She was far more valuable to me alive than dead." He took a step closer to Erin. and spoke in a low voice "But you presume that she is dead. What if I told you she is alive?"

Erin took a deep breath. "I have always felt Mother was alive. I never sensed her death. You don't surprise me with that news." She leaned forward in the lantern light.

"Where is my Mother?"

"I think I know where she is located, but I don't know how to reach her," said Brun.

"I am interested, so tell me more," said Erin "but make sure it is the absolute truth. One falsehood, and you will taste my sword."

"Before I tell you any more, I want an agreement from you," Brun said. "I want you to grant me a complete pardon for all crimes that I may have committed."

"Why should I grant that?"

"Because if you don't then I will not tell you any more information; and then my Amelia will kill your mother."

"Amelia? Amelia is too inept to do anything on her own," Erin said, and spat in contempt.

"My little Amelia is not as forceful as you," Brun said, "but she has a friend … an advisor … who is her inseparable companion. Pequa is her name."

"I have heard of Pequa. Where did she come from? I don't recall anyone in Freeland City with that name."

Brun smiled ruefully. "Pequa showed up about four years ago. I don't know where she came from. She is lovely, and became one of my … lady friends. She was intoxicating! I desired to please her at all costs." He shook his head and smiled, remembering. "She was very interested in your family. It was at her urging that I poisoned your father and attempted to have you killed. She urged me to consort with your mother." Brun scowled. "But then, Pequa befriended Amelia and no longer sees me, except when she wants something. And now Amelia has cut me out also, and only listens to Pequa. 'Pequa says this!' 'Pequa says that!'" he said, imitating Amelia's whiny voice.

"I was happy with my arrangement with Therin. I could make her do what I wanted, as long as it seemed like what I wanted was for the good of the people. She could sense the truth, so I had to maneuver carefully, but it was possible to do."

"Do you still do favors for Pequa?" Alec asked.

"Yes, sometimes. I miss her, now that she spends all her time with Amelia. But if Pequa asks me to do something, I want to do it. I must admit that I have a weakness for her. When Pequa touches me, I have no choice except to do what she wants."

Erin gasped and thought to Alec, *Pequa sounds like an elf.*

That makes sense and would explain a lot of things, thought Alec back to her. *It sounds like Pequa has the powers of the elf coercers — both Brun and Amelia do everything that she wills them to do.*

"What hold does she have over Amelia? Why does Amelia want to please Pequa?" Alec asked.

Brun sighed. "Amelia is addicted to purple mushrooms. That is hard to admit. I didn't think that could happen to my child. But it did. I think Pequa keeps her supplied and does something to enhance the effects."

"But enough of Pequa. What happened to Mother?" Erin asked impatiently.

"Pequa has three bodyguards with her most of the time. One night, Amelia let Pequa and her three men into the Residence. They killed Therin's personal guardsmen. Then Pequa captured Therin and took her away. Next, she came to my residence. She told me to make it look like Queen Therin had been assassinated. I did what she wanted. The Residence was a bloody mess, and I couldn't disguise the blood and dead guards! I invented a story about attackers from the Grasslands attempting to kill the Queen and Amelia. No one believed the story, but the riders close by were loyal to me and they suppressed any opposition. Most of the riders loyal to the Queen were still with you out in the Grasslands."

"So no one questioned Mother's 'death'?" Erin asked. "How could that be?"

"As head of the Council, I wrote a Proclamation stating that Queen Therin was dead, and pronounced Amelia Queen. Of course the Council approved it!" He paused, and coughed. "I may have added a provision that anyone who questioned the Proclamation was subject to imprisonment. Of course no one did."

"So that's how little Amelia became Queen," Erin spat.

"Well, she sure wasn't going to get there on her own," Brun replied angrily. "At first, I could manipulate Amelia, and she behaved. She did what the Council directed. But, over time she became more and more irrational. One day she turned on me and dissolved the Council. The riders who I thought were loyal to me turned out to be loyal only to Pequa! They would not support me! In fact, they captured me and brought me in chains to Amelia, and she ordered them to behead me! Fortunately, Pequa intervened, and Amelia postponed the sentence. I haven't seen her since.

"Now, Amelia does whatever she wants. She rules only to benefit herself and her friends. Some of them have moved into the Residence with her and all they do is have parties and partake of purple mushroom and gamble. Pequa lets Amelia run wild and rarely pays any attention unless she wants her to do something specific. I cannot influence Amelia anymore. Occasionally Pequa will come to me and give me instructions; as long as I do what she wants, my life is pretty good. Pequa makes me tell her what I have been doing.

If I have not done what she wants the pain is awful. If I have carried out her will, then the reward is ecstasy."

"So, I repeat," said Erin, "Why are you here?"

Brun continued, "You want to know why I am here? Because Pequa told me to come here. She told me to come and tell you about your mother."

"There is only one reason she would do that," said Alec.

"I agree," said Brun. "There is only one reason. She is using Therin as the bait in a trap. They want me to send you into that trap. They assume you will be so interested in rescuing your mother that you will go readily."

"So, again, where is Mother?" asked Erin.

"First, the agreement."

"And if I don't agree?"

Brun shrugged his shoulders. "Then I will not tell you where the Queen is. I cannot return to Amelia, and you will not have me, so I will die and keep her location secret. I know that you can sense the truth like your mother could, so you know that I am ready to make that choice."

Erin closed her eyes. *He is right,* she thought to Alec. *I do not see another way.*

"All right! I must rescue Mother."

"This does not make any sense. Why would Pequa merely capture and imprison Queen Therin instead of killing her?" interjected Alec.

Brun looked at him and scowled. "I struggled with that also, and decided that it is not the Queen's fate that concerns Pequa. It is Erin." He looked directly at his step-daughter. "I have seen how you can make fire come from your sword, and can make the Truth Stone turn almost clear. I think that means you have abilities greater than your mother's – even greater than your grandmother's. I think that Pequa, whatever her intentions are, is afraid of you."

Erin could sense that Brun was speaking the truth.

"Pequa and her guardsmen thought they had eliminated you. If your Consort here had not appeared out of thin air, with your father dead no one would have ever rescued you – you would have been a mindless nomad slave or dead. Either way, you would not be a concern to her."

Erin sat in the flickering lantern light and thought a long time as everyone watched her. Finally, she said, "I will meet your terms – but only if we are able to rescue Mother and she is alive. Also, I want you to promise never to be involved in governing Theland in any way, and I want you out of my family. I want you to renounce your consort with Mother, and get out of her life."

Brun also took his time to think over Erin's offer, staring at his hands. After a few long moments he spoke. "You give me a poor option, but I guess I'm not going to do any better." He threw his head back. "I don't know precisely where your mother is, but I can venture a sound guess. You may not know that I have a hillside grotto outside the walls of Freeland City. It used to be a mine, back in the days of my grandmother's mother. I showed it to Pequa – we used to tryst there occasionally. Since Amelia has ascended the throne Pequa has made several trips to the grotto without me, and now has forbidden me to travel to it. I am reasonably certain your mother is being held there. I built a deep dungeon in the hillside years ago to hold special prisoners. That is where I would have put Therin.

"But I have heard from my friends that Pequa has had her guardsmen and some other workers modifying the dungeon – I doubt that now you could escape it, even if you reached it and found your mother there. I have heard that one of her guardsmen now lives at the grotto, and that she has spies watching your riders, as well as watching me. She and her henchmen will have plenty of warning if you choose to approach that area."

"Tell me where it is," said Erin sternly, "and I will determine the risk."

≈ ≈ ≈ ≈

Erin held a long discussion with Alec. "We should leave tonight to rescue Mother."

"That is what Pequa and her clutchmen want us to do, and I think they are ready to stop us if we do that. We don't know how many more elves she has brought to the grotto. If they know that you listened to Brun tonight, then they know you will try to rescue your mother." Alec was quiet for a while, stroking his beard and thinking. Then, he spoke. "We need a distraction. We will put out a rumor that you had Brun beheaded for killing your mother, and that you acted without even taking the time to listen to his worthless plea for your leniency. Then you will stay here and be very visible, while I take Brun and free the Queen."

Erin thought for a moment and then said, "It is a good plan. Let's do it. The only thing I don't like is that I cannot be in two places at once to help you free Mother."

"Maybe you can, maybe you can," Alec said.

≈ ≈ ≈ ≈

"Let's ride," said Erin, calling to Ferd, the bright morning sun cutting across her bustling campsite. Erin and a tall man who looked somewhat like Alec took the lead, followed by Ferd and an escort party of twenty riders. The group rode along the River Ryn towards Freeland City, greeting other travelers and loudly hailing the residents of the next village as they passed. Erin was satisfied that their passage was noted; word would quickly get to any spies in the area.

As they rode, Erin instructed her riders. "Some of you are new to Freeland City, my home. In the center of town is Justice Square, and within the Square rests the Stone of Truth. We are going to the Stone so that I can show my people who I am – their Princess. Justice Square is a distance from the royal Residence, so we should not encounter Amelia. If we do, I will handle her.

"Remember these are our sisters and brothers. Treat everyone with respect."

They encountered no opposition as they reached the gates of Freeland City. The people watched with excitement as the royal procession marched through the town. Some waved to Erin, and then quickly looked around to see if their indiscretion had been noticed. Erin could sense a feeling of awe from the crowds towards her, and an underlying dislike of Amelia and her capricious decisions.

Erin led her procession on a long route circling through town, announcing at every opportunity that she would make a proclamation at Justice Square. Her group reached the entryway to Justice Square as the sun reached midmorning; two of the five moons hung low in the morning sky. A crowd had assembled on the Square in anticipation of Erin's proclamation.

Justice Square remained unchanged since Erin last visited it; the black half-sphere of the Stone of Truth reflected a thin line of sunlight over its platform. At least Amelia hasn't removed the Stone, thought Erin darkly, if even she were able to.

One of the riders unfurled the Princess' banner and led the way into the Square, followed by Erin, the tall rider, and Ferd. The crowd parted for them as they crossed the pavement. Two of Amelia's guardsmen were standing in front of the platform. Erin motioned for her force to dismount, and she walked up to the guardsmen. They stared past her.

"I am Erin, Princess of Theland. I come to the Stone of Truth to show my people the rightful truth."

One guardsman looked at her and replied, "Her Majesty Queen Amelia does not permit any to step onto the platform without her permission."

Erin focused through the tricrystal in her sword. She sensed the lines clear and strengthen. It wasn't the crispness she had when Alec supplied her dark energy, but it was enough. She twisted the lines of energy, and both guards collapsed, falling to their knees. Two riders grabbed the men and slid them out of the way; Erin stepped onto the platform. Erin walked up to the Stone and touched it.

The Stone brought back memories. Erin had walked on this platform ever since she was a child, sometimes standing by her mother as she coaxed color into the Stone, sometimes with her mother as she sought justice. The Stone was cold in the morning air, but Erin's touch brought a feeling of warmth.

Responding to her touch, the Stone slowly began to change color, then rapidly turned from black to solid white. Erin pushed on the Stone, like Alec had taught her, with dark energy. The Stone continued to change until it was crystal clear; now she could see through it, and she expanded her senses into the Stone. She suddenly felt herself soaring in the air. She was looking down on the world as she floated freely. Below her were forests and fields. She sensed an unsuspecting drunglet wandering somewhere below, and thought of swooping down on it. Then her sense of the present returned, and she was staring at the clear globe.

Erin could hear the cheers from the people in the Square. She let them go on for a while and then motioned for quiet.

"I am Erin, Princess of Theland, daughter of Queen Therin, and I have returned from the War on the Grasslands." As she spoke, the stone changed from its clear color and glowed with a golden hue. Erin stopped and used the Stone to sense the feelings of the people standing before her. Her senses expanded, and she could feel their hopes and dreams – most wanted peace and a chance to live their lives and raise their families without fear; but most were very apprehensive. Erin could tell that the crowd did not like Amelia, but feared the results of any confrontation.

Erin continued, "I intend to avenge my Mother's treatment. I will seek out and deal with those who have usurped the throne and abused their power, and I will assume my rightful role as your Princess and ruler to help my people." The stone continued to glow with a golden hue.

Many of the people assembled before her cheered, but she could also hear the people muttering among themselves and could detect the anger in the crowd towards Amelia. Then she saw a commotion at the far entry to the Square. Several guardsmen were whipping people and pushing them aside to open a corridor. Behind the guards were two sedan chairs, each borne by four people with long poles yoked across their shoulders. Erin could sense that Amelia was riding in the first sedan chair and another woman was in the second. A cadre of additional guardsmen and courtiers came along behind the chairs.

Erin stood on the platform in quiet anticipation. She had not planned to face Amelia today, but she was ready. The crowd understood that a confrontation was coming and opened a pathway for Amelia and her entourage to approach Erin. The people carrying the sedan chair brought it to the front of the platform and knelt.

Amelia looked at Erin from her place on the chair. "Sister, I am glad to see you." The stone turned from gold to brown. "I am pleased that you have come to worship me. You and your lackeys may come and bow at my feet, and then I will decide your fate." The Stone turned almost black. "Since you have been gone, we have made a few changes. Opposing my right to rule is treasonous, and carries a penalty of death."

"Amelia, you are accused of abusing the Queen's power. In front of the Stone of Truth, how do you answer?"

Amelia looked at the Stone. "I could never make that stupid thing work, and Pequa always told me the truth part was just an accidental capability." The Stone glowed bright gold. "I cannot abuse my power. I am the Queen! And I can do anything that I want!" The stone turned black.

"Stop that stupid stone trick, before I punish you," she whined. "I am Queen, oh yes, I am! And we have the writ that says Erin abdicated, don't we Daddy?" She turned and looked around. "Oh, maybe I had him beheaded. We can ask his head at dinner tonight, but I am sure that he told me I was the rightful Queen." Amelia quit mumbling to herself and tuned to the other sedan chair. "Pequa, come here and look at all my faithless vassals," Amelia said, pointing at the crowd.

"Yes, your Majesty, they are faithless and deceitful," said the second woman.

Now Erin looked closely at the woman in the other chair. "You are an elf!" she exclaimed.

The tall woman stood and started directly at Erin.

"Of course, I am an elf," Pequa sneered. "I have come to help her Highness Queen Amelia achieve her full glory! I ask little in return, just a small thing – a promise that the Queen will pay a small tribute to the elves." The stone glowed brightly golden, and the crowd gasped with shock at the revelation. Very few of the citizens of Freeland City had ever seen a known elf, and some covered their faces in fear, peeking at the tall dark-haired woman between their fingers. Pequa looked at Erin, then pointed at the Stone. "You are too stupid to know what you have – what you can do. That is a Master Dragon Stone, and yet you use it for mundane things like indicating truth."

Pequa looked at the two men following her chair and said, "Kill her."

The two men stepped forward. Five of Erin's riders stepped in the way. Pequa's two moved with precision, and within the blink of an eye four of the riders were down. Erin watched in astonishment. *They are anticipating my riders' moves. These must be two of Pequa's clutchmen.* Erin drew her sword and let the two come onto the platform towards her. They moved with coordinated precision, one on each side of her. Erin circled to keep them together, and the fight was on. She attacked, and they blocked her thrust and countered with a blow that barely missed. She relaxed and started feeling their intentions. The normally crisp feeling of anticipation became fuzzy, and she noted the hesitation in her opponents also. Erin continued to fight using her sense of rightness as well as her ability to anticipate. With two opponents anticipating her moves she was rapidly tiring and would eventually wear out before her opponents. She needed to change things to her advantage.

Out of the corner of her eye, she saw Pequa staring intently. *Pequa is sensing my reactions and feeding it to her clutchmen. That is how they do this.* Erin thrust at one of the clutchmen and then turned her blade. She focused as much dark energy as she could find and made her runes on the side flash. The momentary flash distracted Pequa, and for an instant, the fuzzy feeling of anticipation turned crisp. Erin took the instant and slashed before Pequa recovered her senses. One of the clutchmen was down. Erin turned towards the second as the fuzzy sense returned. *I can beat this guy, one on one.*

The second clutchman retreated but Erin didn't let him escape. In desperation, the clutchman launched a frantic attack that almost broke through Erin's defense. The attack used all the reserve energy of the clutchman. When it didn't succeed, the clutchman seemed an instant slower. Erin took advantage of the slowing and finished the clutchman.

From her vantage point on the platform, Erin looked across the square. Amelia and Pequa were retreating on the far side of the square. Erin's riders were still fighting with a few of Amelia's guardsmen, but they were winning. Except for the four downed riders that the clutchmen had initially taken out, all her riders were holding their own. Erin jumped off the platform to help her riders finish the remaining battles.

36 – The Grotto

Alec and Brun left the riders' camp quietly before the sun was up, taking Hank and Rhor with them. They looked like a typical team on a dawn patrol; they did not want anyone in the camp or the nearby village to mark their leaving as anything unusual. As dawn came, the quartet headed towards a tributary to the Ryn. This time of year the water was not particularly high, and Brun knew of an upstream ford. The group crossed the river and rode down a small path towards the Evening Mountains.

They rode for most of the morning; the terrain changed from the valley floor to the rolling hills that preceded the mountains. Between two of the hills, they came to a side trail. Brun pointed. "It is only a couple of els further."

"Will it be guarded?" asked Alec.

"Of course," said Brun.

"Then it is time to obscure ourselves. We should leave our mounts here." Alec and Brun dismounted and gave the trogus leads to Rhor.

"I do not expect to return this way," Alec said to Hank. "Wait here until evening. If we have not returned, then take the trogus and go back to camp. We will meet you there."

Alec focused, and the world became fuzzy. "Stay close to me," he said to Brun, "and be quiet."

They walked silently along the path. Brun motioned to Alec. Alec could see a guard watching the path from an elevated post. They walked carefully forward, and the guard continued to watch the path with no reaction.

They continued to follow the path as it ran between two low hills; they crossed a small meadow with a large wooded area behind it. At the end of the meadow, the trail ran through a narrow opening between two rocky bluffs.

As they approached the narrow passage, Burn stopped to rest, looking relieved. "The grotto compound is just past the bluff. If Pequa's guards had noticed us, this is where they would have attacked us." He gazed up at the rock face. "Just ahead, at the narrows, there is a hidden gate that can be closed to stop riders from going any farther; then they are vulnerable to attack from the rocks above or from the woods on either side. A few well-placed defenders here can protect the grotto against an army."

Alec looked around. "I see what you mean," he said.

"There is a barracks about an el past the gate. That's where the guards will be staying. I think that there are about forty of them, from what I am told, but they will count on sentries to warn them if anyone approaches. That gives them plenty of time to get to their stations, so they don't need to come this far out here, except when they change the guard shift."

"What else is over there?" asked Alec.

"My grotto residence is set further back by an old mine pond. Very picturesque. The main mine shaft is on the other side of the pond. Back when this was a working mine, they used the water from the mine pond to rinse and sort the ore. The dungeon I built to hold my captives is near the barracks, carved into the hillside. I suspect that is where the Queen is held."

Alec looked around. "Is there a clearing near here that we can use, where the guards can't see us?"

Brun pointed, "There used to be a clearing in those trees, where they harvested mine timbers. I haven't been over there in quite some time."

"Perfect," said Alec. "Show it to me."

Brun led him through some underbrush to a large clearing. One side was protected by a steep hill and the other sides were ringed by the woods. Alec smiled. "This looks like a good place to stage our riders."

Alec took off his backpack and pulled out the portal-control hex rod. He created a simple circle, checking to make sure the dimensions were adequate. He motioned for Brun to stand next to him in the center of the circle. "Join me. I don't trust you enough to leave you here alone." The world dimmed, went black, and returned. The two of them were standing inside a large circle drawn in the middle of the rider camp. Brun looked around in amazement.

Thom came up to them, carefully staying outside the circle. "The Princess just returned a few minutes ago. I will send a runner to fetch her. The others are ready."

Erin came up quickly, armed and ready. "Did everything go smoothly?" she asked Alec.

He nodded. "How about with you?"

"A minor encounter with Amelia and her minions but nothing difficult," Erin replied. Alec could sense that wasn't the whole truth but didn't press the issue.

"What should we do with Brun?"

"I don't want to take him. We would have to assign a rider to watch him, and we will probably need all our people for more important tasks. I will be able to sense Mother's location, so he won't add anything."

Brun looked relieved at the decision. He obviously was disconcerted about his abrupt arrival in the middle of the camp. He cleared his throat.

"Beware," he said. "There are traps in the dungeon, and Pequa's workers may have added things that I do not know about."

Erin glared at Brun, letting her anger sink in. Then she looked at Thom. "You are in charge here in camp until I return. I will honor my word to free him," jerking her thumb towards Brun, "when I return. In the meantime, keep him in chains. If I do not return, execute him for his many crimes."

Brun shook his head in resignation, "I have told you all I know, but I don't think you will return. You have sealed my death warrant."

$$\approx \ \approx \ \approx \ \approx$$

After her step-father was led off in chains, Erin said to Alec, "I will believe Brun, and we will take forty riders with us. Without the element of surprise, we probably don't have enough riders to recover Mother alive, but if we can surprise them we should be able to easily beat them with even numbers."

Erin hand-picked the riders she wanted, led by Ferd, and Alec cycled the portal repeatedly until all the riders stood in the secluded clearing near the grotto. Not sure how they had arrived there, they looked around in surprise as Ferd moved them into position.

Erin sensed the area. "Mother is here, I know it," she said with elation. "There is no one in the building with her."

Then Erin turned to Ferd. "Brun told the truth on the number of defenders. Most of the guardsmen are in the barracks, except for a few that seem to be patrolling. I sense some activity; it must be time for a shift change. Ferd, you stay here with the riders. Alec and I are going to get Mother. If the guardsmen start pouring out of their barracks, or if Alec sends a signal, attack them."

They waited and saw three guardsmen wander down the path. Shortly three other guardsmen straggled back along the path.

They look like they could be drones, thought Alec to himself.

"Are you ready my Dear Wizard?" Erin said, and squeezed his hand.

With a slight bow, Alec took her hand, kissed it, and then created an obscuring field. They carefully walked out of the woods to the path leading to the grotto, and through the narrow passage between the two bluffs. On the far side of the passage Alec saw the substantial gate that was completely out of view from the meadow. They entered the grotto compound and stopped to look around.

"Mother is in the basement of that building," Erin whispered, pointing across the pond.

Alec responded, "Brun said that is the old mine building. He thought your mother would be in the dungeon on the other side of the barracks house."

"No, I sense her under the mine building."

The two of them carefully walked across the open area, shielded by the obscuring lens, to the old mine building. No cries of alarm marked their passage. They came to the door on the outside of the building. Erin pushed on the door, but it didn't budge. "Your turn, my Great Wizard."

Alec released the obscuring field. *Focus.* The locks on the door shifted slightly, and he pushed on the door. It reluctantly slid open. "Let's get inside before someone sees us," he said.

Once they were both inside, Alec pushed the door closed. *Focus.* "I locked it." He pushed on the door, and it would not move. "They will have a hard time opening that door now."

"Mother is underneath us," Erin interjected, not interested in the state of the door.

Erin led the way into the building. The building was made of stone; the cold stone floor was slightly mossy with age. A trickle of water ran through a trough cut into the stone floor on one side of the room. Small slit windows provided the only light; leaving a pattern of small strips of light against the dark walls. "This must have been the processing room for the old mine," whispered Alec.

They carefully crossed the dark room, then in a far corner came to a shaft cut straight down into the rock. A crude ladder was attached to the side of the shaft, and a large hopper and aging hoist were positioned overhead.

"Mother is down there," Erin exclaimed. She slid into the opening and started down the ladder into the black maw of the shaft.

Alec pulled a light globe from his backpack and focused dark energy into it; the glow from the globe dimly illuminated the ladder and barely lit the bottom of the shaft.

"There is a passage cut into the rocky hillside down here," she said. "Bring your light down."

Alec descended the ladder and joined Erin at the bottom. Water dripped from the rocks leaving a cold, wet and slick floor. "This passageway must have been cut along a vein of ore as they mined," Alec mused. "That's probably why it is neither straight nor level."

They followed the passage. There were several small rooms and side shafts cut into the passage, some used for storage of old mine equipment or newer treasures, and some empty. At each of these, Erin stopped and sensed, then continued moving down the main passage. They came to a door on the side of the passage.

"Mother is behind the door, I can sense her."

Erin pushed on the door with her shoulder, and it opened. The opened door released a rod that clanged into a metal plate; the sound echoed through the chambers for a long time.

"I think I set off an alarm," said Erin. "They will know we are here. You should give the signal to the riders."

Alec focused. A red flare burst in the air above the clearing where Ferd was stationed, making a loud bang! The sound was audible to them, even deep in the mine.

"You can't do anything without making a show, can you," Erin joked, then ran ahead through the dark passage. After a few turns in the old mine shaft, they came to a small cavern; a natural crack in the rock allowed a faint sliver of light into the chamber.

Queen Therin was chained to a metal ring embedded in the cavern wall.

"Mother!" Erin ran to her mother and hugged her.

"Erin! Daughter!" the Queen said, in a barely-audible voice.

"My Queen," said Alec as he grabbed her hand.

Queen Therin was very weak, slipping in and out of consciousness, but very much alive. Alec started pushing a little dark energy into her. The Queen's breathing improved, and her face regained a little color. Then Alec noticed the chains holding her in place.

"Hold still, and I will remove the chains."

Focus. The chains split into pieces and fell to the floor. The Queen looked relieved.

"My children! I am so glad to see you! Thank goodness; I had given up hope of ever being rescued. They left me chained here in the dark and the cold. Occasionally they come and give me some food." Alec rubbed her arms where the chains had bound her, gradually restoring feeling to her limbs.

Erin just held her mother without saying anything, letting her tears wash over them both.

Then, a loud clattering reverberated through the halls and chambers of the mine.

"That's not good! Let's get Mother out of here," Erin said with conviction.

"I fear that I am too weak to walk," the Queen said.

"We can carry you," Erin said, and Alec hoisted the frail woman onto his back. With the help of the light globe they retraced their steps through the mine's passageways back to towards the entry shaft. Alec was about to address the issue of how they would get the Queen back up the ladder, when it became obvious that it was no longer an issue. The last few arns of the passageway were filled with dirt and rocks spilling from the shaft.

"They must have released that hopper above the shaft, and filled it with rock," Alec said. "They think they have sealed off the exit and buried us in here!" He gently placed Queen Therin on the mine floor and eyed the pile of rubble. "Those rocks will take a while for me to remove but they shouldn't prevent us from escaping."

The Queen tugged on his trouser leg. "I am getting wet," she said, and her voice trembled as she started to shiver.

Alec looked down. The previously-damp floor was now covered with water, and the water was rapidly rising. Erin quickly helped her mother to her feet.

"They have filled in the entrance, and I think they are flooding the tunnel," said Alec, stating the obvious.

Alec could feel the concentrations of dark energy around him. "I think they have opened a sluice gate in the mill pond and are draining it into the mine. Help me Erin – let's see if we can stop the water flow."

Erin put her hands on Alec's arm and helped him feel the rightness. The already cold water became noticeably colder, and then the flow stopped.

"I think we have temporarily solved that problem," Alec said. "Now we need to tackle the next one."

The water had reached almost waist deep, and Queen Therin was shivering noticeably. "What did you do?" the Queen asked.

"We froze the water at a narrow point in the mine shaft," Alec explained. "It will stop the flow of water for a time, until the ice dam melts."

"We need to get Mother out of this water," Erin said, with real concern. "She won't be able to withstand this cold for long."

Focus. Alec converted a few of the rocks filling the vertical shaft to air, and they blew out of the way. With a significant effort, he created a small opening all the way up the shaft. Then the rocks in the shaft shifted and fell into the opening he had created. "Hmmpf," he muttered to himself. "I thought more of the rock would move." He tried again with the same effect. "I need a better plan. At this rate, it will take a day or so to remove all of those rocks. "

"Mother is not doing well," said Erin. "We need to do something to get her out of this water."

Alec looked at the queen. She was shivering uncontrollably and was getting whiter and whiter, her breath coming in short ragged gasps.

Focus. Alec moved enough of the rocks to create a small dry platform above the level of the water. Erin pulled her mother onto it. Then Alec heated several rocks around the edge of the platform, warming the place where the Queen lay.

"Listen," Alec said. The sound of falling water increased. "I think our ice dam just failed."

"It's too bad that you can't just whisk us out of here like we did to get here," quipped Erin.

"It sure is," answered Alec, and then he thought, *What an idiot. Of course I can.*

Alec edged off the dry shelf and back into the water. He created a small stone platform submerged in the rising water. "Join me here," he said, and Erin hugged her mother close as the two slid into the waist-deep water. The Queen winced as she reentered the icy water. Erin held her upright, standing as close to Alec as they could.

Alec fumbled around in his backpack, unable to see the contents in the murky darkness; then he could feel what he needed. He grabbed the hex rod and held it in front of him.

Focus, and the world went black. The light returned, now the brightness of sunlight, and the icy water crashed off the platform onto the grass of the forest clearing. They were standing near the grotto, where he had ported the riders. The Queen blinked and then covered her eyes to shield them, unaccustomed to sunlight after her time in captivity, still shivering from her immersion in the cold water, and uncertain as to how she had left the mine.

"I sense only our riders. Let's join them," said Erin.

They hailed their riders. In the distance, Alec could see several of the riders trying to knock down the door to the mine building.

Ferd quickly ran back to Erin and reported. "We have killed or driven off the local guardsmen, and we now control the compound. Several of them escaped, including the man who seems to be Petra's personal guard. I worry she have more things planned."

"You have done well," the Queen said looking at Ferd from beneath her hand.

For the first time, Ferd looked at the soaking-wet, shivering woman huddled next to Erin. He gasped with joy as he recognized the figure.

"My Queen! Your Highness! We were told you were dead." Ferd broke all protocol by enveloping the Queen in a great bear-hug.

"And well she might yet be if we don't get her something warm and dry," said Erin. "Find me some blankets and dry clothes. She fell into icy water, is freezing cold, and hasn't eaten for days. We need some food and hot broth as well." Ferd helped them carry the Queen into the grotto residence.

The riders went scurrying around trying to find suitable things, delighted at the news that their beloved Queen Therin had been found alive. Soon they had a roaring fire warming the great room, and two of the riders quickly carried the Queen to a chair by the hearth. Another rider brought warm blankets, and Erin helped her mother discard her wet rags and helped warm her with her own body heat while someone else came with dry clothes. Brun had apparently kept the grotto well-stocked, and finding food was not a problem.

Alec grasped his medallion and pushed dark energy into the Queen. Soon, with warmth, dry clothing, and nourishment, her condition stabilized, but she was still at risk and very weak. Erin helped Alec sense the rightness of his healing.

"How are we going to get Mother back to our camp by Freeland City?" Erin asked him in a low voice, hoping that the dozing Queen wouldn't hear.

"Our original plan was to port home. Now that won't work because I reset the other end of the portal to the mine shaft. I don't think there are enough trogus here for all of us to ride home. I could go with a few riders and reset the portal when I got back at our base, but I'm not sure your mother will make it through the night without me continuing to strengthen her."

"Mother is most important! You need to stay here and help her," said Erin. Alec nodded in agreement, his eyes never leaving Queen Therin's pale face.

Erin turned to Ferd. "We may have to spend the night here. I don't think that Mother can travel in her current state, and we can't use the portal to return to our base. We had to use the portal to escape the trap they set for us in the mine, and now the other end is deep in the mine shaft. But we may need to deploy some riders. How many trogus do we have?"

"We captured ten. There were more, but Queen Amelia's riders escaped on them," Ferd reported. "By now Hank would have returned to camp with the mounts you rode in on."

"Then send four of our riders back to our base. Have them return with a large force tomorrow, including a carriage for the Queen. We want to return Queen Therin to her royal Residence in style."

"Will do, Princess. We should be able to return with force before midday tomorrow."

"That will give Mother the night to recover. I don't like the idea of having to spend a night here, but that is probably the best plan. We will expect you then," replied Erin.

Erin curled up under the blankets with her mother, continuing to warm her through the night with her body heat. Alec spent the night focusing dark energy and strengthening the Queen. Early in the evening, he was concerned that she might not survive, but by late in the night she was showing much more strength. When the morning light filtered over the hill, the Queen was moving about on her own.

≈ ≈ ≈ ≈

A rider came running into the great room as they ate breakfast. "Princess, we have a problem. Our scouts have detected intruders massing at the entrance to the canyon. They appear to be Queen Amelia's riders."

"How long before they are here?"

"Probably within the first half of the morning."

"How many are they?"

"We think there are over a hundred riders and that is not the worst of it. We have sighted a dragon in the sky!" Erin and Alec looked at each other.

We haven't had a dragon in generations, and now we have two in one week! Erin thought. *But I guess it is possible that it is the same dragon, and that we are seeing her twice.*

They left the grotto hall; Erin efficiently organized the defense. The area was built to be held by a small force, and Erin took advantage of its features. The Queen remained in the building with Ferd and a few riders.

Erin deployed the rest of the riders around the opening where the path went through the gap between the two hills. The riders quickly found the prepared defensive positions on the hillside. They would be outnumbered, but Erin was convinced that between their defensive position, Alec's abilities, and her riders' better skills and training, they had a good chance to holdout until additional riders arrived from her base camp.

She kissed her mother's forehead, then left the grotto to be with her riders.

37 – The Queen Returns

Amelia's scouts rode up the path to the grotto and stopped at the edge of the woods waiting for the main force to arrive. Soon a team of twenty of Amelia's riders rode up. The riders looked scraggly and poorly disciplined. Erin sensed they were more bullies than soldiers; they seemed confident that mounted men with swords could beat any dismounted people, no matter how skilled they were at fighting. Erin could sense that the leader thought this was his chance for glory.

Without any hesitation, the leader spurred his trogus forward along the path. The rest of his riders came storming behind him. The slapping sound of trogus paws echoed and reverberated through the trees. Erin signaled for her riders to wait.

The first of the trogus entered the narrow gap with the others not far behind. Erin motioned, and the heavy gate slid closed, blocking the way out of the narrows.

Now, she thought to Alec.

Focus! A gray fog enveloped everything in the narrow passageway, and shapes became indistinguishable in the mist. Positioned above on the edge of the rocky bluff, Erin's riders threw rocks and spears down on Amelia's riders. The riders, blind in the fog, collided and their trogus snarled and fought with each other. As the mist blew away the carnage in the gap was apparent.

"Report," requested Erin.

"No lost riders. Two are injured but can still fight. We think we got fifteen of Amelia's riders. The last five fled before we could dispatch them. What arrogant fools! They tried to attack on trogus through that narrow gap against trained opponents. I wish we had fog like that more often. It made it impossible for them to see us and we could hear their thrashing."

"Listen," one of Erin's scouts signaled; and they could hear the sounds of a large group approaching. Soon they could see them coming through the trees and across the meadow, more or less following the path to the grotto. As they funneled into the narrow gap the front riders could see the carnage before them and stopped, reluctant to approach within spear-throw range. With the front riders stopped, the other riders bunched up behind them in an unruly mass, with trogus braying and men shouting.

A carriage was in the middle of the Amelia's riders. The carriage driver whipped the drungs, and with reluctance, the drungs pushed their way through the mass of milling trogus. The trogus growled at the drungs but the carriage driver's whip made a space through the throng of animals and men. The carriage stopped in the middle of the path when it reached the front riders, near the side of the bluff. Two figures stepped out of the carriage. Alec immediately recognized them both: Amelia and Pequa.

A herald whistled the royal introduction. A chair was brought out and placed in the shade of the trees near the clearing, and Amelia sat down, Pequa close by her side. Servants scurried to put an awning over Amelia's chair. Next, a servant brought a cup and a basket of food for Amelia.

Pequa stood in anticipation, staring out at the clearing and then up at the sky.

She looks like she's waiting for something, thought Alec. Erin began to look around, trying to sense what Pequa was waiting for.

After a long moment of suspense, the sky darkened. The riders and servants began to scatter, running into the cover of the trees or milling about at the edge of the clearing. And then, there it was.

The dragon! thought Alec. He could feel the draw of dark energy as the large beast landed on the path in front of Pequa. The dragon landed precisely, belying her size, appearing to hover for a moment before she touched the ground with her legs. She gave one final flap with her wings as she looked around with a curious expression. The final flap stirred up dust and blew up a minor whirlwind, sending a gust towards Amelia's chair and upsetting her basket.

Amelia looked up angrily. "Off with its head," she shouted. "How dare the ugly brute disturb my breakfast."

Pequa was obviously annoyed with Amelia. "Oh, shut up, we have important things to do."

Amelia looked at Pequa with astonishment. "Who do you think you are! How can you think to speak to me with such insolence! I put up with your snarly cur behavior because you have been useful to me, but now this ... insult! ... is too much. Come and bow down and beg my forgiveness." Amelia popped a small fruit into her mouth. "If you beg enough, I will have you beaten and not beheaded," she said, through her mouthful of fruit.

Petra stepped forward to Amelia's chair and slapped her. "Foolish girl! I am tired of you!" Pequa pointed towards the grotto and the place where Erin was concealed. "She is my real concern! As soon as I finish her off, I will teach you your place."

Amelia reared back in shock, hand to her face, and squalled, "I am the Queen! You don't talk to me that way! Off with your head!"

Pequa walked over to Amelia, grabbed her by the shoulders, and shook her. "Ha! Don't make me laugh. You are a worthless little drone girl! Not good enough for anything. When I eliminate the House of Lian, no one can protect this little backwater land from us elves, or from our dragon! Then you will learn to respect your betters! I will enjoy watching you suffer ten times over for the trouble you have caused me."

"Take her! Help me!" Amelia looked around and saw that none of the riders stepped forward to help her. "Off with her head!" No one moved.

Pequa's clutchman stepped up and grabbed Amelia by the hair. He jerked her off her chair and shoved her face into the dirt.

"Stay there until you are told to do otherwise," he snarled at her.

Amelia lay on the ground sobbing loudly; the clutchman kicked her and then stood beside Pequa. Pequa looked at the dragon, and in response the beast slowly started walking towards the narrow gap. It barely fit through the space. With her head, the dragon pushed the dead trogus and riders out of the way and slithered up to the gate. The dragon leaned against the gate, and the wood groaned. Alec focused and reinforced the wood with dark energy. The dragon leaned further against the gate, and the wood continued to groan but held the beast's weight. Alec continued to strengthen the wood. Then with a great crack, the hinge between the wood and the rock failed, and the gate fell aside. The dragon's head pushed the failed gate out of the way.

Erin sensed the dragon. *It is the same beast that we met before,* she thought to Alec. She could feel the different minds swirling inside the dragon. The entwined lines that linked the minds seemed tighter than ever before. *Help me,* she thought to Alec.

Alec let dark energy flow into Erin. Now Erin felt that if she could find the right place, she could unsnarl the entwined lines. She used the dark energy from Alec to help change the lines. She pushed energy through her sword towards the dragon. At the edge of her senses was the feeling of rightness.

She could not capture the rightness; it stood tantalizingly just beyond her reach.

Erin's effort relaxed the lines a little, and she could feel a great loneliness and feeling of isolation coming from the dragon. Erin echoed how a Princess also was lonely and isolated in the same way. Erin stepped forward and walked towards the dragon. *Trust my feeling,* she thought to Alec.

The dragon watched Erin approach; Erin walked up and touched the dragon with the flat of her sword. Dark energy swirled. Alec pushed dark energy into the sword and Erin used it to soothe the dragon, stroking the creature's scales with the flat blade. Erin felt the entwined lines relax slightly more. The feeling of rightness stayed just beyond her reach.

Erin was one with the dragon. The dragon almost purred. Erin shared memories with the dragon: Erin saw a memory from within the dragon of no one caring for her since before she had come to this world. A time long ago sprung to her mind – a time before the elves came and took her mother and father away. Erin saw the dragon's memory of a little girl running free in the grass with her friend. She remembered tripping and scraping her knee and she cried. Her friend had held her, and father had used dark energy to heal the scrape. They had cared. The dragon embraced the feeling of peace and caring. It was the same feeling that Erin's dark energy gave the dragon.

Then Erin felt the lines tightening within the dragon's mind. The dragon looked confused and bellowed a pleading call, then backed out of the gap until she was even with Pequa. There she stopped.

≈ ≈ ≈ ≈

An envoy pulled a parley flag out and planted it in the ground beside Pequa. Erin looked at Alec. "She wants to talk, so we might as well go to her."

The two of them walked through the gap and walked along the edge of the woods until they reached Pequa. Pequa stood looking at them with disgust. "I was hoping to come here to celebrate your demise, but now I will have an even better opportunity – I can watch your death. I give you one chance to surrender. If you surrender, I will allow your riders to join Queen Amelia's riders. Otherwise, they will all die with you today."

Erin could sense the anger in her riders. "My riders would prefer to die than to join her," Erin said sharply

A loud howl from the dragon interrupted their conversation. Now that Pequa wasn't standing over her, Amelia had quit sobbing and crawled over to her food basket. After fumbling through the contents, she pulled a pouch out of the basket and opened it. The rich smell of ripe purple mushrooms permeated the air. The dragon sniffed and headed in Amelia's direction.

"No, you fool!" shouted Pequa. "I told the servants not to let you bring those. They are irresistible to the dragon!"

The dragon had identified the source of the delicious aroma and shoved the carriage out of the way to reach Amelia's pavilion. The carriage careened into the ditch, splintering into pieces. With one delicate flick, using the very end of her long tongue, the dragon pulled half of Amelia's purple mushroom out of the pouch and into her mouth.

Amelia looked at her half-empty stash with shock. Then she screamed at the dragon, "I am the Queen. These are my mushrooms! Give them back!"

The dragon flicked her tongue a second time. This time Amelia reacted in time and pulled the pouch away. "No! Leave this alone, or I will have you beheaded. Now – begone!"

The dragon flicked her tongue again, reaching for the purple mushrooms. Amelia grabbed a spear from one of her attendants and swung at the dragon's tongue. Her clumsy stroke wasn't hard enough to harm the beast, but it did divert the tip of her tongue enough to miss the mushrooms. Amelia held the pouch behind her back and stood pointing the spear at the dragon. The dragon let out a great bellow and raised herself to her full height. Amelia stood in front of the huge creature, spear pointed upwards, protecting her mushrooms.

The dragon opened her mouth, and Amelia lunged towards the dragon with the spear, screaming angrily. One snap and the dragon pulled Amelia up by the spear and into her mouth; then the dragon spit. Amelia's head went in one direction and her body in another, followed by the broken spear. Now that the annoying person was out of the way, the dragon quickly flicked her tongue to get the remainder of the purple mushrooms.

Erin and Alec watched the encounter without moving from their position. "Too bad she didn't care for her people like she cared for her mushrooms. If she had, she might have made a good queen," Alec said sardonically.

Pequa watched while the dragon ate the purple delicacies, then motioned to the great beast. The dragon reluctantly responded.

Erin sensed the lines inside the dragon. The lines were becoming tighter and tighter. She sensed anger in the dragon. Erin felt the dragon thinking, *No, Mother, no, this is a friend. I have a friend, and I cannot kill a friend.*

"Kill her."

No Mother.

The thought was interrupted by intense pain.

No, Mother, do not make me.

The pain increased. Erin could sense the dragon's pain. The reptilian brain only wanted the pain to end and now saw Erin as the source of the pain. Suddenly Erin was no longer linked with the dragon. The giant mouth raised and opened and started to snap towards Erin. Erin anticipated the dragon's action and at the last minute rolled away. The mouth closed on empty air. The dragon turned and looked long and hard at Pequa.

Pequa laughed and said to Erin, "You fool! If you had learned to align yourself with the Dragon Stone, you could have taken the dragon from me and made it your slave. Instead, the dragon will be your death."

Erin felt the dragon's pain increase. The dragon let loose a great angry bellow, and Erin felt the lines twist tighter. She sensed resignation from the dragon – the beast had to obey the Mother elf.

Erin backed away from the dragon. She thought to Alec, *Pequa controls the dragon and is forcing it to kill us.*

I have an idea, Alec thought back. *See if we can maneuver the dragon into the woods.*

Erin dashed into the woods followed closely by Alec. The dragon lumbered after them, angrily knocking down trees as it moved.

It is herding us, thought Alec. *It will knock down trees until we are trapped!*

The dragon sensed Erin's location and headed towards her. Erin ran further into the woods and the dragon continued to follow, creating a wide path of fallen trees. Erin sensed the dragon and could feel the twisted lines of force that were compelling the dragon to respond. She tried to untwist the lines, but they were too heavy for her to move.

Try to lead the dragon towards the clearing, Alec urged.

The dragon continued to follow Erin; there was no opportunity to get close to the dragon without being dismembered by falling trees. As they backed towards the clearing, Erin and Alec separated. The dragon continued to follow Erin. Erin tried to sense the dragon and tried to think about purple mushrooms. The dragon continued its charge through the trees, upending them and letting them fall with a crash, following Erin as she retreated through the woods.

Erin drew her sword and turned to face the dragon. She tried to push thoughts of purple mushrooms to the dragon. When the dragon reached the edge of the clearing she slithered towards Erin, moved closer, and raised her head. Erin could see into the great gaping mouth and see the crumbs of purple mushrooms stuck to the long teeth.

Make it come a few more paces forward, thought Alec.

Erin backed away from the dragon, still thinking of purple mushrooms. She sensed the twisted lines inside the dragon and tried again to untwist them, but the lines were too thick for her to move. The dragon stepped forward and opened her mouth, tongue flicking in anticipation. Erin stood still, letting the dragon approach.

Focus. The dragon snapped toward Erin and she quickly jumped backwards; the portal circle in the clearing opened just front of her feet – light dimmed and started to go black. The great dragon stood half inside and half outside the portal. Time froze as the portal tried to respond to the immense energy of the dragon. Alec started sweating and felt the energy try to rebound towards him. He felt the world in black and white for what seemed like an eternity until the portal reshaped itself around the dragon and the dragon suddenly vanished.

Where the dragon had been, a torrent of water poured out. The outline of the dragon's head and tail were replaced with rock from the cave dropping dully onto the clearing floor.

"You did it," yelled Erin in relief. "You ported the dragon into the cave!"

"Yes, and hopefully it is dead," said Alec.

"I can sense her in the cave. She is very alive and very angry because she was expecting purple mushrooms. She is trying to dig her way out, but I think it will take a while. Let's see if we can end this battle before the dragon frees herself."

≈ ≈ ≈ ≈

They could hear the sounds of battle, the ringing of swords, the snorting and snarling of trogus, and battle whistles reverberating. "Our riders have arrived," exclaimed Erin in delight.

Erin stopped and sensed the surroundings. "Pequa and her clutchman have fled and are heading away from us, back to the Elf Mountains. We should go to Mother. Our riders can take care of the remainder of Amelia's riders. They couldn't handle the threats posed by Pequa or the dragon, but now that they are both gone, neither is a problem."

They returned to the grotto residence. Queen Therin was resting; she was still very weak but improving. Erin excitedly told her mother about the dragon and the death of Amelia, and what Pequa had told her about the Truth Stone. The Queen listened in amazement.

A short while later Ferd entered. "My Queen, it is wonderful to see you alive. I apologize. We were preparing a carriage for you, but I must tell you that it is not yet ready. Our scouts told us that Amelia had many riders headed to this area, and we were very concerned about your safety. We thought it was most important to arrive as quickly as possible. I hope we were not too late."

The Queen replied, "Your timing was exquisite. I am glad to see you and my riders – or should I say, 'Erin's riders'?"

"The Princess is our leader, but we will always be your riders, my Queen," Ferd responded, and Erin nodded in agreement.

Queen Therin smiled weakly from her couch. "We will have a carriage available to take you back to your rightful place, the Residence at Freeland City," Ferd continued. "The carriage will be available later today."

They spent another night at the grotto before trying to move the Queen. Erin could sense the dragon making slow progress digging its way out of the hillside, but Alec calculated that it would take several days to succeed.

Alec wondered, "Should we try to kill the dragon before it escapes?"

Erin was very firm, "No. The dragon is not going to attack us or anyone else unless Pequa is close by and forces an attack and Pequa has left. The dragon is not a vicious beast; but she has been misused and abused."

As they started their trip back to Freeland City, Erin announced to all the riders, "It is time to retake our rightful place in the leadership of Theland. Queen Therin has been rescued, and we are going to return her to her Residence and the throne of Theland. Ride for the Queen!"

A great cheer went up from the riders. "Hail to the Queen," they chanted, followed by "Hail to the Princess, our leader."

≈ ≈ ≈ ≈

Early afternoon the procession entered the gates of Freeland City. The first stop was Justice Square. Erin helped Queen Therin to the platform; there they stood and stared at the Stone of Truth several minutes before finally putting their hands on it. Word of the Queen's arrival spread like wildfire, and a crowd of citizens was rapidly forming in the Square. Then, in front of her people, Queen Therin firmly declared that she was the rightful ruler of Therin and was resuming her reign. Erin vowed silently to better understand the Stone and learn of its dragon properties. The Stone of Truth shone with a golden hue, and the people cheered.

Then the Queen's procession moved to the Residence. Alec helped the Queen from her carriage, and they walked to the grand double doors of the audience chamber. Erin stood before the doors and looked at them. She had opened these doors a thousand times. Standing there made her think of all the good that her mother had done and the waste and anguish that Amelia's capriciousness had caused in such a short time, directed by Pequa. The anger built in Erin. She would dedicate her life to repair the damage that the elves had wrought. She would not allow her mother's efforts to be in vain.

The thought gave her courage as she pushed opened the doors and stepped inside. Amelia's minions had made a mess of the room, but at the far end of the chamber was the carved chair Queen Therin had always used. The Queen walked slowly across the room and sat in her chair. Erin waited until her mother was seated and then she also walked across the chamber and stood in front of the Queen, her head bowed. Erin felt the weight of her people as she had never felt before. They would eventually be her responsibility. She sensed Alec behind her. He let her stand in front of her mother for a long time, and then he put his arm around her. She felt the warmth and the strength that he provided.

"Mother, I will never be as good a leader as you, but I will support you until death and then, if it is my honor to take my turn, I will do my best to care for our people." She leaned on Alec, mentally and physically exhausted. There were a thousand things that needed her attention from minor personal items to major decisions, and without Alec, she didn't know where she would find the energy for any of them.

The Residence personnel quickly materialized and were soon at work clearing away the trash left behind by Amelia, cleaning the furnishings, filling the lanterns, and polishing the floors. In a few days it would again be the royal Residence that Erin remembered.

The Queen was too weak to greet anyone, so she asked Erin to fill in for her. Ferd brought Colin back from his place of banishment in the city's jail tower; Colin was overjoyed to see his mother alive and unharmed, and spent the rest of the day tending to her. Erin and Alec stood in the audience chamber greeting the many well-wishers and hearing tales of Amelia's excesses and pledges of service to Queen Therin and Erin.

Finally, the two of them were alone. Alec could feel that the responsibility of leading her people was weighing heavily upon Erin. He took her in his arms and said, "I will be here to support you. You are a great leader, and one day you will be a great ruler of our people."

"It is nice to be home," said Erin, nestling in his arms. "It is too bad you don't have more portals. They are a convenient way to travel across Theland. We could have brought Mother home more quickly if you had more of them."

"That is one of the things I want to do," Alec said. "I think I can figure out how to make more portals. Once I train a few wizards to handle the routine requests around here, I will be able to think about how to make portals."

"The Chief Wizard is a fitting role for you," Erin said, mostly to convince herself. "But I wish you would reconsider Mother's request and serve as head of the Council."

Alec shook his head. "You can sense as well as I can that heading the Council is not my skill. The head of the Council must work with all the people and cajole them until they agree. I am too impatient to do that. Especially now that your Mother has taken to my idea of letting the people select half of the Council Members."

"I know you are right – but you are so much easier to work with than the grumpy old men who will end up on the Council."

"Leading the Council might be an excellent task for Colin. He is good at that sort of stuff."

Erin nodded, and then added, "By the way, you know that the Chief Wizard will have to be a Council Member."

Alec groaned in protest.

Erin laughed and put her finger on his lips to silence him. "We will discuss the Council another day. Tonight, we need to celebrate our victory. I know of a suite in the Residence that has a large tub and right now I would love a hot, soaking bath. I could use the assistance of a Great Wizard."

Alec looked at her expectantly, kissed her fingertips, and asked, "What type of assistance might you want from a Great Wizard?"

"Why to heat the water of course!" Then with a sly smile, Erin added, "But there might be some other things I need a great wizard to do also."

The End of the First Book

Background Information

Lists

The following lists of characters, places, and other terms may aid the reader's understanding of this book.

List of Characters	
Alec	Scientist; dark energy researcher; consort of Princess Erin
Alder; Dr. Alder	Lead researcher for dark energy at the North Atlantic Institute
Aldermen; The Alder	Foreign army massed on the Grasslands
Amelia	Brun's daughter; Erin's step-sister
Bon	Theland rider
Brun	Theland Councilman, consort of Queen Therin, and Erin's step-father
Brar	Brun's younger son
Brunder	Brun's older son, and suitor of Erin
Celeste	Sarah's daughter
Colin	Erin's younger brother
Cryl	Theland rider
Debor, Major	Gott military officer at Winding Pass (deceased)
Devin	Erin's brother (deceased)
Devin, Consort	Erin's father (deceased)
Drone Master	Elf Mother responsible for training drones
Elia	Ancestral elf mother
Erin; Princess Erin	Princess of Theland
Ferd	Queen Therin's lead rider
First Mother	Lian, the ancestral First Queen of Theland
First Queen	Lian, the ancestral First Queen of Theland
Gryg	Nomad tribe of the Grasslands
Gwyn	Ancestral elf mother
Harl	Town Marshal; freed slave
Hank	Theland lead rider
Henra	Elf Mother healed by Alec
Ilave	Boy living in a village on the Grasslands
Jitsu	Gambler at an inn on the Grasslands
Kara	Elf Mother; coercer
Kirkdar, Commander	Theland military officer under Amelia
Lily	Woman who befriends Erin
Leon	One of Queen Therin's Guardsmen (deceased)
Leonder	Leon's son; a scholar; Erin's former boyfriend (deceased)
Levor, Captain	Gott military officer in charge of the Winding Pass garrison
Lian	Historic ancestral elf; First Mother; First Queen;
Marta	Elf Mother responsible for Erin's capture; coercer
Mawn, General	Gott military officer in charge of the Raner Pass garrison
Nikka	Theland rider
Nomads	Un-governed tribes living on the Grasslands
Original Five	Five ancestral elves who founded Theland 500 years ago

Pequa	Amelia's advisor; elf coercer
Rawl, Lord	Gott nobleman
Rhor	Theland rider
Sarah	Alec's girlfriend at the Lab
Siara	Ancestral elf mother
Smink, Captain	Gott military officer at Winding Pass (deceased)
Syna	Ancestral elf; mother of Lian
Therin; Queen Therin	Ruler of Theland; Erin's mother
Thom	Erin's lead rider
Urgan, Sgt.	Theland military officer in charge of a garrison near Winding Pass
Varra	Elf Mother; coercer; speaker for the Disca
Voy, Major	Gott military officer at Raner Pass and aide to General Mawn
Zag	Captured Alderman
Zari	Brunder's girlfriend
Zera	Elf Mother serving as Erin's host; empath

List of Places

Aleinte Escarpment	Ridge in the foothills of the Elf Mountains
Arose	Large town on the Grasslands
Betin	Town on the Grasslands
Cantin	Town on the Grasslands
Elf Mountains	Uncharted mountain range separating Theland from the elf lands
Evening Mountains	Uninhabited mountain range between Theland and the Grasslands
Freeland City	Capital city of Theland
Gott	Land adjoining Theland; ally of Theland
Gott City	Capital city of Gott
Grasslands	Un-governed lands adjoining Theland
Grotto	Compound owned by Brun outside of Freeland City; formerly a mine
Institute	North Atlantic Institute, science research laboratory in the US northeast
Justice Square	Plaza in the center of Freeland City where the queen metes justice
Lab; Laboratory	Dark energy research center at the North Atlantic Institute
Land of the Five Moons	Orb term for the planet where Theland is located; Nevia
Lashon	Land near Theland; an ally of Gott
Mt. Eras	Mountain peak in the Evening Mountains, on the border of Theland
Nevia	Orb term for the planet where Theland is located
New Haven	Capital city of the elf lands
North Atlantic Institute	Science research laboratory in the U.S. northeast
Octavin	Land near Theland
Raner Pass	Main pass in the Evening Mountains in Gott, leading to the Grasslands
Residence, the	Royal residence (palace) of Queen Therin in Freeland City
Ryn River	Large central river running the length of Theland
Theland	Erin's homeland
Winding Pass	Small pass in the Evening Mountains in Gott, leading to the Grasslands

List of Terms

Amulet	Small device, generally worn about the neck, that cancels dark energy
Arn	Distance roughly equal to the length of a person's arm, or a normal pace

Black Wizard	Wizard who uses dark energy for evil purposes
Blue thorn poison	Quick-acting strong poison
Book of Queens	Ancestral Theland document, read only by the Queen or her daughter
Bounder	Small, antelope-like animal of the Grasslands used as a food source
Clutch	Group of male elves, usually three, bound to a specific elf Mother
Clutch Mother	See 'Mother'
Clutchman	Male elf bonded to an elf Mother
Coercer	Elf Mother who can bend a subject's will
Council	Governing body of Theland
Cross-breed	Person of mixed blood, with both elf and orb genes
Cull	Activity where elves raid orbs communities to acquire drones (slaves)
Dark Energy	Fundamental energy of the multiverse; has positive and negative forms
Disca	Governing body of the elves
Dragon	Large flying serpentine beast, having a complex brain
Dragon Queen	Ancestral mythological being
Dragon's blood	Bloodline of the ancestral Dragon Queen
Drones	People (orbs) enslaved by the elves, usually men
Drung	Ox-like beast of burden often used for pulling wagons
Drunglet	Small pony-like mount
El	Distance roughly equivalent to two-thirds of a mile or one kilometer
Elves	Population of beings living in an area adjacent to Theland
Empath	Elf Mother who can sense a subject's feelings (emotions)
Founding, The	Ancestral founding of Theland as a separate colony
Freshling	Elf child
Hyra	Small wolf- or jackal-like creature on the Grasslands
Jinja Root	Plant medicine used for birth control
Lead rider	Military officer in charge of other riders
Medallion	Small device, generally worn about the neck, that collects dark energy
Mother (elf)	Female elf
Negative dark energy	Anti-energy equivalent of positive dark energy
Orbs	Population of non-elf beings (including humans)
Portal	Means to use dark energy to move from place to place
Prairie skarn	Small venomous animal found on the Grasslands
Purple mushroom	Highly-addictive hallucinogenic
Rider	Person riding a trogus; military cavalryman
Seer	Theland woman with certain powers who can discern the future
Seft	Day of the week
Stone of Truth	Spherical stone in Justice Square that changes color
Tricrystals	Small crystals that can transmit dark energy
Trogus	Large cat-like animal used as a mount by military cavalry
Truth Stone	See 'Stone of Truth'
Wizard	Person who uses dark energy; or who exhibits magical properties

A Brief Discussion of Dark Energy

From Alec's college notes on the fundamentals of dark energy.

- Dark energy is the background energy of the universe.

- It is free-floating but can be concentrated and focused into other forms – ordinary matter, heat, motion, weather control, etc.

- It can also be used to bend light or create a vacuum.

- Dark energy has two forms: positive and negative (anti-dark-energy).

- Using positive dark energy to create matter or cause another effect requires three things: a source of concentrated dark energy, a focus, and a director (person).

- The director uses mental energy and a tricrystal (in a medallion or another object) to focus and coalesce dark energy. When the desired effect is obtained, the director releases the mental focus.

- To create an object, the director must be able to visualize the object and how it works.

- Positive dark energy is somehow related to time; the details are not fully known.

- Negative dark energy fields exhibit lines of force. In theory these can be twisted or otherwise manipulated to affect the mental stability of another person (another director), but this has not yet been demonstrated.

- In areas with a low background field of dark energy, it will take longer to obtain results – mechanical concentrators can be used to increase the dark energy field.

- Loss of focus too early can result in an explosion, which can be fatal to the director or others in the vicinity.

For more details, see the information at TheDarkEnergyChronicles.com.

A Brief Discussion of Elves, Orbs, and Other Beings

Alec and Erin learned of elves, orbs, and the wars between the races from *The Book of Queens* and from their visit to the elf city. Here are some of the main points.

For more details, see the information at TheDarkEnergyChronicles.com.

Elves

The elves are an ancient race and are found on many worlds.

An adult female elf is called a "Mother." Each Mother forms a "clutch" instead of a family group. Each clutch is headed by a Mother, and includes her three male-elf clutchmen, and possibly additional male-elf apprentices. The Mother controls her clutch through telepathic commands.

Elves reproduce by laying eggs. A Mother lays eggs twice in her lifetime; there are always four eggs, usually three male and one female. Mother elves do not raise their young. The eggs are tended in a Hatchery, using dark energy, until the "freshling" is ready to emerge. The freshlings are raised in a communal school until they become adults.

Each Mother elf has a dominant "talent" that first emerges when she reaches adulthood. "Coercers" are the top talent and can mentally bend other beings to their will; "empaths" have the ability to sense emotions and actions. There are many other types of talents. Some Mothers have more than one talent.

Elves can sense negative dark energy, but not positive dark energy.

Mother elves are addicted to negative dark energy. They need to arouse strong emotions in order to sense it, best generated by sex, torture, or killing.

Mother elves wear a special ring that allows them to use negative dark energy to communicate and perform unusual feats. When not wearing her ring, a Mother can control an orb through touch.

Orbs

The orbs are an ancient race and are found on many worlds; orbs are more abundant than elves.

Elves despise orbs and the two races have been at war for millions of years.

Humans on Earth are a lost, or wild, herd of orbs.

Orbs civilizations tend to be unstable over time.

All orbs reproduce as humans do, and raise their own young.

Elves establish breeding populations of orbs on new worlds or new territories, called "herds," and cull them from time to time to obtain "drones" to become slaves.

Orbs can sense positive dark energy, often by using a tool such as a medallion or a tricrystal, but not negative dark energy.

If an orb is touched by an elf Mother, the orb has an overwhelming desire to do what the Mother wants; however, if an orb is wearing a ring, the orb is not affected.

Cross-Breeds

A cross-breed results from a union between an elf and an orb. Descendants of cross-breeds may also be cross-breeds.

Cross-breeds are fairly common because elves will often couple with orbs or cross-breeds for sexual gratification.

Elves fear and hate cross-breeds, and usually eliminate female cross-breeds.

Cross-breeds reproduce as orbs do. If she has children, a female cross-breed will generally have three: a male, then a female, then another male.

Cross-breeds may exhibit characteristics of both elves and orbs; for example, they may have the ability to sense and use both positive and negative dark energy, especially if using a medallion or a tricrystal.

Drones

Drones are slaves who serve the elves and may be either an orb or a cross-breed.

Drones are almost always male.

Drones are created by banding an orb or cross-breed with a special neckpiece. The drone is then under the mental control of the elf Mother.

The drone will feel excruciating pain if the Mother's wishes are not carried out, and exquisite pleasure if her wishes are met.

Compliant drones are necessary in elf society because they carry out all mundane tasks. Elf technology depends on positive dark energy; because elves cannot sense or control this, they use drones to operate all equipment. Drones are also used for non-technical tasks, such as farming.

The neckpiece controls the drone; if the neckpiece is removed, the drone will slowly revert to its former self.

Made in the USA
Monee, IL
14 February 2022

91296002R00252